Staying the Course

By Steven F. Deslippe

This is a work of inspired pure fiction.

Names, characters, places, incidents, and remote possibilities, either are the product of the author's wild imagination or are used fictitiously, and any actual resemblance to persons, living, dead or existing in ethereal form, business establishments, events, or locales, is entirely coincidental.

© 2017

Edited By: Edit This One, LLC., Fairfax, IA.
www.editthisone.com

Published By: Edit This One, LLC d/b/a Wordy Gerty Publishing

Wordy Gerty

Publishing

The original image used and modified for the cover of this novel was taken from the website www.pixabay.com, whereas it has been released free of copyrights under Creative Commons Zero (CC0).

ISBN 978-0-9981046-5-2

Acknowledgements

*** A special thanks to Tina Rosekrans (www.editthisone.com, LLC) for taking the time to proof read, make suggestions and edit this novel. Without her help, this novel more than likely would never see the light of day and it would probably just stay on my computer for no one else to read. ***

*** I would also like to acknowledge those authors whose work I not only thoroughly enjoy reading, but have inspired me to work hard at this craft and put forth the best possible story I could — Steve Perry, Stephanie (S.D.) Perry, Nyx Smith, Diane Carey, William Shatner, Stieg Larsson, Sherrilyn Kenyon, Laura K. Hamilton, Kevin J. Anderson, Kristine Kathryn Rusch, David R. George III, Dayton Ward, Michael A. Martin, David Alan Mack, Una McCormack, Keith R.A. DeCandido, Jana Oliver, Kristen Beyer & Christopher L. Bennett. ***

*** This book is dedicated to the memory of my second cousin, whose life was senselessly cut way too short. ***

R.I.P.

Nathan T. Deslippe
August 03, 1989 - August 28, 2016

~ Be the person you want to be remembered as ~

Author's note

In order for the reader to not feel that they may have somehow missed something important from the previous two novels, I have created a brief backstory. My reason for doing this is to bring to light the fact that during the twenty-five year period in which Antonio Marcone had been incarcerated, Louie Mazotti led a double life.

Luckily, the consequences of his doing this did not come back to bite him in the ass. And now, with Louie's two closest associates no longer alive, his secret need not be guarded so closely — a secret that will eventually emerge and become an essential part of the continuing Fate's End series.

Backstory

Right from the beginning, unlike his fellow associate, Louie was all right with this new direction that Antonio had decided to take the organization. It was a nice change of pace for him not to have to worry about whether or not the authorities were going to be watching them, harassing them, or unexpectedly breaking down their door — both he and Sal were after all, just as guilty for not only the numerous crimes that resulted in their boss being sent to jail, but for the deaths of three police officers, and the attempted murder of another. If it hadn't been for a lot of careful planning and a bit of blind luck being on their side on that fateful night, the outcome might have been a lot different — but it all worked out just like they had hoped. They got what they wanted out of the explosion; that being the deaths of three irrelevant cops, and an unambiguous message sent.

After only a few years into the 'new direction' of the D.U.O., Louie started to get that itch to go back to the way things were — but he wasn't about to overstep his authority and go behind Antonio's back. That, he knew, wouldn't be a smart thing for him to do, as his boss would certainly make him pay for his defiance. Knowing his luck, he'd be bumped on down the organizational ladder and full control of the daily operations would then be handed over to Sal. Having to take orders from his rival throughout the remainder of Antonio's incarceration would be the worst form of living hell imaginable — he'd much rather put a bullet in his own head and go to the land of fire and brimstone ahead of schedule.

Those past few years without really any liberty to push beyond the limits of the law had actually caused him to look deep within himself and search for a solution that would satisfy both his want and his obligations. He surprised himself when the answer to his dilemma wasn't that hard to find. It however, came with an immense risk. There was no justifiable reason for him to do this, but venturing out on his own was nevertheless, a tempting option.

Louie's goal since the day he had become a high-ranking member of the Detroit Underworld Organization was to one day take over control of it — that, clearly wasn't going to happen for a very long time. However, windows of opportunity don't come around that often, and one seemed to be right there in front of him at the moment. Climbing through it was certainly appealing, but also a bit scary, not knowing what was waiting for him on the other side or what the repercussion might be because of his actions. He had an important decision to make.

Loyalty or prosperity; which one was most important to him? If he didn't take that risk, would another opportunity like it ever come around again? He doubted it. But for him to take that rather large leap of faith, a few problems stood in his way that he would first have to deal with — those being, finding a way to successfully pull the wool over Antonio's and Sal's eyes.

If he were actually able to do so, a bit of freedom that had never been there before would be attained and he would be able to freely make his own decisions. No longer would he be just a 'Yes' man; a tool to be used as a means to accomplish someone else's goal — he would be his own boss.

As he contemplated doing this, one thing kept coming to the surface for which he was unsure how to deal with — the moment where either Sal or Antonio learned of his breaking the number one rule. Louie believed that he could survive his boss's wrath, but his rival would undoubtedly use that knowledge in order to enact a power play of his own. No way could he ever give the man the ammunition that was needed to throw him under the bus and then run over him with it as many times as he felt like it.

In order to ensure that his tracks were covered, he had to be even more cautious than Antonio was being. There were plenty of low-risk opportunities out there Louie could explore that would allow him some personal gain; he honestly was tired of riding the coattails of someone else's success. No timetable needed to be set, as he was in no rush to attain the goals he believed he could one day achieve. A slow, methodical, patiently implored strategy would not only bring him the success he believed he could attain, but it would also minimize the potential of his entire venture blowing up in his face.

In his heart, he knew that when his boss finally got released from prison, it would only be a matter of time before the man's ego became his undoing. At that point, he would make the decision as to what direction he would then want the remainder of his life to take. Yes, the D.U.O. would have rightfully become his, since he was the next in line, but if by then he had assembled a significant financial portfolio, he had no qualms about dissolving the organization and putting it to bed forever.

Once his decision had been made to take that leap of faith, Chicago was where Louie went in order to look for that first business opportunity. There, nobody knew who he was — and there, he had a clean slate. Yes, it would have been easier for him to do this in Detroit, as he knew the city like the back of his hand, but staying in his own backyard was not a smart thing to do; Sal knew just as many people as he did, so the chances of the bastard learning what he was up to were rather good.

Almost immediately, he felt as if Chicago was where he belonged all along — especially when he had wandered through University Village, an area of the city also known as Little Italy. It reminded him so much of his place of birth in Modena; a place that he had gone back to many times during his youth but strangely, never during his adulthood — and he longed to go back there again someday. Soon, he hoped.

Louie's initial plan had only been to seek out business opportunities throughout the Midwestern States, maybe even possibly venturing up into parts of Canada, but his first visit to Chicago had scrapped that notion. His need for personal gain suddenly felt less important, as he had inadvertently found a place where he fit in. The Windy City had somehow allowed him to relax and enjoy the people in and around it — and his usually disquieting thoughts never seemed to be there. While in Chicago, he was at peace. He didn't have any ambitions, any commitments, or responsibilities to fulfill. The only certainty he knew he had was that his freedom away from the life he committed himself to was short and that he would eventually have to return to what awaited him in the Motor City.

Twice a month, Louie would return; not just to get away for the weekend, have some fun, or explore a business opportunity if it happened to come his way, but Chicago was quickly becoming his second home. In fact, if the necessary cards ever fell into place, this was where he had decided he would put down roots. But that was a very big if; too many variables were still out there that could get in the way of that ever happening.

Each time Louie went to the Windy City, he knew that Sal was doing his damndest to try and figure out where he had gone and why. Antonio, he did not believe had any suspicions that he was in essence, 'moonlighting' — but it was only going to be a matter of time before Sal put a bug in his ear. And once that happened, whether or not the entire truth was learned, his days away from his chosen life would probably be over. At that point, he would have no other choice but to come clean — and the only way there would be for him to ever save his manhood from being removed would be to then bequeath to the organization whatever assets he would have so far accumulated.

As each day went by, Louie hoped and prayed that such a scenario would not take place. Not just because his surreptitious life would come to an abrupt end, but because his trips had unexpectedly become something other than just a monthly getaway. Something had happened to him near the end of that first year of visits — it became a blessing and a curse at the same time and had changed his life forever, and he knew that he could never divulge what it was to anyone as such a revelation could ultimately ruin everything that he was a part of and more.

For that reason, the D.U.O. had suddenly become priority one to him once again. No longer did it make sense for him to venture out on his own and take a risk; he was content to stay in the position he had long ago earned. What happened had caused him to see things in a completely different light. He suddenly realized that his responsibilities within the organization had to be taken even more seriously than he ever had before. Whatever Antonio would ask of him, he made sure the task was completed, believing it was just one more thing that helped to ensure the D.U.O. would be in a position to become the empire it was destined to become. Louie hadn't suddenly had a change of heart; an even more selfish reason was the motivation behind his decision.

If Antonio or Sal were to ever find out his little secret, unimaginable consequences could be the result. It also incessantly jeopardized the continued existence of the Detroit Underworld

Organization. Oddly enough, the very thing that had unexpectedly brought a whole new purpose and joy to Louie Mazotti's existence could ultimately destroy it.

~ We are just one of many pieces that are being played out in a strategic and elaborate game. The moves that are made may not always seem logical, but are intended for a reason, which we may never understand nor fully are able to accept. When the game has finally reached its conclusion, we then have no other choice but to stand there dumbfounded. Not only are we then left scratching our heads and wondering how in the hell it happened, but we also begin to wonder how it was that we did not see it coming. ~

Prologue

Sunday, September 07, 2014

A few beads of sweat trickled off his brow, caused by the unseasonably hot temperature — the kind of heat that is usually felt in late July, as he casually walked down the streets of Chicago toward the same place he had gone to every time he came here to visit. It was because of his love for baseball, his only self admitted obsession next to his work that he had accidently found a quaint little Italian restaurant called La Famiglia Restaurant Giardino one afternoon following a Cubs game — the place was just down a block or so from the recently renovated, historic Wrigley Field. From the moment Louie had walked inside the establishment, it felt like he had literally been brought back in time. The aroma induced so many memories of his youth and how much enjoyment his Nonna got whenever she would cook for her grandchildren.

Of course, the place was filled with people that he did not know, but within only a few moments, he felt accepted. By the end of his first visit, those who were regulars of the restaurant had treated him as if he was now part of their extended family. He hadn't expected what had happened that day, but for the first time in his adult life he felt like a normal, average, everyday human being. No one gave him strange looks like they did when he walked into any place of business in Detroit, and no one even seemed to care about who the usual Louie Mazotti was.

Because of the anonymity that he had been granted, he determined that the La Famiglia Restaurant Giardino was now his new favorite place in the world — and not just because of the hospitality he received, or because the food there was as authentic and delicious as an Italian meal should be, there was a personal reason why Louie could not wait to return. That first day, not only had a 'rare jewel' served him, she had easily warmed up his incessantly cold heart.

Mirella Santori was her name, and from the moment that she had greeted him at his table, Louie had become smitten. She was physically everything that he had ever imagined his perfect, ideal woman would be. Her light-brown eyes only invited kindness, and her soft, soothing voice could easily grab and hold anyone's attention. The wavy long red/brown hair and well proportioned, toned figure she possessed had uncharacteristically caused Louie on several occasions to visualize his hands gently caressing every inch of her inviting body. She wasn't that tall, but she was far from petite — and she was the kind of woman who could easily draw the attention of any man away from the woman he was with. But to him, it was that mesmerizing walk of hers that had been the determining factor. At some point, Louie believed that he was going to go out with her. However, this usually confident and assertive man suddenly found himself experiencing something that was foreign to him — cold feet. It wasn't until he had visited the restaurant for the third time that he was finally ready to take that next step with Mirella beyond that of him just being a customer.

Although she was ten years younger, Mirella could see that Louie had an old world charm that she had to admit she liked. She didn't say yes the first time that Louie had asked her out, because she could easily tell that he was the kind of man who usually got what he wanted and would simply not accept her rejection. She also could tell that he was the kind of man who would show her the respect that she deserved, conduct himself as a gentleman should, and would return numerous times and try his luck again until he succeeded. Yes, it was somewhat mean of her to toy with Louie's heart like that, for she too could not deny that she was attracted to him, but when it came to letting someone capture her heart, she wanted it to be a man who would not stop at anything to get what he so desired.

Finally, after two months and five more visits, she had agreed to go out on a date with him; a date that quickly evolved from being a mutual attraction, to a friendship, to realizing that there was a connection, to developing feelings. All of which she had hoped would occur, but never did she image that those things would all happen within only a month of their first date.

As with all relationships: the direction, the success, and the longevity; the main ingredients needed are trust and communication. Louie knew that it would be very difficult for him to have any kind of normal relationship with someone, as his life was extremely complicated — he had hoped that Mirella was the kind of person who might one day understand and be able to accept it. But there was no guarantee that she would. Therefore, Louie had to prepare himself for the likelihood that he was going to get kicked to the curb. Still, he held out hope. He believed that she was the one that he had waited his whole life to find, to have a family with, and spend the rest of his life with. So instead of waiting for enough time to pass by; enough time for Mirella Santori to fall madly in love with him, and then have her heart broken when she finally found out the truth, Louie decided to take a chance, come clean, and be honest with her after only their first month of seeing each other.

He had made the decision a long time ago never to question the path he had chosen to walk. He was a member of the Detroit Underworld Organization, and ideally, Louie hoped that Mirella could see beyond what he was a part of and accept him for who he was on the inside — the kind of man who would love her with all his heart and do anything she would ever ask of him. What he had hoped for though, did not occur — she ended it right there. To say that her reaction to what Louie had revealed about his life was that of total shock would certainly be an understatement. There was no discussion afterward and no willingness from her to listen to an explanation that would validate his choices. She instead, abruptly slammed that proverbial door in his face.

Alone in the park with the surrounding nature, Louie just stood there befuddled. He could not think of anything to say; he just blankly watched as Mirella turned her back to him and walked away, out of his life forever.

His heartbreak did not stop him from continuing to visit Chicago — although he no longer went to the La Famiglia Restaurant Giardino. That was until the opening game of the following season for the Cubs. After the game was over, Louie decided that it was time to go and see Mirella. He had hoped that with the six months that had passed since his revelation that enough time would have gone by where she would at least allow him an opportunity to explain his side of the story and be able to have a normal adult conversation with him about the last night that they had been together.

To his shocking surprise, Louie had come to find out as soon as he arrived at the restaurant that Mirella no longer worked there. He inquired with the manager about her whereabouts and was devastated to find out that she had quit shortly after everything that had happened. Disheartened, he turned away from the manager with the intent to leave the restaurant when another waitress, one that Louie had remembered seeing there several times in the past, stopped him just before he walked out the front door. She looked at him with a sympathetic smile and handed him a note — and then without saying a word, she left Louie standing alone by the entrance of the establishment.

With trepidation, he looked at the note, fully expecting his heart to be broken again.

"Louie,

I hope that you don't hate me because of my decision to never see you again. However, something has come up and it is urgent that I speak with you about it.

Please call me,

Mirella"

Unsure how he should feel in that moment, Louie's mind began to erroneously speculate as to the reason why Mirella Santori was now reaching out to him after all the time that had passed. Was she sick? Was she still pissed off at him? Had she had a change of heart and realized just how much she had missed him? Those were questions that were suddenly dancing around inside of Louie's head. The sudden willingness of her wanting to get in contact with him had grabbed his curiosity, his fears, and his hope, so he promptly stepped outside the restaurant, re-read the phone number on the bottom of the note, and called her.

Mirella didn't tell him that much over the phone, only that she needed to speak with him in person, so he disconnected his call and got into his car. It was about a thirty minute drive to get to her place; an address that took him into a part of the city that looked to be just on the outskirts of the projects — he did not feel comfortable here, as he could easily see just how much attention his new black Mercedes SLS AMG was attracting.

As he approached Mirella's front door, Louie started to get real nervous — why that was, he had not a clue. Nothing had ever made him feel this way about anything before. In his line of work he had to be on point, prepared, and confident — anything could happen at any time and he had to be able to quickly adapt. The lack of self-assuredness in that moment was foreign to him. Louie did not like the feeling whatsoever. He needed to find a way to gain control of his sudden nervousness before he saw Mirella again.

His heart was pounding so hard it felt as if it was ready to break out of his chest. He knew that it was the uncertainty in his thoughts that was causing this to happen; an uncertainty that was of course, brought on because of the apprehensiveness that Louie could sense during the brief conversation he had on the phone with Mirella. It wasn't until she answered her door, that he immediately understood everything, why the anxiety had been there, and why he had sensed what he did when they spoke.

She stood there with a smile on her face — not a, I miss you smile, but a smile that said, 'Hello, I'm glad you are here'. She then stepped aside and graciously invited Louie into her home. Once he was completely inside, he took a moment and looked her over. That was when he was able to confirm what he originally thought he had seen when Mirella had first answered her door — she was almost seven months pregnant.

"And before you ask, Louie… Yes, I am carrying your baby."

With that confirmation now set in stone, he realized in that moment that he was going to be something that he had always wanted to be, but never thought was in the cards — a father. This now forced him to acknowledge that his life was going to be very different from this moment forward. It already was way more different than anyone else's, but he now recognized that he would have to approach the way he lived it in a manner more typical of everyone else. He knew that he would no longer be able to live on the edge of insanity. Instead, he would have to use discretion and common sense with everything that he did or was asked to do, as he now had even more on his plate than just the responsibilities that came with the position he held within the D.U.O. — and he knew that there was no way in hell that he could ever let anyone know about his child.

This miracle was both a blessing and a curse for Louie. Not only did this make him the happiest man in the world, it now placed an invisible target on his back; a target that he could never let anyone see. All the pressures that were a standard part of his life had just increased by tenfold — he just hoped that what was just added to the weight already sitting on his shoulders would not one day become the reason why everything that ever mattered to him was forever taken away.

―――――――――――――○○―――――

Present day, 2035

Maxwell had absolutely no idea if time where he was coincided with time in the land of the living. But by judging what little he had so far been able to see of what was happening on earth by using the Apollo's Stone, he deduced that he had been in Nefieti's Netherworld for at least a month.

Although he was eager to learn, Maxwell couldn't even begin to fathom everything that the otherworldly object was capable of. Each day, he tried and he tried and he tried, but he had failed to come anywhere close to understanding its true nature, let alone figure out how to at least leave the angel's realm. He could have allowed his frustrations to mount, but doing so he knew would not accomplish a damn thing. He had to be doing something wrong; emotions and thoughts after all, were what allowed the Apollo's Stone to work. But no matter how hard Maxwell tried to control both, either a memory or a reminder of some unfinished business would surface in his thoughts and disrupt the balance that he was trying to achieve.

All that he wanted to do was visit his son. He understood that he hadn't been given the stone for that specific purpose, but he simply wanted Sabastian to know that he had not been abandoned; that his father would be there to help guide him along the same path that he himself had prematurely stepped off of.

His ability to fully understand the Apollo's Stone so far hadn't been a complete failure, as he was successfully able to use it to spook Antonio. He would have liked to have been able to do more, as he owed the bastard a lot for what he had done to his family and friends, but he was content with what little he was able to do, because it was enough to set off a chain of events that culminated in a conclusion that he felt was more than deserved. However, the death of Antonio Marcone would have been more satisfying to Maxwell had it been at the hands of his son, and not the man whose own guilt did not, in his eyes, deserve any form of absolution. Nevertheless, the end did justify the means, as the soul of an evil bastard would soon, if not already, end up right where it belonged — Hell.

For the first time in his life — or death, Maxwell felt no undeserved pressures. And as he sat there in his manifested apartment and continued to study the Apollo's Stone, it finally hit him as to why he had so far failed to understand the object. It wasn't for his lack of trying; it clearly wasn't supposed to be easy to master. In fact, he had come to the conclusion that the mystical object was testing him and every bit of his quintessence.

Before he would be able to do what he had been brought to this realm to do, he had to approach the dilemma he found himself wrestling with in a manner completely different than any other problem he ever had to solve before. Somehow, he needed to find a way to literally become one with the stone.

With that belief, Maxwell had to assume that the otherworldly object's capabilities were far greater than what he had first imagined. He doubted that he would be able to ever control the universe with it, but he was fairly certain that in time, he would be able to manipulate and influence a situation or a destined path — that alone, was good enough for him.

Upon reflection, there was nothing about Maxwell's existence for him to complain about. All now appeared to be good in the preverbal world except — he felt it had been unfair that his wife, Sylvia, was only allowed to stay with him for a mere twenty-four hours his first day in the Netherworld. He hadn't seen her in a quarter century, and that brief visit just wasn't enough to make up for all of the lost time. It did though, allow for Maxwell to solidify what he had always believed in his heart — the love they had for one another was indeed eternal.

Two days after his wife had returned to Heaven, Maxwell finally had a chance to speak with Nefieti and ask him to confirm how it was even possible for his wife to visit. The angel's answer was simple — his love had brought her to him. Love of course, is an emotion — the Apollo's Stone harnesses that. But then the angel told him it wasn't just his love that had been responsible for bringing his wife to him — there was another very important factor at work. No, the stars did not need to align, but a full moon needed to appear. And whenever that took place, according to Nefieti, an aperture will temporarily open up between every existing realm there is. This 'corridor' was the only way that an eternal soul could be moved from one realm to another by either the Fates, the Almighty Lord, the Prince of Darkness, any of the numerous ancient Deity's, or anyone in possession of an Apollo's Stone that does not have any restrictions placed upon it by a being of divine continuity.

After hearing this information, Maxwell could only come to one conclusion — the Apollo's Stone that he had been given, was free of restrictions. Now, it was up to him to master its abilities so that he could not only summon his wife whenever an aperture opened up, but complete the pending task for which he was brought to this realm — and if the opportunity were to present itself afterward, he would use the otherworldly item to try and make things right with his son.

He was surprised that he was feeling as tired as he was. That wasn't something that he ever expected to feel again, considering that he was already dead — he could only assume that the reason for this feeling was because he still had possession of his own soul. Nevertheless, he got up from his bed, went into his living room and then, using the Apollo's Stone, did what he did everyday — he looked in on his son. Each time he did this though, it got harder and harder for him as he wanted so desperately to go where Sabastian was, hug him, and tell him how much he loved him. But he knew that would not be possible, as the potential consequences that could result from his selfishness were enough to dissuade him from taking such a risk — not only could his unexpected appearance from beyond the grave alter his son's true destiny, but Maxwell in turn, did not want to experience what it was like to be reprimanded by a pissed off eternal being.

Sabastian was an adult, and he unfortunately, just had to live his life without his father ever being a part of it. Like any other parent, he just had to observe his son from the sidelines and cheer him on.

After spending about a half an hour observing his boy, Maxwell decided to spy on the last of the enemy. If he only knew how to use the Apollo's Stone for more than just keeping watch or for haunting someone, via either their dream or a physical conduit like a mirror, a television, a computer or a vid-cell screen, he'd pay Louie a personal visit — for the lone purpose of rattling the man's cage. But Maxwell had yet to get a good read on Nefieti, and unlike his old boss, Christopher White, he was not yet sure if he could get away with pushing a few of the angel's buttons. So until he knew for sure just what kind of a 'boss' he now had, and until he was more proficient with the otherworldly object, Maxwell decided to play it safe and just spy on the enemy.

Immediately, he realized that the Sicilian bastard wasn't in Detroit — he was in Chicago — along with a woman and a young man. At first, Maxwell was unsure as to what was going on, but after about a half an hour of watching their interaction with each other, only one conclusion could be had — the damn asshole had gone and procreated. This was not good. No longer was there only one enemy left to deal with, as one was now potentially waiting in the wings. If Maxwell had known about this sooner, he would have dealt with the situation long before he punched his one-way ticket to the afterlife. But as he sat there observing Louie's naïve offspring, he knew that if he were to have taken it upon himself to implement some preventative measures, he would have become no different than the enemy he for so long, fought against. Not only that, he would have involuntarily taken that first step in the direction of where the Gates of Hell lie.

Just his thinking the way that he was, suddenly caused the Apollo's Stone to no longer allow him to see what was going on; it had turned snowy like an old analogue television that was unable to tune into any channel. His first thought was to throw the stone in annoyance, but instead of acting on a childish impulse, Maxwell set the Apollo's Stone down onto his coffee table and called out to Nefieti, as he now had a few questions that he wanted answers to. He honestly didn't think in that moment that his summons would be heard, but two seconds later, the angel was sitting directly across from him.

"I've just discovered something that may one day prevent my son from fulfilling his destiny. It is my responsibility to ensure that possibility never takes place. Show me how to use the Apollo's Stone so that I can either go to Louie Mazotti or bring him here. He and I need to have a heartfelt talk."

Nefieti didn't believe that for one second. "Um… first off, you are in no position to demand anything of me. Secondly… the Fates would not take too kindly to me allowing you to implement a preventative measure in order to assure that a prospective occurrence does not take place. And lastly, it's a little late for you to try and strike a deal with the enemy."

"It's never too late. Had I gone straight to heaven then yes, it would be too late. But was it not you who said that the Fates stepped in and were responsible for my redirection to this realm? And was it not you who gave this otherworldly object to me in order to complete a task? Therefore, I can only conclude that I am going to be asked to do something that by all accounts, should just be left well enough alone."

Nefieti could do nothing but smile. "Your assertion is correct."

Maxwell got up from his seat and walked about his manifested apartment. After taking a few seconds to organize his thoughts, he said, "You know… whenever I was working on a difficult case, I had to rely on my gut quite often to point me in the right direction or to make a difficult choice. And very rarely, did it fail me. Now, it's telling me that what you are refusing to allow me to do is exactly what you want me to do for you. This pending task of mine I know has something to do with Louie Mazotti and the path that he is currently walking; a path that you want me to change."

"You are a very perceptive individual, Mr. Banks."

"So then… what's the problem? Let me have a chat with the bastard."

"Not on your terms."

Maxwell was getting frustrated; he hated not having any dirt on someone he could use to hold over their head. "How is it that you can interfere with an individual's destiny to achieve your wants, but I can't assure that my one and only son stays on his destined path?"

"Your son, all on his own, had found his way back onto his original intended path, and Louie Mazotti has already begun to stray from his."

"How so? No matter what he does, he will eventually end up in Hell."

"As it stands now, he won't."

"What? What do you mean? The man is guilty of numerous crimes!"

"That is true, but not one of those ever involved his killing someone. Well.., other than putting a bullet into the back of a terrorist's head, Louie Mazotti has never once gotten innocent blood spilled on his hands; he used his brains while his associate was the one who used his brawn."

Maxwell was furious. Had he any alcohol in his manifested apartment, he'd pour himself a double shot to help ease his mental pain. Since he didn't, the only thing he could do was pace the room. "So let me get this straight. Even after everything the bastard has done and been associated with, when his time is up, he is going to Heaven?"

"No. Purgatory is his current destination."

"The bastard deserves to rot in Hell!"

"I agree… and that is why you are here."

It was at that moment when he realized why he was brought to the Netherworld. Louie's offspring had been the cause of him straying from his original destined path and Maxwell had been chosen to put the asshole back on it. That, he had no problem doing. "Then let's get started. Show me how to use the Apollo's Stone so that I can nudge the bastard in the direction that will take him to where he deserves to end up."

That declaration was what Nefieti was waiting to hear. Now, it was only going to be a matter of time before he got what he wanted, and Louie's son started on down the path that he was destined to walk. "I'm sorry, but I cannot. This is your task. Like you told me earlier, you relied on your gut to help you whenever you faced a dilemma. I suggest that you do the same when it comes to figuring out the stone."

Maxwell simply could not question the angel's words, as they were indeed his own. For that reason, he had to concede. "Ok, fine. But don't expect a miracle to happen anytime soon."

"I don't believe in miracles. You, however, have been known to pull more than just one rabbit out of your ass at a time. And when you do it again, you will undoubtedly relish in the stone's capabilities. You'll also understand why I could not help you."

Nefieti was about to flash himself out of the manifested apartment when Maxwell said, "Hold on a minute. Would it be possible instead to bring Terrance Burrelli's soul to this realm? I would like to have a conversation with him."

"I would too had he done the same thing to my wife and son. But as you know an aperture first needs to be open before a soul can be transferred between realms. That being said, I couldn't request it because the man's soul is currently in the possession of the Fates."

"Why is that? His soul should have had a one-way ticket to Hell."

"If he hadn't done what he had before his life ended, then that is where it would have gone."

"What are you talking about, Angel? The man killed my wife and kidnapped my son. Hell should be his eternal home."

"It was supposed to be, but that changed because of the decision he made before he died. It is why the location of Terrance Burelli's eternal stay is now under review."

"The man does not deserve a stay of execution. There is no doubting his guilt."

"He admittedly made some bad choices early on as an adult. Afterward, he did everything that he could to put his past behind him and live an honorable life. And in the end, he not only tried to make things right, he repented his sins to the one person he hurt the most. I know that you may not agree, but there was a lot more good than bad in the man's fifty-one years on earth, and that was all that was needed to place the man's final destination under review."

Maxwell was getting frustrated. It almost sounded to him as if this fallen angel was defending what Terrance Burelli had done. "No matter what good the man had accumulatively done in his life, killing someone and kidnapping another is something that cannot be swept under the rug."

"But brownie points are certainly earned when you save someone's life."

That confused Maxwell. It wasn't until Nefieti picked up the Apollo's Stone and used it to show him the last few minutes of Terrance Burelli's life that he finally understood. The man had showed up at Thibault's by the River and done what Maxwell had been unable to do — he killed Antonio Marcone and saved his son's life in the process. "But... he kidnapped my son and killed my wife. If he hadn't done what he had, then...."

"You have no idea whether or not your life would have been filled with nothing but happiness had Sabastian not been kidnapped and your wife not killed. Everything happens for a specific reason; reasons that can sometimes be difficult to accept and understand."

Maxwell sat down on his favorite La-z-boy and allowed the angel's words to sink in. He knew that Nefieti was right, even though he felt like trying to prove him wrong. In his heart he believed that, had his family not been taken from him, his life would have turned out as perfect as he could have ever hoped for — but without the ability to see for himself what could have been, Maxwell had to concede to the angel's point.

"I know that this isn't going to change your opinion of the man, but just so you know, Terrance Burelli's decision all those years ago was one that he regretted his entire life. It caused him to continually look over his shoulder, scared that what he had done was not only going to catch up to him, but ruin the respected career he had built. Nevertheless, his path ended up exactly where it was supposed to."

"I'm never going to get a chance to confront Terrance Burelli, am I?"

"That, I do not know. It all depends upon where his eternal resting place ends up being. If he is sent to Hell, then the answer is no."

With those words, Maxwell understood that an opportunity to confront the man might never come his way. Therefore, he needed to find a way to move beyond what took place. He had to put his personal wants aside and do what was being asked of him. He needed to focus on what was important and learn how to use the Apollo's Stone in ways other than it being just a means to see what was going on in the land of the living. He needed to learn how to summon a particular soul to his 'holodeck' on command — and he needed to learn how to transport himself back to earth. Only then, would he be able to accomplish what was expected of him. "Ok… I was just so angry when I learned everything I had."

"That's understandable. However, I would appreciate it if you didn't interrupt my afternoon nap again."

"You sleep?"

"No. But I like the feeling of resting in a large comfortable bed. I may be an immortal being, but I sure as hell am not going to stay on my feet for all of eternity."

Maxwell couldn't fault the angel for wanting some creature comforts, so he gave Nefieti his word that he would not call out to him in anger again, or bring up the name of Terrance Burelli — though that promise did not mean that he would not summon the angel again if something else came up that he simply did not agree with.

After the angel flashed himself back to his domain, Maxwell walked over to where Nefieti had set down the Apollo's Stone, picked it up, then sat on the edge of his couch and admired its beautiful, dancing colors. He could sit there all day and look at it. Never was the swirl pattern the same. It constantly changed according to whatever mood he was in — he just wished that it were as easy as a simple thought to get it to do what he wanted to do.

After spending a little bit of time reviewing his conversation with the angel, Maxwell came to a conclusion — one that had not previously crossed his mind. The immortal being he now believed, had a hidden agenda of some kind. In time, he was sure he would learn what that was. And even though he was being given an opportunity to do something that no one else probably ever has had before, it irked him somewhat that he was being used as a means for someone else's gain.

Wanting not to dwell on his supposition, as it would certainly get in the way of completing his assigned task, Maxwell closed his eyes and again tried to return to earth. Nothing — well, not exactly nothing happened. For the first time ever, he had gone somewhere. At least, he initially thought he had — that was until he realized that he was still in his small corner of Nefieti's realm. Although the area no longer looked like his apartment, it was very familiar to him — it was his childhood home; one of the few places from his past where he was always happy. No one was there; the house was empty. Still, Maxwell could not help but smile.

A few moments later, his surroundings vanished. They were immediately replaced with his manifested apartment. The trip down memory lane had been short, but it was one that Maxwell was certain he was going to return to once he had mastered the Apollo's Stone.

After a few moments spent clearing his thoughts, he decided to try again to leave where he was. Maxwell wasn't ready to confront his enemy, but he was ready to see what he could and could not do in an ethereal form. This time, instead of just letting his emotions control the object, and while at the same time, trying to keep his mind clear, he interjected one distinct thought in hopes that it would be the key component needed for him to return to earth.

Sure enough, it was. He had finally succeeded. He had actually felt his body leave the Netherworld and appear right where he wanted to. He wasn't visible, but Maxwell knew that it would not take too long for his presence to become known. He had no intention of doing any harm to anyone, but he now had the opportunity to find out what he could and could not do in an ethereal-like form.

In that moment, Maxwell felt that the logical thing for him to do next was to test the boundaries of his new found abilities. It was mean of him, but he didn't care. No better a target was there to test those abilities on than the ones who were long overdue to be harassed — those low-life pieces of crap: dealers, pimps, and common criminals, that used the streets of Detroit to do their business.

1

It was a very strange feeling for Sabastian the moment he had opened the door to his father's apartment. Maybe the essence of Maxwell Banks had been left behind? He just did not know. Although he had fully accepted that he was his long lost son, it still did not feel quite right that he was about to enter into the residence of someone whom he was bound to by DNA, but did not otherwise know.

Sydney had offered to accompany him because he had thought that being there with his nephew would help to ease whatever fear may be inside. But alone is what Sabastian wanted to be, as this was a moment that he wanted to experience on his own. He could have just sat there and listened to his uncle and Savanna tell him stories about his father, but for him to truly learn what Maxwell Banks was all about, he had to search that out for himself — and then maybe when that had been accomplished, he'd be able to figure out what he, Sabastian Banks, was supposed to become.

Upon his entering of the apartment, a slight chill ran down his spine. He wasn't the kind of person who would normally believe in the supernatural, but he was someone who always kept an open mind. Was the spirit of his father right there in the apartment with him at this very moment? Had his father's spirit been there to watch over and protect him at 'Thibault's By the River', or had fate simply intervened in order to assure that his destiny was fulfilled? It was highly unlikely that answers to those questions would be revealed. Nevertheless, he wanted to believe that Maxwell Banks had been there, because he knew that he should have died that night when Antonio stood over him with a gun pointed at the back of his head.

While in anticipation of his own death, a bizarre feeling had enveloped him. It was one that Sabastian had never experienced before; his gut was telling him not to worry because he was going to be the one walking away from that restaurant and not Antonio. His gut had been right.

Upon reflection, Sabastian knew that he had to look at what had happened to him in a pragmatic way. His instincts were what had saved him, not an influence from beyond the grave or from some other unknown entity. Still, he had to believe that in some strange way, Maxwell Banks' legacy was slowly nudging him along his destined path — and he was okay with that, as he honestly felt that he was far from ready to step completely onto it and walking it all by himself.

As Sabastian made his way through the living room area of his father's apartment, his hesitancy slowly began to dissipate — but that still didn't make this any easier. Absorbing his surroundings and trying to figure out what kind of man his father may have been was turning out to be more difficult than what he had first assumed it would be. There weren't too many material things present, just the basic items that you would find in any man's bachelor apartment: a few trinkets, books, magazines, pictures; nothing that Sabastian could assume were sentimental or of a personal nature.

After spending about a half an hour looking through the majority of his father's apartment, the only thing that was left for him to see was the lone bedroom, the most private of spaces that the majority of people tended to have. A bit of that earlier hesitation had returned to Sabastian as he slowly opened up the door. Almost immediately, his eyes were drawn to the black and white oil painting of his parents' wedding day that had hung above the queen-sized, four poster antique brass bed. He curiously made his way closer to the head of the bed and then gazed at the perfect representation of his mother and father. Carefully, he leaned forward across the head of the bed and removed the painting from the wall — he then sat down on the edge of it and studied the portrait.

As his fingertips gently touched the surface of the painting, a flood of emotions enveloped him; the same flood of emotions that he had felt when he had visited his parents' gravesite not too long ago. He had never known these people, and he never will, but with this painting that he now had in his hands, he surely would never forget them.

Sabastian could not take his eyes off of the portrait, as his thoughts took him to the land of unanswerable questions. What would his life have been like if everything that happened had not? Would he

2

be more like his mother or father? Would he have actually followed in his father's footsteps and become a police officer? Would he have even considered joining the military? Would he have gone off to college and earned a degree? Would he have been married by now and had children of his own? The only thing he knew for sure, was that his life would have turned out to be much different if his parents were still alive and a part of it today.

The longer that Sabastian stayed in his father's apartment, the more he realized that he was beginning to feel at home — this was where he belonged. Now, better late than never, this was where he was supposed to be. He leaned forward, gently kissed the portrait, and again touched the surface of it. Yes, this was just an inanimate object, but in that moment he felt it was the only way that he could physically connect with his parents.

After a moment in quiet thought, he returned the painting to where it had been hanging, left the bedroom, and walked toward the front door of the apartment. After crossing its threshold and locking the door, he stood there for a second and smiled. *'No longer do I have any doubts. This is where I belong.'*

He felt like his life was speeding by at a rate faster than what he was physically able to keep up with. Much of it had been lived with a slight sense of evil purpose — although he would not readily admit that to himself. A normal life is what he never knew — and there were many times that he wished he had one. The closest that he would ever come to feeling like he was living one was when he had made the time to travel to Chicago in order to visit his one and only son; a son who knew him only as, Uncle Louie.

After being made aware that the woman whom he had a brief relationship with had become pregnant with his child, and knowing that she, Mirella Santori wanted nothing to do with the lifestyle he had chosen to live, Louie had made a difficult decision. It was a decision that still pained him inside to this day — but at the time, he had felt that it was the only way for him to stay a part of his child's life. It sucked, but he knew that he had no other choice.

The agreement he had made with his son's mother was straightforward. Louie would be allowed to be a part of Marco's life

3

so long as he kept one important thing a secret. He would simply be known as a good family friend — an unofficial uncle. The agreement also included a promise from him that he would take Mirella out of the lower-class neighborhood that she had been living in and financially support her and their son — it was an arrangement that wasn't the most ideal for Louie, but he understood that it was necessary, as his son needed a continual positive influence. That couldn't happen without the agreement being made, because Louie's chosen way of life wasn't one that a young child needed to be exposed to. Therefore, the only logical choice that he had was to become someone else whenever he was around Marco. It certainly wasn't what he wanted, but it was the only way in which he could be any kind of father figure at all to his son.

In the back of his mind, he knew without a shadow of a doubt that a day would eventually come when all that was believed would be discovered as being a lie. And when that day happened, he was certain that Mirella's insistence was one that she was going to regret imposing — keeping the truth hidden from her son was most certainly going to backfire. And when that took place, Louie knew that it was going to cause her more heartache than what she could ever imagine. It wasn't what he wished upon the mother of his son, but Mirella had made her bed, and only she could lie deep in the deceit she had insisted upon.

A week had gone by since Louie had miraculously escaped with his life in yet another situation handled badly — a situation that Maxwell Banks' offspring, Sabastian, had again gone and stuck his nose in. How Louie had gotten so lucky, he did not know? Thankfully, he had been close enough to the front exit of the restaurant that he was able to crawl unnoticed out through the unlocked door. Once he was outside, he took a quick look through the glass front door into the restaurant to see what was happening. And although he was concerned about Antonio's safety, he was still feeling the effects of the sonic micro-burst. Because of this, his accurate perception of what was actually taking place could not be assured. All that he remembered seeing was his boss with a gun in his hand pointed at Sabastian's head — he was completely unaware of what Terrance Burelli was about to do.

Before Louie could fully regain his senses, what was taking place inside the restaurant was over — it was too late for him to do anything. Antonio had been a longtime friend of his, and Louie knew that he should have risked his own wellbeing and gone back inside to support his boss. But he didn't, and Antonio had lost his life.

It had taken a good five minutes after he had left the restaurant before the haze that had been lingering inside of his head, cleared. It was only then that Louie recognized things had forever changed. What he had first thought about doing twenty-some years ago had just been done for him. That window had opened right back up and was inviting him to step right on through.

The day that Louie honestly thought would never come had. The Detroit Underworld Organization was now finally his to run. Through unfortunate circumstances, he was now the new boss — but he was also the boss of a clearly fractured organization. It would take a lot of work on his part and a lot of convincing of the remaining lower ranking members of the D.U.O. that the organization could be salvaged and restructured, strengthened, and run like a real professional operation — not an ego driven clusterfuck like it had been. It wouldn't happen overnight, but Louie was confident that he could make it happen.

After spending a few days relaxing in the company of his son, Louie decided that Marco's twentieth birthday, which was less than a month away, would be the day that he would break his promise to Mirella and finally tell his son the entire truth that he was actually his biological father and not his uncle. This was a decision that he had been pondering over for years, one that hadn't been easy for him to make. Louie knew in his heart that he was going to go back on his word one day, but he just didn't want to wait until he was old and on his deathbed for that to take place. Therefore, his son's upcoming birthday seemed to be the perfect day for such a revelation. The reason for that was simple; in Louie's eyes, Marco would officially become an adult and he deserved to be treated as such.

What had also made this difficult decision much easier for him was that Sal and Antonio were no longer intertwined in his life. The consequences that could have occurred if either one of them were to have found out about Marco, would have been unfathomable. Fortunately, the possibility of that taking place was no longer there. Still, doing everything that he could over the years to prevent them from ever learning of his secret had been extremely taxing on him. There had even been a couple of instances when Marco's existence had almost come out. Thankfully, that had not occurred — although Louie was pretty sure that Sal had found out the truth at some point and had just been waiting for the right moment to let the cat out of the bag.

"You want to do what, Louie?"

"Listen, Mirella. I've had to live this lie about my son for almost twenty years. He is now a sophomore in college, and I think that it is time he knows the truth."

"No way! You made a promise to me and I expect you to keep it."

"I'm not getting any younger. I want to be able to have a real father/son relationship with Marco and I can't do that pretending to be his uncle."

Mirella stood up from the synth-leather sofa she had been sitting on and turned her back to Louie. She then purposefully walked into the den and poured herself a rock glass of kiwi-infused vodka from behind the bar. In the depths of her soul, she knew that Louie was going to spring this on her one day, but she had honestly hoped that he would have continued to be the upstanding man he had always been and stuck to his promise to never reveal the truth. She had absolutely no idea what she would do if Louie did go back on his word — she only knew that it would ruin her near perfect world.

Mirella returned to the living room with her drink in hand, set it down on the coffee table in front of her, and then looked seriously into Louie's eyes. "I always knew that this day would come, but I am begging you not to tell Marco that you're his father. I don't want him to ever find out what you are and what you are involved with. If he finds out the truth, then it is only a matter of time before he finds out everything else about you."

"Is that really so bad?"

"Yes!"

Louie got up from where he had been seated and sat down next to Mirella on the sofa. "There could not have been a better mother to raise and influence my son than you. Marco is ready to handle the truth."

"I'm not ready for the truth to come out." Mirella took a healthy sip of her drink and tried her best to relax; she found it very difficult to do so. "Listen, Louie. We both rushed into a relationship with each other all those years ago and now we have a son because of it. Don't get me wrong… Marco is the best thing that has ever happen to me. And I'm also thankful that you were man enough to tell me everything about you and what you were involved with right from the beginning. If you hadn't done that, I probably would have fallen madly in love with you and then ended up hating your guts. You've been nothing but gracious, kind, and generous to me and to Marco, but I am begging you, Louie, not to go back on your word."

He never expected that this conversation would go smoothly or that there would be some possible give in her stance. Even after all these years, he still cared tremendously about Mirella — and he too, would have probably fallen deeply in love with her. But she was right about one thing; Louie's chosen life would have caused more damage than could ever be repaired if it had become known before now. His decision to tell Mirella everything about him early on was the right one, even though it continually hurt him throughout the years. But at least he had been able to stay a small part of his son's life; a part that he knew he had to continue to play as Marco's 'uncle' if he wanted to stay in the picture.

Because he still cared deeply for Mirella, and didn't wish to hurt her, Louie made another decision. For the moment, he would continue to honor the promise he made and keep the truth hidden from his son. How long that would be for though, he was unsure. "Ok.., I won't say anything." He then walked toward the entrance of the home, removed his spring jacket from the coat rack, and put it on. Louie was just about to leave when Marco opened up the front door.

"Hey, Uncle Louie. What are you leaving for?"

"I have some business that I have to tend to, so I can't stay."

"Ah… that's too bad. I was gonna ask you if you could help me out with my studies? We have what our professor calls a pre-exam cram session on Friday in preparation for our upcoming finals. I'm still having some difficulty with some parts of my business management class and I don't want to be lost."

"I'm sorry, Marco. I wouldn't normally hesitate to stay and help you, but today is just not a good day. You said that your session isn't until Friday, so I'll see if I can clear up my schedule and stop by on Thursday evening."

"That would be awesome."

Louie smiled at his son. "I will try my best."

"You always do… and I will completely understand if you can't make it."

Louie then unexpectedly gave his son a warm embrace; an embrace that seemed a bit different than the ones that Marco had ever received from him before. Thinking nothing of it, he stood there by the front door and watched his 'uncle' walk down the sidewalk, get into his car, and then leave. Then, turning to his mother, Marco asked, "Is it me, or does Uncle Louie seem to be a bit off today?"

"He has had a lot of personal things on his mind as of late that he has been struggling to deal with. I'm sure he'll be fine in a few days, so it's nothing that you need to worry about."

Accepting his mother's words of assurance, Marco took his schoolwork and headed up the stairs; Mirella pounded back the remainder of her vodka as she walked into the kitchen. She hated to lie like that to her son, but in her mind, a lie was better than the truth when it came to her son's father and what she feared it would do to him if he ever found out — and what it would do to her if that were to ever happened.

After spending the morning at his father's apartment, then a few hours at the gym, Sabastian went to the agency, hoping that his uncle would be there because he wanted to have a family chat with him. But upon his arrival, he discovered that Sydney wasn't — what was there instead, was the delicious smelling lunch that Savanna had arranged to have delivered.

"So does anyone know where my uncle is at?" Sabastian asked just before he took a bite of his roast beef and Swiss sub.

"He told me that he had a hot date tonight, so he was going to get his hair cut. I'm sure he'll come here after that."

He set his sandwich down on the edge of Savanna's desk and went over to the sim-caf machine to pour himself a fresh cup. Since his father's death, the amount of calls to the office had become few and far between — it led Sabastian to believe that word had already begun to spread of Maxwell's untimely passing.

Since then, Savanna has spent the majority of her days tying up loose ends. She even had to deal with a request from the Union Revenue Service to provide documentation of travel expenses that her old boss had claimed over the previous five years; expenses that had nothing to do with an actual client, but were part of the ongoing search for his missing son. So when the vid-phone had unexpectedly rung right in the middle of their lunch, it had startled Savanna — it was almost as if she never expected the agency to get a call again. To her relief, it wasn't another call from someone wanting money or documentation; it was instead a personal call for Sabastian.

"Hello, Grandma. Hold on a minute and I'll have Savanna transfer your call to my fath… another office so that we can have some privacy." It felt a bit weird to Sabastian in that moment; not just because he had greeted Edith Burelli the way that he did with Savanna right there beside him, but because he had partially made reference to his paternal father. And although she was not his maternal grandmother, he had loved this woman his entire life as if she was — that, as far as Sabastian was concerned, would never change. "It's only been a week, Grandma, since I saw you last. So… what's up?"

"T.J… Um, I mean.., Sabastian. A clerk from the A.C.U. Military Base in Houston called here looking for you. I can only assume that you never forwarded your new number to them?"

"Yeah, I never had a chance to do that. A lot has been going on in my life, so I haven't done a lot of the things that I need to do. So.., what did they want?"

"I don't know. I was just asked to try and get a hold of you and then get you to call them back as soon as possible."

Sabastian thanked his grandmother; told her that he loved her, disconnected his call, and then he called the Ameri-Can Union Military Base. Sabastian's conversation had been fairly brief, and after it was finished, he left his father's office and returned to Savanna's desk. To his pleasant surprise, his uncle Sydney was now there.

As happy as he should have been to see his uncle, disappointment could clearly be seen on his face. He sat back down in the chair he had earlier been in, took another bite of his roast beef sub, then a healthy sip of his sim-caf — for some reason, neither tasted the same as they had only a few minutes ago. The call that he had just made, and the information that he had just been given, was something that he knew was one day, destined to occur — but in all honesty, he never expected it to happen so soon. He had just only recently returned to a normal life (if you can call the events that took place not too long ago, normal) and didn't want to break the hearts of his recently reunited family. However, Sabastian could not think of a legitimate reason to delay his soon to be unpopular news to those in the room, so he cleared his throat and spoke, "Um… I'm afraid that I have to leave for a while. I've just received an emergency recall notice. I have to be back at the military base in Houston by tomorrow evening."

"Why? Did you not change your status from active to reserve?"

"I did, Uncle Sydney. But because of the specific skill set I have, I am needed for an emergency deployment."

"What kind of emergency deployment?"

"I honestly don't know all the details yet, Savanna. I guess I'll find out from my new platoon commander, whoever that may now be, and get the full details when I get there. I just hope that they are not gonna send me to some backwater, third world country to search for some drug lord or something."

"Let's hope that is not the case." Sydney leaned over from his seat and gave his nephew a hug. Although these unexpected hugs from his uncle still felt a bit weird to him, Sabastian just accepted them as his way of saying how much his uncle was thrilled that he had come back into his life, that his uncle loved him, and that he was only trying to make up for all of the time lost.

After finishing his lunch, Sabastian excused himself, took the remainder of his sim-caf, and went back into his father's office. The moment he claimed the seat behind the desk, several potential scenarios quickly formed in his mind; some of which he was okay with, most of which he was not. Then again, that was only his mind trying to convince him that as soon as he stepped foot back onto a military base, his old life was going to return and attempt to permanently push aside his new one.

Because Sabastian was unwilling to give up what he now had, he picked up the vid-phone that was on the desk and called the office of his new platoon's commander; his ex-father's former office. He knew that his negative thoughts had no basis for what was really waiting for him once he returned to Houston — nonetheless, some insight would be welcomed. Having a bit more information at hand before he left would not only help to put his mind at ease, he would be able to do the same for those who were waiting patiently on the other side of his father's office door.

To Sabastian's surprise, Captain E.J. Swilling answered his call. He first confirmed to Sabastian that he was the one who would be replacing Terrance Burelli as leader of the Special North American Freedom Unit, and then he explained to him the reasoning behind why he had been recalled. After hearing what the captain had to say, none of Sabastian's concerns were removed. There was nothing that he could do about it though, so after disconnecting his call, he polished off the last drop of his sim-caf, sat back, and thought. Five minutes later, he still could not find a logical reason as to why he was being asked to serve again.

A very light, warm rain had been falling all day long. The droplets themselves had been reduced to a size so small that the light mist felt almost nonexistent; it was so light that you really didn't notice at all that you were still getting wet — but then again, the environment that Mother Nature chose this day to create, only helped to enhance the beauty that made up the ten acres of the Byakko Gardens.

She hadn't found many places during her life where she had enjoyed spending time alone. And even though her first visit here had only been for a few brief days, Jerrelle had instantly felt at peace. It could have just been the reassurance that she felt with her half-sister being close by; seeing that the gardens were above the secret headquarters of the Extremist Clandestine Liberation Organization, but there was something tranquil about the actual grounds that had made her completely forget about her unconventional life as she took in the peacefulness that surrounded her.

After what had happened at 'Thibault's by the River', Jerrelle had spent the following few days with Sabastian in San Antonio. She was disappointed that they had lost the golden opportunity they had that night to finish what they had started together. One of their targets had somehow slipped away and disappeared during the chaos — but she also knew that a time would come when Louie Mazotti would unexpectedly cross their path again. And when that happened, she and Sabastian would then resume their mission of completing what her friend's father had started all those years ago.

Whether or not he would admit it, Sabastian needed some time alone so that he not only could begin to get on with his new life, but find the answers to all the questions that only he could search for. Easily recognizing this, Jerrelle decided that it was best for her to just step aside for the time being so that he could do what needed to be done. Besides, she knew that it would not take her friend too long before he found what few pieces of his life were still missing — seeing that it was his curiosity in the first place that had led him to discover who he really was.

In the meantime, Jerrelle used some of her not-so-honest winnings from her successful night of gambling at the New Book Cadillac Casino and booked herself a vacation; the first one that she had ever been able to afford. During her sister's brief cameo appearance that same night at Thibault's, Jerrelle had made sure that she would be able to make direct contact with Bai Lin whenever she wanted to, as she sure as hell did not want to have to go through the same painful bullshit each time she had wanted to see her sister. So when Jerrelle had arrived in Japan this time, she was thankful that Bai Lin had been waiting for her just outside the airport terminal.

Sitting on a carved stone bench in the garden, Jerrelle was looking at nothing in particular. Once the light rain had finally dissipated, a thin patch of fog had begun to form on the ground. *'Well, isn't that just a bit of irony?'* Her time in the garden up until that point had done a lot to relax her, but she was also cognizant of the fact that her thoughts were still as foggy as the ground around her.

Her adventure with Sabastian had been good and bad. The good being that her badly fractured friendship with him had been permanently mended; the bad had been the loss of the one and only

12

person she had ever admitted to herself that she had truly cared about. She had done a good job under the circumstances to push aside the pain of Helfred's unnecessary death while she helped her friend try to accomplish his goal. But now that they had put a halt to their mission as her emotions were pushing their way to the surface. They desperately wanted to be released, yet her strong personality was being its usual self and resisting what needed to happen — she believed that she was nowhere near ready to move on.

As the light fog began to expand to encase her feet, Jerrelle leaned her head forward and observed that gentle act of nature. She watched the intermittent drops of water that still existed in the air, fall — but there were also drops that were much larger than what she had seen around her just a few minutes ago, now cutting through the remnants of Mother Nature's act. In that moment, she thought the rain was going to pick up again — but after a few seconds, she realized that was not the case. Those larger drops had actually come from her, as they were her own falling tears — her emotions had overpowered her habitual defense mechanism.

No longer did Jerrelle have the mental strength to fight it. The hurt inside her shot right to the surface and slammed against her like a typhoon swallowing up an entire shoreline. The floodgates had burst open. This was something that she had only experienced once before in her life — and that was when she was a teenager, right after her mother had been senselessly murdered. Soon afterward, that was when Jerrelle started to build her wall, as never again did she want to feel so vulnerable; so helpless.

Up until today, the foundation of that wall had stayed solid. Now, its first crack had become visible. The usually thick-skinned, tough exterior that she always portrayed had softened. She felt embarrassed and like a fool.

Jerrelle had sat there on top of the carved stone bench for nearly an hour — although she was unsure how much of that she had spent crying. If her sister had not come looking for her, she probably would have just stayed there grieving until the wee hours of the next morning.

Gently, Bai Lin placed her hand on her sister's shoulder as she sat down next to her. She looked caringly into Jerrelle's bloodshot and glossy eyes, and could see the deep hurt that her sister was in. Without having to speak a word, she took her sister in her arms and held her. The comfort of the embrace was exactly what Jerrelle had needed at that moment, for Bai Lin knew that her sister's tears were not quite done yet. For that reason, she didn't speak a word; she just sat there and held her, allowing her all the time that she needed. She had never seen her sister like this before, and it tugged at her own heart to see the immense pain that Jerrelle was suffering through. Unfortunately, Bai Lin knew that there was nothing that she could do to help take that away. Only time could do that.

As the sun was setting, Bai Lin looked into her sister's eyes and could see that Jerrelle was all cried out and exhausted, so she helped her up off of the stone bench and walked her to the cleverly camouflaged secret entrance to the underground headquarters of the Extremist Clandestine Liberation. Once they had made it to the bottom of the spiral staircase, she led her sister to a private room, and then escorted her over to the futon that had been prepared. There, Bai Lin encouraged her to lie down and get some rest. In all honestly, she doubted that her sister would be able to do that. Nevertheless, she shut off the light and left Jerrelle alone with her congealed thoughts.

2

Louie returned to his apartment; the one that he had been renting since Marco was old enough to leave the ever-watchful eye of his mother. Though his trips to Chicago had been few and far between over the years, he didn't want to stay in a hotel room every time he would visit, or impose on Mirella to stay at her place. He simply wanted a semi-permanent residence of his own so that he could spend some quality time alone with his son whenever he was in town.

Once inside, he went straight to his small apartment-sized fridge and grabbed himself a beer. He wasn't like Antonio when it came to alcohol. For him, expensive spirits were something that he would drink only on occasion — usually when he needed to take the edge off his work related stress. The rest of the time, he preferred to drink a good ice-cold brew.

Next, he went over to his digital music player and selected some classical piano to listen to. As the soothing sounds of the Steinway filled his apartment, he took a healthy first sip of his beer, then he walked out onto his balcony — there, he stood at the railing and stared out across the street at the adjacent Wicker Park. Although he enjoyed watching the dogs running and playing leash free, he found it difficult most of the time to observe the socialization of all the families that used the recreational area. Every time he saw a father and son together: playing catch, throwing a Frisbee, a football, or kicking a soccer ball around, or chasing each other in a game of tag, it just ate away at his heart. Yes, nothing was stopping him from doing all those things with Marco, but not being able to act like a normal father while engaging in such activities was just as bad as having to deal with Sal for all those years while Antonio had been locked up.

After finishing off his beer, Louie headed back inside his apartment. Again, the thought of telling Marco the truth had re-entered his mind, but he was a man of his word and his selfish thoughts had to be put aside — at least for the time being. *'One day, my son will know the truth... and I do believe that he will accept me for who I am and not judge me for what I do.'* Louie then placed the empty beer bottle onto the kitchen counter and made a long-overdue business decision. *'I think that it is time to begin the process of re-structuring the organization.'* He then walked over to the coffee table in the living room where he had left his vid-cell, picked it up, and called the one person whom he knew he wanted as his right hand man; his number one. He had several options to choose from, but none of the lower ranked members of the D.U.O. had impressed him enough over the years to be promoted. The person that he wanted by his side to take over the responsibilities that he once had, lived overseas in China; Zhin Wi, the top associate of the D.U.O.'s Asian affiliate.

Louie's call was unexpected; so was the news pertaining to everything else that had recently happened — including the untimely deaths of Sal and Antonio. To say that he wasn't flattered would be a lie, but China was Zhin Wi's home and he wasn't sure that he wanted to leave it all behind. However, he knew it was his track record that was the reason why Louie was now reaching out to him with this once in a lifetime offer; an offer that he immediately realized he'd be utterly stupid to turn down.

After hearing those words he had hoped to hear in response to his offer, Louie disconnected his call and instantly felt at ease knowing that he had just taken that first step. With his chosen right-hand man now scheduled to arrive in Chicago in just a few short days, it was only going to be a matter of time before the D.U.O. was back in business and continuing on in the direction that Antonio had first put it in more than a quarter century ago.

Now feeling a bit better that he had made the decision to get back to work, Louie returned to his refrigerator and grabbed another beer. At that exact same moment, his vid-cell rang. Only three people had his personal vid-cell number, and two were no longer alive. The other person was Mirella Santori — but that wasn't who was calling him.

Louie was just a bit perturbed, as he did not recognize the number on his phone's display. A solicitor was one thing, as they would call from time to time. However, if this call ended up being from one of the organization's clients, then Louie was going to rip them a new one. They had no right finding and then calling his personal vid-cell number without first having his permission to do so.

After a few seconds of contemplation, he recognized that the unknown call was from the area code that was associated with Puerto Rico. He didn't know anyone personally who lived there, but he was aware of a few past clients that conducted their business from that former unincorporated territory of the United States of America.

When the United States decided to amalgamate with Canada, Puerto Rico had also been invited to join. Surprisingly, its government and its people overwhelmingly decided against it — a decision that to this day still baffled many within the Union.

Inside, Louie was pissed — but he wasn't about to chastise the individual on the other end. Open-mindedness was what was needed until he had all the facts; only then would he decide whether or not the call would continue or be disconnected, as the person calling him just happened to be someone whom Louie remembered well and actually liked — and yes, he was a past client of theirs.

No hello. No how are you. No what's new — the man's first words were a well thought out apology for making contact with him the way that he did. He then followed that by informing Louie that he had tried on numerous occasions to contact the D.U.O through regular channels, but none of the messages that he had left had been returned. He then again apologized for the way that he went about contacting Louie; insisting that he had only done this because he didn't know any other way to get in touch, as he and his organization were desperately in need of a shipment of high quality merchandise before the week's end.

In this business that Louie inherited, one's own desperation becomes another's intrigue — but he wasn't about to let his curiosity erase the fact that this person had broken the number one rule. Then again, Antonio's rules no longer applied. Rules can be broken, rules can be re-written, rules can be loosely interpreted, and rules can simply be thrown out the window. Maybe it was time that Louie amended the entire rulebook.

After taking a swig of his fresh beer, an uncertainty appeared in his thoughts. Was Louie really ready to conduct business with a client? At least, this one he knew — and trusted. When the time

17

finally came to bring the D.U.O. back to life, the smart thing for him to do would be to start all over from scratch and accumulate his own list of clients; keeping only a few of the old ones that had no real risk attached to them. In that moment, Louie decided that now was as good a time as any to see if he could pull off a small business deal all by himself without the help of his currently dismantled organization — it wasn't like he hadn't coordinated a deal before. So he informed the caller that the D.U.O. was in the midst of a restructuring phase, and that he wasn't sure if he would be able to fill his request by week's end. Louie did however, promise that he would make a few calls and then get back to him within the next forty-eight hours, at which point he would let him know whether or not he could complete his request.

Although the client wasn't too happy with the presented conditions, he agreed to give Louie the necessary time that he claimed he needed to try and arrange the shipment of merchandise he was asking for. What wasn't known, nor was he willing to declare his reasons, was that the man was in a bind, as there wasn't another supplier out there willing to sell to him and his organization — that fact was the lone reason why this individual was willing to accept what he actually felt was an unnecessary delay.

After Louie had disconnected his call, he opened up his fridge and took out a third beer — that was something that he normally did not do, but he was by himself and he wanted to enjoy his day. Soon, his life would return to the way it used to be and he would no longer be able to indulge himself — he after all, was now the boss of an underground criminal organization.

With his fresh beer in hand, he went back out to his balcony, cracked it open, tossed the cap over the railing, and then relished in the sensation of the beer freely flowing down his already well lubricated throat. Halfway through it, he decided to take up a seat on the antique wood and cast iron bench beside the balcony door. There, he then flipped open his vid-cell and dialed a number. Within two rings, Louie's call was answered — and like it had always been every time Louie talked to this man, his face stayed concealed. "Hey, this is Louie. I know you weren't expecting a call from us for a while, but things have changed. Can you get access to our supplies? I just had an unexpected request for a shipment of our best military grade hardware."

"I think so, Louie. Although getting them on the road afterward might not be that easy. As you know, all of our transportation specialists are off on 'vacation'."

"I am aware of that, Casper. This isn't something that has to be done; I only want to see how difficult it would be right now."

After quietly working in a subcontracted capacity for the D.U.O. for two and a half decades, the trust and the comfort that was there between the two could not be denied. However, knowing who he was working for and what they had no qualms about doing if they felt it to be necessary, Casper had chosen to keep his real identity a secret. The D.U.O. had after all, killed James 'Jimbo' Lewis — the man who not only had been responsible for his recruitment, but had been someone whom Casper had known since he was a troubled teen. "Ok. But I got a feeling that Antonio won't be happy with my report."

"You don't have to worry about Antonio anymore. He is no longer alive. I am in charge of the D.U.O. now." Louie wasn't sure, but in that moment, he believed that a small weight had just been lifted off of Casper's shoulders, as a definite exhale could be heard on the other end of his call.

"For you, I will do my best."

"I know that you will." Louie then proceeded to inform his 'employee' of what the requested merchandise would be.

Casper took a moment and thought about what he needed to do to complete the order. Once he had everything organized in his head, he said, "Not everything your client is asking for is available in one location. Unfortunately, it's in three. This will probably take me two, maybe even three days to not only assemble everything that the client wants, but to figure out a way to get everything shipped to where they want it to end up."

"How would you move the merchandise?"

"As it stands right now, the only option we have would be to contract this out."

That wasn't what Louie wanted to hear. Bringing in someone to do a task that would normally be handled internally was a risk that should not be taken. But under the circumstances, he understood why

19

Casper had said that — the last thing he wanted was to prematurely call everyone back to work. He wanted to do this slowly and restructure certain aspects of the organization where it was needed. If he called his transport specialists back to work, he'd have to also make sure that the proper people were in place to back them up if an issue arose. That was just too much stuff for him right now to have to worry about without his trusted associates in place to help assure that everything went off without a hitch. "Do what you have to do, Casper, to complete the order. I'm not worried about your ability to stay discrete in the process."

"Thank you, sir. So where does the client need the merchandise shipped to?"

"Tijuana, Mexico."

"No problem. And for the record, I am glad that Antonio is no longer alive. With you, I no longer have to worry about waking up one day and discovering that I have become a playing piece in one of his famous games."

Louie could not help but chuckle. Casper's military career had been mediocre at best before he became involved with the Detroit Underworld Organization. But from that moment onward, he had a motivation to him that had all but removed the inadequacies he had been labeled with. And as far as Louie was concerned, the man had been the M.V.P. of the D.U.O. on multiple occasions over the years. If only Louie knew who he really was, he would actually consider inviting Casper to join his team. But where he was, Louie knew that he was just too valuable a player to promote. He needed him to stay put and continue to do what he had been doing. And so long as he didn't screw them over, their asset was going to be a well-compensated individual who would have a lifelong place on Louie's payroll.

"Hey T.J.!" greeted a handful of Sabastian's army buddies the moment he entered the barracks at the A.C.U. Military Base. He had been T.J. his whole life; now it just seemed strange for someone to call him that. Although he was still getting used to being called Sabastian; knowing more now about who he was, where he came from, and the situation surrounding the first quarter century of his life, has made the adjustment a lot easier than he thought it would be. Still, that adjustment for others who knew him well was certainly going to take some time, of which Sabastian was more than willing to give them. For now though, he just ignored the faux pas, as the army buddies that he had lived and trained with for years, had no idea that his life had taken a complete three-sixty.

"Hey, guys. It's good to see everyone again."

"So… you have some explaining to do," Richard Atwater said, as he walked up to his old friend and placed his right arm around his shoulder. He, like Sabastian, had been adopted at birth, but then had lost his mother when he was five years of age from a sudden stroke. From the first day they had met each other, a close friendship had been formed; a friendship that grew when each other realized that they had a lot of things in common, including growing up with only a father.

"What do you mean?"

"Um… like why did you decide to leave the active service and go on the reserve list?"

"Yeah! Why did you do that, T.J.?" Ben Fraisure and Jeff Tranter said almost simultaneously.

'So much for a seamless return,' Sabastian thought. 'I guess I might as well get this over with now.' Sabastian set his supply bag down on top of his old bunk, pulled himself up onto it, and gathered the attention of the entire platoon. He then began the daunting task of explaining a brief censorial version of the events that led to the discovery of his true identity and the sad fact that their platoon leader, Major Terrance Burelli, had lost his life. Sabastian was very careful as he told his story, because he did not want to divulge any information that surrounded the actual circumstances of his ex-father's involvement. He had no desire to tarnish the man's legacy; he only told them that Terrance had helped him with his 'mission' and had died in an unfortunate accident.

There was a lot of mumbling; a lot of chatter amongst those in the platoon once Sabastian was done telling his unbelievable story. Most of them weren't sure what to think. They all knew, liked, and had trusted their fellow soldier. And now, the person that they knew well, was not who they had thought him to always be. His name wasn't just different, but the person they knew was different. He was no longer a young man with no worries; he was now a young man who had inherited a shitload of crap and taken the initiative to try and correct what had happened to him and the family he was born into.

Those in Sabastian's platoon each felt a strange sense of pride in their fellow soldier; their friend, for doing something that not one of them were sure that they could take on and accomplish if the situation had been theirs instead. One by one, they each walked up to their brethren and shook his hand, welcoming him back to their platoon — and it was this gesture by each of Sabastian's fellow soldiers that made him realize he had always had another family, had always had this tight bond of brotherhood with these twenty-nine other guys who would have, if he had actually asked them, been right there alongside him and gone up against Antonio Marcone and his organization.

As he looked amongst his peers, his second 'family', a sense of humility consumed him. Shortly thereafter, Sabastian realized that sadness had filled the room. Their respected leader no longer was with them, and it caused an uncertainty in each and every one of his fellow soldiers — of which he was unsure how to remove.

As much as he was willing to forgive Terrance Burelli, there admittedly was still a bit of resentment within Sabastian — time, he was certain, would eliminate that. However, in the eyes of everyone else in the barracks, sadness was there. The Major had been their commanding officer since the first day that this elite group of Union soldiers had been assembled — and they had accomplished so much together. But like life itself, things happen and things change. Sabastian knew that if their platoon were to continue to grow and succeed, they all had to accept the reality of the loss of their leader, move forward, adapt, and make his ex-father proud of each and every one of them.

Sabastian was about to remind them about that exact thing when Captain E.J. Swilling entered. The entire platoon immediately took up their usual positions at attention and listened to their superior as he addressed the unit. First, he confirmed that their platoon leader had unexpectedly passed away. After that, he let everyone else know what Sabastian had learned the previous day over the phone — that Captain Swilling was now their new commanding officer. Right after that, he instructed them to gear up and prepare for a new assignment.

An hour later, the entire unit was collectively sitting aboard a military transport plane waiting for clearance to take off. It was during this time that Captain Swilling explained in full detail to the entire platoon what exactly it was that their mission to Tijuana, Mexico, was all about. Recently, some information had come to light concerning the A.R.M. (the **A**merican **R**ecovery **M**ission was a organization whose lone objective was to find a way of undoing what they felt was an egregious error by the United States government — that being, their amalgamation with Canada) that needed to be verified, and then addressed if need be.

After everything was made clear, Sabastian's doubts about being where he was, had resurfaced. It just didn't make sense to him as to why he had been recalled back into active duty, as he felt this mission was something that could easily be handled by the unit without him. He never was one to question the orders of a superior officer, but his mind yearned for some more clarification, so he approached Captain Swilling and said, "Permission to speak freely, sir?"

The captain nodded. "Of course, Lieutenant."

"Now that I know what this unit is being asked to do, I am even more convinced that I am not needed. The parameters of the mission appear to be nowhere near as precarious as I was first lead to believe."

"We have no idea what is waiting for us. Yes, we probably could have done this without you, but there are a few like myself who believe that these individuals we have been tasked to locate pose a much larger threat than what our country's leaders deem."

"I highly doubt that our government has intentionally turned a blind eye to the A.R.M."

"You would think not, but that seems to be the case. The A.R.M. clearly belongs on the terrorist watch list, yet that has not happened."

"Then who is authorizing this mission?"

"I'd rather not say.

After a few moments of thought, Sabastian said, "This is unsanctioned, isn't it?"

"Yes, Lieutenant. It's off the books. If we are able to verify what we have been asked, acknowledgement will then have to be given by those in charge."

Sabastian's rank came with no privileges when it came to knowing who actually issued their orders. However, there was no doubt in his mind that the S.N.A.F.U. has been dragged into a pissing contest between government agencies. Either the Department of Homeland Security or the Union Bureau of Investigation was responsible for this — and if he were a betting man, he was pretty certain that the U.B.I. was the culprit.

"This could easily blow up in the faces of those who have asked us to do this."

"It is a risk that they are willing to take, as it is believed the A.R.M. has intentions of conducting an act of domestic terrorism at the upcoming N.A.T.O. summit in Los Angeles."

Sabastian didn't need to ask why, as he was well aware of the purpose of the A.R.M. Conducting such an unfathomable act would instantly bring their organization into the spotlight and the government would no longer be able to sweep them under the rug. They would immediately be vaulted right up to the top of the terrorist watch list; they also would gain a lot of supporters who feel the same way as they do. A growing dissension amongst its people was a slippery slope that the Union could not afford to let happen.

The S.N.A.F.U. has been on a few of these kinds of assignments before; Sabastian was okay with an immense responsibility being placed upon their shoulders. What he wasn't all right with was being used as a tool in a political agenda — and his gut was telling him that was the case. Even so, the hearsay this mission was based upon was enough that Sabastian could not ignore his obligation. But before he committed himself to being a part of this, he wanted all of the cards to be laid out onto the table. "How large an organization is the A.R.M.?"

"It is unknown. All that we know is that they have a cell in Tijuana. We suspect that they also have others that are spread out across the border of Mexico and maybe even within the southern portion of the Union. There quite possibly could be other sleeper cells in Cuba, the Dominican Republic, Bahamas and Puerto Rico. All of that though, is irrelevant. The mission at hand is to verify whether or not a terrorist plot is planned, then stop it from taking place if it is." The captain took a moment and paused, looking into Sabastian's eyes with a serious, yet respectful stare. "Your... your 'father' was a man held in high regard throughout the military. He took a group of young men and turned them into one of the most elite military groups in the world. These young men," the captain scanned the plane with his eyes to allow Sabastian to understand who he was referring to, "have always, whether or not you knew it, thought of you as the same type of person; the same type of leader that Terrance Burelli was. These men look up to you and respect you the same way they did him."

"Your words are much appreciated, sir."

The captain then leaned forward and lowered his voice so that he could speak to Sabastian in as private a setting as possible. "I don't know everything that has happened to you over the last month, but I only can assume that you have been through a lot."

"I have."

"I know you'd rather be at home right now, but... you are still a part of this unit and I believe that you're not the kind of person to bail on them, just because you have a pass in your back pocket.

That pass the captain was referring to wasn't unequivocally free — it could be revoked. This however, was an instance where he could have used it, as his country was not at war. Nevertheless, no grounds were there for Sabastian to dispute the words spoken to him. He was an honorable man, and he was being asked to do his country a favor.

Next to his ex-father, Captain E.J. Swilling was the most respected of the senior officers the entire base had. A moment of pride enveloped him; the man had thought so much of him and his abilities to personally request his presence on this assignment. Yet, there still was a small part of him that wanted to find a way to convince the captain that this could be accomplished without him; the part that just wanted to forever leave behind whatever ties he had to his fallacious past. "Sir.., I appreciate the vote of confidence, but..."

The Captain put up his hand, signaling Sabastian to stop. "You are needed because you are the best person to lead these men to success. I have no doubt that we will find the cell. Acquiring the information we came looking for though is imperative, and your abilities give us the best chance of doing that."

Sabastian always had difficulty in accepting a personal endorsement. He had never been selfish; he always made sure the credit was distributed equally. Now though, he was following the path he was born to walk and reclaiming the life he had been born to live — and in doing so, it meant that an individual legacy would eventually be created. Had this undeniable support come his way before now, he would not have readily accepted it — now though, he was willing. "Ok. But after we accomplish our mission, I respectfully request to be relieved of duty."

Captain Swilling extended his hand, nodded his head, and smiled. It was that simple gesture that told Sabastian that an agreement had been reached, a mutual respect forged, and that he would be relieved of duty at the conclusion of this assignment.

It had been difficult for Jerrelle to sleep that night. All that her mind would allow her to see was Helfred. Almost from the moment that she had laid her head down on the memory foam pillow, her mind began replaying all of the significant moments that she had experienced with him: the day they met, the first day they kissed, the first day that she knew she wanted to be with him, and the day that separated them both forever; the day in which each of their respective commanding officers had informed them that their relationship had to cease. That day had been one of the hardest Jerrelle had ever experienced in her life — and it was also the same day that she realized just how deep her feelings ran for Helfred.

The day was about as near to being perfect as anyone could ask for: very few, if any clouds were in the sky, the temperature was moderate, and the breeze was slight. Along the coastline and barefoot, both Jerrelle and Helfred walked hand in hand, not caring that the hot sand had begun to leave the bottoms of their feet red. It wasn't until she had inadvertently stepped on a seashell that she became aware of the damage done to the bottoms of her feet.

Helfred, doing the gentlemanly thing that she had never previously experienced from him, picked her up and carried her over to the water's edge for a bit of quick relief. After standing in a few inches of water for about five minutes and looking off in the distance across the Baltic Sea at an ocean liner that was passing by, Jerrelle whispered into Helfred's ear that her feet were feeling better, so they continued on with their romantic walk — this time however, they stayed close to the water's edge.

Two miles later, they stopped when they came upon a grouping of large rocks that was about forty feet long; three quarters of it protruded out into the water. Again, Helfred uncharacteristically picked up Jerrelle, this time setting her down on top of a large boulder. She thanked him for the assistance and then walked across the grouping of rocks until she reached the end of it. Once there, she took up a seat and let her legs dangle over the edge; her feet and ankles had disappeared below the surface of the water.

After sheepishly watching Jerrelle make her way to the end, Helfred hopped up on top of the 'rock pier' and made his way over to her. The moment he sat down beside her, she grabbed his hand and looked at him in a loving gaze; love that she knew she could never verbally profess to him because this day, this perfect day, was going to be the last one that she would ever be allowed to spend with him.

"Helfred, I don't know what to do? I mean, I know that we can't fight this, but I honestly don't understand how both of our commanding officers can insist that they have the legal authority to order us to never see each other again."

"I hate this as much as you do. And I don't agree with this either, but there is nothing that we can do. We are both military officers and we must follow the rules and adhere to any and all policies no matter what our opinion of them may be."

They both had been given the same reason by each of their superiors — although both countries were allies, a possible breach of national security could not be risked, no matter how slim the chances were that that might happen. A strict policy was in place when it came to fraternizing with one of their own, let alone with other members of the service from another country. It wasn't that they both were not trusted members of their respective military units, but it was a longstanding policy that had to be enforced without exception.

27

The two of them just sat there at the end of the rock pier that day and held each other as if neither one of them ever intended to let the other one go. How long they had sat there, neither one knew — nor did either one care. What they both wished for though, was that the inevitable conclusion of the day would take its sweet old time coming. The longer that could be put off, meant the pending heartbreak that awaited them, would not be felt, as neither was sure that they could continue on afterwards.

What they did not want of course, took place. The sun had sunk into the bottom of the ocean, and nature's daily ritual had been completed. This would never happen again. This special day that they had spent together was over. Their being together was also officially over — all because of a set of rules that both selfishly believed should not apply to them. It just did not seem fair.

Still feeling somewhat drained from the previous night, Jerrelle forced herself up off of the futon and then proceeded to take a shower. After that was done, she actually felt a bit more alive — and hungry, so she made her way into the complex and toward where she hoped she'd find the kitchen. Five minutes of roaming throughout the halls and she was certain that she was lost; the complex was huge and it had way too many rooms for her to count. She wondered as she wandered just how many members of the E.C.L. actually called this place their home.

She never was able to find the kitchen, but she luckily found her sister; Bai Lin had been sitting alone in the common area of the complex, relaxing in a dark grey synth-leather chair, and drinking her morning sim-caf.

"Hey, sis. How are you doing this morning?"

"Other than feeling a bit run down, I'm okay. As soon as I find the kitchen and have some breakfast, I'm sure I'll feel better."

"Go back into the hallway, head right, turn left at the second hall and then just follow the smell of bacon. There is no way you can miss the kitchen if you let your nose lead the way."

"Ok… thanks."

"When you're done your breakfast, I have something to speak to you about."

"Oh? What is it?"

"It can wait until after you eat."

Jerrelle left the common room and headed for the kitchen. *'Bai Lin was right, I can smell the bacon... and eggs.'* The smell of that combination was just what she needed to wake up her senses.

After finishing off a healthy plate that consisted of a three egg and cheese omelet, four strips of bacon, a small bowl of steamed rice, some fresh raspberries, and a tall glass of orange juice, Jerrelle went back to the common area to look for Bai Lin — but she wasn't there any longer. The only person who was in the room was a young preteen Asian girl who was reading The New Adventures of Harry Potter on her E-tablet. That was a bit of a surprise, as Jerrelle never suspected that there would be any young children living in the complex. *'Why would someone bring their children to this place and expose them to this type of lifestyle?'* she pondered.

Although Jerrelle's curiosity was clamoring for an answer, she chose not to inquire. Instead, she decided just to ask the preteen if she knew the whereabouts of her sister; the young girl spoke to her before she could even ask.

"If you're looking for Bai Lin, she's not here."

"Thank you, but I can see that. Do you happen to..?"

"No, I don't!"

"Oh? Ok, what is your..?"

"My father told me not to talk to you. He said that even though you are Bai Lin's sister, he still is not sure that he should trust you."

"And who is your father?"

"There is no reason for you to know that. Now, could you please leave me alone? You're taking up what free time I have and I can't focus on my book."

If it had been anybody else but the young daughter of a member of the Extremist Clandestine Liberation who had spoken to Jerrelle that way, she would have walked right up to her, no matter how old she was, and taught her a lesson about respecting others. *'It's not surprising that there is someone in the E.C.L. who doesn't want me here. I will have to be extra careful as to not step on anyone's toes as I don't want to cause any problems... especially for Bai Lin.'* Heeding

29

to the demand of the young girl, Jerrelle left the main common area and walked down the east hall toward the exit that led to the Byakko Gardens. A few seconds later...

"Hey!"

"That caused Jerrelle to stop. She turned to her left and saw her sister sitting at a computer terminal in the small room that appeared to be the compound's library — though the room really only had one small book shelf and two computer terminals. "So you said that you had something you wanted to speak with me about," Jerrelle stated as she entered the room and took the seat next to her sister.

"Yes. I've recently been in contact with our European faction of the E.C.L. and I have been told that Helfred's brother, Nicoli, wishes to speak with you."

A sudden bit of uncertainty enveloped her. Jerrelle had only found out recently that her ex had a brother, but she honestly never expected that they would ever cross paths. She surely didn't expect Nicoli to reach out to her — at least, not so soon after Helfred's death. "I don't think that I'm ready to speak to him."

"I'm sure he understands how difficult this would be for you, but I think that meeting him would be good therapy for you — and also for him."

Jerrelle knew that her sister was right. She had to face her pain head on — and the longer she avoided it, the better the chance that it would eventually consume her and cause her all sorts of other kinds of mental hurt. Her long cry the previous evening had done a lot to release what she had kept bottled up inside, but there were still some deeper emotional scars that had to be healed.

Although still a bit hesitant, Jerrelle gave in to her sister's recommendation and agreed to meet with Helfred's brother. She had to acknowledge that this would probably be the one and only opportunity that she would ever get to apologize to Nicoli for her inability to prevent what had happened. And if she didn't tackle this one, rather large emotional challenge that she still had left to face, then she knew that she would probably try to find some stupid lame excuse to continually avoid the issue altogether.

Happy that her sister had agreed to do this, Bai Lin encouraged Jerrelle to head topside and wait for her at the same stone bench that she had found her sitting on yesterday. Once she was done making the necessary arrangements with Nicoli, Bai Lin then would join her.

As she leaned over and lovingly hugged her half-sister, Jerrelle whispered thanks into her ear. She then released her hold, left the library, and headed in the direction of the exit to the outside gardens above. After crossing the threshold of the exit to the outside world, she headed back to where she had been the night before. Upon her arrival at the stone bench, what she suspected might happen, had not — no desire to cry again, was there.

Smiling inside, Jerrelle reclaimed her spot and decided to use the short time that she was going to have to focus on her thoughts and then gather as much strength as she could. Although she had no idea what Bai Lin's plans were for her today, she had a feeling that another round of unwanted, unbridled emotions would make another appearance at some point — which was probably why her sister had suggested that she head out to the gardens in the first place.

She didn't know how it was even possible, but Jerrelle was almost certain that the Byakko Gardens had some kind of strange healing, soothing properties — a unique characteristic that she was going to take advantage of as much as she could while she was visiting with her sister. Jerrelle was all but certain that her entire being was going to be taxed when she finally had that meeting with Nicoli. Until then, she had hoped that the gardens would help to give her a little bit of extra strength so that she did not become a pathetic sideshow for the whole world to see — that was all she needed was to embarrass herself in front of not only Helfred's brother, but to those who just happened to be around her during that time.

3

Unlike the previous two days, the weather was as near to perfect as anyone could have asked for. The sun was out and its gentle rays had initiated the necessary healing effect needed to help repair the damage that had been done to Jerrelle's heart and soul.

After about ten minutes spent with her eyes closed and her thoughts cleared, she left the stone bench and walked the intricately carved paths throughout the entire gardens; paths that she took the time to become intimately familiar with. Astutely, she studied and admired their beauty and its essence while using the surrounding life that had enveloped her curiosity as a means to draw more strength. She had spent much of the past few days alone with her uncertain thoughts. When she wasn't alone, Bai Lin had been the needed shoulder. Now, Jerrelle felt that she was near the end of her healing journey — little did she know that the last part of it she was about to embark on was going to end up changing her in more ways than she could have ever imagined, and set her on a path she could not have foreseen.

After Jerrelle was done with her walk, she went back over to the stone bench and waited for Bai Lin to arrive. There, she again closed her eyes; this time though, she just listened to her surroundings. Never before did she recall hearing so clearly all of the intricacies of nature. Not only did it fascinate her, it helped to bring peace to her wounded soul. Now, all that she had to do was find a way to bring peace and harmony to her life. She had no idea what it was going to be like once she returned to the real world; she only knew that in order for her to move forward, a lot of the things that made up who she was as a person, had to change.

Keeping her emotions in check had not been as difficult as she had thought it was going to be up until now, and as she patiently sat there waiting for her sister, Helfred returned to her thoughts — she contently beamed this time instead of shedding a tear. Surely, a day would come where she again would feel sadness for her first love, but the man had given her plenty of moments to forever cherish —

especially the one when the two of them first crossed paths with one another.

She knew the military was going to be pure hell once she became a member of its fraternity, but she never expected that her first posting was going to be forty-two hundred miles from home. Thoughts of regret continually popped into her head on a daily basis ever since she had enlisted — nevertheless, her now being a part of the military was, as pointed out to her by her parole officer, the best option on the table.

She had no one else but herself to blame. In hindsight, she should be in jail instead of where she was. For the first time in her life, she was forced to look at the big picture. Yes, this was not where she wanted to spend the next several years of her young life, but an opportunity was clearly there for her, if she really wanted it, to change who she admittedly was: a volatile, angry, resentful, and defying individual. Discipline and a direction — maybe that was all she needed? Then again, it may be that only a medical professional with numerous degrees could figure out why she was the way she was, then determine the best way to fix all of her issues — if that was even at all possible.

Jerrelle had fully expected that her first posting would be in another part of the world after her basic training was completed. There, the next and final phase of her military training would continue, then conclude. Following that, she would be assigned to a permanent unit. Once that happened, she would receive her first official ranking and be considered a full-fledged Union soldier. At that point, her chances of seeing actual combat would increase tremendously — that possibility was the only positive aspect of being in the military that Jerrelle was actually looking forward to.

She had hoped that her first official posting would be in one of the many warmer or exotic countries: Panama, Fiji, Samoa, Canary Islands or even Guam, but when she found out about her assignment, she immediately assumed that the courts had pulled some strings and made it so that she had been given the worst possible one there was. That of course, she knew wasn't the case. Still, she wanted to blame someone for her shitty posting.

Only three weeks in, and Jerrelle was itching to leave the Reagan Training Facility and go see if this wretched part of Berlin that she had been dumped in had any good places to drink. She doubted it, but a cold beer was a good beer no matter what part of the world you were in.

It was early February and the cold air nipped at her face — it seemed much colder to her than it would ever get back home in Detroit. This unpleasant experience gave her one more unfounded reason to generate distaste for a country that she knew absolutely nothing about; a country that Jerrelle's lack of an open mind had all but convinced her before her arrival that she was really going to hate.

She had been walking the sparsely snow covered downtown streets for about fifteen minutes when she saw a bar on the other side that looked as if it was the local hotspot — a place called the Neue Bavarian Hofbrauhaus, where military service personnel were entering at a rather steady pace. She decided right then and there that this was going to be the place she would try out first. And though it appeared to be filled with German Military Officers, she thought that with her being in the service like them, she would at least somewhat fit in amongst the crowd.

She entered the bar, got herself a beer, and then found a somewhat private corner at the far side of the establishment. The music wasn't that loud, though it did irk Jerrelle — as did most of the rock and roll that was being played in Germany at the time.

Like she had hoped, the feeling of not belonging wasn't there. However, the atmosphere inside the place was completely different than what she was used to back home in Detroit. She knew that she should give the place a chance, as no one was giving her strange looks, and her intuition wasn't telling her to watch her back. Nevertheless, she had made up her mind that this German watering hole was not for her. So after only fifteen minutes, her beer was gone, and she was headed toward the front door. When she was about halfway there, she noticed a small commotion developing near the entrance. Not wanting to get too close, Jerrelle stopped and astutely watched; impressed, as the bouncers had quickly and efficiently dealt with the problem.

A few minutes after the issue was taken care of and those involved were escorted out of the establishment, Jerrelle continued her exit from the bar. She turned left and began to walk away in search of another place to have a drink when she heard a commotion in the ally next to the establishment from which she had just left. Her curiosity as always had come forward as she stood there for a moment and assessed the situation. Almost immediately, she had recognized that something was about to go down.

She knew that the logical thing for her to do was to just walk away, as this wasn't her issue nor was she even in her own country — but her gut told her otherwise. Four civilians, three men and one woman, had cornered another man who was in uniform. They obviously had a beef with the German service man, and each looked as if they had the ability to handle themselves rather efficiently and effectively. This was not going to be a fair fight.

It quickly became obvious to Jerrelle that this military man was about to get his ass kicked. She didn't know this individual, but they were 'brothers in arms' — both belonged to the same kind of fraternity and both were from countries that would normally fight on the same side. They were allied soldiers. It wasn't about making this a fair fight; this was all about honor. If there was anything that she had learned since she had joined the military, it was honor amongst men. Exist alone; die anonymously — become one with many, die with an abundance of admiration earned.

It wasn't a matter of choice; it was what she knew she had to do. So Jerrelle took two steps closer and instantly, she recognized the cornered man; he was the one who had moments earlier, been escorted out of the bar. Why that had happened, Jerrelle didn't know — she only knew that she had to help her fellow soldier.

As the group was about to strike, Jerrelle made her presence known, she took an empty beer bottle that she had found lying on the ground next to the side of the building and whipped it at the back of the largest man in the center of the group. "Hey you pieces of crap! You want to leave my brother alone?"

"Your brother?"

"Yes. He is a soldier, as am I. Therefore, he is my allied brother."

35

"Get lost bitch, or we'll have to hurt you too."

Bitch was of course, one of those key words on Jerrelle's list that she hated to hear — and it was usually all that it took for her temper to ignite. With reason now to officially become a part of this situation, she stepped forward, and almost immediately, just as Jerrelle had thought, the lone female of the group walked up to face her first. The woman drew a butterfly knife from her jacket and brandished it at Jerrelle with confidence — that was the woman's first mistake.

"You better know how to use that knife, because if you don't.., I'm gonna make you eat it for dinner." Jerrelle took one more calculated step forward, knowing that the woman would soon make her move. It wouldn't be planned; it would be done on impulse because she arrogantly believed she was going to win this fight.

Right in the middle of Jerrelle's next step forward, the woman lunged. However, right before her foot had touched the ground, Jerrelle had caught the woman's wrist with her right hand, pulled it and the knife it held toward her, and in one motion; she drove her left palm into the woman's face. She broke the woman's nose; her face suddenly looked like a red ink blot. With relative ease, she then bent the woman's wrist backwards, farther than a wrist was intended to bend; the woman had no choice but to drop her weapon.

Jerrelle could have stopped there, but she intended to send a message to those in the peanut gallery who were judiciously watching her, so she continued to bend the woman's wrist back even further until she heard the bones beginning to crack. That unpleasant sound though, was soon drowned out by the ear piercing scream the woman bellowed.

In pain, she fell to her knees and clutched her dangling wrist. In that moment, the woman knew that she had just made the biggest mistake of her life — she also knew that payment for her sins had yet to be completed, even though her eyes clearly begged for mercy.

When it came to a fight, Jerrelle always knew when to stop; she never crossed that line unless the opponent needed a lesson taught. This was one of those instances where an individual had to be knocked off their throne, so Jerrelle sized up the near defenseless woman and then delivered a crescent kick to the side of her head. She could have easily killed the prone woman, but she knew exactly how much force to use in order to render someone unconscious and put them temporarily out of commission.

"That was my wife, you Bitch!" The tallest of the three remaining men said; the same man that Jerrelle had hit with the beer bottle.

The military man, who had been cornered, saw the opening he had hoped for and made his move. Even if this unknown woman had not come along to help him, he had felt that his own abilities were good enough to deal with the unbalanced odds — though he was pretty sure that he would not have walked away from the fight unscathed. Now, this unknown woman, who could obviously handle herself, had swayed the odds even more into his favor.

He took the opening that the three men had given him when they had briefly turned in unison to watch what this unknown woman was doing to their friend, and made his move. He took a few calculated steps off to the right side of the next tallest of the three men, tapped him on his left shoulder and waited. As all people do when they are tapped on their shoulder, he turned around to that side and instantly collapsed as the military man performed a martial arts kick to the side of the man's left knee. He then quickly turned his attention to the friend of the man to his right and saw just in time the baseball bat that had been swung at his head. He ducked just enough to avoid his head being knocked off and used the man's own momentum against him — The military man used both of his hands and thrust them into the man's back, sending him up against the opposite alley wall and into a steel fire door.

Jerrelle had to only see the first move made by her fellow soldier to realize that the man could handle himself quite nicely. What she first thought was going to end with her at least leaving with some sort of injury, no longer seemed certain — the situation had drastically been tilted into their favor.

Facing the disposed woman's husband, Jerrelle cracked a confident smile. She then positioned herself in one of the many attack stances she had, quickly sized up her opponent, and then invited him to make the first move. As he stepped forward, Jerrelle could see the uncertainty in his eyes.

The man picked up a three-foot piece of bent rebar from the alley floor and cautiously approached Jerrelle. After seeing what she had done to his wife, the man knew that this woman wasn't going to be an easy opponent to dispatch. In fact, the confidence that he had when he and his group first entered this alley had all but disappeared. Still, he knew that he had no other choice but to fight this woman. She after all, had beaten the living shit out of his wife. If he didn't fight for her honor, then his own ass was going to be in the doghouse for a very long time.

The man took a few more cautious steps and then made his first move; just like his wife, it was not calculated. He missed badly when he swung the rebar; he also concluded right then and there that he just might have bit off way more than he could chew.

After a few seconds of uncertain thought, the man took another swing at Jerrelle; she calmly deflected it off to the side. The man stood frozen for a moment; it was almost as if Medusa had turned him into a stone statue. The only thing that moved on him was his eyes as they were looking for an escape route. Unfortunately for him, there wasn't one.

With no other viable option left, the man felt desperation sink in. No longer did he hold the rebar like a club; he held it like a dagger and hoped that he just might get lucky.

The man should have learned from watching what had happened to his wife when she lunged at Jerrelle — but he apparently didn't. His intention was to impale her; it was a decision that was going to cost him.

During the man's attempt to stab her, Jerrelle dropped down to the ground and in one fluid motion, drove her right hand into his family jewels. The assailant's eyes instantly bulged to the size of silver dollars as pain like he had never felt before, enveloped his body. A moment later, the man dropped the rebar, fell to his knees, and then cocooned himself into the fetal position.

Inside, Jerrelle felt good, as she hadn't had an excursion like this one in a long time — but this was also the kind of circumstances that had led to her having to enlist in the military in the first place. Still, she felt that her participation in this excursion was justified; it was done for the right reasons — unlike her usual fights. Therefore, *there was nothing within her own conscience that could chastise her for her actions. However, Jerrelle knew that all good things had to come to an end. There was no reason to fight this man anymore. Only a reminder is what he needed so that this individual and his posse of idiot friends would think twice about cornering and outnumbering someone — just because they could.*

After taking a moment to survey the alley, and concluding that no eminent danger was nearby, she returned her attention to the downed man and smiled. A few seconds later, the man attempted to right himself — but before he could get completely up onto his knees, Jerrelle shook her finger side to side in a shaming gesture in front of his unprotected face, then symbolically, waved goodnight to him. Without any reservations whatsoever, she then sent a vicious front kick to the man's glass jaw — he fell straight backwards and joined his wife on the ground, out cold.

Fully expecting that her help was still going to be needed, Jerrelle took a few steps forward, ready to lend a hand. To her amazement, her fellow soldier had taken care of business all on his own — her assistance was not needed, as the man had easily dispatched his two opponents.

After displaying a smile of appreciation, the soldier calmly walked over to Jerrelle, and without even a word being exchanged between the two of them, walked side by side with her out of the alley and down the street. Three blocks later, they came across a tiny little pub that had less than ten people in it. They went inside and sat at a table at the back of the bar. The man, whose debt she knew he'd repay one day without ever talking of it, looked across the table and finally spoke. "What is your name?"

"Jerrelle Dakota Robinson. And yours?"

"Helfred... Helfred Wolfram Nemchieve."

Jerrelle opened up her eyes and she knew at that moment she had found a way to draw strength whenever she needed it — she only had to pull up her memories of the day when Helfred came into her life. For the first time ever, she had not fought out of anger; she instead, had fought in order to prevent an injustice. Her life had forever changed because of it, and it felt good that for once, she had made the right decision.

The jaunt down memory lane had unexpectedly been therapeutic. Bai Lin had been right. These gardens above the E.C.L. compound were special. They had indeed helped Jerrelle to heal; helped her to find her needed strength — and had helped her to find something positive from her memories of Helfred of which she could forever cherish. Because of that, she was now confident that she would finally be able to move forward and, who would have ever thought, contribute to society instead of being the burden that almost everyone she ever knew had claimed she was.

What never should have happened to the organization, had — and his predecessor's unhealthy obsessions were the reason for that outcome. Now, it was up to Louie to put the pieces back together so that the Detroit Underworld Organization could became stronger than ever before. *'The only way for me to fully restore what should have never fallen apart, is to be patient and take this one small step at a time. First, I need to assemble the important parts of the organizational structure. Then once that is done and stabilized, I will be able to bring in the rest of the remaining assets. I may even have to shuffle around or add a few more people to key positions. And unlike Antonio, I won't restrict whom I bring in based on blood. Being open to anyone that can be an asset is what I feel will ultimately make this organization become one of the most revered of its kind in the entire world.'*

Once Louie had made up his mind that that was what he was going to do, he began the process of tracking down some of the important members of the organization that Antonio had sent away before their brief trek across the globe. He wasn't quite ready to bring them in yet; he just wanted to bring them up to date on what was going on. And then in a few weeks time, once he had everything in place, Louie would officially recall them to their duties.

This was the first thing that Antonio should have done once they had returned to the Union from England, but he didn't. He had selfishly wanted instead, to enjoy a few stress-free weeks away from the daily responsibilities that came with running an underground organization. Louie couldn't fault the man for having that desire, but it was an illogical decision on his part because the organization had inadvertently sailed into troubled waters — all because of the way they had chosen to dispose of the enemy. Instead of doing what is expected of any leader; take the helm and then guide them around the storm, Antonio chose to just wait for it to pass. His decision to do that, in Louie's opinion, was what has now given Detroit's law enforcement the opportunity they had long ago sought, to raid their headquarters, gather important information, and then assemble all that they needed to shut them down forever. *'As soon as Zhin Wi gets here, I will have to send him to Detroit ahead of me and have him secure the office… if that is at all possible, and then investigate to see if he can find out whether or not the law is actually in the process of doing what I fear.*

He went over to his fridge, grabbed himself a beer, and headed out to his balcony. Most people have a favorite place to go when they want to relax; for Louie, it was his own balcony, twenty stories up above the street, with nothing there to obscure his view of the city that he loved.

After taking a healthy swig of his beer he removed his vid-cell from his spring jacket pocket; his intent was to begin the task of tracking down the other members of 'his' organization, but before he could even make his first vid-cell call, his apartment doorbell rang. He placed his beer down on the glass coffee table and went back inside his apartment to answer it. "I wasn't expecting you until at least tomorrow morning. Please come on in."

The man at the door was sculpted like an athlete, but had a persona that didn't match that image — he looked and acted more like that of an ancient battle warrior. You could easily tell that he had spent a lot of years training, not in a typical gym, but in various forms of ancient martial arts. His muscles weren't overly large, but they were very much defined. Even at only five-foot, seven inches tall, Zhin Wi displayed an aura of confidence; a natural presence he had that kept people at a safe distance for fear of what he just might, or could do to them.

He was of pure Chinese decent and had a documented bloodline that could be traced all the way back to the Ming Dynasty of the late fourteenth century. His long jet-black hair was always kept in

41

a ponytail, and his eyes were the darkest of brown. The only one distinctive marking he had, was a large scripted tattoo of 'Ming Dynasty' in traditional Chinese font, right across his chest; a tattoo rarely seen unless his shirt was off and he was about to beat your ass. 'It's good to see you again, Louie," he said as he entered the apartment.

"Please make yourself at home, Zhin." Louie went over to his fridge, removed another beer, and handed it to his associate; he then invited him to join him out on the balcony. There they sat, looking out across the city and catching up. By the time their beers were finished, Louie had filled Zhin in about the organization's longstanding history with the Detroit Police Department, the obsession that Antonio had toward Maxwell Banks, and their futile attempts following the man's elimination to get rid of his overzealous son, Sabastian. He then followed that briefing by informing him of the events that had taken place shortly after their return to Detroit, which unfortunately resulted in Antonio's unexpected death.

Wanting at that point to give his associate a few minutes to digest everything he had just been told, Louie left him alone on the balcony, went back inside his apartment, grabbed two final beers, and returned to his seat outside. As he handed Zhin his fresh beer, what bit of doubt that may have been there that his decision to ask his associate to leave China and be his number one, had disappeared. What he believed he saw in the man in that moment was a new sense of purpose — and that was what allowed Louie to feel confident enough to no longer procrastinate doing what he knew he had to do next.

The time had come for him to initialize his reformation plan; a plan that he hoped would not only solidify the Detroit Underworld Organization, but somewhere down the road also have it expand beyond the two geographical locations that it currently resided in.

By the next morning, Louie felt much more at ease. Zhin Wi had pledged to be his personal supporter and right hand man; it was what he had done himself all those years ago when Antonio had selected him to that very position. Yet throughout his tenure, he felt that his ex-boss quite often regretted his choice; a choice that Louie believed the man had made only because at the time, there was no one else within the organization he could trust, other than Sal, who had been more than willing to support his coup in order to get rid of Vance Palmalino.

Just after breakfast the next morning, Zhin had left for Detroit; Louie was again alone in his apartment. His intention this day had been to call and inform the remaining members of the D.U.O. of what his plan was and when each would be recalled to 'work', but then he changed his mind. This no longer was going to be the same Detroit Underworld Organization. There were several members that he knew had always hated the fact that he had jumped right past them on the 'seniority' list and undoubtedly, they would not have any qualms about making things difficult for him. Those individuals and the positions they held, Louie felt needed to be reassessed. It was a task that he wasn't looking forward to, but he knew that it was something he had to do. He was after all, the boss, and those who would now be under his command needed to be on the same page as he. Those whom he did not firmly believe would jump on the bandwagon; their employment would have to be terminated — without just cause.

After a moment of reflective thought, Louie decided to hold off on the reevaluation process until after he heard back from Zhin. Once he was certain the office was safe and secure, he would return to Detroit and then make his decisions: who would stay, and who unfortunately, needed to be silenced because he simply did not trust them. He wanted to soften the reputation a little that the organization had, but before that could happen, he would have to continue on with the old ways in order to assure that those whom he 'fired', did not return somewhere on down the road and attempt to go postal or sell him out to the highest bidder. Killing someone wasn't what Louie wanted to do, but it was something that he knew he was going to have to do to ensure the continued existence of his organization.

Right after ingesting two Tylenol IVs to help eliminate the headache that he had, Louie brought his morning sim-caf to the living room. He then sat in his synth-suede recliner and began to let his mind venture into the future. He could see what he wanted; he could see what he needed to do in order to accomplish just that — and he knew that in no more than one month's time, the Detroit Underworld Organization would be fully operational again. So long as everything that he had planned fell into place, the organization would become more efficient and more profitable than it has ever been before — that, Louie was certain of.

With the G8 conference in Los Angeles just around the corner, Captain Swilling, and those who had requested his help, felt that if their suspicions about the A.R.M. were correct, it would be just too tempting of a target to be ignored. To those who were behind this request, not only was validation expected, they had no misgivings whatsoever about watching those fellow government agencies that did not agree with them, eat a whole lot of humble pie. It was petty on their part, but there seemed to be no other way to be taken seriously when they go out of their way to forewarn them about a pending threat.

According to the assignment the S.N.A.F.U. had been given, the American Recovery Mission's cell was supposedly located somewhere within the vicinity of the River Zone area in Tijuana; an area that was not that far away from the San Diego border. It's not that they had never before had to search out the location of a suspected terrorist organization with little information to go on, but what they had been asked to do was the type of task they hated, as it usually wasted a lot of their valuable time.

This unauthorized mission certainly could all but ruin more than just a few careers if they were to not succeed in accomplishing their objective. Not only that, it could place an unwanted black mark on the reputation of the Special North American Freedom Unit — or worse, be the reason that it gets disbanded. Because of these possibilities, failure just wasn't an option.

During the flight to Mexico, Sabastian's mind stayed busy sorting through all the uncertainty that he still had. The more he had thought about it, the more he began to accept the fact that Captain Swilling was right — his recall notice had been necessary. He remembered being made aware of the A.R.M. during one of their unit's monthly briefings, a few years back. But back then the group had only been classified as being a level four threat (that level was considered to be a non-aggressive, fly by night, activist type of group — generally these kinds of groups just peacefully protested). However, the A.R.M.

had to recently be reclassified and listed as being a level two threat; the same rank that the United Arab League was at. Though no proof was there, the organization had claimed responsibility in a car bombing, just over four months ago that killed the family of a Florida state senator.

Sabastian didn't have a problem with tracking down a suspected terrorist group, as that is what being a member of the S.N.A.F.U. is about. He had faith in himself and his unit, but something in the back of his mind was telling him that they were being fed to the wolves. He had an issue with being used as a pawn in someone's twisted game, as he had just experienced that while going after Antonio Marcone and the D.U.O. At least in that instance, he had control over the decisions he made and was the only one who could accept responsibility if his choices turned out to be the wrong ones.

Like all assignments, he essentially had no freewill and was bound to the orders that were given, even though they had come from a governmental agency that refused to disclose their identity. Was the reasoning given, justified? Sabastian had to assume so — and even if it wasn't, if there was a hidden agenda of some kind behind it, there really wasn't anything that he could do about it. Sure, he could submit a formal complaint, but he was nobody of importance and it would more than likely just be swept underneath the rug. Too bad Terrance Burelli wasn't still alive, as he would have had a major problem with his unit being used as a tool in a pissing contest between government agencies.

Once their plane landed in Tijuana, Sabastian made a decision — he was going to approach this assignment in the same manner that anyone should when all of the necessary information was already acquired. To him, it made sense to approach this in a somewhat cautious and logical manner. Firstly, they needed to gather all of the Intel that they could, thoroughly assess it, and then make a decision based solely upon the facts gathered and not on one's own opinions or speculation.

Maybe it had something to do with the unexpected endorsement from his platoon commander, but Sabastian suddenly felt an abundance of self-confidence; way more than it had ever been in the past. Or maybe, it was because of what he had recently been through, combined with the knowledge of who he really was, that had changed him for the better. Whatever the reason was, Sabastian was willing to accept the responsibility that Captain Swilling had bestowed upon him to be the leader of the platoon while they searched for the American Recovery Mission's cell location. Had this sort of thing been offered to him before now, he undoubtedly would have declined it; not because he didn't think that he could handle it, but he just didn't want the rest of the platoon to assume that he was being handed a leadership role because he was their commanding officer's son.

With this being the first time that he was being given an opportunity to lead, Sabastian was determined not to fail. He fully trusted his fellow brethren and considered them all his friends, but he wasn't about to accept any slacking, lollygagging, or unnecessary screwing around — no excuse of any kind would be accepted when it came to insubordination.

While he was chasing Antonio Marcone halfway around the world, he had learned a valuable lesson that he intended on applying to this mission. A lack of focus during it could become the reason that failure became the result. Were that to happen, it could cause serious repercussions — that was the last thing Sabastian wanted was to have his unit embarrassed or worse, his country. For that reason, he made an unconventional request. He had asked Captain Swilling to allow him to split the platoon up into two groups of fifteen; one led by him and the other one led by the only other person in the platoon who was just like him.

Thankful that his request and his choice of Richard Atwater to be his right-hand man was approved, Sabastian gathered the entire platoon in their temporary command center in a hanger at the airport, informed everyone of the situation, and then reviewed their assignment one more time so that everyone was on the same page. Once his briefing was over, the unit then loaded up everything they needed into two heavily armored transport trucks and each proceeded to head to opposite ends of the city. Once they arrived at their destinations, east and west, they would then begin a blanket search pattern that would slowly make its way to the center of the metropolis. If they found nothing, then they would have to do it all over again; this time by starting at designated points north and south.

It wasn't an efficient way for them to search for their target — especially in a city of one point eight million people, but at least they had been provided with a specific area within the city that they believed their targets might be. Nevertheless, what they were doing was a risky way of trying to find the A.R.M. — they unfortunately, really had no other choice but to use this method.

Sabastian knew that the presence of Union Soldiers combing through the streets of a Mexican city was going to garner some attention; it was also going to set off some alarms. And even if they were lucky enough to actually locate their target, chances were that the A.R.M. would already be aware and would be ready for them. There was nothing that they could do to prevent that possibility. They had to treat them as being a hostile entity and be prepared for the worst — even though the A.R.M. had yet to officially be given the designation of being a terrorist group.

From the moment they began their search through the city streets, the citizens of Tijuana began to show signs of confusion and nervousness; they were uncertain as to why there were fully armed Ameri-Can Union Military men patrolling their home. The people were used to seeing their own Mexican army occasionally on the streets, but never the military of another allied nation. Some citizens took refuge inside the nearest building, some stopped in their tracks as their curiosity took over, but most of the people out and about soon clued into the fact that the Ameri-Can Union Military was there to look for someone or something; they weren't there to do harm to the people of Tijuana.

Thirty minutes into their search, Richard's group came across an old abandoned apartment complex. It was an agreed upon rule that when a building was going to be entered, contact was to be made with the other group before hand to let them know what they were about to do and where they were currently located. The reason for that was so that if something was in the process of going down, all they had to do was call out one word on their radio 'Snafu' and help would instantly be dispatched to their already known location.

The front door to the apartment building had been boarded up, but the rusted chain that had been used to secure the front entrance had been cut, leaving the weathered plywood accessible. This seemed like a possibility to Richard, so he ordered two of his men to cautiously approach the door; they immediately noticed that the sheeted barrier had been left slightly ajar.

Less than three minutes later, those two soldiers returned to their group and reported their findings to Richard.

"This is Godzilla calling Optimus Prime, come in."

"What the hell did you just say?" Sabastian replied, perplexed.

"I am Godzilla, and you are Optimus Prime. You know.., the Transformer?"

"You didn't happen to accidently fall down and whack your head, did you, Richard?"

"Nope! I just figure that we should use a code name when we speak to each other. I am Godzilla because I am a beast among men, and you are a Transformer because you decided to change into someone else that no one who knows you even recognizes."

'Jesus,' Sabastian thought. *'It was bad enough that I have to put up with that new nickname Jerrelle gave me. Now, I have my other friend doing the same — at least I can deal with being called, Sab.'* "Tell you what, just call me Sab and I'll call you… Rat."

"Rat?" Why in the hell would you call me that?"

"I just mashed up the first letter in your first name with the first two in your last name. It's short and it sounds cool to me — besides, your ears and nose remind me of the furry little creature."

Richard wasn't at all too happy at the jab his friend had just took — not just because he thought that Rat was a bit insulting, but because every one of the fourteen soldiers around him had overheard Sabastian and had all gotten a good laugh out of it at his expense. "Listen. The reason I called you is that we are about to enter an abandoned apartment building. It's at 248 Aguacaliente Boulevard. It's hard to miss, seeing that it's eight stories high and most of the windows are boarded up."

"Ok. Just remember to follow procedure and don't do anything stupid.., Rat."

Richard was going to kindly inform his friend that he wasn't one of those who needed to occasionally be reminded about procedures, but being called 'Rat' again by Sabastian was all that it took to cause him to pause his thoughts. That hastily created nickname had given Richard a sudden rash of irritation — and just like a swath of real inflammation, it really bothered him.

Turn about is fair play; he was more than ready to fire back with an insult of his own over the open airwaves and refer to his friend as now being 'Sea bass'tian; a real smelly fish, but he quickly realized that his group of soldiers had already begun to make their way toward the front entrance of the abandoned apartment complex without him — that, Richard couldn't let happen, as he was responsible for them. *'I owe you one, my old friend. Paybacks are more than just a bitch... they are fuckin' necessary.'*

Although the afternoon sun and the typical Mexican dry heat was annoying Sabastian, the lack of an update from Richard was bothering him even more. It had only been twenty minutes since his friend's group had entered the abandoned apartment building to search it, yet he had hoped that by now he would have received a report of some kind. However, since he had yet to hear the codeword come over the radio, his wanting to get a full report admittedly was a bit premature. He knew Richard almost as well as a twin would know their other half and the man's trust has never once been in question. Therefore, he knew that he had to leave well enough alone and stay focused on his own, just as important task.

The afternoon heat wasn't bothering just him; he could clearly see that it was also beginning to affect everyone else, so Sabastian decided that a momentary halt of their search needed to take place in order to give his squadron a fifteen minute rest and rehydration break — that was until something odd off in the distance suddenly caught his attention. If he hadn't been placed in a leadership role, then what he was now looking at, he more than likely would have dismissed as being inconsequential — but his gut was telling him that something was off. Two men, somewhat alike, had exited from a side alleyway, stepped onto the sidewalk, and then headed east; in the opposite direction from where Sabastian and his group currently were.

It was clearly obvious that those men were not native to Mexico, but Sabastian's gut was also telling him that they were not just a pair of random tourists. He was not someone who would normally draw a conclusion based upon what he saw, but if his instincts were correct and these seemingly out-of-place men were actually associated with the A.R.M., then their mission would move into the next phase. For now though, Sabastian was going to treat this situation with kid gloves and take it one calculated step at a time, as the last thing that he wanted was to be responsible for an international incident.

Although he knew that this was probably going to be one of those archetypal long shots, he pulled aside two of his men, Ben Fraisure and Jeff Tranter, and asked them to cautiously investigate the alleyway that those two men had just stepped out from. No sooner had Ben and Jeff left to do that, Sabastian's eyes quickly surveyed the surrounding area and locked onto a three-story office complex that sat directly across from the alleyway in question. Immediately, he recognized that the rooftop would be a perfect place to observe the alley and the adjacent buildings from, so he handpicked another soldier and sent him to take up a surveillance position from up there. Lastly, he ordered the remainder of his group to follow him back a block from where they were at and take up a secluded position in a south side alleyway entrance that he had remembered them passing earlier.

Ten minutes was all it had taken before Sergeants Fraisure and Tranter had returned to where the rest of the platoon had been waiting; they then gave their report. "Shortly after we started to walk down the alley, Jeff noticed two surveillance cameras; one was positioned over a single steel exit door at the back end of the alley, pointed toward the street, and one was halfway down it pointing back toward the door. And although we probably could have jammed their signal so that we could survey the alleyway, we thought it best to error on the side of caution."

"Are cameras the only thing you saw?"

"No. I noticed something which I thought to be a little odd."

"What was it, Ben?"

"The door at the end of the alley seemed to be much wider than one that you would typically see down a back alley exit, and it looked to be custom made out of heavy gauge steel plating... as if the door was installed with the purpose of preventing anyone from ever contemplating trying to break in that way."

"I agree with Ben's assessment," Jeff said. "And… I'm not sure if it is of any relevance, but there was also something I noticed that I thought to be a bit strange."

"Whatever it is that you suspect, I want to hear it," Sabastian said.

"Well… it appears the building, not too long ago, had windows that were recently removed and filled in with cinder block. And the fire escape also looks to have been fairly recently detached."

"What makes you suspect all of that, Jeff?"

"First off, the bricked in windows have yet to show any signs of aging. And most of the cut bolts that would normally secure the fire escape to the building wall do not have any rust on the exposed ends."

Sabastian contemplated the information that was just reported back to him. And although what he now knew didn't prove anything, it did help to solidify the fact that something didn't quite seem right — now, he was more curious than when he first saw those two men exit the alleyway. Whatever was inside that building, he wanted to know — even if it had nothing to do with their assignment. If what was being kept inside that building turned out to be illegal, then his sworn duty as a Union soldier meant that he had a responsibility to report it to the local authorities. Yes, they were in Mexico and not in the Union, but with his being a member of the S.N.A.F.U., provisional jurisdiction was automatically granted by the Policía Federal when it came to assuring the safety and security of the entire continent.

If anything, Sabastian believed that whoever owned the building, wanted to keep whatever was inside a secret — thus the reason for the filled in windows, the fire escape removal, and the large security door. But before he even contemplated satisfying his curiosity, he remembered that he wanted all of his men to follow procedure — that included him. For that reason, Sabastian promptly reported what it was that they were investigating to Captain Swilling. After a quick discussion with him, the captain agreed with his initial assessment — dismissing what they had found without first satisfying their suspicions, could end up being the mistake that Sabastian was adamant he was not going to make.

Fully expecting to receive back specific instructions from Captain Swilling regarding what steps should be taken next, he was once again surprised when he had been told to use his own judgment pertaining to what their next course of action would be. And although he was pleased that his commanding officer had enough faith in him to do that, he could not help but think back to his recent 'failures' overseas. It wasn't just his and Jerrelle's lives this time that were on the line; the entire platoon was his responsibility. Therefore, he had to make sure that the choices he made were ones that did not place any one of his brethren in an unsafe situation — he had to make sure that his assessments were accurate and his decisions correct.

After a few minutes in thought, Sabastian felt confident in the game plan he had assembled. Sergeants Fraisure and Tranter; he instructed them to find a secluded position a few blocks down the street — once they were there, their job was to keep an eye out for the return of those same two suspicious men. He then gave the same order to two more members of the unit to take up a similar position in the opposite direction, just in case the two men had circled around and decided to return from whence they came via the opposite way. After that, he led the remaining members of his unit down to the end of the same alleyway they had been waiting in. Once they got to the open street, they headed east until they arrived directly behind the office complex where Sabastian had previously placed his rooftop surveillance.

After explaining to everyone else what it was that he wanted from them, he dispersed his unit over a three-block radius — this was so that all the angles of the building in question were covered. If the A.R.M were indeed inside, and the S.N.A.F.U.'s presence were to be prematurely discovered, any thought of an escape would be much more difficult to attain.

After the dispersal of his men was complete, Sabastian looked at his watch; it was then that he realized Richard had yet to check in with him. Now, he was getting worried. No, the codeword had yet to be broadcast over their radios, but an immense amount of time had passed since his part of the unit decided to check out the boarded up apartment building. So he picked up his radio and called his friend — five beeps later, he answered. "Hey, Rat! You haven't checked in for like... forever. I was getting worried."

"You know that I would never give you a reason to be worried. But if you call me that stupid name again, you might want to keep one eye open when you sleep in your bunk tonight."

Sabastian knew that Richard's warning contained no real malicious intent. Nevertheless, he decided that his bit of personal fun at his friend's expense had run its course — there was no need for him to continually beat the obvious dead horse. "Ok.., I'll leave that name in the gutter with the rest of its kin and I won't use it again. However, I had every reason to be worried because you entered that building some forty-five minutes ago and I have not heard one single report from you."

"Well… I just didn't think there would be a need to broadcast a boring play-by-play commentary of the non-action that had been taking place on the field."

Richard had a point. Unless there was a real problem, he wasn't required to keep in touch. The huge responsibility that had been placed upon his shoulders was what Sabastian believed was attributing to his worrying. His desire to know everything that was going on was pushing aside the usual patience and trust he had. If he were to ever become a good leader, one that everyone looked up to and admired, he had to have complete faith in those whom he entrusted to take on an assignment. "You're right. So… have you found anything?"

"Nope! We just finished combing through the entire building and, other than a few homeless people, we didn't find jack shit."

"Well, we have. We are just sitting on it right now and gathering information. We need to be sure that this is what I suspect it is before I make a decision about what to do."

"I take it that you have all of the angles covered already?"

"Yup! We have got this place under surveillance better than a toothless redneck on the front porch with a double barrel shot gun in his hand, keeping an eye on his very determined virgin daughter."

Richard could not help but chuckle at Sabastian's analogy. "Do you want us to head over there and give you a hand?"

"Not just yet, Richard. But if we do determine that this building does belong to the A.R.M., then I will call you. I tell you though… if it does and they realize that they have been found, I am certain that the scorching Mexican sun will become the least of our worries."

"I agree. Led mosquitoes are far worse than any unwanted sunburn."

A smile came across Sabastian's face, as Richard's train of thought had been the same as his. That was why he had all but become Sabastian's best friend, his brother from another mother. "Don't worry... we've brought with us plenty of repellant."

No sooner had Sabastian ended his conversation with Richard, his rooftop surveillance man reported that there was now a pick-up truck backing down the alley up to the steel door. After a few moments of uncertain silence, the man continued his report, letting Sabastian know that the driver had gotten out of the pick-up truck, walked to the back, and then removed a tarp that had been covering several wood crates.

It was easy for Sabastian to think that whatever was inside those crates, it was the evidence they needed. But without him actually seeing its contents, he could only assemble a conjecture. His curiosity was urging him to get a closer look; he also had an anomalous feeling that he already knew what they contained — but acting on such an impulse to satisfy his suspicions would defeat the purpose of them being there. He had to be patient and do this by the book. Unlike his mission to take down his family's enemy, an unnecessary risk simply could not be taken in this instance.

Sabastian's eyes on the rooftop continued his report, informing him that the steel door had just opened up, two men exited the building, and the offloading of the crates had begun — he also let it be known the men that had come from inside of the building, also appeared not to be of Mexican heritage.

That bit of information only helped to increase Sabastian's suspicions — although, in no way shape or form did it give him the grounds he was looking for to take the next step. Whatever was going on inside this building, it had to be illegal. Cloned electronics, auto parts, knock-off merchandise, drugs, weapons — those crates that had just been delivered, he felt had to contain one of those items.

What had they actually stumbled upon? If what was taking place within the walls of this building had nothing to do with the

A.R.M., was it really their problem to deal with? The answer to that question of course, was yes. They simply could not turn a blind eye to criminal activity.

Sabastian was at a loss — he suddenly found it difficult to figure out what the next move was that he should make. He thought about calling Captain Swilling again and asking for his advice, but he didn't want to give his commanding officer the impression that he wasn't up to the task. It was time that he stepped up to the plate and did what was being expected of him.

There was a bit of fear on his face; he couldn't let any of his fellow brethren see that. Positive thoughts and confidence was what he needed in order to stay focused on the task he had been given. He could not allow himself to make any kind of stupid mistakes, so he closed his eyes, took a deep breath, and attempted to sort out his still muddled thoughts. At first, he was finding that difficult, but then he found the key that he was certain would allow him to filter them out — his father.

Maxwell Banks had been a man of conviction; a man of strength, a man of determination, and a man of honor — those were the same traits that Sabastian had discovered not too long ago that he also had. He had felt those things suddenly appear during his search for Antonio Marcone, and felt them growing stronger the closer he got to finding out the truth, to reaching his goal, and to settling the score. Now, Sabastian needed to find a way to harness those inherited attributes from his father and use them to help control the situation he had been placed in. Once he was able to do that, he was certain that everything would fall into place, as it should.

4

Once she had finished setting up her sister's meeting with Nicoli, she decided not to immediately head up to the gardens. Bai Lin instead, thought that Jerrelle could use a bit more time alone to get her head on straight, as the last thing she wanted to have something innocuous become the trigger that set off a mental breakdown.

She knew her sister well; it was why Bai Lin had prepared herself for what was surely going to be an objection of epic proportions once she sprung on Jerrelle what her plans were for this day. Hence the reason she delayed meeting her sister topside for as long as she could, knowing that the gardens would help to return her sister back to normal — or as close to normal as was possible.

When Bai Lin finally arrived to where Jerrelle was patiently waiting, what she had hoped to see seemed to have occurred, as her sister immediately produced a warming smile. This was a good sign for Bai Lin. Still, it didn't mean that what she wanted to do this day was going to happen. It may end up coming down to her having to pull rank; a forced sibling ultimatum — something that she was willing to use only if it became absolutely necessary.

As she expected, Jerrelle's answer was an emphatic refusal, but Bai Lin wanted to spend some quality time with her sister beyond the boundaries of the Liberation's compound; she wanted to take her into the city and enjoy the sights and sounds of one of the most beautiful places in the world — Tokyo, Japan. It appeared as if a standoff was about to take place.

When she wanted to, she could be a real pain in the backside — but Bai Lin was her big sister, and Jerrelle loved her very much. She always found it difficult to argue with her — and as much as she did not want to do what was apparently on the agenda, she reluctantly caved in. This wasn't her home after all, and Jerrelle didn't mind exploring new places and seeing the sites — but she was probably one of the few females on the planet that didn't like to shop, as she only did it when she absolutely had to buy something that she needed. Besides,

Jerrelle really didn't care what she wore. So long as her body was covered, her taste in fashion consisted of jeans, a comfortable pair of runners, a t-shirt, and maybe a jacket — and the colors of those had to be monotone.

Once they arrived in the downtown core, Bai Lin took Jerrelle to the Chūō District; a place where they could walk the streets, do some shopping and then later, relax at one of the many cafés and restaurants that were staggered throughout the area. Together, they had spent just under two hours walking and shopping, and yes, Jerrelle did actually buy something; she bought a black synth-suede and leather jacket that was trimmed in forest green. It looked warm and really cool on her — it was also something that Jerrelle desperately needed for the upcoming forecasted colder than normal Detroit winter.

After their shopping was over, Bai Lin picked a small bar / restaurant called Ryū No Su (The Dragon's Den), so that they could both relax and get a bite to eat. This place hadn't been chosen randomly; Bai Lin had brought her sister here for a reason that she had purposely neglected to give, because the surprise that was waiting inside was one that Jerrelle was probably not expecting — at least, not today.

Instead of grabbing a table outside so that they could continue to enjoy the near perfect day together, Bai Lin walked straight inside the restaurant. At first, Jerrelle somewhat protested, but then she quickly gave in for the same reason she had earlier — she didn't wish to argue. Once they had entered the place, instead of heading to one of the many open tables, Bai Lin lead her sister to a table that already had a single occupant. This caused Jerrelle to stop a few feet away from the table, unsure as to why her sister had led her here. She then asked Bai Lin the obvious question. "Um... why are we sitting here when there are a lot of other empty tables?"

"Just pull up a chair and I'll explain."

Jerrelle wasn't the kind of person that liked to humor someone she didn't know with trivial small talk, but she trusted her sister's judgment, so she pulled up a chair directly across from the decently attractive looking man.

"I took you out shopping today in hopes that it would also help you to take your mind off of what you've been going through." Bai

57

Lin produced a smile as she looked across the table at their guest. "Sis... This here is Nicoli Nemchieve."

At that moment, Jerrelle didn't have a clue about how she should feel. Although she was prepared for the fact that Helfred's older brother wanted to meet her, she didn't expect it to be only hours after she had found out. Immediately, her defense mechanisms wanted to kick in; the wall that she would usually erect when she faced a situation that she did not want to deal with was right there for her to hide behind. However, she knew that if she tried to avoid the inevitable; if Helfred were actually here at this moment, he would be extremely disappointed in her for not being the strong, assertive, and fearless person he knew her to be. Never before had she backed down from a challenge, and this one was no different — it just wasn't the kind that she was used to facing. "I... I didn't expect this to happen so soon. I'm not sure if I'm ready for this, Bai Lin?"

"I can only imagine, Jerrelle, how hard this is for you right now. And I am sure you are hurting just as much as I am over the loss of my brother. I asked Bai Lin to bring you here today because this was the only time that I could make available to meet with you."

"I'm so sorry about what happened, Nicoli." At that moment, Jerrelle could feel the emotions that she had worked hard to gain control over, coming back to the surface — the sadness that had been there had apparently never completely left. She took a moment and drew strength from her memories in hopes to keep control over what she felt was only a few seconds from being unleashed. She was face to face with the brother of the only man she had ever loved; she had to stay strong and in control. "I'm... not sure where to begin?"

"My brother once told me that you were the reason he became the man that he was. From the moment he had first met you, his life changed for the better. Before he met you, my brother was a man with no direction or care in the world. He used to just go out, have fun, and get into trouble without even caring if someone ended up getting hurt. You changed his whole outlook on life and gave him that reason he needed to grow up. He took his life and his career in the military seriously the moment you grabbed his heart. Even the day you both were forced apart, he used the strength that you had given him and he continued to grow and evolve into the man he became. He also knew

58

deep down inside that you two would re-connect one day. And that belief is what drove him to become the great man that he was. Thank you for everything that you did for him."

Jerrelle couldn't hold back the tears any longer; the floodgates broke open. She knew that Helfred had changed a lot after they had first met, but she really had no idea as to how much of an effect she had on his life. Now, the guilt that had been there had returned and enveloped every part of her because she had allowed Helfred to accompany her and Sabastian on something that he had no reason to be a part of. "Nicoli, I... I don't even know what to say?"

"You don't have to say anything."

Jerrelle took the offered napkin from her sister and wiped away some of her tears. "Yes, I do." After a few moments spent gaining control of what emotions she could, she wiped away a few more of her tears, found the strength from somewhere within her inner being, and pushed aside her trepidation. She then looked directly at Nicoli and said, "I feel that it is my entire fault that Helfred died. I failed to protect him and I let him join me in a dangerous situation that he had absolutely no business being involved with. I had only asked for his help to gather information, yet he insisted on being with me and helping me. I should have put my foot down and insisted that he not join us. But I didn't... and it cost him his life. I feel solely responsible for what happened to him."

"What were you doing that was so dangerous?" Bai Lin asked.

Jerrelle took a moment and recalled her memories. Once she had assembled the story in her head, she explained in detail, the events which had taken place that had lead to her and Sabastian's arrival in Germany, and then the subsequent events that followed which ended in Helfred's death. After she was done, Jerrelle found it very hard to look into Nicoli's eyes, but when she finally found the courage to do so, she could see a change — hurt and confusion were now anchored to them. "I don't know what else to say, but I'm so sorry."

"I know you are, but my brother is dead and I'll just have to continue on without him. I'll adapt, as I'm sure you will." Nicoli then stood up and looked over at Bai Lin. "I really must be going. Thank you, Bai Lin, for bringing your sister here. And thank you, Jerrelle, for

letting me know what had really happened to my brother. Goodbye."
Nicoli then left the restaurant.

After a few moments of uncomfortable silence, Bai Lin left the table, went to the bar, and returned to their table with two pints of beer in hand. The meeting with Nicoli didn't go quite how Bai Lin had thought it would, but she was pretty sure that Jerrelle was glad it had happened. This was the last obstacle that her sister needed to clear, and now that it was out of the way, she was positive that Jerrelle could complete the healing process and get on with her life.

About forty-five minutes later, their beers were gone and they both left the restaurant with a full stomach. Their intent was to return directly to the E.C.L. compound, but once they got about two blocks away from where they had been, Jerrelle suddenly realized that she had just done something really stupid — she had accidently left her new jacket behind.

Promptly, they both returned to the restaurant; Jerrelle was relieved to see that her purchase was still on the floor right where she had left it. After retrieving the shopping bag, the sisters proceeded to again leave the restaurant. However, no sooner had they taken two steps out the front door, they heard people screaming in the streets. Both had very little time to react, as a car was headed right toward them.

Strictly on instinct, Jerrelle jumped straight up as high as she could to try to avoid as much of the oncoming impact. Bai Lin did what she could as well to avoid being hit by diving off to the left and grabbing the dragon bust that protruded out from the side of the building.

Unfortunately, neither one of them were able to completely avoid being hit by the car. Jerrelle's feet had clipped the top of the car as it crashed through the restaurant's front door; she was sent tumbling forward, head over heels. Bai Lin's legs had also been clipped by the car, knocking her off her brief hanging position — the result of that had sent her entire body back partially inside of the now destroyed front of the building and depositing her unceremoniously on top of a pile of debris.

Chaos ensued; those who had been near this wild and unbelievable situation, jumped right in to help aid those who had become injured. Jerrelle was lucky, as the only injury she really had sustained was a gash and a large welt on the top of her head from her hard landing. After a moment of uncertainty, she was able to stand — she then quickly surveyed the area looking for her sister. The moment she saw her, fear overtook her emotions. Bai Lin was lying in an awkward, contorted position on top of the rubble, halfway inside what was the restaurant's foyer.

"Bai Lin! Bai Lin!" Jerrelle carefully maneuvered herself through the rubble and made her way over to her sister; she hoped and prayed that her worst fears weren't realized. She moved away some of the debris, knelt beside her sister, and then placed her hand on her shoulder. A moment later, Bai Lin slowly began to move; a rush of immense relief ran through Jerrelle's veins once she saw her open up her eyes. She exhaled, and then smiled; she knew right then and there the person that meant the most to her in this world, was going to be all right. "You hurt badly, sis?"

"I think my insides are okay, but… my left knee might be totally fucked."

As more and more strangers began to offer their assistance to those inside the restaurant, Jerrelle, though appreciative, just wanted to leave. "I think we need to get out of here before the emergency vehicles get here, as I don't think that it would be wise for us to go to the hospital."

Bai Lin looked at her sister and could see some blood trickling down the side of Jerrelle's temple. "We are both hurt. We'll stay here and let the paramedics treat our injuries. I'll just make sure that we don't make it all the way to the hospital."

"How are you going to do that?"

Bai Lin then reached over to her emerald charm bracelet, which concealed her micro-communicator, turned it on, and spoke into it. Then, she sent off that brief message she had just recorded, asking for assistance.

"Kuruma no nakaniha untenshu ga imasen!" Shouted a man who had went over to help the driver of the car.

"What did he just say, Bai Lin?"

"He said that there is no driver inside the car."

"No driver?" Jerrelle looked at her sister; both of them seemed just a bit perplexed that no one had apparently been behind the wheel of the car that had almost killed them.

A few moments later, the emergency vehicles had arrived. Once the sisters' injuries had been tended to, they were both placed into the ambulance for transport to the hospital — little did the EMS attendants know that the relatively short trip they were taking was not going to be as straightforward as they expected it to be.

He knew that he would soon be gone and that it would be quite a long while before he would have this chance again to see his son, so Louie made sure that his promise to help Marco with his studies on Thursday was kept. When he had arrived at his son's home, only Mirella was there. She invited him in and asked him to join her in the kitchen. "Marco was hoping that you'd come by today."

"I wasn't too sure at first if I'd be able to because as you know, things have a tendency to change. And with the way things are developing, I'm almost certain that I won't be back in Chicago anytime soon. Therefore, I postponed a couple of things that did not require my immediate attention in order to make sure that I could see my son one more time before I went back to Detroit."

"Oh... I didn't expect you to be going back already?"

"I wasn't planning on it, but I am. I know you'd prefer not to be made aware of anything that I do, so I'll just tell you that I'm now needed and have to return to work."

Mirella wasn't sure how she should feel about this revelation. On one hand, she was glad that Louie was leaving because with each day that he was around her son, the risk that he would break his promise and reveal the truth, increased. But she was also sad because unlike a lot of single mothers, he had made a genuine effort to be a part of his son's life. He had also turned out to be a very positive influence on Marco, which was something that Mirella feared wasn't going to be the case. "When will you be leaving?"

"I'm not exactly sure. I'm waiting for some confirmation from a colleague first... but I'm pretty sure that I'll be gone by week's end."

"Marco will be upset that you are leaving. You did tell him after all that you were going to be in Chicago for a few months."

"I know. Unfortunately, promises sometimes have to be broken." Louie intentionally paused for a few moments so that his words, he hoped, helped to keep the fear alive in Mirella's thoughts that he might not keep his word after all. "How do you feel about it?"

"Me? I know that things happen and promises sometime can't be kept, but…"

"But you are admittedly happy, aren't you, that I am leaving early because you are afraid that the longer I stay here, the greater the chances are that I'll tell Marco the truth that…"

"The truth? What do you mean tell me the truth?"

Both Mirella and Louie froze, surprised that Marco had quietly returned home without either of them being made aware of his entrance. They looked at each other, uncertain that their secret might have just been unintentionally revealed.

"What's going on here, Mom? Uncle Louie?"

As Louie was about to answer Marco's question, he could see Mirella's eyes pleading with him not to do it; not to break her heart and destroy her son's life. "…the truth is that I have been called back to work already, much earlier than I had anticipated, so today will be my last visit for a while. I didn't want to tell you this because I know how much you were looking forward to us spending a lot of quality time together over the next little while."

"You can't be serious? You told me that you had a lot of vacation time built up and that it would be a few months before you would be called back to work."

"I know, Marco, but things have changed within the company and I am needed. I do have some time tonight though, so I can help you with your studies."

Showing the obvious signs of disappointment and dejection, Marco turned away from his mother and 'uncle' and headed up to his room. "That's okay; I'm all studied out anyway. I'm just going to go and take a nap… and don't bother calling me for dinner, Mom. I'm not hungry."

Louie was about to get up and follow his son to his room when Mirella touched his arm. "Just let him go. I know you want to make sure that he is all right… and I'm sure he will be. If you go up to his room, he will only fire question after question at you about why you are really leaving and…"

"And like I just said… You are afraid that I will accidently let it slip out about me being his father. Come on, Mirella. We've been through this a million times. I will not go back on my promise to you." Louie was pissed off — and he was getting tired of Mirella not trusting him to keep his word. Almost from day one, he had to fight to hold back the bitterness that was there due to the ultimatum that his son's mother had given him. Trust is what Louie expected out of those who worked with and for him, and trust is what he thought he had long ago earned from Mirella — but that apparently was not the case. So he got up from his seat in the kitchen, put on his windbreaker, and headed to the front door.

"Louie, wait! You don't have to leave."

"Yes, I do. It's obvious after all these years that you still don't trust me to keep our little secret. Well, you don't need to worry anymore because I have now decided that it will be better for my son that I not come around here anymore. But, be aware that the day will come when Marco will find out that I am his father. And when that happens, you will have wished that we had told him the truth a lot earlier, because I guarantee you that he will not be happy with you for hiding it from him." Without another word said, Louie left the house.

Mirella just stood there at the threshold of her home, while the cool fall breeze blew up against her exposed legs and arms, staring at her son's father as he got into his car. In the back of her mind, she knew that Louie was right. Marco would probably have accepted the truth a lot easier had he been told it when he was younger. *'It's too late to tell him now,'* she thought. *'He's going to hate me no matter what when the truth comes out. And I have absolutely no idea what the hell I am going to do when the shit finally does hit the fan.'*

Minus the presence of the deliberately positioned military, the streets of Tijuana continued on with its daily routine of pedestrians, traffic, and idiosyncratic sounds. At first, the Union Military's presence had caused a slight bit of uneasiness with the residents of the city. They were used to seeing tourists among them, so when soldiers from another country suddenly appeared walking their neighborhood, confusion had disrupted the norm. After a while, Sabastian and his men had almost seamlessly begun to blend in. The looks of uncertainty by the people of Tijuana had diminished and the calm of everyday life had all but basically returned. This was something that could be sensed and Sabastian now felt a bit more confident that their presence had not yet been made aware of to the A.R.M. — that was if the supposed terrorist group was indeed inside the building they were keeping watch over.

Part of being a soldier in the S.N.A.F.U. was adapting to your surroundings, being patient, and waiting for the right moment to conduct a well-timed surgical strike — which was something that Sabastian had a refresher course in not too long ago. During his recent period of personal uncertainty, there had been a few situations when he just rushed in with guns drawn and no game plan. The results could have been disastrous. His actions then had been coerced by his emotions; fueled by the hatred he inherited for Antonio Marcone.

Drawing on that experience, he recognized that his emotions could easily be taken to a level of almost shear panic if he allowed it. Thankfully, Sabastian now felt that he was able to find the balance that he needed between emotion and logic so that his mind didn't allow him to start thinking along the lines of what if 'this happens', and what will 'then happen' because of my decision. And so that sort of second-guessing never took place, he was adamant that any call he made, he first had to be one hundred percent comfortable with it.

What he assumed might happen, had — a change in everyone else around him was taking place. Impatience was growing within those who were a part of his group. He and this platoon had been on many missions before, but it had been nearly two months since they had last been called upon, so it was easy to understand everyone's eagerness to get the information they came here looking for.

Knowing that it was his job to make sure that everyone was on the same page, Sabastian stopped thinking about all of the sudden variables that could come into play and started to focus on one thing — being the anointed leader. So he left his post, walked over to where each soldier had been patiently waiting, and had a brief discussion with them. As soon as he had finished giving his encouragement to the last two soldiers in their group, he received a radio transmission from Jeff

Trantor. Remembering that he had sent Jeff and Ben Fraisure four blocks up the street to keep an eye out for the two individuals who had earlier left the alleyway, he anxiously answered his radio call as he was walking back to his original position. "Go ahead, Sergeant."

"I just wanted to give you a heads up. Those two guys are headed back your way. Do you want us to follow them?"

"That would be a big negative," Sabastian said. "I want you both to head one block south and head over to where I am behind the building that is across from the one in question."

"Ok. But what are we going to do to find out if these men are indeed members of the A.R.M.?"

"Don't worry about that. I think I finally have that figured out." Sabastian ended his conversation just as he had returned to his post. Immediately, he handed his rifle over to Sergeant Eric Anadeg; the soldier that he had chosen to pair up with. Eric was a Native North American who was named in honor of his parents favorite movie, 'The Crow', because their last name means 'Crow' and the movie's main character's name was Eric — he was also the newest member of the S.N.A.F.U. and Sabastian had thought it was best to keep the 'Probie' close to him and make sure that the young man's inexperience wasn't the reason that an avoidable mistake was made.

Hastily, Sabastian removed his small backpack and set it down on the sidewalk. The one thing that he had learned while looking for Antonio Marcone was that situations might arise where you may have to improvise. He had thought that he was prepared for that possibility, but it never crossed his mind to bring a digital camera — then again, he doubted that his Captain would have authorized it.

After opening up his backpack, Sabastian removed a plain white T-shirt, a pair of knee-length jean shorts, a new pair of Nike Ultimate's, and a pair of dark Ray Ban III sunglasses. He then quickly stripped out of his military uniform and changed his clothes.

Eric stood there somewhat dumbfounded; he had no idea what the leader of his unit was doing, nor did he think that it was his place to inquire — he was the newbie after all, and he did not want to cross the line that everyone understood.

Seeing how confused and uncomfortable the young man must be, Sabastian simply smiled, then said, "I know what I am doing is against regulations, but we don't have time to think of a plan. We need to find out who those guys are... so I'll be back in a few minutes."

Now that he was disguised as a tourist, Sabastian walked up the street, turned, and then headed north. At the end of the block, he crossed the intersection that brought him over to the same side of the street the building was on that they had under surveillance. From there, he started to walk east toward the two oncoming individuals he had deemed suspicious. Sabastian's objective was simple; pretend while in mid-walk that he was on his vid-cell and in the middle of a heated argument. It was his intention to sell the image that he was just an average Joe who was mad at his girlfriend, when in actual fact, what he was doing was placing himself into a position to take a few quick vid-cell pics of the two men as they passed by him on the sidewalk.

When Sabastian reached the next street corner, he stopped. There was no reason for him to continue on in the direction that he had been walking, as at the opposite corner, his targets were waiting to cross at the light. When the light changed, Sabastian stayed where he was and acted as if the world around him did not exist; only the pretend conversation that he was having on his vid-cell was what was important at that moment.

The two men crossed the street and walked right passed Sabastian; little did they know that their pictures had just been taken with a perfectly placed vid-cell. A few seconds later, once those two men were halfway down the block, Sabastian looked at his candid shots — he smiled at just how good his rapid un-aimed vid-cell pictures had turned out.

Stoked that he had been able to accomplish what he had set out to do, Sabastian returned to his post, stripped out of his civilian clothing, and redressed into his military uniform.

"I know we are in Mexico, but... you're supposed to be on the beach before you parade around in public, half naked."

Sabastian just looked at Jeff and Ben with a brazen and twisted look on his face; he had not a comeback for them from his usual stocked arsenal of witted remarks — which perplexed him.

After deciding not to try and come up with something clever; fearing that he'd probably end up coming across as a dimwitted fool, he just buttoned up the last button on his uniform and repacked his 'tourist clothes'. Once that was done, Sabastian took another brief moment and looked over the pictures that he had taken. He honestly didn't expect what he had just done to work like it had, but thinking outside the box like that was something he now realized he needed to do more often whenever the situation warranted itself.

"So what are you going to do with these pictures? Tape a copy of them to the lid of your footlocker?" Ben asked.

"No, you moron! I'm going to send them off to a friend of mine. And if we get lucky, he'll be able to find out for us who they are." Sabastian then proceeded to call his father's agency. "Hey, Savanna. Is Baylor there?"

"I'm glad you called, Sabastian. We were getting so worried about you. Where are you right now?"

"You know that I can't tell you that… but I really need to talk to Baylor."

"Sure, he's in your father's office. Hang on."

'He's in my father's office again,' Sabastian thought. 'I think it's time that boy gets a computer of his own.'

"What's up, Sab?"

"You're not gonna start calling me Sab too, are you?"

"I am. Jerrelle told me that you think it's a cool nickname, and I like it better than Sabastian. So again… what's up, Sab?"

After a slight exhale of annoyance, he said, "I'm going to send you a few pictures. I need you to work your magic, hack into the San Antonio Police forensics lab, and pirate their facial recognition software."

"Um… no! We've been through this before. As of this moment, I refuse to hack into any government server ever again… even if your intentions are good."

"Listen, Baylor. I really need to find out who these men are."

Baylor decided in that moment that he was going to take this opportunity and have a little harmless fun and argue with his friend. He could have told Sabastian that he didn't need to hack into the forensics lab, but that would be spoiling the surprise he had — and he didn't want to do that just yet. "How bad do you need to know? I mean, you still owe me one considering that you had me hack into the main server at the Detroit Police Department. And then you had the nerve to tell me that you might not even need the info that I had gathered for you. I think that I have risked my anal virginity for you enough in my lifetime."

Sabastian had never had a reason in the past to truly get pissed off at Baylor. Under normal circumstances, he would have just brushed off his friend's attempt at being a pain in his ass, but he wasn't there in the same room with him — he was in another country and he didn't have time to deal with the way that his friend was acting. In fact, Sabastian was just about to verbally rip Baylor that new asshole he had always been afraid of getting, when he realized in that moment that his friend was actually laughing. Instantly, Sabastian relaxed, remembering that he had always had trouble keeping a straight face whenever he was trying to pull one over on him. "You know, I was only seconds away from really getting pissed off at you. Thankfully, you can't bullshit worth a damn."

"I know. I just couldn't resist the urge to try and mess with you. But just so you know, I don't need to hack into the forensics lab. When Captain Lutherage extended the offer to help you in any way that he could, I couldn't resist asking him if he'd be willing to give us a full copy of their facial recognition software. Seeing that this is a detective agency, I just assumed that you may need to use that technology one day on a future case."

"You were being a little presumptuous there, bud."

"Maybe? But I do happen to know you a little bit better than anyone else."

A bit of gratitude enveloped his soul. The thought of following in his father's footsteps had never really crossed Sabastian's mind before. The only thing he thought he was going to do was to finish walking the same path that Maxwell Banks had. Becoming a private detective though, most certainly appealed to him. He did after all, not only have the lineage, but a military background that would most certainly come in handy. This deliberate suggestion from his friend was definitely something that Sabastian needed to seriously consider once he had completed what his father had started. "I am glad that you and I are best buds, Baylor." Sabastian then sent him the images.

Happy that his old friend had asked for his assistance with something again, Baylor fired up the facial recognition program, and then transferred the incoming photos to the desktop computer. However, there was one small problem that he had neglected to disclose to Sabastian — he hadn't yet taken the time to learn how to use the program. However, there was no time for excuses; he just needed to get to work and learn what he needed to learn. It wasn't that complicated of a program, but Baylor was pretty sure that Sabastian needed to know who these two men were as soon as it was possible — anything much longer than yesterday would not be acceptable.

As the chaos around the destroyed restaurant began to subside, police and emergency workers took control of the area and tended to the victims of this unexpected and spectacular accident. A good majority of the patrons who had been inside the establishment had sustained minor injuries from flying debris; one person unfortunately, had lost her life. She just happened to be in the wrong place at the wrong time — and she was the same waitress who had greeted and served Jerrelle and Bai Lin.

Where the waitress had been standing at the time, the trajectory of the wayward vehicle would not have hit her, but a table that had been in the direct path of the car, was sent flying right toward her — she didn't have a chance, as it smashed into her. The force of the impact caused her neck to be broken, and she died before the EMS could get her stabilized.

Bai Lin and Jerrelle both knew how lucky they were to have escaped serious injury. The sisters could have simply left the chaotic scene, but they admittedly were not the kind of people who could easily blend in with a crowd. The last thing they needed was to have someone draw an unwarranted conclusion as they left, based solely upon the way they looked.

They were both victims of this tragedy, so it made sense to stick around, receive onsite treatment for their injuries, and then leave the same way any victim normally would — in an ambulance.

As soon as the E.C.L. had received Bai Lin's encoded message, they used their G.P.S. tracking system and honed in on the unique, dedicated tracking marker that was a part of Bai Lin's micro-communicator. Since a hospital was one of those places where records of individuals were easily attainable, they needed to ensure that their fellow Liberation member did not make it there. They just could not risk the possibility of Bai Lin's identity and association being discovered — someone might have an issue with a member of the E.C.L. and make things difficult for her, or someone might panic and call the police once Jerrelle's extensive criminal record came to light. Therefore, the ambulance that was carrying both of the sisters had to be stopped.

About three blocks before the hospital, in three black Nissan Titan III pickup trucks, members of the E.C.L. strategically set up a rolling box. What they were doing certainly caught the ambulance driver by surprise. He didn't know what to do, as he could not maneuver the ambulance away from the moving trap. The driver had no choice; he had to follow the urging of the three trucks and complied with what they wanted, so he slowed down the ambulance and brought it to a complete stop.

The driver was not only frustrated, but pissed. However, before he could give these people a piece of his mind, a Winchester 70A Magnum Rifle with an attached laser sight appeared out the center back window of the lead black truck. Fearing for his life, the driver slowly removed his hands from the steering wheel and raised them in acknowledgement that he understood the message that was being sent. The driver then silently said a pray, hoping that his life wasn't about to be over.

Six members of the E.C.L., covered from head to toe in what appeared to be black ninja-like riot gear, got out of the three trucks, had their weapons drawn, and then surrounded the ambulance. They were quick and precise as they opened up the back of the vehicle — they then forcefully removed Jerrelle and Bai Lin. This was done on purpose; to make what was going on look like an actual kidnapping, even though it was really just a rescue.

Once Bai Lin and Jerrelle were secured separately inside two of the black trucks, all three of the vehicles promptly left the area, each in a different direction. This had left the ambulance attendants scratching their heads; it also had caused Jerrelle's anger to rise. She wasn't at all happy that she and her sister were unceremoniously yanked out of the back of an emergency vehicle like a third-world prisoner of war. In fact, the Tasmanian devil that lived inside of her started to come to life; she desperately wanted to give them all a piece of her mind for the way they had been treated — but she didn't, as the last thing Jerrelle wanted to do was to make things more complicated for her sister.

Had she known in advance the reasoning for the treatment they received, she probably would not have gotten so pissed off, but she wasn't a member of the E.C.L. and she wasn't privy to their method of operations. Initially, she thought that their treatment was due to the situation they found themselves a part of and that Bai Lin was being blamed for it. Come to find out, this was just one of the different procedures that the Liberation used when it came to retrieving one of their own. While she was in Japan and in her sister's company, Jerrelle just needed to remind herself that she was only along for the ride and that she needed to keep her opinions to herself and her emotions in check.

In hindsight, she realized that she was lucky, as the E.C.L. did not have to extract her from the situation — she could have been left to fend for herself and deal with the authorities that the hospital surely would have alerted once they looked into her background. Therefore, she could only come to one conclusion — the Liberation had accepted her as being something other than just someone with a visitor's pass.

Fifteen minutes after their rescue...

Inside, what looked comparable to that of a hospital examination room, Bai Lin and Jerrelle sat; each was having their injuries reassessed. Shortly after that had began, the leader of the E.C.L., Orochi Bushido, unexpectedly entered.

Had he ever held a regular job, his age would thus qualify him to collect a pension. His physical appearance though, wouldn't corroborate that fact as he looked only to be maybe in his mid fifties. He possessed an heir of regalness and his presence garnered the kind of attention and respect that was well deserved.

72

Slightly less than six foot tall he stood, and it was easy to see that the man kept himself in peak physical condition. His hair was uniformly gray — except for the odd strand of solid black tucked between it, not at all thinning, and cut and styled appropriately for someone of his stature. Surprisingly, his body bared no visible scars; it only had the traditional E.C.L. dragon tattoo that everyone in the Liberation sported — it covered his entire left forearm. Besides the design, size, and placement on the body of the dragon tattoo, Orochi's had a distinction unlike any others that only he was allowed to have — it contained the Japanese word 'Rīdā', along with 'III', cleverly hidden within the artwork. These elements were what signified that he was the third leader of the Extremist Clandestine Liberation.

Whenever a situation like what had just happened would occur, it was the responsibility of each member of the E.C.L. to clean up his or her own mess. So before her leader had a chance to remind her of that, Bai Lin lowered her head in shame and asked for forgiveness for failing to do what was expected of her — be fully aware of her surroundings at all time.

Orochi walked over to Bai Lin, and with his left hand, gently lifted her head up so that he could look her in the eyes. "I do not believe that you are responsible for what took place."

"I feel that I am, oh great one. And I will graciously accept whatever punishment you feel is necessary for my incompetence and for bringing disgrace to the Liberation."

"Nonsense! I will not accept your insistence to shoulder the blame. I am aware of what had happened, and in my opinion, this just appears to be a random, unavoidable accident."

"I don't think so,' Jerrelle said, as she gingerly got off of the examining table. "With all due respect, I know that I am just a visitor here, but I think that what happened was actually an attack on my sister."

"And what makes you think that?"

Jerrelle looked at her sister and then she looked over at Orochi. "A few moments into the chaos, a man went over to the car to check on the driver. We both heard him state that there was no driver inside it."

"No driver? How is that possible?"

"I'm not sure, but I do have an idea as to how that could have occurred." Jerrelle then went on to explain what she was thinking. She started by giving the Extremist Clandestine Liberation leader a brief recap about her recent cross-continental adventure with her friend, Sabastian. Then, she went on to explain that Governor Christopher White, her friend's father's ex-boss and longtime friend, had informed them of the last conversation that took place between he and Maxwell Banks in which he had learned about the Communist Revolutionary Assembly Party acquiring some military grade microchips, called S.M.A.R.T., from the head of the Detroit Underworld Organization.

Jerrelle followed that with a pause, as she wanted to take a moment and see if she could gauge what Orochi was now thinking. She was no expert in reading people, but she believed that the man was keeping an open mind and was interested in what he was hearing, so she decided to let her opinion be known that she thought it was possible these same S.M.A.R.T. microchips could have been used to intentionally send the unmanned car to kill Bai Lin.

Orochi sat back and reviewed everything that had just been presented to him. As unlikely as it seemed, he had heard rumors about the existence of these microchips. And like a lot of others who were a part of the underground world, he had dismissed it as being only a theoretical possibility that was still several decades away from coming to fruition. Now, he had to accept the likelihood that it did indeed currently exist.

Just because Bai Lin's sister was not a member of their organization, didn't automatically mean that she was someone whom he should be leery of — after all, she had let them know about Antonio Marcone's hasty retreat to Japan. Therefore, he felt that there was no reason to dismiss her opinion. As improbable as it was, no other explanation seemed to be there. "Ok. Until a reason can be found as to why there was no driver behind the wheel, your hypothesis is the one that I will have someone follow up on. If it does turn out to be true, and that someone is out there looking to kill Bai Lin, then they will be dealt with accordingly." What Orochi did not share with Jerrelle, which was none of her concern anyway, was that those who would have provided that individual or organization with the

S.M.A.R.T. technology will be considered just as guilty as those who used it for said intended purpose.

Satisfied with the information he had come to obtain, Orochi turned and then headed toward the exit of the medical ward of the E.C.L. compound. Just as he was about to cross the threshold he stopped, turned back around, and looked at Jerrelle, "Before I go, I want to apologize. There is no acceptable reason for my granddaughter's behavior toward you. I believe that it was her father who encouraged it, as he seems to like to question my judgment when it comes to opening up our doors to those from the outside world — even when it is to the immediate family of one of our own members."

"That's all right," Jerrelle said, with a smile. "No harm done."

Orochi bowed his head in respect, and then left the medical ward.

Both the sisters just sat there, unsure. A lot had just happened that seemed somewhat difficult for them to understand — at least, the leader of the Liberation had made it clear that no responsibility for the incident would be directed at Bai Lin. Still, something didn't seem right. But that didn't mean that they could deliberately knock down every door they came across until they found the right individual who could give them the answers they sought. Instead, what they had to do was focus on only two things — resting and recuperating. Bai Lin's knee after all, was pretty messed up, and Jerrelle's head was throbbing. "How is it that every time I come to Japan to visit you, I end up with a massive headache?"

Bai Lin didn't say a word, she just laughed.

"So… do you think that you'll be up to going back to that restaurant tomorrow?" Jerrelle asked.

"What? Why would you want to go back?"

"Because I forgot my new jacket there… again."

5

~ Sometimes the choices we make come with a deep regret soon afterward. Left unaddressed, that regret just might end up causing you to do something unbefitting of who you really are. And unless you can find a way to free your own guilt, an even bigger regret will occur on the day that you leave this world. ~

He wasn't sure if he was doing this in spite of Mirella, but Louie had decided once he had left her place that he wasn't going to let his lifelong feelings for her stop him from living the remainder of his life the way he wanted; the way he should have been all along. So as soon as he returned to his apartment, he turned on his laptop, and searched the area's escort services. This was something that he had never done before, but Louie was in an atypical mood — he really wanted a piece of ass, thinking that it would help to alleviate his frustration.

Once he found a sight that looked to be one of the higher-class services, he spent a few moments browsing their 'menu' of ladies. *'There is nothing wrong with doing this,'* he thought to himself. *'Sal used to do this all the time… though his preferred company was usually just shy of being legal.'* The more he studied the site, the more trepidation began to consume him. Usually, whenever Louie set out to do something, he never changed his mind. Understandably, he was starting to have second thoughts about paying for sex.

'Sex… that is all it would be. I mean, it's been more than four presidential terms since I have last used my bed for something other than sleeping.' He was about to give up on this crazy idea of his, when the second last escort's profile on the site caught his eye; she instantly garnered his full attention. This woman was more than perfect in the physical sense: her long dark hair, her European facial features, her perfectly toned body, her well placed assets, her award winning smile, and even those unique tiny diamond studded single piercings on the center backside of each of her hands, made her as close to a real

goddess as any man could ever wish for. Everything about her looks was exactly what Louie had liked when it came to his ideal woman. In fact, he had to admit that this escort was the best looking woman that he had seen since the day he had first laid eyes on Mirella.

There was no going back if he did this. He would be one of the millions of men that ever walked the earth who had paid for sex. If he was going to take the plunge, this was the woman with whom it would be.

Although he was still feeling a bit apprehensive, Louie picked up his vid-cell, contemplated for a brief moment, and then did it — he called the escort service. He was told by the woman who answered his call that it would be about an hour before his 'date' would arrive, which gave Louie just enough time to accomplish everything that he felt needed to be done.

This evening obviously wasn't going to be one of those romantic ones, but Louie still thought of himself as a gentleman. He always had respect for women, no matter what kind of life they had chosen to live — even those who had chosen to work in the kind of profession that his 'date' did. Besides, he was in no position to judge someone on the choices they had made. His decision to live his life as a member of the D.U.O. was a prime example of something that a lot of people could not understand, nor could accept. So even though his 'date' tonight was what it was, he was adamant on showing her that he was nothing but pure class and that she was way above the low-level her chosen profession ranked on the scale of highly respected careers.

Louie had dimmed the lights, put on some of his favorite piano music, and lit a few strategically placed scented candles throughout his apartment. When she had arrived, she was even more beautiful in person than what Louie had imagined. This young woman could easily make any man of any age happy: happy for one night, or happy for a lifetime.

A genuine smile instantly appeared on her slightly tanned, flawless face; within moments of entering the apartment, she knew that her client was trying to make this evening seem like more than it actually was. The reservations that usually would accompany her when she initially met a client had promptly disappeared — that almost never took place until at least halfway through the allotted time.

77

The gentleman inside of Louie came forward as he walked up behind his 'date' and began to assist her with the removal of her knee-length, real leather jacket; with care, he hung it up in the closet next to the front door. Once he closed the door to the closet, he took his 'date' by the arm and walked her to the living room, introducing himself along the way as 'Daniel' (he had decided that he did not want this woman to know his real name, so he used his middle one instead). She introduced herself as 'Madelyn', which Louie could only assume was an alias.

Seeing that tonight was only a business agreement and not a real date, Louie removed his billfold from his suit jacket pocket and paid the lady her fee. She smiled, thanked him, and then proceeded to explain to Louie everything that she would and would not do. Kissing on the lips was the one thing that was out of the question, as that was something she only did with clients of hers that she had known for a very long time, trusted, and had grown fond of.

Fully understanding and accepting the ground rules that she had just laid out for him, Louie offered Madelyn his hand; she willingly took it. He then led her to his bedroom; he only had two hours with her and wanted to get his money's worth.

As she entered the room, Madelyn's blue /green eyes lit up as she again noticed the effort that Louie had made to make her feel special. The chocolate flowers were something that she had never received from anyone before in all the years she had been in her line of work — and the champagne was Krug, Clos du Mesnil, circa 2006; she recognized the brand and knew that it had cost her client almost a thousand dollars for the thirty-year old bottle.

Right then and there, Madelyn understood that this man had high expectations for the evening — and she was more than happy to make that come to fruition. She even entertained the thought of maybe staying past the agreed time. Though time was money, she, not the escort service, called the shots when it came to how much extra time she could spend with a client — she had earned that right. Besides, her client this evening was actually still a pretty damn good-looking man for one who was rapidly approaching the age for which a retirement community, where the weather is always at least satisfactory, was right around the corner. He also seemed to possess an old world charm —

that is what allowed Madelyn to believe her client was not only a real gentleman, but that he would treat her like a treasured heirloom. In fact, she already felt so comfortable with this man that she was beginning to think she might even enjoy herself as well this evening.

Louie walked over to the table where the champagne sat, picked up the bottle, both glasses, and invited Madelyn to join him out on his bedroom balcony. He then popped the cork and smiled as the champagne poured itself out and over the edge of the balcony. They both shared a brief laugh, as twenty stories below an unexpected passerby received a slight shower from the expensive alcohol.

Louie could not help but take a moment and absorb the beauty that was in front of him. Standing there under the moonlit sky with a woman who could make any man his age feel like a teenager again, he could not help but be brought back to a time when he had experienced what it was like to finally become a man. He had lost his virginity to a woman who was nearly the same age as his own mother, two days after his seventeenth birthday, in an almost similar situation (he had delivered a box of items to a lady friend of the family late one night, and she had somehow coerced him onto the balcony to admire the harvest moon). In a strange sort of way, Louie felt as if he was revisiting an important moment in his past.

Without even watching what he was doing, Louie expertly filled both glasses with the expensive champagne — only because his eyes were locked onto something more intoxicating. In a chivalrous manner, he handed Madelyn her drink, set the bottle down, and with a genuine smile on his face, he toasted the evening. It was then that Louie felt something that he hadn't since the day he finally asked Mirella on a date — nervousness.

With the evening's perfect ambiance as a backdrop, and near perfection standing right in front of him, Louie stood there inert. He was a lost soul, captivated and confused at the same time. He was in the company of a woman more beautiful than he could ever remember being this close to in years, and he could not for the life of him remember what to do next.

Three modest sips of the champagne and two trifling toasts later, Madelyn took Louie's hand — only because she could see that he was hesitant to take that next step. She then led him back into his bedroom, set hers then his glass of champagne down onto the nightstand, and then began to remove his suit jacket. After laying it across the arm of the nearby chair, she took two steps back and proceeded to slowly unbutton her blouse, letting Louie enjoy the moment; a moment that she could only assume he hadn't experienced in a number of years.

Not wishing to tease her client for too long, she undid the last button and draped her blouse across the front corner of Louie's bed. Then, turning her back to him and bending forward as she did it, slowly unzipped her skirt — she let it fall meaninglessly to the ground, stepped out of it, then turned back around to display what little was left that could still be classified as clothing.

Standing there nearly naked was his 'date', wearing only a matching set of under garments the likes of which Louie had never before seen on a woman; underwear that for all intensive purposes, left very little to the imagination. Her perfectly tanned body, accentuated by her red and black laced bra and panties, immediately intensified the joy that he knew awaited him — and when Madelyn encouraged him to come closer to her, he almost had a heart attack.

A moment of expected hesitation consumed him; he wasn't young anymore, and a one-night stand with this woman was surely going to kill him. Nevertheless, Louie decided that he would be willing to accept that kind of fate if it were to befall him — one can only hope that when they die, the last breath they would take would be during a moment of pure happiness.

Gathering the courage that he needed, Louie walked up to Madelyn and gently placed his hands on her shoulders. His heart began to race; he was only moments away from having sex with this beautiful young woman, a woman who was young enough to be his own daughter.

With her guidance, she led Louie's hands from her shoulders and brought them down to her breasts. She could sense the anticipation he had, as well as the hesitancy that was so obviously there. And although her client had not made any personal details known to her, Madelyn could tell that the sensation of touching a woman's bare skin was somewhat unfamiliar. Strangely, her client seemed to be treating this moment like a teenage boy would who had suddenly discovered that his initial perception of what a woman's body was truly like was nowhere near accurate and that his own magazine collection, internet education, and imagination, had failed to fully prepare him for reality and what he was about to experience.

With it becoming blatantly obvious that her client had somehow forgotten that there was more to a woman than what his hands were currently glued to, Madelyn laid her own hands over top of his, smiled, and then guided them down to her hips. Next, she turned around and placed her backside up against Louie's manhood, closed her eyes, and then began the process of getting him to stand at 'full attention'. Within only a few seconds, she had accomplished that — she also had his.

After inhaling a deep breath, Madelyn encouraged Louie to unclip her bra. For some reason though, hesitancy was still there. However, only a few moments had to pass before Louie finally found the courage to take that next step, so he slid his fingers under the straps and followed the lingerie down to the middle of her back, stopping at the center clip. The memory of that day on the balcony with his mother's friend returned; he was hesitant then as well to unclip her bra. Unlike that day though, he no longer was a naïve, scared young man; he was a man of many years, and nothing had ever prevented him from attaining what he wanted or set out to do.

After pushing aside what little trepidation was still present, Louie undid the clips on Madelyn's bra. He knew immediately that a small taste of heaven awaited him, but he suddenly couldn't move. All that he had to do was remove the straps from her shoulders and he would just be one step away from doing what he was paying this woman for — but something caused his hands to begin to shake. Already, Louie was admittedly nervous; that though, he knew, wasn't the reason why he was now wavering. Standing behind this woman and touching her nakedness, felt foreign to him. This was all wrong. It felt like he was contaminating the deep feelings inside of him that he once had for Mirella; feelings that he long since locked away. This escort had somehow triggered emotions in him that he had purposely suppressed; emotions that he had to acknowledge right then and there were much stronger than what he had ever thought they had been.

He didn't deny that at one time, he had fallen hard for Mirella; which was why he had agreed to do what she had asked him to do all those years ago. But it took a beautiful, tempting woman like Madelyn, to make Louie finally realize that he still, and had always been in love with the mother of his son. *'As much as I want to do this… and die trying, I just can't.'*

Louie refastened Madelyn's bra, bent over and picked up her skirt off of the floor, grabbed her blouse from the corner of his bed, and handed them back to her. "I'm sorry. As beautiful of a woman as you are, and as memorable of a night as I believe tonight would be, I just can't do this."

Madelyn had never in all the years she had been an escort had a client change his mind — not this far into it. Many times she had to help a client gain the courage they needed to have sex with her, but with this man, she could see that there was a deeper reason as to why he was changing his mind.

Once she finished putting her clothes back on, she walked over to Louie and gently grabbed his hand, looked into his conflicted eyes, and immediately could tell that he had a deeply wounded soul. "I may not be an expert, but I can tell that there is a true love in your life that you know in your heart you can never be with."

Louie didn't respond to Madelyn's observation; he just stood there in silent acknowledgement.

"You must be a very strong willed individual to have to live your life with such a burden, Daniel." Madelyn gave Louie a consoling smile, let go of his hand, and then left the bedroom. While in thought, Louie stood there and watched her walk down the hall toward his living room. She was mostly correct in her observations; his burden was what had made him do this tonight — and he was not going to let his burden turn him into a shell of a man. As of this moment, Louie swore to himself that he was going to take back his life; the one that existed outside of the secret world he professed a lifelong commitment to.

"Hang on a moment!" Louie made his way to the front door of his apartment, just as Madelyn was removing her jacket from the closet. Louie took it from her, and being the gentleman he knew he was, helped her put it on. He then reached into his front pocket and removed his money clip, removed another five hundred union dollars from it, and attempted to give it to her. "Please take this to make up for my wasting your time."

"You did not waste my time, Daniel. It is not often that I come across a real gentleman in my line of work." She placed her hand on top of Louie's and closed his hand over top of the money. "That extra money is not necessary — thank you for being who you are."

Compliments directed at Louie were few and far between. And although he didn't even know this woman, there was something about her that he did like, so he asked Madelyn to wait there at the front door and he went back into his bedroom. He returned a few moments later with the box of chocolate flowers. "I know this isn't much, but I saw your eyes drawn to these when you first walked into my bedroom." The smile she produced as she accepted the chocolates only confirmed Louie's decision not to go through with what he had initially intended to do with this beautiful young lady. In fact, he chose right there to make her an open offer that he hoped she would one day accept. "I will be heading back home to Detroit within the next few days. If you are ever in my city and need help with anything, please make contact with me and I will be more than glad to help."

"Thank you for the gracious offer, Daniel, but I think that it will be very hard for me to ever find you, because I'm pretty sure that you withheld your real name from me."

"I did. My name is Louie Daniel Mazotti."

"It's nice to officially meet you, Louie. My name is actually Madelyn.., Madelyn Kinsworth." She stepped forward and embraced Louie in a friendly hug and lightly kissed him on the cheek. She then left his apartment and disappeared into the elevator.

He stood there a few moments after Madelyn had left and thought. *'If I had only met that woman years ago under any other circumstances, I would have rescued her from her chosen life and treated her the way she deserves to be treated.'* Louie then closed his apartment door and went back inside, grabbed the bottle of champagne, his glass from the bedroom nightstand, and went outside to sit on his balcony to enjoy the remainder of it and the evening all by himself.

An hour ago, the streets of Tijuana were filled with people going about their everyday business. At the same time, Sabastian and his group had halted their search for the A.R.M. cell location in order to take up watch of a building that had snagged their curiosity. Oddly now, very few people were left walking about the streets — and the majority of those seemed to be in a hurry to leave the area. Like an animal scurrying to find shelter because it knows that a terrible storm is approaching or a natural disaster is about to occur, that's what seemed to be unfolding right in front of them.

An uneasy feeling suddenly enveloped Sabastian. Either the people of this city somehow knew that the American Union Military were within minutes of conducting a raid, or they knew that those who were inside the building they had been keeping an eye on, were about to ambush his half of the platoon. Whatever the reason for the rapidly developing tension in the air, he knew that he could not allow those under his command be affected by it — so he turned on his com-link and addressed the unit. After each of them responded in succession with the affirmation that Sabastian expected, he looked at Eric Anadeg, and without any words needing to be exchanged, knew that his fellow soldier would not let him down.

His gut was telling him to just make the call — even without the hard evidence that they needed. Sabastian was certain that they had found the cell, but the last thing that he wanted to do was to make a very regrettable mistake. He couldn't fail, and he could not disappoint those who had faith in him: Captain Swilling, his unit, his family, friends, and yes, even his ex-father.

Again, Sabastian was feeling uncertain of what he should do next. Thankfully, he did not have to search for an answer to his dilemma as his vid-cell surprisingly rang — it was Baylor calling him back. He really didn't expect his friend to return his call so quickly, because it had only been roughly thirty minutes since he had sent those pictures of the suspicious individuals to him. "You couldn't have called at a better time, bud."

"Wow! Since when did you start missing me?"

"Only when I need something from you and well… things are changing here rather quickly. I hope you were able to identify those two men for me?"

"I have and… man, this facial recognition software is really fuckin' cool. Do you know that I can even take a child's picture and it can project what that child will look like when they get older?"

"Listen, Baylor, I really don't have time to chat. Can you just please tell me who these two men are?"

"Sure. They are Quinton and Jarious Harvin. Both men have an extensive rap sheet: petty theft, possession of a controlled substance, disorderly conduct, and a few weapons charges."

"They are brothers?"

"Yes! Quinton is the oldest."

"Is there anything else?"

"Of course. Savanna was able to find out that they are both linked to the American Recovery Mission; an organization that some within the government firmly believe is a radical terrorist group."

This was exactly the confirmation that Sabastian had hoped for. Though this still didn't give them the undeniable proof that they had found the Tijuana cell, it did give them the grounds they needed to finally take that next step.

Sabastian thanked his old friend for a job well done and then disconnected his call. Immediately afterward, he picked up his radio, called Richard Atwater, and quickly explained to him everything that he now knew — he then followed that by requesting that his half of the platoon join Sabastian's as fast as they possibly could.

With the other half of the S.N.A.F.U. now on their way to join them, the uneasiness that had enveloped Sabastian only a few moments earlier, had dissipated. He felt much more confident that this uncertain mission just might produce the results they had come here looking for. Admittedly, he had been skeptical; now, the supposition that had been there by those who were behind their deployment, seemed correct.

Twenty minutes later, Richard's group had joined up with his. After a few minutes of conversation with his friend, Sabastian recalled the soldier that he had previously assigned to do surveillance on top of the three-story office complex. Richard then ordered the platoon's sniper, a soldier named Stanley Zeikulliamon, a.k.a. 'Zeik', two blocks further back from their current position, to the rooftop of an office building, six flights up, that had a clear line of sight to the back alley door of the building in question. Zeik had been the only soldier in the history of the Houston Military Base to ever register a perfect score in all three assessments: closed quarter's combat, long range targeting, and the supposedly unwinnable assault and rescue test — that portion of the test has affectionately been dubbed by those within the S.N.A.F.U. as their version of the Kobayashi Maru (A no-win situation caused by a set of rules that can only be won by changing the rules, in effect, cheating). It is this test where a single soldier has two options: either construct a plan that will allow them to extricate a group of hostages safely, one at a time, or hastily perform a direct attack on the terrorist group. If they chose the first scenario, time will not be on their side, as the obliviousness of the enemy would not last for long. If they chose the second option, the likelihood will be that the terrorists would have executed all of the hostages long before the soldier could take them all out. The whole purpose of such a test is to determine the kind of choices you'd make and the type of leader you one day could become.

Somehow, Zeik had become the first, and still the only one to ever succeed in that test. To this day, those who created it to be unwinnable firmly believe that he had cheated. But those, like Sabastian and Richard who knew their brethren well, knew he had something that they only wished each had — an IQ of nearly one hundred and fifty, which he used every bit of that day.

After recalling all of his men from their positions, Sabastian then assigned four of them to assist four of Richard's men in quietly clearing the streets in and around the suspected structure. The remaining soldiers from both groups were then divided into three groups whose assignments were geared to their specialty. In only a matter of minutes, they were going to storm the building from the back, the front, the rooftop, and then secure it.

Working under the assumption that their anonymity was no longer there, Sabastian decided to do what he had initially swore he wasn't going to do — attack without a solid game plan. They didn't have all the viable proof they should have had; they didn't have enough information to justify what they intended to do. All they had as a reason for what they were about to do, was what they had suspiciously seen being delivered to the building and the confirmed identities of two men and their supposed association with the A.R.M.

What doubt that was still there, could not be compared to the doubt he had when he first chose to go against Antonio Marcone. No game was being played; no breadcrumbs were being laid down for him to follow into a trap. It wasn't just he and Jerrelle; Sabastian had twenty-nine of his fellow soldiers there to back him up. If anything, they had the upper hand in this entire situation. They were all ready for this; this was what they have been trained for. This was no different than any other situation that they have been faced with in the past. A quick, decisive, and surgical surprise strike was what they needed to execute in order for them to succeed — which he firmly believed they were going to.

Once everyone was in their assigned positions, Sabastian gave the order. It began with Zeik using his Beretta CNML 86-B, air compressed mini scud launcher to blow open the building's alleyway steel access door. At the exact same moment, the group on the rooftop and the group at the back of the building set off the charges they had planted against the back exit door and around the frames of the two large black painted skylights, blowing all of them to smithereens. The group on the rooftop then repelled down into the building, as the remainder of their platoon entered through the alley and back shattered doorways.

Chaos ensued as the fifteen members of the A.R.M. inside the building panicked. They weren't prepared for anything quite like this; smoke canisters tossed inside the building caused sudden panic to erupt. Those few who had already been in possession of a handgun, fired hastily through the billowing smoke; those who did not have a weapon, became desperate to obtain one in order to defend themselves from the inbound soldiers. Hastily, The Harvin brothers had pried open one of the recently delivered wood crates in order to obtain the assault weapons that were inside — that ended up being a mistake on their part as they had stupidly forgotten that none of the weapons shipped to them had come already preloaded with ammunition, as it was in a separate crate.

Smartly, both Quinton and Jarious set their weapons down onto the ground, went down to their knees, and placed their hands upon their heads, as they did not wish to be mistaken for being a hostile enemy. The rest of the members of the A.R.M. followed their lead, as it quickly became apparent to each that they now found themselves in a no-win situation.

The organized assault on the building could not have gone any better. Now, they just needed to determine whether or not their suspicions were correct. With a content feeling running through his veins, Sabastian surveyed the rather large room. His brethren had quickly bound the suspected terrorists with zip ties and secured all access points, while Ben Fraisure, Jeff Tranter, and Eric Anadeg, were checking the few adjoining rooms — everything seemed to be covered.

Because Sabastian was already aware of the identities of two of the cell members, the logical choice was to start questioning one of them first. He wanted to know if the A.R.M. was indeed planning an attack against the upcoming G8 conference, if there were any additional cells and where they were located, and who and where the leader of their group was — so he asked Richard to help him escort Quinton Harvin outside to the front of the building.

Once they were there, they forced the man to sit down in an old wooden chair that Sabastian had placed in the middle of the sidewalk. Richard then zip tied Quinton's hands to each arm of the chair while Sabastian openly invited those citizens of Tijuana who just happened to be lingering around to come forward and witness what was about to take place. "Don't think that we're being nice here by bringing you outside so that you can enjoy the sun. There is a sniper on the top of that office building a few blocks over that has his rifle pointed at your head."

In order to verify his statement, Sabastian removed his vid-cell from his back pocket, stood behind Quinton, used his free hand to point at the man's forehead, and then took a selfie with him. After that was done, he scrolled to the image and showed it to his prisoner.

That picture was all it took for Quinton to realize that this union soldier was not bluffing. It was then that his cockiness and over confidence disappeared — and when his eyes locked onto where the laser sight was coming from; on top of the building across the way, he nearly needed to change his underwear.

"I've brought you outside so that you can confess your involvement with the A.R.M. and confess to me what it is exactly that you are planning when it comes to the upcoming G8 conference. And if you don't give me the information that I am looking for, then I'm sure we can make these people who are gathering around, believe that you are the one who is supplying all the illegal drugs to their children and that you are also a high-ranking member of the Cardona drug cartel. I'm sure that these fine citizens of Tijuana would be more than willing to stone you to death while you sit here restrained."

"You can't do this! You are an American soldier!"

"I am a Union soldier."

"And I am an American who wants nothing more than to restore the United States back to the strong independent country that it once was."

Richard, who had stayed off to the side after he had tied Quinton to the chair, moved around front to stand next to Sabastian. He looked the man right in his eyes and said, "Do you know anything about a possible a terrorist attack during the upcoming G8 conference?"

The arrogance that Quinton boasted earlier, returned. "It is not an attack, it is a cleansing of the political bureaucrats that have become misguided and led to believe that a united North America is what will save us from our supposed self-destruction. We have to stop this before the provisional ten-year period is over and the United States of America officially merges with Canada. And it is up to us to give Mexico all the excuses that it needs to forget about ever officially joining this fiasco."

"You're just like a typical terrorist. You have blinders on and choose to see only what you want. Mexico has already provisionally agreed to join… as has Greenland and the Bahamas. And it won't be long before many more of the island countries in the Caribbean become a part of the Union."

"If the borders are continually removed, then we as Americans will lose everything our ancestors fought to become. The only good thing that could ever come from countries like Mexico joining the

Union would be that all of our homes will be clean, our lawns will be maintained, and our fields will be worked."

Those stereotypical words were all that Sabastian needed to hear to know that this man and the group that he belonged to were a bunch of dangerous, misinformed, narrow-minded people on a very misguided mission. They definitely needed to be stopped before they did something that history would never forget. So Sabastian leaned in close to Richard and whispered a few unexpected words into his ear.

Acknowledging his unusual request, Richard left Sabastian alone to deal with Quinton Harvin.

"I have only two more questions for you. And I hope that you will at least answer them truthfully. Where did you get those military weapons?"

The man just sat there laughing under his own breath; he had no intention of appeasing his captor. "Let's just say that it feels good every time we kill a supporter of the Union with weapons that have been stolen right out from underneath their noses."

"Stolen?" Sabastian paused, as a random thought suddenly appeared. *'Could the D.U.O. have been the ones who had supplied the A.R.M. with these weapons? They have been known to supply other factious groups in the past. But then again, the shipment of arms that the A.R.M. had just received could not have come from them. They had to have come from someone else because the D.U.O. is in total chaos right now.'* Whoever supplied the A.R.M. with these weapons, Sabastian knew was irrelevant at that moment. However, this was something that he would have to look into at a later date. And if he happened to find out that there was a connection between the D.U.O. and the A.R.M., then this information needed to be brought to the Union Bureau of Investigation.

As the curiosity continued to grow in the streets around them, Sabastian determined that now was the perfect time to ask the all-important question. "Ok, if you co-operate, I will not leave you to judgment of the people that, as you can plainly see, have curiously gathered around. Who and where is the leader of the A.R.M.?"

"You don't honestly think that I am going to throw him under the bus?"

That was the sort of response that Sabastian expected, so he leaned in closer to Quinton, grabbed the arms of his chair and pulled him a few feet forward, spun his chair one hundred and eighty degrees so that he was facing the building, and then grabbed the back of the chair and leaned him backwards so that he could see what was up above.

Immediately, Quinton let out a panic filled scream when he saw that his younger brother, Jarious, was gagged and dangling upside down over the edge of the building by a rope that was looped around his ankles.

Sabastian had no intention of letting Jarious fall to his death, but he wasn't about to let Quinton know that. The fear of losing a brother, a person who he was probably very close to, was all that he assumed it would take to get the answers that were needed. Such a tactic wasn't something that he would ever use as a civilian, but Sabastian was back in the military right now and he had a job to do; the safety and security of his country called for such immoral methods to be implored. "I will ask you again, Quinton. Who and where is the leader of the A.R.M.?"

Unsure if this crazy military man was bluffing or not, he caved in — somewhat. He did not reveal who was behind the leadership of the A.R.M., but he did tell him that the main cell location was in the country that was once an unincorporated territory of the United States of America and had refused when offered the opportunity to join the Union — that country being Puerto Rico.

Satisfied that he had acquired enough information, Sabastian signaled for his men to pull Jarious back up over the edge of the building — he then cut Quinton's bindings and escorted the man back inside. Once the brothers were secured with the rest of the members of the A.R.M., he made a call to Captain Swilling and filled him in on everything that had happened. Ideally, Sabastian would have liked to have acquired the name of the man in charge, but he would have had to cross the line much further than he already had in order to accomplish that goal.

Within a half hour, their transportation had arrived and all the captured members of the A.R.M. were officially taken into custody. The recently revised patriot act gave the S.N.A.F.U. grounds to do this because these individuals not only had been in possession of stolen military weaponry, but also were connected to a plot to conduct domestic terrorism against the Ameri-Can Union.

Just before sunset, the entire unit was back aboard a plane and headed back home to Houston. Once they landed on Union soil, the captured members of the A.R.M. were then subsequently transported to the Davidian Compound; a new military detention facility just outside of Waco, Texas. This heavily secured facility was located on the same famous grounds where David Koresh's religious cult had once existed — a somewhat ironic place for the Union to keep high-risk prisoners and right-wing fundamentalists secured.

With his assignment now over, Sabastian felt that he could finally relax; a sense of pride also consumed him as he reflected at length while riding on the Greyhound bus from Houston back to San Antonio. This had been the first time he had been given the opportunity to command a unit; a responsibility that he wasn't sure he actually deserved to be given, but once Sabastian started to review the events that had taken place, he was able to understand why his C.O. had insisted that his presence was required for this mission. Captain Swilling had apparently seen something in him that he had never before been able to see — that was until now.

Two men had ultimately helped to shape his life. Sabastian had inherited all of his biological father's traits: his instincts, his drive and determination, his uncanny ability to deal with any unforeseen variable, the ability to push right past any obstacle that was in his way, and accomplish whatever it was that he had set out to do. Then, there was the steady influence that Terrance Burelli had on him. From that fateful day when he had sunken his ex-father's classic car into Lake Erie, all throughout his years in the military, the man had done all that he could to prepare him and make sure that 'his son' walked the path that he believed his 'son' had been born to take.

Though still not yet absolving him of his sins, Sabastian was now willing to open up his heart just a little bit more for the man who had raised him. In retrospect, he now began to understand Terrance's motivation: his insistence that he work hard, his unwillingness to accept failure from him, and his belief that Sabastian could become something far beyond what was ever thought attainable. That was all done to make sure that he was fully prepared for the day in which he found out the truth; it had been Terrance's way of making restitution for the very regrettable mistake he had made all those years ago.

Captain Swilling had been right — Sabastian was the correct choice to lead that mission, and he now felt a sense of pride within himself. He knew that his father, Maxwell Banks, had been there with him since the beginning and guiding him on his journey of discovery. And he now knew that Terrance Burelli was also with him in some capacity. The only thing that Sabastian could have wished for during his mission was that his 'adopted father' had still been alive to see him accomplish what he had just done, because he knew that Terrance would have been as proud as any biological father would be.

This past month had been one for the record books. Never before had Jerrelle been in a situation where she truly had felt that her life had been in danger — even her three years in the service had been relatively hazard free. Not once during that time had she ever thought she wasn't going to survive, but all that changed the day Sabastian came back into her life. During their time chasing Antonio Marcone all over the world, they had placed themselves into situations that could have easily ended badly. And even though in each of those instances the odds may not have seemed in their favor, Jerrelle still believed that they would not only find a way to survive, but accomplish the 'mission' that she agreed to become a part of. However, upon reflection, she was seriously beginning to wonder if she had somehow used up all her luck. Within a one month span, she had come close to dying four times — the last close call being an 'accident'; an accident in which she was all but certain wasn't one at all.

The more she thought about it, the more she began to believe that there was someone out there who wanted to kill her half-sister. Her formulated logic made sense — it was her sister after all, who had brought to the attention of the E.C.L. the fact that the D.U.O. had been in Japan, then the Liberation used that knowledge to discover that Antonio Marcone had a secret slush fund hidden in a bank account in China; a bank account that they had freely helped themselves to.

Those known facts didn't prove anything, but they did help to harden her own belief that Bai Lin's life was in danger.

She had initially planned on flying back home to Detroit tomorrow. Now, there was no way that Jerrelle was going to leave her sister's side; there was no way that she was going to let anyone harm her only living flesh and blood. She was going to stick closer to her than Bai Lin's own shadow.

She walked into her half-sister's incensed filled private room in the E.C.L. compound, producing a smile the moment Bai Lin acknowledged her entrance, and then sat down next to her on the bed. Her sister looked like she had been through a war, but she'd be the first one to insist that she had in the past, been hurt far worse.

Clearly, her knee was messed up, as it was braced and was resting on top of a pillow. That however, wasn't the only visible injury that she had suffered yesterday, as across her shoulder and back area was plastered a rather large bandage; it covered the lengthy gash that she had received from some falling debris.

Being confined to her bed for a period of time wasn't something that she was all too upset about, as she understood the necessity to rest and recover. What infuriated her more than anything had in years was something she could not have prevented — the deep and long gash down her back, as it threatened to permanently disfigure her large dragon tattoo. The one neck of the beast that wrapped over her shoulder was completely severed — and because of the size of the gash, the potential was there for an infection to develop. If that were to happen, her beautiful piece of art would undoubtedly be forever ruined. Therefore, she needed to do everything she possibly could to assure that the gash healed without any clear evidence that an injury to the area had ever occurred.

To minimize any chance of getting an infection, Bai Lin was going to have to use every form of ancient Japanese healing method that she knew, because tattooing over a freshly healed scar was one thing, but finding an artist, who had the talent to make a nasty scar disappear, would be near impossible.

"How are you feeling today, sis?"

If it had been anyone else other than her sister, Bai Lin would have stayed under the covers. Instead, she propped herself up and leaned back up against the headboard. She sat there unfazed, wearing nothing above the waist. "Physically, I've felt a hell of a lot worse than this before."

"You know, I've been thinking…"

"About?"

"…about staying here for a little while longer. At least, until you get back on your feet again."

"I love you too, but you don't have to caudle me, Mama Bear. I'm a big girl and I can take care of myself."

"I know you can. That's not the point. As much as I know that the E.C.L. will protect you, I'm convinced that there is someone out there who wants to kill you. And I'm not gonna let that happen."

"You and your unsubstantiated beliefs are one day going to blow up in your face. What happened was an accident. No one wants to kill me."

"Excuse me if I don't feel the same way as you." Remember, the E.C.L. did steal from a D.U.O. account. And I am willing to bet that they have since learned of this and.., they after all, do know of my association with Sabastian. They also wouldn't have to dig too deep to discover your existence and affiliation. The obvious conclusion they would then draw would be that you were the one who told the E.C.L. about Antonio Marcone being in Japan a few weeks ago. And since we are aware of their accessibility to that S.M.A.R.T. technology, it makes sense to me that they are out to kill you."

Bai Lin just sat back and quietly thought, sifting through her sister's outrageous conjecture — one of many that Bai Lin knew Jerrelle was famous for presenting. In the past, her sister had always been right, or near enough to being right with her hypotheses, but this time, she was pretty sure that her sister had completely missed the mark. "Listen, sis.., anything is possible. But until facts surface that prove otherwise, I believe what Bushido believes."

"Fine! Until your Liberation can verify that belief though, I am not going anywhere."

"Yes, you are. And don't make me pull rank on you!"

"What the hell do you mean, pull rank?"

"I mean that since I am the older sister, I out rank you. And because of this, I am telling you that there is no need for you to stay here any longer than what you had originally planned."

Unsure of how to respond to her sister's declaration, Jerrelle just sat there dumfounded. Bai Lin had never, ever thrown her out; had never asked her to leave, had never sent her on her way, and had never before pulled rank. "Are you blaming me for this?"

"Oh shut up, Jerrelle. That is the stupidest thing that you have ever asked me. I love you now the same as I always have and always will. You have a life to get back to, and my being laid up here is not enough of an excuse for you to stay."

"A small tear formed in the corner of her eye. Jerrelle knew that her sister was right — she wasn't needed. Bai Lin had a lot of company and a lot of protection. She would be fine.

Feeling somewhat unwanted, Jerrelle lifted herself off of the bed and moved closer to Bai Lin. Careful as not to touch her wounded shoulder, she leaned over and gave her sister a long, loving, somewhat smothering embrace. She then left the room and went back to hers to begin packing — but not before suggesting that her sister at least put a bra on if she was going to sit up in her bed the next time someone came in the room for a visit.

By this time tomorrow, Jerrelle was going to be on a flight back to Detroit; back to her own world where she belonged — but she would also be thousands of miles away, constantly worrying about Bai Lin's safety. Never before had she found herself in a situation like this — it was certainly going to be one of the more difficult segments in her life that she was going to have to find a way to adapt to — but she knew that she would, just like she always did whenever things got tough.

The champagne did what it was supposed to do — it soothed the pain; not from the rash decision he had made last night, which he knew had been the right one, but the decision that he had made twenty years ago.

Louie could be a real son of a bitch if he wanted to; which was the persona he chose to project while he was immersed in the world of the Detroit Underworld Organization. But away from that life, he knew deep down that he was a kind and caring man; a man whose two lives were starting to butt heads with each other. For some strange reason, he was now finding it very difficult to keep them both separated like he had been able to do in the past.

With the road he travelled now veering off in two completely different directions instead of side by side, Louie was well aware that the 'evil' half of him would soon dominate over the other one. Once that took place, his already blackening soul would no longer allow any good to surface. At that point, he would only care about one thing — and he knew that he would have no regrets afterward about breaking his promise to Mirella. However, the potential was also there that he would unintentionally do something in the process to hurt his son. For that reason, Louie needed to find a way to restore that balance in his life.

Unknowingly, he had taken that first step last night when he touched the nearly naked escort. It had been a very uncomfortable moment for him in which Louie then realized the huge mistake he had made all those years ago when he let Mirella Santori dictate the terms for which he could stay a part of his son's life. Unfortunately, there wasn't anything he could do to change that decision from long ago — what's done is done. The only thing that mattered now was to lay the foundation for the future; a future in which he resolutely believed his son was going to be a big part of.

After Madelyn had left, Louie sat on his balcony for three straight hours thinking about his life and contemplating his choices while finishing off the entire bottle of Krug, Clos du Mesnil. This morning, he was now paying for his binge, as the room was not only spinning, it felt like the entire apartment was a cabin on a cruise liner sailing directly into the eye of a hurricane.

Carefully, Louie swung his legs over the edge of the bed, sat up, and took a moment to gather his bearings before he dared to move. He wasn't a young college student who could drink his buddy under the table; he was a man of many years and his body was way out of practice when it came to handling that much alcohol — the thirty-year-old, one thousand dollar champagne, had all but drained the life out of him.

After making sure that his two feet were firmly planted on the ground, Louie sauntered over to his refrigerator where he luckily had a few bottles of Gatorade stashed. *'I'm thinking that I am going to need at least two of these, a big breakfast, and two days of quiet isolation before I can somewhat function normally again.'* After pounding back the first one and then taking two extra strength Tylenol IV's for good measure, Louie decided that he should next make his way to the bathroom and take a long, cold shower. Before he even got halfway down the hallway though, his vid-cell rang — it not only caused his nerves to dance, but his brain to ache.

"Um... Ah... Hello!"

"You don't sound too good, Louie."

"I had a rough night, Zhin."

"What happened?"

"Nothing happened, it was self-inflicted."

Although Zhin Wi had been a longstanding member of the D.U.O., and had been stationed the entire time on the opposite side of the world, it didn't mean that he was not aware of every aspect of the organization and every personal issue that affected his new boss. Unlike those recently departed associates, Zhin was smart enough to figure out that Louie had a secret life outside of his obligations; a life that he respected and chose only to be aware of — he refused to be educated further on it or to use that as leverage in order to achieve a personal gain of some kind.

Without prying into what had happened last night, Zhin just said, "Well, I hope you feel better. Anyhow... the reason I called is that I have finished my assignment and I will be on my way back to Chicago shortly."

Carefully, Louie found a seat and took a moment to gather his thoughts. "Tell me everything you found out... and could you do me a favor and talk quietly, as everything sounds very loud to me right at this moment."

"Of course." Zhin then began his report; it was one that had a lot of good news and a bit of bad. The good news at least, did a lot to help ease the hangover that Louie was suffering through. According to Zhin, the Detroit Police Department had spent nearly a week combing through the offices of the D.U.O., looking for that one key piece of evidence that they needed to permanently shut down the organization; just like Louie had predicted — and just like he had hoped, they found nothing. Antonio had been smart. Sometimes, his cautiousness seemed more like blatant paranoia. The man, when it came to all of his personal investments and involvements, had decided a long time ago to keep offsite all of the pertinent information about the D.U.O. In hindsight, that had actually been a smart move — and Louie knew that the only way there was to access the personal palm-top that stored all of that information was to go where it was kept; locked securely in a hidden safe at their safe house retreat in Ann Arbor, Michigan.

The safe house wasn't used very often, as its main purpose was as a backup place in case the need arose to temporarily conduct their daily operations somewhere other than the main office. And other than a month before the D.U.O. officially moved their headquarters from the basement of the pawnshop to the New Book Cadillac Hotel, or by Sal whenever he would pay for some company, the place was never used.

The only problem that Louie saw now was that he didn't have the combination to the safe. Getting access to it, and learning all the secrets that were inside about the D.U.O. that Antonio had intentionally kept from him and Sal was now priority number one. As long as he had been a part of the organization, he had known that there were aspects of the organization that his former boss chose not to share — the man always felt the need to have control over everything, and limiting his trusted associate's access to vital information was another way of doing just that. But now that Louie was in charge, he wanted to know what those secrets were.

On a sad note, Zhin reported that he was able to locate Roy Chevalier, but upon entering his residence, he had found the man dead by what appeared to him to be a self-inflicted gunshot wound — although he couldn't tell for sure because the body had already started to decompose.

Louie was heartbroken at hearing that news. Roy had been a reliable person who had helped him numerous times in the past and he had never disappointed him. Even in death, Roy hadn't disappointed him — he apparently took his own life, protecting what he knew about the organization. Next to Zhin, Roy was the only other obvious choice that Louie had considered bringing into the organization full time. But now, with this unexpected news, Louie would have to find another 'specialist' when it came to the acquisition and distribution of information.

"I want you to stay there in Detroit, Zhin, and I'll meet you there tomorrow. Since our offices are now a disaster, thanks to those tactless cops, I want you to begin the daunting task of straightening them up? I don't expect you to get it all done by the time I get there, but I would like for you to at least start by straightening up Antonio's old office. I'll call the hotel and inform our manager about what's going on, just so that she is aware and does not panic."

"Ok, I'll see you sometime tomorrow."

Louie disconnected his call, called the hotel's manager to inform her of what he wanted from them, and then headed to the bathroom to take that cold shower. Even though that first Gatorade and the Tylenols were beginning to kick in, he still felt the need to shock his system back into a normal existence.

Twenty minutes later, he left the bathroom feeling much better. Wrapped in his bath towel, Louie went back to his refrigerator and grabbed himself another Gatorade — but before he could take a sip of it, his vid-cell rang again. Louie went back over to where his phone was at and sat down on his sofa, took a look at his caller ID, and once again, he didn't recognize the number or the area code.

Louie was not happy. Another person, whom he did not know personally, had somehow been able to access his personal unlisted vid-cell number, and then assumed that it would be all right to call him. *'I'm gonna have to either get a new number or find a way to block these unwanted calls.'*

Just like before, he thought about not answering, but something inside of his still 'not too clear' mind had influenced his curiosity. "Hello?"

"Yes... Hello. Is this Louie Mazotti?"

"To whom am I speaking?"

"I'd rather not say right now. But I do have some information for you that I think you'll be interested in."

"Why would I want to listen to someone who, without my consent, has somehow found out what my unlisted number is and

100

called me with what I can only assume will be either a bribe or some form of malicious intent?"

"I can understand why that would be your assumption, sir. My intentions though, are genuine."

Louie was seriously thinking about telling this man off and ending the call. In his eyes, someone with no hidden agenda would at least show their face. But once again, his curiosity was urging him to give the man a chance to explain the reason for his call.

The caller knew that the window he had opened wasn't going to stay that way for much longer. So he said, "I know that your time is valuable, but I am only asking for a few minutes of it."

Again, the temptation was there for him to just hang up, but he didn't. "The clock is ticking, so get to the purpose of this call."

"Thank you. You see.., yesterday I made a choice that has unfortunately, made me an enemy to my people. I let my fury dictate my actions because of someone's unexpected admission, someone whom I already had some animosity toward. With what I have now done, I cannot fix, nor will it ever be forgiven. For that reason, I must now place myself in exile."

Unsure if this person calling him was actually a lunatic or just someone with guilt issues, Louie once again contemplated hanging up — but just like before, his curiosity was preventing it. "When it comes to stories, my attention span is rather short. If you don't get to your point soon, I am going to disconnect this call."

After a moment of awkward silence, the caller continued. "You see... up until yesterday, I was a high-ranking member of the European faction of the Extremist Clandestine Liberation. I made a choice to seek revenge upon a person for their involvement in the death of a member of my family. Unfortunately, another member of the Liberation was in the way of my attempt at revenge. And because of my actions, I have placed myself in a position where I must go into exile before the E.C.L. figures out that I am responsible for what had happened."

"So why are you telling me this?"

"Because the person I was seeking revenge against is also an associate of a man with whom I know you are familiar with."

"And who might that be?"

"Sabastian Banks. It is his friend, Jerrelle Robinson that I want my revenge against."

For once, Louie's curiosity had paid off. He paused for a moment and took a healthy swig of his Gatorade, then asked the obvious question. "Why do you want her dead?"

"Because… I hold her personally responsible for the death of my younger brother. He was with Jerrelle and Sabastian in Germany, helping them with their stupid idea of revenge against your organization, when he was killed."

It now all made sense to Louie. This man had sought him out with the sole purpose of offering up Jerrelle and Sabastian to him on a silver platter. *'This man probably knows enough to help me finish the job that Antonio had started. This may turn out to be a good day after all.'* "Before this conversation goes any further, I want to know your name."

"My name is Nicoli Nemchieve."

He should have become instantly nervous, but Louie strangely, felt relaxed. He was well aware of who this man was, but only through his renowned reputation. For this man to throw away everything that he had worked for, just to seek revenge, meant that he was also capable of unethical acts — and Louie knew that he could use such a man to his advantage. "Mr. Nemchieve, I am going back home to Detroit tomorrow. Why don't you fly there and then we can meet face to face and continue with this discussion."

"I will do just that. I look forward to meeting you in person, Mr. Mazotti."

Once a meeting time and place was agreed upon, Louie disconnected his call and went out to his balcony; the scene of last night's drunken binge. He stood there staring out into the city, finishing off his second Gatorade, and oblivious to the fact that he was still only wearing his bath towel — at least he was twenty stories up and didn't give a shit if it was only the soaring birds that saw his half-naked, old body.

Even after receiving congratulatory words and handshakes from his peers, as well as praise from Captain Swilling for a job well done, Sabastian still found it somewhat hard to accept full credit for what had just been accomplished. It did feel good to once again serve his country, albeit for only a few days — maybe, just maybe, his decision to go on reserve status was the wrong one. Was he even ready to take on the rather large responsibility that he knew was his destiny? Or maybe, in the world he had been immersed in for seven years, was where he was supposed to stay for a while longer?

Upon reflection, Sabastian realized that the short stint he just had outside of the military had done him a world of good. If the assignment had been handed to him just a few weeks earlier, he more than likely would have failed to complete it. Everything that he had been through, from the first day that he had found out who he really was, to the day Antonio Marcone had met his maker, was exactly the unforeseen experience that he needed. It had allowed him to gain the kind of self-confidence that he admittedly had always lacked. That sudden exposure to the life that he was always meant to live was the boost that he needed. The belief that was now there, most certainly could be attributed to the reason why he had been able to successfully lead the platoon to victory — even if it was only a small one.

Sabastian entered into his father's detective agency, feeling happier than he had in a very long time — and it clearly showed the moment his uncle had seen him walk through the door. Sydney quickly walked over to his nephew and gave him a big bear hug; the first hug that Sabastian finally felt comfortable receiving. "I'm so glad that you're here. We were all so worried."

Savanna approached Sabastian with a fresh cup of real English tea with a teaspoon of lemon rum. She placed it on her desk and gave Sabastian a hug and a kiss on his cheek — she then gave him the tea. "Thank God you made it back in one piece."

"It feels good to be home."

That was a declaration that both Sydney and Savanna did not expect to hear from him — at least, not so soon. "Did I just hear you say what I thought you said?"

"Yes, you did. Before I got my recall, I was going to tell everyone…"

"Tell everyone what?" Baylor asked, as he entered the main lobby area.

"I was going to tell everyone that I have decided to permanently move here from Ohio and live in my father's apartment... if that is all right with everyone?"

Elation filled the room as Sydney and Savanna smiled at each other. Sabastian moving down to San Antonio was something they both had secretly wanted since the very moment they first found out that he was Maxwell's long lost son, yet neither one of them felt that they had the right to encourage him to do so. Again, Savanna gave Sabastian a hug, but this time she whispered into his ear "I had a feeling that you would come home to us... I'm so happy."

"What about me, bud?"

"What about you, Baylor?"

"Did you even consider my feelings when you made your decision to move down here?"

"I just figured that you'd follow me, seeing that you've been here in San Antonio for almost a month now. Don't you like it here?"

"Well... I do, but that's not the point. You just should not assume that I am going to do something because you think I will."

Sabastian could not help but shake his head. He loved the man like a brother and it was times like these that Baylor's harmless pouting drove him nuts — but then again, he knew that his friend only did it because he could get away with it. "Could this lobby area be re-arranged so that we can put in another desk somewhere for Baylor to use?"

"Sure, I guess... but might I ask why?"

"I have decided to take over my father's business. I believe I have what it takes to be a private detective. Therefore, Baylor needs to have his own space to work instead of my new office." Sabastian turned and looked in the direction of his father's old office, indicating to everyone in the room what he was referring to.

"Well then, I think we need to celebrate the official re-opening of the 'Banks Detective Agency' by me taking everyone out to dinner tonight."

"Sounds good to me, Uncle Sydney." A good meal is what Sabastian really needed. His diet had been terrible the past month and now that he knew where he wanted his life to continue, he was ready for a bit of normality.

He quickly drank his English tea, savoring every delicious drop, and then placed the empty cup beside the sink in the kitchen nook at the back of the lobby area. They were all about to leave and go get that dinner when his vid-cell rang. To his pleasant surprise, it was Jerrelle calling.

"Hey, Sab.., I'm glad you answered my call. I just wanted to let you know that I'm leaving Japan and heading back to Detroit in the morning."

Sabastian was already aware of his friend's vacation schedule. He knew that she was due back in Detroit tomorrow, but he also knew her well enough to sense that something was wrong, so he excused himself and went directly into 'his' new office. At first, his old friend was very reluctant to tell him what had happened, so Sabastian took over the conversation and began to fill her in on everything that had happened to him over the past few days: his temporary recall into the service, his deployment to Tijuana, the faith that had been given to him by Captain Swilling to lead the platoon, and the success of the mission.

After he had finished with his story, he was surprised at how effortless it had been for him to get Jerrelle to open up to him and tell him everything that had happened to her and her sister. Once she was finished, Sabastian could easily understand the conflict that she was wrestling with in her mind. Whether she would admit it or not, he knew that she was still dealing with the loss of Helfred. And now, she had to come to terms with the fact that she almost lost her sister.

As much as Jerrelle tried to persuade Sabastian that she was fine, he wasn't about to believe her claim — and that was all it took for an idea to emerge, of which he was unsure she would agree to. No way was he going to let his friend go back home and attempt to cope with everything that she had recently been through, alone. He knew her well enough to know that she'd either just worry herself to death, or go out to some bar, get drunk, and beat up some sorry-ass fool that looked at her the wrong way, just to release her frustrations — so Sabastian did everything in his power to convince his old friend to change her flight plans and fly to San Antonio instead.

For the second time in the span of only a few minutes, Sabastian was surprised; a brief point / counterpoint session was all it took before Jerrelle agreed to his idea. So, with his friend now fully committed to fly to San Antonio, he exited his office and left for dinner with Sydney, Savanna, and Baylor; a dinner that he was hoping would not last all evening, as he needed to go back to his father's, now his new apartment, and spend some time organizing the place in order for it to be ready for his company — it just would not be right to expect Jerrelle to stay at a hotel after insisting that she come to San Antonio.

Several weeks earlier...

A rash decision is all that it took and the life of Jason Hernandez had forever changed. One moment he was the manager of the New Book Cadillac Casino, a position that he had worked hard to get, and the next, he was a fugitive — of sorts.

He had never in his wildest dreams expected that a life altering opportunity would essentially be tossed into his lap like it had. Nothing should ever come that easy. But there it was — his extraction from the quagmire that he had been stuck in for nearly twenty years, had just taken place. In fact, Jason had been only one of a half a dozen employees still working at the casino that had also worked previously at the Greektown Casino before the takeover had happened.

He kept telling himself that the decision he made is what anyone would have done had they been presented with the same offer. To be able to break completely free of being associated with a mob organization was unheard of. You had either earned their trust and were expected to take what you knew to your grave or you were killed because they felt that you were a liability — the latter happened far more often than what the other did.

He knew that he was one of those who would be deemed a liability, as proven by his willingness to sell them out. Did he regret his decision? No, as Jason had wanted out for a very long time. And now that he had made the decision to walk away, it undoubtedly was going to come with a very steep price having to be paid — he just prayed that the collection of his debt would not take place for a very long time. Yes, he was going to be constantly looking over his shoulder, wondering if he had made the right decision; wondering if he had foolishly placed his family in danger, and wondering if the D.U.O. would ever find out that it was he who had actually sold them out. That was why he and his family could not stay in Detroit, nor could risk staying anywhere within the boundaries of the Union. Jason had to move them far beyond that barrier and take them some place where Antonio Marcone would never consider looking — he hoped.

At first, he wasn't sure where that place would be, that was until he had discovered during his hasty research that his family's homeland of Puerto Rico had an open offer on the table that came with no restrictions and no questions.

With the recent independent separation from any association to the former United States, Puerto Rico was now a place where current Union citizens had an option. That same ten-year window that the Union had in place before the United States and Canada officially became an amalgamated country; Puerto Rico was giving any family with an ancestral history of prior citizenship in that country, an opportunity to move back home.

Although Jason's wife had vehemently objected at first to his sudden desire to move their family out of the Union, she eventually relented after a long discussion had taken place. He also however, made sure that specific details were not shared during that conversation so that the enormity of what he had done did not come to light, as he just was not yet ready to confess everything.

Camilla, Jason's wife, had never been comfortable with the fact that her husband had worked for a company that was owned and operated by the mob, but it had been an excellent paying job and it had allowed them to live a decent life without them ever having any financial issues to worry over — their family always had whatever they needed.

Honestly, she had never expected her husband to suddenly quit his job. What he had done had taken a lot of courage to cut his ties to the casino, but what upset her more than his wanting to leave their home was that he had quit his job without first consulting her. Nevertheless, it had been done — Jason was her husband and Camilla was going to support him and his decision because she loved him with all her heart.

So they packed up as much of their lives as they could, and forty-eight hours later, they were on their way to their new home; a home that Jason prayed would never be found by anyone associated with the D.U.O., as the last thing that he wanted to do was come clean and explain to his wife the real reason why he had quit his job. He hoped it was a secret he would be able to take to his grave — so long as his death wasn't followed by his family's elimination in retaliation to his rash decision.

6

It looked like a tornado had ripped through the offices of the top floor of the New Book Cadillac Hotel. Every single room had been thoroughly searched through and nothing was left undisturbed. The security measures that had been taken to prevent unauthorized personnel from gaining access to the D.U.O. offices were apparently obsolete — even the access panel in the elevator, of which a key was needed in order to get to the top floor, had been ripped open and bypassed. This was something that would have to change and be upgraded; the security procedures themselves would also have to be overhauled so that something like this would never happen again.

As Louie walked through the chaos, his heart sank. Most of his recent life had been spent here, and it suddenly felt like someone had thrown his body to the ground, stomped a mud hole in it, straddled it, and then had the audacity to relieve themselves all over him — Louie felt humiliated and insulted all at the same time. The only solace that he could take from the disaster was that nothing appeared to have been destroyed — it was just thrown all over the damn place without any sort of regard.

He made his way through the mess until he arrived at his old office. Once Louie entered, his jaw dropped. Inside, it looked like a three-day frat party had taken place. He never expected that his personal workspace would have already been tended to, as Antonio's office was priority. Nevertheless, what he saw actually pissed him off.

He found a somewhat open path amongst the clutter and made his way over to his desk, picked up his knocked over office chair, and then sat in it. Abhorrently, he looked at the disgusting mess in the room: a rather large pile of garbage lay up against the wall by the office door, numerous pizza boxes were scattered across his favorite couch, fast food bags and wrappers had been balled up and were lying on the ground near the waste basket — it had been moved away from the side of his desk and placed upon a chair up against another wall and obviously used for an impromptu game of basketball. Donut boxes and a half a dozen half empty Tim Hortons sim-caf cups were left on the far corner of his desk, and even a condom wrapper was lying on the floor under his desk, almost exactly where his feet would normally touch the ground. *'Those damn cops are fuckin' pigs!'* His first impulse was to get up and gather up all of the trash, but Louie's responsibility wasn't to houseclean, it was to get 'his' organization back in proper working order before he did anything else.

The pit in his stomach that he felt appear when he had first stepped foot back on the top floor, suddenly opened up even wider when he remembered one very important thing — his hidden safe. Hoping and praying that it had not been discovered and rummaged through, Louie completely removed the bottom drawer of his desk and, to his relief, the floor mounted safe appeared not to have been touched — there was nothing about the D.U.O. inside the safe, only what was most important and sentimental to him, as the last thing that he ever wanted was to think that there was a possibility that someone had become aware of his closely guarded secrets. The few items that were inside that safe: personal pictures, a copy of Marco's birth certificate, and the deed to Mirella's house, not only could be used as a means to destroy him professionally, but could be used against those whom he loved in order to drive an implicit knife right through his heart.

As he started to go through the safe's contents to verify that everything was indeed still in there, Louie took a moment and looked at the most recent picture of him and his son; the one that was taken at Marco's high school graduation. A flood of memories immediately overtook his mind, as that day had been the happiest moment in his life. And that day, Louie also had a revelation — his son was becoming a man. That was also the day that he first began to envision the possibility that, in only a few short years, if things were to fall into its proper place, his son would end up right where he truly belonged; by his side and learning everything he needed to know to follow in his father's footsteps.

Yes, Louie was alone in his office, but he didn't want to take a chance of anyone walking in during his stroll down memory lane, so he promptly returned the picture and the rest of his personal items back into the safe, locked it, and replaced the drawer over top of it. He then got up from his chair, left his office, and the mess that was still inside it, and headed for Antonio's old office. As he entered it, he saw that Zhin, and two maids from the casino's hotel, were just about done with their cleaning of the office — and although nothing was in order, the garbage was gone and the important items were gathered up and in neat piles.

"Welcome back, Louie."

"Thank you, Zhin."

"I know that access to this floor is supposed to be limited to just a handful of trusted staff members, but under the circumstances, I felt that the only way to quickly get this office back in working order was to bring in a few people from the hotel's cleaning staff to help. I hope that you are not upset with me for making that decision?"

"Not at all. You did what was necessary."

"I was hoping to get more of it done before you got back, but Antonio's office was a disaster area. It still needs to be thoroughly cleaned, vacuumed and then completely wiped down. Apparently, the local authorities do not have a budget when it comes to fingerprint powder, as it was covering every inch of this room."

As the two maids were leaving with the last few bags of trash, Zhin asked them to head on over to the next office and get started on cleaning it. However, right before they left, Louie made sure to thank them both for a job well done and told them to take an hour paid break for lunch before they continued on with their cleaning. He also asked them when they got to his old office, to do him a favor and sterilize his desk, as he was almost certain that the police had used it for something other than being a place to set down their coffee.

After Zhin had closed the office door, Louie made his way behind Antonio's, now his new desk, sat down, and then called the hotel's manager; he had something important that he wished to speak with her about in person. Five minutes after he had requested that she come up to Antonio's old office, a somewhat tall, middle-aged woman, dressed in an expensive business suit, entered — Louie openly encouraged her to take a seat. "Ms. Connie Yale. I must say that I have always been impressed with your style... and I'm not just talking about your wardrobe choices. You've been working for us for almost twenty years and, whether or not you were aware, I've been paying close attention to the way you go about your work. I have been

111

nothing but impressed with your dedication and your discretion. I am also aware that you do know exactly what this office..." Louie opened his hands in a gesture to symbolize the meaning behind his statement, "...is all about and you have kept the veil of secrecy pertaining to it. That shows me the dedication you have to not only your job, but to those who sign your paycheck. Therefore, since our casino manager has decided to abruptly leave us, an important position needs to be filled with someone who would never even contemplate throwing this organization under the bus.

With those words, Connie had a pretty good idea where this conversation was headed. She however, was unsure if she wanted to give up what she already had, for a position that paid the same, but came with more headaches.

"Ms. Yale... Not a single doubt exists in my mind that you are the most qualified person to handle a job for which an immense amount of responsibility will be placed upon your shoulders. For that reason, I am formally offering you the newly created position of Executive Director of Operations, where you will be in charge of both the casino and the hotel."

That she never saw coming. She thought that she was going to be offered Jason Hernandez' old job, not be offered one where she would have to oversee everything. A smile of elation promptly appeared on her face. This kind of position was something way more than what Connie Yale had ever aspired to achieve. She had been content with the position she currently held, but never in her wildest dreams did she ever fathom the possibility of being offered an executive position. Her hard work and dedication had just been rewarded — she was flabbergasted, to say the least. "Thank you very much, Mr. Mazotti. I accept and I won't let you down," she said as she stood up and shook Louie's hand. "If there is ever anything else that you need from me, please don't hesitate to ask."

"There is one thing that I would like for you to do."

"Certainly, Mr. Mazotti."

"My associate," Louie motioned with his head toward Zhin, "has informed the two maids that are up here right now cleaning the offices, of the discretion that is expected of them pertaining to the fact that the entire organization is run from this floor, and that any

112

'company' information they may accidently become privy to, is to be kept in confidence. All that I ask is that you remind them that if they happen to speak about their time up here that their employment would immediately be terminated and their deportation guaranteed."

"Mr. Wi was with me and the hotel's assistant manager when they each signed a confidentiality agreement before they were sent up here to clean, but I will again remind them of the responsibility that they now have to keep to themselves what they may unexpectedly learn while up here."

"If you feel that they can do that, you may then let them know that this floor will be their responsibility to keep clean from this moment forward."

"I'm sure they will appreciate that." Connie then stood up and excused herself; her intent was to leave her boss's new office, but Louie's unexpected request kept her right there.

"Before you go, Ms. Yale, I would like to ask you something. Would you happen to have any idea as to where Jason Hernandez might have gone? He is not at his home and we um… need to find him so that we can send him his last paycheck. I mean, his bank deposit did not take place due to a closed account and we have tried to call him but his phone is no longer in service." Of course that was a bold faced lie, but Louie wasn't about to admit to his new executive director that they were looking for the man so that they could kill him — even though he was pretty sure that she was somewhat aware of what had taken place and was relatively certain what the ex-manager's fate was soon to be.

Connie didn't have to think long before she decided to tell Louie what she knew; knowing that the information she had would only solidify the trust the man had just given to her. She had always found it difficult whenever she had to work with Jason on something. In fact, there had been times when he was a complete asshole to her. Therefore, Connie felt that this moment was the perfect time to leave the man with a well-deserved parting gift. "I have been told by some of the casino employees that they heard through the proverbial grapevine that he had decided to move out of Detroit. Though as to where, I'm not exactly sure. But if I was a betting woman, I'd guess that he went back to his native homeland of Puerto Rico."

"What makes you think that?"

"Both he and his wife's families are originally from there. Also, Puerto Rico now has an open return policy for those who do have roots there."

Louie leaned back in his chair and contemplated the opinion of his new executive. *'So... it may not be Cuba like Terrence said. It figures that fucker just might have been lying.'* "Thank you, Connie. We'll look into that possibility. For now, why don't you head over to Jason's old office and take the remainder of the day, or however long you may need, and do whatever you want to it to make it your own. Oh and... the decision will be yours as to who is going to replace Jason as the casino's manager, as well as your old position."

"Thank you, sir. And like I said, I will not let you down."

"I know you won't. That is why I promoted you."

After his new executive director left the office, Louie went over to the mini bar to pour himself a drink — to his surprise the bar was empty. *'Shit! Those fuckin' cops must have stolen all of Antonio's rare and expensive liquor.'* He removed his wallet, took out the hotel's business credit card from within, and handed it over to Zhin. Louie then took a moment, made a list of everything that he wanted to have stocked in the bar, and asked Zhin if he could go out and replenish the liquor supply.

Once his principal associate had left, Louie decided to take a few minutes and relax, so he stretched himself out on the same black synth-leather couch that Zhin had been sitting on. He hadn't intended to fall asleep, but two minutes later, Louie was out like a light.

Within a matter of moments, the spring shower had stopped and the sun came out from behind the clouds, drying the ground almost as fast as the rain had stopped. The umbrellas were quickly put away and the patio furniture on all of the outdoor cafés and restaurants no longer were layered with what had fallen from above. The sudden change outside was enough incentive to modify everyone's initial outlook on the day, luring those who had earlier accepted it as being a wash-out, to venture out of their shelters and sample just a bit of what remained before the evening came upon them.

Louie had been content to spend the entire day in his office, but the welcomed, unexpected change in the weather was all that it took to pull him out of his isolation; he was rather hungry and decided to go and grab himself some dinner. So he got in the elevator, stepped out once it arrived at the ground floor, and headed out the front doors of the New Book Cadillac Hotel.

He only had to walk a few blocks in order to get to his favorite place, an establishment that just happened to be owned by the D.U.O. — the Old World Café & Restaurant. Once he got there, Louie decided to sit outside on the patio so that he could not only enjoy the surroundings of the city, but get some much needed fresh air — he had after all, been in a self-imposed lockdown for the last few days, trying desperately to restore the D.U.O. to an actual functioning mob organization.

He hadn't been seated for more than a few minutes before one of his favorite caffeinated drinks, espresso with a half shot of Frangelico, and a menu, suddenly appeared. Louie was baffled, as he could not recall someone bringing this to him. Admittedly, his mind had been distracted with not only his objective, but also by this usually peaceful part of the city that strangely seemed to have a whole different vibe to it than usual.

Thinking nothing of it, he just dismissed this uncertainty as being inconsequential; he had more important things on his plate to be concerned about at the moment. So Louie picked up his drink, closed his eyes, inhaled the aroma, and let its intoxicating bliss invade his senses — this was as close to heaven as he believed he was ever going to get.

After savoring his first sip, he could feel the stresses that normally were there, secede. Shortly afterward, an unusual peacefulness surrounded him — that hadn't happened in decades. Venturing away from the office for a bit had turned out to be the right decision for Louie — his batteries were quickly recharging. Whatever the remainder of the day brought, he now felt ready to tackle it with confidence.

He placed his espresso down on the table, opened up his eyes, and disbelief promptly enveloped him. He froze. A piece of his past was now sitting right across the table from him; a piece of his past that

*should no longer exist. He could not move, nor could he even speak —
Louie was being held there in place by shock.*

"What's wrong? Don't you recognize me?"

"This is impossible? You are dead!"

*"You're right, I am dead... and you are the only one left alive
who had a part in that."*

"You're not real. This isn't real."

"Right now, Louie, this moment is real."

*He didn't know what to do. A big part of him wanted to reach
across the table and wrap his hands around this man's throat and try
to kill him again, but logic stopped him. No reason was there as to
why Maxwell Banks should now be in his presence. Yet, the man
somehow was — and Louie wanted to know why. "Let me guess...
Since you couldn't kill me, you've decided to haunt me instead."*

*"Correct. I will haunt you whenever I feel it to be necessary.
Today however, I have decided to come here to only remind you of my
declaration, right before you and Sal ended my life."*

*Louie took a moment and reviewed his memory. Maxwell had
all but guaranteed that a day would come when karma would cash in
the debt it was owed. However, just because it now appeared that the
man's long lost son was the one who was doing the collecting, didn't
mean that he was going to pay up. "That will never happen, Max. I
am the kind of person who would only kill those who deserve death.
And unlike Antonio, I won't obsess for years over someone before I
decide to end their life."*

*"Your affirmation is irrelevant. Antonio's debt has been
transferred over to you. Long ago, you were grafted onto his family
tree... just like he claimed I had been. And the only way that you are
going to be separated from that graft is when your branch has rotted
and fallen to the ground."*

*Louie took a calming sip of his espresso, set it down, and then
gazed vehemently over at his ethereal enemy. He, like his predecessor,
did not believe in fate. In fact, he knew the promise that Maxwell was
making was just as empty as the one that he had declared just before
his life ended. "I have already planted new roots. And soon, the
organizational tree will extend out further and become stronger than it
has ever been before. No one is going to be able to stop me and no*

116

one, not even your impetuous son, will ever collect on the debt you believe is owed."

"Turning a blind eye to what is fated to happen is not the smartest thing to do. You, Louie Mazotti, I know are no fool... but you clearly are narrow minded."

"And you are clearly mistaken. The events of the future are not yet written in stone. They easily can be controlled and manipulated so that they end the way I want them to."

"You're full of shit, and you know it. You can't change destiny. The path that one is born to walk will eventually be taken. Though my son started out on a completely different one, he eventually found the one he was supposed to be on. And now, he is fulfilling my prophecy. Antonio and Sal are already in Hell because of him and it will only be a matter of time before you join them."

Whether or not this was real, Louie had no choice but to acknowledge that Maxwell was right. And it was solely up to him to do everything that was in his power to find and then eliminate Sabastian before the young man had a chance to make his father's words come true. Originally, he had intended to just ignore the fact that the young man was alive and he was content to just wait until Maxwell's son had made the first move before he did anything in response. Now, Louie knew that he had to be the aggressor.

He finished off the remainder of his espresso, set the empty cup down onto the table, and said, "You may honestly believe that Sabastian will finish what you were unable to, but I can assure you that will not happen." Louie's vid-cell unexpectedly rang.

"I think that you should answer that, as I'm pretty sure that you'll want to hear what the person on the other end of your vid-cell has to say."

Reluctantly, Louie answered his call. "Mr. Louie Mazotti..." said a deep, baritone, evil sounding voice; a voice that instantly made the gray hairs on the back of Louie's neck stands on their ends. "You are fated to join the millions who are already damned for all eternity; to be forever tormented and tortured, right alongside your former colleagues."

Maxwell just sat there and laughed at a very shocked and confused Louie. Up until now, there hadn't been anything about what he was experiencing that had convinced him all of this was real. That Chinook-like chill down his spine was not like anything that he had ever experienced before. And that deep voice, though he had never heard it before in his life, he knew for certain who it belonged to — it suddenly made him realize that everything Maxwell was telling him, had to be taken seriously.

It infuriated him that his enemy seemed to have somehow gained the ability to return to earth; it also annoyed him that the man had come back with the sole purpose of reminding him about some unfounded prophecy — whose ass did he have to kiss in order to do this?

His eerie call abruptly ended; with a cold, blank stare, Louie looked right at his enemy and said, "If burning in hell alongside my former associates is to be my final destination, then I have no problem going down in flames. But rest assured that your offspring will perish right along with me.

Not wanting to give the enemy a chance to refute his declaration, he threw his vid-cell at him — his throw missed Maxwell and smashed up against the light post that had been directly behind him. Louie then promptly grabbed the edge of the table and flipped it at his adversary; his plan was to then attack the man, but he paused when he realized that his enemy was no longer there. He looked around and discovered in that moment no one else was on the patio, no one was walking the street, and no traffic was flowing — neither were there any signs of Mother Nature's existence.

Feeling stupid, Louie bent down and righted the table that he had flipped over. Just as he was about to turn and walk back to his office, the smashed vid-cell suddenly re-assembled itself and flew directly into his right hand. If this whole situation hadn't been weird enough, then that had just capped off his twilight zone-like experience.

Knowing that a logical explanation would not be found, Louie just placed the phone into his back pocket and then left the patio. After taking two steps down the sidewalk, his vid-cell rang again. Fearing that maybe it was the devil calling him back, Louie stepped over toward a street side garbage container. There, he took his cell and tossed it into the trash; it promptly flew right back up and rested in the *palm of his hand. He again tried to toss it back into the garbage, but this time the phone seemed to be stuck right to him.*

He couldn't shake it loose; it just stayed there and kept on ringing and ringing and ringing. For a brief moment, he thought about slamming his hand onto the ground in order to smash his phone — but it would probably reassemble itself again. Frustrated, Louie tried to shut the cell off — that didn't work. He had no idea what to do; it appeared that he had no other option but to take this call.

When he finally looked at the call display and saw what he did, 1-666-LUCIFER, it all but confirmed who he feared was waiting for him on the other end. Maxwell was apparently right. Louie's fate was already sealed.

The sound of the office vid-phone ringing woke him. Promptly, he got up from the couch and walked behind the desk, sat down in Antonio's old chair, and answered his call; it was the hotel receptionist, letting him know that Nicoli Nemchieve was here to see him. "Have him go into Otto's (that was the name of the small café and lounge inside the hotel) and tell him that I'll meet him down there in about ten minutes." Louie disconnected his call and then walked into the private bathroom that was connected to the office so that he could freshen up a bit — his dream had rattled him and he needed to make sure that he was back to normal before he met with Nicoli.

A few minutes later, Louie was ready to leave his office when Zhin returned with a large box full of the requested liquor supplies. *'Perfect timing,'* Louie thought. "Zhin... I have a small task for you."

Once he understood exactly what it was that his new boss wanted from him, he brought the liquor supplies over to the wet bar and began stocking it. As he was doing this, Louie left the office and headed over to the elevators. While on his way down to the ground floor of the hotel, he tried to erase the memory of his unsettling dream, as the last thing that he wanted was to give off the wrong impression. Nicoli was a very smart man and Louie knew that any hint of his being off his game could cause him to change his mind. If that were to happen, the results he had hoped for from this meeting would not occur, and it would then force him to take a much longer road when it came to achieving his goals.

When the elevator doors opened up at the ground floor, Louie stepped out into the lobby, took a few deep, methodical breaths, and determined that he was about as relaxed as he was going to get — it was time to get down to business.

Although he had absolutely no idea what Nicoli looked like, he figured that it would be relatively easy for him to determine whom the man was. And sure enough, the moment that he entered Otto's he spotted him.

Sitting alone with his back to the wall at the far end of the café was a man of purpose. Just by looking at him, it was easy to tell he was fully aware of his entire surroundings and that he wasn't the kind of man who let anything insignificant distract him. When standing fully erect, Nicoli appeared to be roughly six and a half feet tall and weighed somewhere between two hundred and fifty, maybe sixty pounds. His hair was cut short and styled nicely, mostly black in color, but it also was noticeably mixed with several strands of grey throughout. His entire body was cut solidly, and what little skin he showed, was slightly tanned. He also had two very visible marks — the first one being a tattoo of the ancient Germanic Mythological God 'Tiw' (Tiw is the God of warfare and battle. Unlike the Japanese members of the E.C.L. who all sport some kind of dragon tattoo, the European Members of the Liberation all have a choice of which ancient God from their ancestral lineage they tattooed on their body). The second identifiable mark he had, was a light blotch-like, one inch by two inch vertical birthmark on the side of his face that sat centered between the outside of his right eye and his ear — had his sideburns not been as long as they were, the birthmark would surely be noticed much more easily.

Knowing that the next few seconds would determine whether or not this meeting went well, Louie cautiously walked up to Nicoli and sat directly across the table from him. Without a handshake or an introduction, both he and Nicoli remained quiet for a few moments while each sized up the other.

"Nicoli, I presume?"

"Mr. Mazotti. I am glad that we are meeting face to face like this."

"Although your call did catch me off guard, I am not someone who would blatantly dismiss an opportunity that may unexpectedly present itself. Therefore, I invited you here to Detroit for two reasons. The first, of course, is that I am very interested in hearing what it is that you know. And secondly, I want to let you know that I am hoping after our meeting has concluded that a mutual agreement between us might be worked out."

Nicoli smiled inside as he had a feeling that Louie Mazotti wanted more than just information from him. "I appreciate your willingness to hear me out... and I too am more than willing to see what else may come from this."

Louie called the waitress over to their table and she took their drink order. During that time, while their view was being slightly obscured by the waitress, Zhin slipped into the lounge. He then quickly found himself a semi-concealed table and kept his eye on the meeting, just like his boss had asked him to.

"I'm sure you are aware that organizations such as the D.U.O. don't normally accept unsolicited offers such as the one you made. I however, unlike my predecessor, am not so closed-minded. I am more than willing to work with you so that both of our wants are attained."

"I'm glad to hear that."

"Before I commit to anything though, I would appreciate it if you would first humor me and elaborate more on what happened to put you in the situation you now find yourself in."

"With all due respect, I would rather keep the details of it from you. I will say this though... It will only be a matter of time before the Liberation learns what I am guilty of. And once that happens, I will become a wanted man who will be hunted, and more than likely killed for my incompetence. That certainty means my days on this earth are numbered, so I have decided that it is best I expand my options in order for me to attain my desired revenge against Jerrelle Dakota Robinson. That is why I reached out to you."

Louie listened intently to what Nicoli was saying; not one hint of deceit seemed to be in his voice. That was an encouraging sign.

"If and when we both achieve our wants, and my own death has yet to take place, we can then discuss the possibility of a future working relationship."

121

Both hatred and guilt were certainly present in this man. No longer did he want to know the details to the events that put Nicoli Nemchieve in the position where he felt that he had to make a difficult choice. Louie had been down a similar road himself — he was just thankful that his decision had not cost him everything he had worked so hard to achieve.

Deciding in that moment that he no longer needed to pry into Nicoli's past, he took a sip of his freshly delivered drink and contemplated his next move. It was easy for him to see that the man sitting directly across from him had all the physical attributes that Sal and Terrance Burelli had. But unlike them, this man appeared to have a working brain. Still, what Louie had so far learned from Nicoli, wasn't yet enough for him to make a commitment — the last thing he wanted was to make a mistake and then have to deal with another pain in his ass.

"Mr. Mazotti.., I suspect that I am probably the only one outside of your organization with firsthand knowledge of whom the individuals were that are indirectly responsible for the deaths of your two former associates, Salvador Batiste and Antonio Marcone. For that reason, having me on your side is only logical."

"That's a rather presumptuous statement... but accurate nonetheless."

Nicoli could not help but smile. "If you decided to accept my proposition, and we succeed in our endeavors, then I will have no problem giving you firsthand information about the E.C.L. as well as other underground networks that operate throughout Europe."

"You honestly would have no problem selling them all out?"

"Like I said before, I eventually will be a dead man. So until that happens, F.U. to them all."

"You certainly have balls, Mr. Nemchieve. I must commend you for being willing to take such a risk in coming here and making me this kind of an offer."

"It was an easy decision for me to make. You are a very smart man; one that I believe can spot, and will not dismiss a golden opportunity, simply because there is a potential risk attached to it.

Louie had to smile; it was a purposely displayed acknowledgment to Nicoli's own perception of who he believed himself to be. "Is information the only thing that you have to offer?"

"No. Besides my own physical abilities, I still have some trusted connections. They are what have allowed me to become aware of your usual business practices... such as your main source of income being that of stealing military weapons and selling them and other highly requested, sensitive items to third world counties, dictators, and other underground groups. My connections will undoubtedly make it a bit easier to acquire things that your clients request as well as other items that they may have believed were unattainable."

"Items such as what?"

Nicoli slipped his hand into his pocket and removed a small silver steel box. He opened it up and showed it to Louie. And although he instantly knew what it was, and had used its existence to lure Maxwell Banks to his death, Louie had never before seen it in person. "How did you get your hands on this S.M.A.R.T. chip?"

"As of now, I'd rather not tell you. I say though, that this is not the only one I have, as a small supply of them is currently at my disposal."

Louie sat back and contemplated everything that Nicoli had said to him. For its entire existence, the D.U.O. was very selective when it came to working with individuals outside of the family — and never before had they considered hiring a rogue member from another underground organization. This however, Louie felt, was a completely different situation in itself.

Nicoli was soon to become the enemy of an organization in which one of its members was connected to someone who was connected to the offspring of his enemy. Louie also knew that he just could not procrastinate too long when it came to finding Sal's replacement. As many times as he had busted his balls and had butted heads with the man over the years, he understood the value of having someone like him within the organization. Physically, Nicoli was everything that he needed to fill that position, but trusting him was one thing that he still wasn't too sure about.

Louie turned his body a few degrees and made a quick, small hand gesture to have Zhin come and join them; his associate approached the table and stood only a few inches away from Nicoli.

Intimidation was something that never worked on Nicoli; he stood up immediately and looked down upon Zhin. Just by comparing the two, Zhin was obviously the smaller and more normal looking, but what he lacked in size, he made up for in ability. Wagering money on Nicoli was no sure thing if the two of them were to get into a fight, as Zhin was proficient in every ancient martial arts discipline and he feared no one — no matter what their size.

After a few tense moments where Louie wasn't sure what was going to happen next, Zhin slowly backed away from Nicoli, leaned over to his boss, and whispered into his ear. He then took up a seat between the two.

As Nicoli was sitting back down, Louie said, "My associate concurs with my initial assessment. Mr. Nemchieve, I conditionally accept your proposal." Satisfied that the first part of this meeting was safely over, he called the waitress over to his table and encouraged everyone to order some food.

From the moment they placed their orders, to the completion of their meals, Louie was able to gather a much more in-depth evaluation of the type of character that Nicoli was — and he liked what he had learned. He was thrilled that his instincts to invite the man to Detroit had been the correct one. Now, he just had to find something for him to do in order to test, and assess his abilities and loyalty.

Tomorrow, Maxwell had been told, was when the next aperture between realms was going to open up. And when that occurred, his heart and the Apollo's Stone he hoped, was going to bring his wife back to him. If he could throw a welcome home party when she arrived, he would. Instead, the two of them would just have to celebrate alone.

Although he still had not been able to fully figure out everything that the Apollo's Stone would allow him to do, like making an actual ethereal appearance on earth, or physically being able to influence someone into doing something, Maxwell had at least figured out how to invade and take over someone's dreams.

Ethically, it didn't seem right to do that. But the more that he had thought about it, the more he had come to realize that he was only doing what the D.U.O. had done to him — they had invaded and took over his world. Therefore, a little poetic justice only seemed fair. Besides, the oath that he took to uphold the law no longer applied; only the laws of nature did — which he was willing to continually manipulate until the last of the three assholes got what was coming to him.

With time to kill, Maxwell decided that he wanted to leave his manifested apartment and go somewhere. So he closed his eyes, drew on his emotions, and organized his thoughts. There was one place where he wanted to go that he hadn't been to in years — Mackinac Island.

Within a few seconds, he was there. His apartment was gone, replaced by the grounds that were a part of the Old Mackinac Point Lighthouse. It was here at this beautiful historic building in which he and Sylvia were looking out across the straits of Mackinac, when she first gave him the news that had forever changed his life — it was in this special place that he had found out he was going to be a father.

Maxwell made his way over toward the backside of the historic property then stopped once he had arrived near the middle of the white wooden fence that surrounded the lighthouse; there he leaned his back up against it and looked at the cargo ships and other vessels that were out on the water. It wasn't real, but that didn't matter to him. In his mind, it was. That was why he had manifested it. Other than the day that his and Sylvia's path had first crossed, and the birth of his son, this particular place was one of the few good memories that Maxwell had had in his life.

"Well… this isn't the Bahamas, but the view is nice."

Maxwell turned to his right and saw that Nefieti was standing just a few feet away from him and doing the exact same thing he was. "A place doesn't have to be tropical to be beautiful."

"I agree… but I would prefer a tropical drink in my hand, the warm sun, a light breeze, and a tanned woman lying topless on the beach next to me."

"Hum? I never realized that an angel could have the same sort of fantasies as any other human being."

"Just because I am much older than any recorded moment in earth's history, does not mean that I have nothing left to my imagination. Every once in awhile, creating such a scenario as a beautiful woman on a beach on a beautiful sunny day helps to remind me of what heaven used to be like."

"Heaven has beaches?"

"No… it was just a metaphor."

Maxwell had a feeling that sadness lingered in Nefieti's soul; he also suspected there was still some pain that would probably never go away. He had no idea what the angel's story was, but it was easy for him to speculate that something had to have happened in order for him to be relegated to being the devil's welcoming committee. Nevertheless, his old juvenile ways decided in that moment to rear its ugly head and he chose to push a few of Nefieti's buttons. "Why would you even fantasize about a naked woman on a beach when your boss's domain is just as warm and a stone's throw away? I mean… I am sure that you could find any wench there who would be not only willing to disrobe for you upon command, but satisfy any urges or kinky request you may have."

The look that Nefieti gave Maxwell was one that he just could not figure out. However, he realized in that moment that he needed to remind himself that this angel was in essence, his boss. Yes, he was already dead, but it honestly never crossed Maxwell's mind that pissing off the immortal being might result in ramifications far worse than what his current corporal existence was.

Unlike any job, he simply could not get fired. In fact, Maxwell's mind quickly assembled multiple undesirable scenarios — including the possibility that the angel just might incinerate him right where he sat.

"I am all for the occasional bit of good natured ribbing, but I am warning you to choose your topic of ridicule wisely, as I generally don't tolerate an immature brand of humor."

"I'll remember that."

"Oh and just so you know… your being dead and here does not mean that you are immune to being on the receiving end of any type of physical pain or psychological torture." A sadistic grin immediately appeared on the angel's face; this time, Maxwell could easily read what Nefieti was thinking. However, before he was able to assure the angel that he would comply with his forewarning, he found himself no longer in front of the lighthouse — he was in a place that no one would ever put on his or her bucket list.

It was beyond hot, smelled of sulfur, rotten eggs, and even molten metal. Desperate-sounding moans came from every possible direction there was, and the suffering of millions of damned souls could be felt deep within his bones. Like the open white space that Maxwell had first been brought to after he had died, the expanse of this realm had no walls, no ceiling, and no end in sight. But unlike the white expanse, this place certainly felt enclosed. Maxwell immediately wanted out. He didn't belong here. It was worse than he could have ever imagined. In fact, for the first time in his existence, corporal and ethereal, he felt utter remorse — and he had learned his lesson.

He cried out to Nefieti, wanting to sincerely apologize for the insensitive remark he had made, but the angel did not answer him. He cried out again, and again the immortal being did not respond. Then off in the distance, something caught Maxwell's attention. Hundreds of 'things' were headed in his direction. He had no clue what they were. It wasn't until they started to get a little closer that he was able to determine they were short, human like creatures — every one of them looked the same. They each had hair that was snow white and long, had short, devil-like horns on their foreheads, and their skin was rough and textured and had a grayish tinge to it. If Maxwell didn't know any better, he'd swear that this was Lucifer's welcoming party.

Instinctively, Maxwell reached for his gun. Of course, it was not there — and even if it was, it was highly unlikely that a weapon pointed at the approaching army of demonic minions would cause them to stop their forward progress. In fact, he doubted very much that bullets would even harm these nefarious-looking creatures.

Maxwell stood there with immense regret. He had been given a second chance to make things right and his reputation for ill-timed childish behavior had ruined it for him. Apparently, his destined eternal resting place had just changed — all because he had opened up his mouth at the wrong moment in what he thought was just a little friendly bantering among friends.

Now only a few meters away, were the army of minions. What was going to happen once they got to him, he had not a clue — he only knew that he wasn't going to resist. His doing so would simply be futile, so Maxwell lowered himself to the ground, sat cross-legged, closed his eye, and waited for the inevitable.

A few moments later, he felt a cool breeze on his face. He opened up his eyes and realized that he was back in his manifested surroundings of the Old Mackinac Point Lighthouse. He turned his head and looked over at Nefieti; Nefieti was laughing.

"What's so funny?"

"Sorry, but I could not resist giving you a taste of your own medicine."

Maxwell was not impressed that this servant of the Lord of Darkness had decided to give him a preview of what Hell was like. If it weren't for the fact that this fallen angel was in the influential position that he was, Maxwell would have punched the entity in his perfect, angelic face, for what he had done. But in hindsight, Maxwell deserved what had just happened to him. "Ok... I no longer will crack jokes pertaining to your personal life, as long as you promise to never send me for another visit to that place again."

"I promise... unless you do something stupid and earn yourself a one-way ticket." Nefieti extended his hand; Maxwell accepted it, sealing a promise between the two. "But just for the record, what you saw wasn't Lucifer's kingdom... I sent you to the Amaranthine."

"The what?"

"The Amaranthine is a never ending desert that surrounds Hell. Once Lucifer has decided to move on from torturing a specific soul, usually right after a millennia or so has passed, that dilapidated soul will then be exiled to the Amaranthine for the remainder of all eternity."

It didn't matter that Nefieti had shown Maxwell what he had, as it was enough to deter him from ever giving the angel a reason to contemplate doing it again. Even from the outskirts, having an idea now of what the worst possible place was for him to spend all of eternity in was the kick in the butt that he needed. This task that he had been given, Maxwell had admittedly not taken that seriously. He had been content up until now to just watch over his son, have an

128

occasional visit by his deceased wife whenever that was possible, and have a little fun at his enemy's expense. However, the opportunity that Maxwell had been given was one that very few, he assumed, would ever get. Therefore, he decided at that moment that he would not squander it. Hell, or any subsection of it, was not where he ultimately wanted to end up; Heaven was.

"You're welcome, by the way."

"For what?" Maxwell said, uncertain.

"I normally would not help anyone who has been assigned a task by the Fates, but it was actually fun to pretend to be my boss when you invaded Louie's dream."

"Thank you for that, as it definitely helped to get the point across."

"It did... now Louie is much closer to getting back on the path that he was always destined to walk. So long as you continue to do what you are supposed to, his soul will end up where it is supposed to.., when it is supposed to." Nefieti did not say another word. He vanished and left Maxwell alone to enjoy his surroundings.

Of all the places that he had ever been to, this was one of his favorites. In fact, there was a time when he had even contemplated possibly moving to Mackinac Island when he and Sylvia were ready to retire. Of course, that dream got squashed a long time ago. Nevertheless, pleasant memories were filling his soul as he enjoyed his surroundings.

"I love this place too."

Maxwell turned his head toward the voice he knew all so well. A genuine smile instantly appeared on his face — he again, was no longer there alone. "I... didn't expect to see you until tomorrow."

Sylvia grabbed a hold of her husband's hand and smiled. "The aperture just opened up. I could not wait to come here to be with you and to get an update on everything that our son has been doing."

"Of course... but we only have twenty-four hours to spend together and I would rather just be in your arms the entire time."

Sylvia stepped closer to her husband and then wrapped her tiny arms around his waist. She then pressed herself tightly up against his chest, looked up into his joy-filled eyes, and said, "From what I have been told, the Fates are very happy with your first intrusion into

Louie's dreams. So as a reward for a job well done, they are allowing me to stay here a little longer."

"Really? For how long?"

"Until you complete your assignment."

That unexpected revelation was all that Maxwell needed to hear. It gave him that last bit of incentive he needed to not only fulfill his agreement with Nefieti, but to refrain from ever doing something childish again. No longer was the need there for him to have fun at someone else's expense. For the first time since he could remember, Maxwell's mind was completely clear of any unnecessary distractions and it was one hundred percent focused — and he was now more determined than ever to make the last of those responsible, pay the piper.

Home — that lone word had more of a meaning now than ever before. Sabastian had grown up under the watch and guidance of two people who had loved him, but there had been many times during his teen years that he often wondered what the true nature of his existence was. It had taken his uncertain mind and a lack of disclosure by the man who had raised him, to force himself into finding out the truth. And now that it was out, he knew exactly where he belonged.

Sabastian walked through the door to his father's old apartment with his Uncle Sydney right behind him. As he made his way through the living room to the kitchen, the stress and the pressure that had been there, was suddenly alleviated. With a content feeling consuming him, he opened up the fridge, cleared out all the expired items, and replaced the contents with something very important — BEER! He and his uncle had decided while at the restaurant that tonight was the night that they were going to spend some quality time together by rechristening the apartment and telling stories. Well, mostly it was going to be Sydney telling the stories, as other than what Professor Sung had already told him, this was the only way possible for Sabastian to learn what his father was all about.

They cracked open their first beers, toasted to Maxwell's memory, and then they both headed to the living room. "Ok, Uncle Sydney. What I first want to know is how did my parents meet?"

"Almost the same way your father met Savanna. He had been on a case and your mother ended up becoming an unsuspecting victim. What happened was…"

Standing on the banks of the frozen Rideau Canal, in Ottawa, Maxwell was enjoying his day off. Unlike most Canadians, he didn't know how to skate, so he just stood there and watched everyone going up and down, back and forth on the famous landmark. The sun was out, yet there was still a bite to the air; a winter's day that was typical for the region. Being an R.C.M.P. Officer of only four years, Maxwell's days off was still few and far between. However, he had just been promoted to detective and knew that with such a promotion meant that he would be on call, twenty-four seven. If there was an open case and a lead came in, then he would be back at work; which is exactly what had happened.

Maxwell had only taken a few drinks of his large black Tim Hortons coffee when his cell phone rang. Sure enough, it was his captain calling. From the first day of his promotion, he had been assigned to a six-officer team to try to locate a man, Gerald Sellick, who had been suspected in three home invasions of helpless senior citizens, one of which ended in a brutal murder. Those instances had all taken place in a span of just less than two weeks. But since then, nothing had occurred over the past month… until today. An anonymous tip had just come in, alerting the police to the fact that a man had been seen scoping out a house over the past few days; a house that belonged to a single, elderly woman.

Because the house just happened to be only four blocks away from where Maxwell currently was, he had been sent there alone to investigate the report further. When he had arrived at the residence, he took several quick glances through the front and side windows of the home, as well as a gander at the back of the property. To him, nothing seemed to be out of the ordinary, but that didn't mean that the report was false.

Somewhat perturbed that he had been dragged away from his day off to investigate a lead that produced no results, he made his way back to his car. Once there, Maxwell got inside and sat there staring aimlessly out the still partially frost covered front windshield. After a few moments of quiet contemplation, he took a sip of his now nearly ice cold coffee, then spit it right back in the cup.

Desperately wanting a fresh cup, he was about to leave and go get one when he realized that he first needed to call in his report — he hesitated. He didn't know why, but all of a sudden, something just didn't feel right. It wasn't the cold, it wasn't the quiet, and it wasn't the insistence of the anonymous tipster that Gerald Sellick had been seen in the area — Maxwell just had this odd feeling in his gut that he had missed something, so he left his car again and decided to check the immediate surrounding neighborhood.

Twenty minutes later, and after finally being satisfied that the area was clear, Maxwell made his way back to his car. Just before he opened up the driver's side door, he stopped. It wasn't his gut this time that caused him to do this, it was a scream that cut right through the bitter cold air — it was promptly followed by a loud crash.

Maxwell knew that the noise had come from inside of the house which he had earlier searched its perimeter, but instead of opening up his car door and reaching for the police radio or using his cell phone to call for backup like procedure had said he should, both his curiosity and instincts urged him to go immediately to the home.

With his gun in his right hand, Maxwell was all set to kick in the front door of the place, but stopped when he surprisingly noticed that the front door had been left ajar — it had been physically opened by a foreign object; a pry bar that he saw lying on the cushion of the chair that was just off to the side.

After a few cautious moments, Maxwell stepped inside the residence. But before he even had a chance to identify himself, his heart sunk — he saw the reason for the scream and loud crash. There, on the floor, was an elderly woman pinned underneath the wreckage of a fallen, rather large oak china cabinet.

Assuming that what he was looking at was the result of foul play and not an accident, Maxwell cautiously moved in closer to check and see if the woman was still alive. He then knelt down and placed his hand on her neck, hoping to feel a pulse. There was none — she was dead.

It was then that Maxwell reached into his coat pocket to retrieve his cell so that he could call this incident in. However, his

132

ears promptly drew his attention away from doing that. Turning toward the front of the home, he straight away saw a middle-aged man standing down at the end of the hallway with what looked to be some obvious personal items of the elderly woman's, in his hands.

The man didn't freeze the moment that he had seen Maxwell. Instead, he dropped what he had been holding and took off for the front door — on his way out he retrieved his pry bar.

To stop the man, Maxwell could have simply shot him — but his life hadn't been in danger. Also, he had just gotten his promotion, and having a reprimand placed on his record for the unnecessary use of a firearm was something that he just did not want.

The only choice he had at that moment was to follow the suspect. This time though, as he did that, Maxwell retrieved his cell phone from his pocket and quickly called in his report, informing them that he was now in foot pursuit. The trail could have gone cold in a hurry just by his taking the time to phone in what was going on, but he had a lot of tracking experience; experience that he had learned as a boy from his own father, an avid big game hunter.

As he thought, it hadn't taken Maxwell long to find the trail the suspect had made — which ironically, lead him right back in the direction of the Rideau Canal. The suspect was smart; he was trying to blend in and hide in plain sight by working his way over to the most crowded area of the place. However, it only took Maxwell a few minutes of searching before he again found the suspect. And then once he had clearly seen the man's face, he knew that it was Gerald Sellick.

As concealed as Maxwell could make himself, he slowly made his way through the multitude of people toward the suspect. He knew that this was not a good scenario for him to be in at that moment; the smart thing for him to do was to wait for his backup — that after all, was procedure.

Though he had been trained for situations such as this, in Maxwell's racing mind, this whole thing was not playing out the exact way the police manual said it should. He felt strongly that the suspect was going to do something stupid — and if he did, the whole area would be unceremoniously thrown into a large scene of mass chaos. So he made a difficult decision. He and he alone had to be the one to take out the suspect as quickly as he could — and hopefully without incident.

As he finally jockeyed himself into a good enough position to announce who he was, Gerald sensed his presence — the man reacted as any desperate individual would and he darted straight toward the nearest unsuspecting person. There, sitting on a bench, was a young woman who had been oblivious to her surroundings; she had just finished removing her skates and was about to put her boots back on when she was grabbed and forced into becoming a human shield.

Cautiously, Maxwell continued his approach; that was until he had seen Gerald place the end of the pry bar up against where the frightened woman's carotid artery was. It wasn't a sharp object, but it would still do the job.

After a few surprising screams, the crowd of people finally recognized what was going on — some of the people around the situation began to panic, but most of them quickly dispersed, giving Maxwell a clear view of the suspect and his frightened hostage.

The sirens in the distance closed in. In Maxwell's head, everything was now moving in slow motion. His training and hunting experience quickly reminded him to stay patient — his gut though, was telling him that if he did not act quickly, Gerald Sellick would be responsible for another unnecessary death. He simply could not let that happen.

Maxwell felt confident in his abilities; confident that he would put the life of this innocent woman at risk in order to put an end to this. He firmly believed that he had the advantage, as he could see the panic begin to develop in Gerald's eyes; the same kind of panic and desperation that a cornered animal would display. But that also meant the suspect was susceptible to making an illogical decision. It was why Maxwell had to be the one to make the first move. He could not trust that the suspect would listen, co-operate, or do the right thing. It was the fear for his own survival that had caused Gerald Sellick to take a hostage in the first place. He knew that he had put himself into a no win situation and he did the only desperate thing that he could think of by grabbing someone for no other reason than to have a bargaining chip. And although he knew that the odds of this working out for him were not that favorable, he did it anyway because that was the only move he had left.

When Maxwell finally recognized that the right moment had come, he took a few cautious steps forward, looking only into Gerald's eyes and straight through into his soul. He could tell just how lost the man was and that he was looking for a way out of this without having to give up. "Be smart and let your hostage go. You've already killed two people; don't add another to that list."

"I didn't mean to, I swear!"

Whether or not that was the truth, was irrelevant to Maxwell. Any attempt to negotiate with this unstable man, he knew, was going to be a futile effort — it would only delay the mental bomb that was sure to go off in Gerald's head.

As the moments passed by, Maxwell could see the desperation grow in the man. Even in the cold temperature, beads of sweat had begun to run down his forehead — the hand holding the pry bar, had also started shaking. This was not going to end well if something wasn't done soon, so Maxwell decided that it was time to nudge the suspect near the edge of that proverbial cliff in hopes to have a reason to act. So he took another step closer, fully expecting the suspect to react in a defensive manner — and he did.

Gerald removed the pry bar from his hostage's neck — albeit only a few centimeters. At the exact same moment, he barked out an order to stay back — that was the opening Maxwell had wanted, and without a second thought, fired his gun at the suspect, taking him down with one shot to the right shoulder.

Roughly a minute later, his police brethren had finally arrived. Once they had secured the scene, Maxwell made his way over to the still hysterical young woman — she had not moved a muscle since she had fallen to the ground and tucked herself into a tight ball. He knelt down on his knees, wanting only to make sure that she was all right — but before he could say anything to her, she jumped into his arms and cried.

This was a first for Maxwell, having to console a victim. He wasn't sure what he should do or say to this young woman — all that he could think of was to ask her name. As she looked into his heroic eyes, she replied, "My name is Sylvia."

135

"…So my father actually saved my mother's life?"

"Yup! If he hadn't been called to investigate that lead, then that chain of events would not have taken place and you would not be here today."

Sabastian finished off his beer and went back to the fridge with a smile on his face. He quickly reviewed what his uncle had just told him, and in that moment, he was proud of his father for what he had done — he had saved his mother's life. "So if that hadn't happened that day, do you think my father and mother would have eventually met in some other way?"

"That, Sabastian, is a question that I don't think could ever be answered. Nevertheless, I am glad that things happened the way they did, because if they had not, then you would not be a part of my life. I know that you've only been around it for a little while now and I'm sure that you still have many questions that you want answered, but I can tell you this… There is more of your father in you than you realize. I can see it, and I'm sure you'll eventually see it too. You will come to discover more about who your father was in time all on your own."

Sabastian took out two more beers from the fridge, brought them back into the living room, and he and his uncle toasted his father/Sydney's brother once again. A half an hour later, his uncle went home, leaving him all alone in his father's, now his new apartment — his new home.

With the remainder of his beer in hand, Sabastian headed toward the bedroom — and just like the first time he had entered the room, the painting of his parent's wedding day snagged his attention. A smile instantly grew on his face as he finally had some kind of idea as to what kind of man his father was, and what kind of man he himself was destined to become.

After finishing off his beer, Sabastian placed the empty bottle on the nightstand and went to bed for the first time in his new home, content, and with no lingering questions that really needed to be answered.

Things were going to be different this time around; it was a promise made to himself that Louie planned on keeping. Unlike Antonio, he wasn't going to let his ego or a need for vengeance obscure his vision, or anything trivial as such get in the way of making the D.U.O. more successful and profitable than it had ever been before.

The first few essential parts that were needed to reinitialize the organization had been assembled. And although there were numerous members that Antonio had sent into hiding that were crucial to the cause, Louie decided that now was not the time to track them down. To him, it made sense to just begin with only a skeleton crew and take things slow, use the opportunity of essentially having a clean slate to work with, and confirm whether or not his choices of Zhin Wi and Nicoli Nemchieve to be his two trusted associates were the right ones before bringing anyone else back into the fold.

His recent confrontational dream with Maxwell Banks had been very unsettling. Was there more to this than what he deemed it to be; a stressed caused nightmare. He did not know? Louie never was one to believe in premonitions, but he just wanted to make sure that his onetime enemy's prophecy didn't come true before the weight of running an entire underground operation was plopped into his lap. So before he did anything else, Sabastian and his street trash sidekick needed to be completely eliminated from the picture — as did his now ex-employee, Jason Hernandez. In essence, that man was only a loose end — but his apparent betrayal had to be dealt with nonetheless. Why he had done this, Louie didn't know, but he had a feeling that there were certain variables such as: money, his family, and the lack of a conscience that were the deciding factors in his decision to sell them out. Had he been in the same boat as Jason, he might have done the same thing — but he simply could not ignore the choice that the man had made. Not only would it send the wrong message to anyone else that might consider doing something similar in the future, but also the ex-manager was well aware of too many intimate and incriminating details about the Detroit Underworld Organization. So for that reason alone, the man absolutely needed to be tracked down and dealt with, as only then could Louie officially take the first step toward rebuilding 'his' inherited empire.

Over the years, Louie had spent a lot of time thinking of ways to make the D.U.O. grow, but it wasn't until his recent brief hiatus that he finally believed his own ideas had the chance to become a reality. So with Zhin and Nicoli following right behind him, he entered his new, clean office, and went straight over to his newly stocked bar. Instead of grabbing what he usually drank; beer, he poured himself and his associates each a healthy rock glass of Walker's Club; a special rye whiskey created to commemorated Hiram Walker's one hundred and seventy-fifth anniversary, and to pay homage to what the brand was originally named before it got changed, five years into its initial production, to Canadian Club.

With his drink in hand, he walked over to his new office chair; he was surprisingly content, considering what now had to be done. As he sat down behind his desk, his associates followed suit, each taking up a seat across from him. After taking a moment to savor the uniqueness of the whiskey's flavor, Louie opened up the top drawer of the desk and removed a real Cuban cigar. Instead of preparing it to be smoked, he placed it just to the right of his vid-phone — now was not the time to light it up, as unequivocal victory had not yet been achieved. It was placed there simply so that Louie had a reminder; success was within his reach, so long as he did not lose his focus between then and now. "Not long ago, a man that I've never really trusted told my predecessor that our former casino manager, Jason Hernandez, had returned to Cuba in order to try and buy the freedom of his family. If this declaration were to be true, then going there to find and deal with the backstabber would undoubtedly be an arduous task. It's not that I don't have faith in the two of you, but because some first-rate, and highly expensive forged documents would be needed in order to gain admittance into Cuba. For me to authorize such expenses, some evidence would be needed that he was indeed there." Louie paused for a moment and took another sip of his whiskey. "I, however, personally do not believe that he is there. Our newly appointed executive director of this hotel and casino has countered that ancestral claim, declaring instead that he is in fact from Puerto Rico. It is there that she suspects he has taken up refuge because of their open door policy for anyone to return whose roots can be traced back to that country."

"Does she know this as being a fact or is she just speculating?"

"It is pure speculation, Zhin, but it's all we have right now."

"I know that I'm new here," Nicoli said, "but… is it really worth taking an unnecessary risk in order to hunt down and silence a former casino employee? I can understand doing that if he had been associated with the D.U.O., but he's just a fool who chose money over loyalty.

"He's much more than just that. He has intimate knowledge about this organization. Therefore, a chance cannot be taken that he will stay silent and bring what he knows with him to his grave. We have to ensure that happens."

"Louie is right," Zhin affirmed. "Assumptions cannot be made, but assurances have to be garnered."

After taking a moment to make sure that what he wanted to do was the right move to make, Louie finished off his whiskey and continued. "What I would like, Zhin, is for you to go to my old office, which is now yours by the way, and confirm whether or not Jason Hernandez' family has left Detroit. If he has and it turns out that he has gone to Puerto Rico, as Connie Yale has suggested, then I need for you to find out where in that country he is."

"And once I find this out, I can assume that you would want me to go there and eliminate him."

"Once you have those facts, then yes… and you'll take Nicoli with you." Louie turned and focused his attention toward his newest recruit. "You understand that this assignment is also a test. Upon its completion, I fully expect to have no lingering doubts about my decision to accept your offer."

"Rest assured that I have already played what cards I had on the table; I always wear my intentions on my sleeves and I do not go back on my word."

Louie actually believed him. Nevertheless, there was no harm in having the man prove his worth.

Wanting to get working on his assignment, Zhin politely excused himself so that he could begin his research. As his number one associate was leaving, Louie got up from his seat and went back over to his liquor cabinet where he poured not only himself another glass of Walker's Club, but one more for Nicoli. "We have a bit of time before Zhin returns with his findings… so I think that we should use our free time to get to know each other some more." A ring of the two glasses echoed in the office, a sincere smile on Louie's face appeared, and the continued sharing of personal information about each other, began.

Thirty minutes later, Zhin had returned to Louie's office with the confirmation that he had been asked to find — Jason Hernandez had indeed hastily left his Detroit home and subsequently booked a last minute flight for his family to Puerto Rico. Immediately after making Louie aware of his findings, he and Nicoli left the office and headed straight to the airport.

Right after they left, Louie polished off the remainder of his whiskey, and then took a walk — to his old office. There, he spent about an hour packing up his personal belongings and promptly moved them down the hall to his new workspace. Temporarily, he took the picture he had of his son on his graduation day and placed it on the edge of his desk. If only for a few minutes, Louie wanted to feel like a real father by displaying the picture for all to see. He was so proud of his only offspring, and having to hide his son's existence from the world hurt him almost as much as it did keeping the truth from Marco. *'One day my son, you will know the truth. And I look forward to the day that you will be here by my side, learning what is necessary to follow in my footsteps.'*

7

For the first time since everything had happened, since his life had done a complete three-sixty, Sabastian woke up feeling like a normal human being. He left his new place and headed directly to his father's agency, now his agency. Today was the first day that he was going to work; his military career was on the back burner and he was starting a new career as a private investigator.

After the obligatory good mornings were exchanged, he headed straight to his office, turned on his vid-phone, and called Captain Lutherage. He wanted to let him know about his decision to take over his father's business, and he wanted to make sure that he would have the backing and support of the San Antonio Police Department if and when he would ever need them.

After his brief and encouraging discussion with the captain had been completed, Sabastian walked out of his office and into the lobby area where Savanna was waiting with a fresh cup of real English tea with lemon rum for him. "I assume that you had a good night with your uncle?"

"Yes, I did. It was the first night I felt relaxed and was able to get in a full night's sleep."

"I'm glad things are beginning to settle into place for you."

"As am I." Sabastian then thanked Savanna for his tea and he went right back into his office. There, he lounged back into his chair and inhaled the aroma that came from his cup. He was about to take his first sip from it, when the picture that was on the corner of the desk of him as a newborn baby being held by his parents, grabbed his attention. The more he looked at any picture of his parents, the more he felt closer to them; not as close as actually being able to physically and emotionally bond with them, but as close as he possibly could without ever having known them. A bit of sadness promptly filled his soul; all because he knew that he was going to have to live the remainder of his life without their guidance, their encouragement, or the words 'I love you' ever being spoken by them.

His vid-phone unexpectedly rang, causing his private moment to be interrupted; it was Savanna calling him to let him know that the Governor of Michigan was on hold. Befuddlement was what became of his thoughts. There was no obvious reason for his father's old friend to be reaching out to him. Nevertheless, Sabastian could only assume that it had to be important.

As Savanna patched his call through, he took that long anticipated first sip of his tea. After a few seconds, and another sip, Sabastian was ready to speak with Christopher White. "Hello, Governor. What can I do for you?"

"Hello, Sabastian. I just wanted to let you know that I have been informed by my sources with the Detroit Police Department that Louie Mazotti was seen this morning entering the New Book Cadillac Hotel."

That was a bit of good news for Sabastian; what he feared, had apparently not happened. He exhaled in relief, now knowing that the enemy had not disappeared to some backwater country, or simply gone underground. But as anxious as he suddenly became to put this whole situation to rest, there was one thing that he knew was much more important than that. With what his friend had recently been through, and the attempt the other day on her sister's life, he knew that Jerrelle's wellbeing first needed be assured.

At the conclusion of his conversation with his father's ex-boss, he leaned back in his chair and sunk into thought. He was a bit unsure as to what to do next. He could sit there all day and drink tea, but that would be a blatant waste of an entire day. What he needed was a case to work on, but the chances of that showing up at the agency's doorstep this day was rather slim, so Sabastian fired up his computer — he should have remembered that it was password protected.

He could have sat there for a while and tried to figure out what his father's passwords were, but he was certain that he would get rather annoyed within only a few minutes of failed attempts, so Sabastian called Baylor into his office and asked him to do what he could to bypass the security and remove all the passwords. That way, he would have easy access to all of the computer's contents without having any hoops to jump through.

Knowing that Baylor had previously accessed the computer, (unbeknownst to him, Savanna had informed him of what the passwords were), he left his friend alone in his office and went into the lobby, pulled up a chair next to Savanna's desk, and finished off his morning tea.

The door to the agency opened up just as Sabastian was drinking the last of it. And although the hurt was not noticeably apparent upon her face, his eyes could see it, as a somewhat disheartened looking Jerrelle stood at the threshold. Never before had he seen his friend look the way she did at that moment. He definitely had his work cut out for him. If he didn't do something to help her with her uncertainty, then Sabastian knew that Jerrelle would surely convince herself that her sister was still in danger, and that she would soon lose the only other person in her life she had left who meant more to her than anything else in the world.

With genuine concern for his old friend, he walked over to her and welcomed her in a warm embrace. Under normal circumstances, Jerrelle would not have allowed her friend to get that close and do such a thing like that to her in front of other people, but that stoic persona that she usually portrayed was nowhere to be found.

With his arm around her, Sabastian walked his friend into the lobby area, sat her down in a chair in front of Savanna's desk, and then went over to the sim-caf machine to get her a fresh cup. Upon returning with the hot drink, he sat down next to her, placed his reassuring hand on her shoulder, and informed her of the news he had received just a few minutes earlier from Governor White. "However... I'm not going to worry about Louie Mazotti right now, as it is your wellbeing that is most important. Before I even consider going after him, I need to make sure that you are going to be all right."

"I'll be fine. Once I'm convinced that my sister is no longer in danger, I'll be back to my normal self. It's just... I really didn't want to leave Bai Lin alone. She made me come home."

"She's not alone, and you know it. I know you feel the need to protect your sister because she's all that you have left... and I understand your concern, but she will be fine. I'm sure that the E.C.L. is doing everything that they can to find out who is responsible for that attack."

"I know. It's just..."

"You're not going to lose your sister, Jerrelle. You're only feeling this way because of your recent loss of Helfred."

"I think I have pretty much come to terms with his death, Sab. I actually met his brother, Nicoli, the other day, and I had a chance to speak to him about what had happened."

"Did that help you ease any of your pain?"

"Yes, it surprisingly did. Meeting him helped me alleviate some of the guilt that was beginning to eat away at me. Now, it's just my sister's safety that is making me crazy."

"You just have to have faith in her fellow Liberation members to do what they are supposed to do... watch each other's back."

Baylor walked out of Sabastian's office and over to his new desk. He sat in his chair and began to work on his own computer. "Your computer is now password free, Sab. Unfortunately, there is no longer a dedicated secured line to Governor White's Office. It's a small price to pay, I'm afraid, for my doing what you asked."

"That's okay. Thank you, bud."

"Did he just call you, Sab?"

"Yeesss! And thanks a lot for starting that."

"No problem. And you're welcome."

After returning his empty cup of tea to the back kitchen nook, Sabastian invited Jerrelle to join him in his new office. Once inside, he closed the door and spent just over an hour talking about this, that, and everything else. By the time their chat had ended, Sabastian could see a bit of the old Jerrelle returning.

They both decided that they were hungry, so they exited Sabastian's office; their intent was to leave and go out by themselves to get some lunch, but before they could cross the threshold to the agency, Savanna's vid-phone rang. *"My first case, maybe,'* Sabastian thought. But it wasn't — it was though, a personal call for him. So he went back into his office alone and answered it. Fifteen minutes later, he returned to the lobby area and asked Jerrelle to take a seat.

It's amazing that in a span of only a few minutes how much things can change. One moment, everything seems to be back on the right track, and the next thing you know, something unexpected impedes your path, causing you to unwillingly have to retreat or

144

detour. It wasn't what Sabastian wanted to do, but he was a man of honor and he was being asked to once again dust off his uniform.

He sat next to his old friend and looked into her eyes, as he wanted to be sure that she was ready for the news that he was about to tell her, ready to take on another adventure, and ready to go back and be a part of something that had left a sour taste in her mouth. "I just got off the phone with Captain Swilling, and… upon the completion of my last assignment, I had a sneaking suspicion that my return to civilian life would be relatively short; that I would be getting another call in the near future to go back and help finish off what we started."

"You're being recalled again?"

"Yes, Savanna. Well, sort of."

"Sort of?" Jerrelle asked.

"Yeah, um… It is being assumed now that the American Recovery Mission has become aware of what happened to their cell in Tijuana. Therefore, the natural course of action for them to take would be to either go deep underground and disappear for a while, or do something unspeakable in retaliation; the latter of which needs to be assured of not taking place. Therefore, those who were responsible for the S.N.A.F.U.'s last deployment have now requested that we find and flush out, then apprehend the leaders of the A.R.M."

"Why are you needed? Can they not do this minus one person?"

"They could, Uncle Sydney, but… It has been requested that only the best soldiers be given this assignment."

Silence filled the room; Jerrelle immediately knew that her old friend was holding something back. "What are you not sharing with us, Sab?"

"Deadwood!"

"What's that, Savanna asked."

Jerrelle knew what that term meant — and she didn't think that it was her place to let the others in the room with them, know. Personally, she wasn't too keen on the idea of her friend being asked to be a part of such a mission. However, it came with the territory. Being asked to participate in a Deadwood mission was something that every member of the S.N.A.F.U. knew was a possibility, and would have had to be okay with it before joining the elite fraternity.

145

"It's the term we use when we are sent on an unofficial mission that is deemed to be very dangerous, wherein we were to fail, our participation in it, and our association with the unit, would not be acknowledged, nor would we be rescued."

"Disposable heroes," Sydney said.

"Yes, we would be considered that."

Savanna nearly had a panic attack; Sydney didn't know what to think. Sabastian had only recently come back to them and they wanted to do everything they could to protect him so that he remained a part of their lives for a very long time. However, he also knew that his nephew had long been a big part of something that he admittedly, was very proud of — they had no right to tell him to refuse the assignment because of what could happen."

"Just be careful."

"What do you mean, Sydney? It's not all right this time for him to go. You can't go, Sabastian."

"We can't stop him, Savanna. He is not only a carbon copy of his father he is a Union Soldier. His paths still run parallel; and right now, he needs to walk back down the one that shaped him into the man that he has become today."

Sabastian could not help but smile at his uncle's endorsement.

"I hope that they're not expecting you to do this alone?"

"As I said earlier, only the best have been asked to do this."

"How many will be with you?"

"Two."

"That's it?" Baylor asked.

"Yes.., but don't worry, as I trust them both to watch my back more than anyone else in the world."

Those words caused Jerrelle's head to tilt off to the side; there was now no doubt in her mind that her old friend was about to spring a surprise on her that she did not want. "Who is going with you?"

"My best friend in the unit, Richard Atwater, and… you are."

"Oh, hell no! What in the fuck did you volunteer me for?"

"Because… when we raided the cell in Tijuana, we were able to recover a big shipment of stolen military weapons; weapons that I would bet your casino winnings on were acquired directly from the Detroit Underworld Organization."

146

"Do you know that for sure?" Jerrelle asked.

"No, I don't. I know that the D.U.O. was still in shambles only a week ago, but with Louie now confirmed as being back in Detroit, I would bet that those guns in the hands of the A.R.M. were his first shipment as sole proprietor."

Jerrelle didn't like hearing the possibility of what Sabastian was assuming. In her mind, she was the only one allowed to have a working theory and trust it to be somewhat plausible.

As the days and weeks had gone by, she had seen the confidence in her friend growing. Now, it was obvious to Jerrelle that Sabastian had finally taken full control of his life and that he was now convinced that the Detroit Underworld Organization were somehow connected to the American Recovery Mission.

She had promised her friend when they first reconnected back in Detroit to stand by his side, and then she reaffirmed her position in Germany right after she had lost Helfred. His fight was her fight, and she was going to see it to the end. If Louie had sent those guns to the A.R.M., then it was her obligation to go with Sabastian and find out whether or not he did supply them. And even though Jerrelle had been dishonorably discharged from the military, she still took pride in her country. Her short fuse was what had ruined her military career, and now this was a chance for her to make up for that rather large mistake — how could she even think of refusing an opportunity to make things right. "Ok, Sab.., I'm in. When do we have to leave?"

"Tomorrow morning. First, we'll drive to Houston, meet up with Richard at the base, and then we will be going to the docks. As a precautionary measure, we will not be flying into Puerto Rico. Instead, we will be posing as tourists and will be going there via a cruise ship."

"Why?"

"If they have not gone underground, then chances are that they will be expecting us. If so, the obvious travel routes, or the abandoned Union military airstrip, will undoubtedly be monitored. It may seem a bit overly cautious by going there this way, but it is better that we travel as inconspicuously as possible then to have an unwanted welcoming party waiting for us upon our arrival."

"You can't very well take military grade weapons with you on a cruise ship, Sab."

"We will be travelling unarmed, Baylor. Once we get to Puerto Rico, we will pick up our rental vehicle and then head straight to where there is a secret Union military depot to pick up our awaiting weapons and other essentials." Sabastian could see that Savanna was listening intently to everything that was being said and it was obvious to him that she was still very uncomfortable with the idea of him going off the grid on an unsanctioned mission, so he got up from his chair and walked around to her side of the desk, leaned over, and gave her a reassuring hug. "Don't worry about me. I will be fine."

"I know. It's just I wish that this part of your past would be over. I'm afraid of losing you like I lost your father."

"Don't worry... If anyone is going to shoot him, it will be me for dragging my ass into this mess."

Those words shouldn't have been reassuring, yet they were. It was then that Savanna realized Jerrelle would make sure that Sabastian came home to them in one piece.

Sydney, by all rights, should have been just as scared for the safety of his nephew, but he was contently smiling instead. Sabastian was continuing on his own journey of discovery; finding out exactly who he was, and what his father was all about. Maxwell never hesitated to help someone in need and had always performed his duty when he was a police officer to the utmost of his ability. His nephew had that same fire and desire. Duty was calling; his country needed him. Sydney could not have been any prouder in that moment, so he walked up to Sabastian, gave him that obligatory man hug, wished him good luck, and asked him to stay safe.

As he looked back upon the events of the past and reflected, Louie realized just how lucky he had been. Had Sal, the Sicilian bastard known of Marco's existence, it would have been only a matter of time before the man either used that knowledge as leverage to get what he wanted, or thrown him under the bus in order to vault himself to the head of the class. Had he done the latter, Antonio undoubtedly would have ripped him a new one — or worse, treated him in the same manner he would anyone else who failed him and have him eliminated.

Now that both of his former associates were resting comfortably six feet underground, it was tempting to just say 'screw it' and reveal his secret — but Louie knew that it was best he keep it closely guarded for the time being. His wants and needs had to be pushed aside for the greater good of the organization. Being the boss now meant that even more discretion had to be used. He had to be careful and cognizant of whom he did business with, as well as those whose lone objective was to ruin him — being the oblivious child of someone in a position of power in an underground organization, is all the ammunition that anyone would ever need to do that. And although Louie had always known that the potential was there for this to occur, it wasn't until the escort, Madelyn Kinsworth, came to his Chicago apartment that he finally realized his own heart had become the organization's Achilles heel. All that it took was one look at the prostitute's exposed backside and Louie not only was able to finally admit to himself the true love that he had felt for Mirella, but he finally understood her side of the whole situation — too much was at stake for everyone involved.

Louie had convinced himself that he did not need the comforts of another woman to fill the hole in his life that he believed was there. For some odd reason though, he was unable to see that Mirella and Marco had always done that for him. Just like his being secretly Marco's father, he and Mirella could have continued on in a clandestine relationship, and that supposed hole would have never appeared. What was important now, was that both of them stayed safe. Still, Louie could not stop wondering how different his life would have been had his son, right from the very beginning, been made fully aware of the truth.

And unwanted inner debate was brewing, leaving more debris of uncertainty scattered throughout Louie's brain — it was almost as if a category five tornado had just touched down. He needed to find a way to clear a path through it all, so Louie walked over to his wet bar to grab himself a morning drink, hoping that it would help him to think a little better — but he soon realized that a bottle of beer, or whiskey on the rocks, was not the answer. He wasn't hung over and needed some hair of the dog; he needed to wake up and not confuse his mind even more.

Instead of numbing his thoughts, Louie put on his spring jacket and left his office to go and get himself an espresso with just a touch of

Frangelico. He could have easily called the hotel's kitchen and had Connie Yale bring him up the drink, but she wasn't a waitress or his personal servant — she had a casino and hotel to run and had more important things to do than to be at his beckon call whenever he needed something that he could easily get for himself.

He left his office, headed down to the ground floor, and on down the sidewalk he went to the Old World Café & Restaurant. Two steps toward the place and Louie's memory of his recent dream came to the forefront. He hesitated for a moment and briefly thought about going across the street and back two blocks to a different café — but that one didn't have alcohol and Louie wanted to add a little touch to his caffeine. This left him with no other choice — and it also left him questioning his own sanity. He stupidly feared what might be waiting for him again, even though he knew that what he had experienced was just a dream.

When he arrived at his destination, he scanned the patio; Maxwell wasn't sitting anywhere. He then opened up the front door, scanned the room, and found it to only have six people inside who weren't employees. The coast looked clear.

He wasn't usually a paranoid individual, but Louie wasn't about to take any chances. Once he had made it to the service counter, he ordered the largest espresso with Frangelico that he could get and then positioned himself so that he could keep an eye on the entire café while he waited. Less than two minutes later, he had his espresso and he was out the door.

Because his mind had been so focused on what he feared could have happened to him again, Louie ended up unintentionally walking right past the New Book Cadillac Hotel. By the time his wits had returned, he was standing across the street from Comerica Park. Baseball — next to his work, it was his only other admitted obsession.

There were no games going on, as it was mid October and the Detroit Tigers were not in the playoffs. Yet, he found himself crossing the street, drawn to the allure of the beautiful ballpark. He wasn't sure what had possessed him to be led astray, but he didn't bother to understand it either.

He walked down one side of the park, turned, and then walked down the other, stopping when he reached Woodward Ave. There, he stood right in front of the only open area of the ballpark that fully exposed the entire field to the city.

Up to the wrought iron gate, Louie went. There, he stared out across centerfield at the empty facility, imagining himself being inside with his son — something he had always wanted to do. He had taken Marco to a few ballgames before in Chicago, but it didn't feel the same. Just once, he wanted to take his boy to a game as father and son, not 'uncle' and 'nephew' — it hurt him more than he ever thought it should, having to project a false persona in order to do something as simple as spending a day with your own offspring.

Staring out at the vastness of the unoccupied playing field was what had done it — the hope he had that everything would eventually work itself out, no longer was there. He truly wanted to keep his word, but a dose of reality suddenly smacked him hard in the face. Louie was no spring chicken, and he had somehow avoided meeting his maker on numerous occasions. Chances were that whatever luck he had left, wouldn't be enough to save him the next time.

He just didn't care anymore. His days on this earth were clearly numbered and he didn't want to waste any more of them without his son by his side. It was selfish, but so what. Yes, Mirella was going to be heartbroken, but he felt it was now time that she take a turn with the emotional suffering.

After finishing off his large espresso, Louie headed back to his office. The temptation was certainly there to immediately pour himself and then pound back a good stiff drink upon his arrival, but he knew that was not a good idea; he needed to keep his thoughts clear, as some important things needed to be dealt with before he could move forward with the life he now wanted to live.

During his short walk from the ballpark, Louie had reaffirmed his decision; it was one that was going to result in him being forever hated. No, he was not going to change his mind again — he was going to break his promise. This was certainly going to result in some irreparable consequences, but life is all about choices, and the choices made don't always have to please everyone.

Right after Zhin and Nicoli returned from their current assignment, Louie was going to go back to Chicago. He had taken care of Mirella Santori for twenty years, and as far as he was concerned, it was time that she took care of herself. No longer was Louie going to be the 'bad guy' and protect a secret that they both were responsible for producing — it was time that she owned up to her part in this mess that she willingly created because she was not strong enough all those years ago to handle Louie's honesty.

Upon arriving at the top floor, Louie walked straight to his office and then over to his desk. There, he picked up his son's graduation picture and looked at it as he made his way over to his only office window. His thoughts went right back to where they were less than ten minutes ago as he could clearly see Comerica Park from where he stood. What would it be like to take his son to a baseball game, just like any normal father would? What would it be like to just walk the city and hang out with him? Soon, he would be old enough to legally drink — and yes, that was another milestone in the young man's life that Louie didn't want to miss. He had missed out on many of those in the past, and he didn't want to miss out on anymore.

With his decision now set in stone, and no more doubt lingering about that could cause him to change his mind one more time, Louie took a few moments and put together a game plan, as he wanted to be ready when the world finally found out that he had a son; he wanted to make sure that this revelation did not become his or the organizations undoing.

While in the midst of figuring all of that out, his vid-phone rang. He went back to his desk, set the photo of his son's graduation down, and then answered his call.

"I'm sorry for bothering you, Mr. Mazotti," the hotel's front desk clerk said, "but I have a young woman down here who is insisting on seeing you."

"You know that you are not supposed to verify to anyone who walks in off of the street that my office is in this hotel."

"I know that, sir, and I'm sorry. But I thought that you might make an exception this time. She said that she tracked you down because you told her to look you up if she ever needed help with anything."

"What is this woman's name?"

"Madelyn Kinsworth."

Louie never expected to hear the escort's name again. He honestly thought that she would be like almost every other person who had once introduced him or herself in passing, never to be heard from or seen again — and he certainly had never told Madelyn how to find him. He had only told her he would help her as a kind, goodwill gesture. Yet somehow, she had found him. Louie wasn't really happy about that. He wasn't mad, but he wasn't happy. In the brief time that he had spent with Madelyn, he had taken a liking to her.

While in mid-conversation with the hotel's front reception desk, Louie took the photo of Marco and placed it in the bottom drawer of his desk. Once he had done that, an odd feeling overcame him — he suddenly felt a little perturbed that this escort had been able to locate him with such ease. How she had done this, Louie had not a clue. What bothered him the most about it though, was that if she could locate him this easily, anyone else with half a brain could. First, his private vid-cell number had been learned, then his location. Somehow, he'd have to find a way to prevent these occurrences from ever happening again, as the last thing he wanted was to erase his identity, then pack up the organization and move it to a secret underground bunker or worse, some small undeveloped island halfway around the world. "Tell her to wait for me inside Otto's. I'll be down there in a few minutes."

"Ok, Mr. Mazotti."

Ten minutes later, Louie walked into the lounge and instantly understood why Madelyn had sought his help. His heart sunk as he took a few steps closer to her. There she sat with an obviously disheveled appearance; it seemed as if she had gotten into a bad car accident or something. She looked ashamed and she hid her beautiful blue / green eyes with dark sunglasses. That near perfect face of hers was now swollen, cut, and bruised. The only thing that Louie could think of in that moment was to take Madelyn by the hand, lift her up out of the chair, and hug her. He had only known this woman for less than a half hour, but in that short period of time, he had felt a strange connection to her. There was something in her honest soul that touched his. There was something special about this woman that he could easily sense. That must have been why his instincts had chosen her that night. Now, she needed his help and Louie was going to give it to her.

The moment she saw Louie, the obvious sadness that showed, dissipated — albeit only on the outside. She stood up, and as if they were long lost friends, reached out her arms and willingly embraced him. A tear trickled down her face; but she didn't care if anyone saw it. Madelyn had been through what no one should ever have to experience. She was hurt in more ways than one — and to deny that fact would simply mean that she would be lying to herself. She couldn't turn to her family for help; she couldn't turn to the law either. That was why she had come to Detroit in search of a man whom she barely knew.

Louie placed her right hand into the crook of his elbow and escorted her over to the hotel elevators. Once inside, they rode it all the way to the top floor. From there, he led her to his office, opened up the door, invited her inside, and encouraged her to take a seat on the couch that was over against the back wall. He then excused himself and headed over to his wet bar where he poured two identical small glasses of Walker's Club on the rocks — so much for not wanting to drink this early in the day.

No sooner had Louie returned and taken up a seat beside her; Madelyn started to tell him her heart wrenching story. "Two days after we first met, I received a request to do a bachelor party with another girl. When we work a party like that, we usually bring a bodyguard. Anyway, shortly after we got there, we realized that it wasn't a bachelor party, but instead, an initiation for four frat boys from the University of Chicago. All that we were paid for that night was to strip and dance for them, but half way through doing that, one of the guys in the room opened up a door to the adjacent room and then four more guys came out. Immediately, they went straight over to our bodyguard and subdued him — they put a rag over his mouth until he passed out. Two of them then gagged him, tied him up, and dragged him in the other room. The other two guys grabbed the other girl and dragged her as well into that same adjacent room."

Louie didn't have to hear the rest of the story, as he knew exactly what Madelyn was going to tell him — but he let her continue

154

on anyway because he knew that she needed to begin to heal from the traumatic experience that she had just been though.

"I've had men force themselves on me before and make me do things that I didn't want to do. It unfortunately is a part of my profession that I have to deal with when it happens. But I've never before had four guys beat me up and repeatedly rape me." Madelyn paused as her emotions began to take over — she took a healthy sip of her rye, hoping that it would help her to settle down.

His seeing the tears begin to trickle down her bruised face, tugged at his heart. Louie admittedly could be a cold-hearted bastard, but he'd never do, nor would he ever order anyone to do to a woman what had happened to Madelyn and her fellow escort.

After he offered her his handkerchief, he got up and walked back over to his wet bar — and even though he knew that Madelyn wasn't close to being ready for a refill, he felt that another round would be appreciated, so he poured two more glasses of Walker's Club and returned to the couch. "I don't know if you'll need this second drink or not, but it is here if you want it. You also don't have to finish telling me your story. You didn't deserve what happened to you."

"Thank you, Louie. I knew almost immediately that you were much different than any other man I have met through my work… and I am glad that we never slept together that night."

"As am I, Madelyn. Although I feel that it is you who I should thank. Because of you, I was able to realize what the important things are in my life. And you also made me realize the rather large mistake that I had made many, many years ago. I had accepted a situation, which I thought at the time, was the right thing for me to do. But now in hindsight, after some serious soul searching, I firmly believe that I caved in too easily and I should have stood my ground. Thank you, Madelyn, for allowing me to finally see the mistake I made."

A small smile appeared on her face — although she was clearly unsure of what she had done to help Louie. She only knew that she felt safe; felt like a normal woman around him, not like an object to rent for an hour or two.

Even though he had encouraged her not to finish telling him her story, Madelyn wanted to. If anything, telling someone what had happened would at least allow her to start to heal. So she took one last sip of her first rye, leaving only the ice in the glass, looked at Louie, and continued on with her story, telling him that the four guys who were left in the room with her had tied both of her wrists to the bed posts, gagged her, and then each of them took turns. When they were done, all four of them went into the other room and switched places with their other four frat brothers.

Madelyn had lost all track of time that night; she only knew that it was early morning when all eight of those young men had finished and left. Unlike the other girl she had come with, she was at least able to gather up enough strength to get up off the bed. Then, placing her hand around her fellow escort's shoulder, she helped her up off of her bed, helped her to get dressed, and then they left.

One more person was unaccounted for that morning — their bodyguard. She was unsure as to what had happened to him, but Madelyn's only concern at that moment was to leave the nightmare that she and the other girl had somehow barely lived through.

On the inside, Louie was fuming. He couldn't ever remember feeling this much internal rage — not even toward a difficult client, and never even at his archrival, Sal. Madelyn and her fellow escort did not deserve what had happened to them and he was determined to make those responsible, pay. Louie was admittedly far from a saint, but to him, a woman was the most sacred and beautiful gift that the Almighty Lord could ever give to a man; a gift that should be cherished, adored, and respected. If he were to ever do what would be considered a good deed in his lifetime, revenge on Madelyn's behalf would be it.

Louie got up from his seat, went back over to his desk, and then called down to the hotel's front desk; when the clerk answered, he instructed them not to rent out the presidential suite to anyone until further notice. He then asked that the key be given to Connie Yale. Five minutes later, his new executive arrived with what Louie had asked for. "Before you leave, do you know if we happen to have any new job openings presently within the casino or hotel?"

"There more than likely is, Mr. Mazotti, but I wouldn't know off the top of my head what positions there are that need to be filled."

"Could you please find out and then let me know?"

"Of course. Now if you'll excuse me, I would like to go and finish organizing my new office."

After Connie left, Louie escorted Madelyn over to the hotel's presidential suite; it was one floor down and at the opposite side of the hotel from where his office was. When they arrived, he handed her the key and encouraged her to enter. "This suite is for you to use as long as you like. You've been through a lot, so feel free to relax and enjoy all that is here."

She sat down on the extra long, synth-suede couch, and took in the enormity of the living area. Louie sat down beside her and tried to gaze into her damaged soul. He could see the pain that she was in, but he could also see the strength that she possessed. It was then that he believed time was all that it was going to take before Madelyn would recover and return to being the person whom he had first met. "So... how did you find me anyway? I never told you where in Detroit I was."

"Those chocolate flowers are how I found you."

"Huh?"

"After you gave me those flowers, I decided that I wanted to save them for another time, so I put them in my fridge. Then, after all that happened to me, I remembered the offer you had made. However, I could only remember your first name. Louie is not that uncommon of a name, so trying to find you using conventional means would be no different than me trying to find the proverbial needle in a haystack.

I was about to give up when I saw stamped on the side of the box the name of the place that the flowers came from, so I went there and asked the clerk if he could tell me who had purchased them. At first, the clerk didn't want to do that, claiming that it was company policy to keep all customer information private. I begged him, but he just would not budge. That was until I removed my glasses so that I could see into my wallet, as my intent was to try and bribe the clerk for the information. It was then that he saw the damage to my face; he immediately changed his mind. I don't know if he suddenly felt sorry for me or not, but he relented and told me that you had purchased those chocolates with a company Master Express card that was registered to this casino. So I came here in hopes that I would find you."

157

Louie could not help but smile at Madelyn's resourcefulness. "I'm glad that you were able to find me. Is there anything you need before I go?"

"Well... yes and no. I was hoping that since I see that you are involved with this casino, that maybe you might know some people who would do me a favor.

"What kind of favor?"

"Do you know anyone who would be willing to pay back those assholes that did this to me? I mean... I can't really go to the police; they'll just ignore the fact that a prostitute got her ass beat and raped. They'll just tell me that I got what I deserved."

Louie had decided long before he was asked that he would do this for Madelyn. But he wasn't about to go ahead with any sort of payback unless she had first given him her blessing. Now that she was officially asking for that kind of help, he was more than willing to do it for her." I can arrange what you want, Madelyn.., but there is one thing that you should know about me first."

"Ok. What is it?"

"Although I am directly involved with this casino and hotel; it is, as am I, a part of the D.U.O."

"The D.U.O.?"

"The Detroit Underworld Organization."

Madelyn still didn't quite understand.

"It is Detroit's version of the mob."

That was something that Madelyn wasn't expecting. She had pegged Louie as being a very successful businessman; a man in position of power, not someone who would be classified as a criminal. In that moment, she began to second-guess her decision to seek out Louie for his help. *'What have I gotten myself into,'* she thought? But there was something about him that made her feel comfortable; made her feel safe. It dawned on her in that moment that if anyone could pay back those fucking bastards for what they had done to her, then a man with such ties could. "Um... are you the boss?"

"Yes."

After being a part of a disreputable world for seven years, she had unknowingly just walked right up to the front door of another — yet, that didn't seem to bother her as much as it should. In that moment, she made a decision. Yes, she was certain that it was going to cost her, but she was also willing to pay whatever fee would come from her request because revenge was the only thing on her mind. "If you do this for me, Louie, I will do anything you ask of me in return. I'll even be your woman if you choose."

That was definitely a tempting offer from Madelyn. Although her beauty; her hanging off of his arm would most certainly compliment his stature, he wasn't sure that he wanted to get involved in another relationship — but if he were to with this woman, it would strictly be a business arrangement. "Just relax and enjoy the amenities provided. Try to allow yourself to forget everything and just focus on recovering from your ordeal. As it stands right now, it will be at least a few days before I can do anything for you, as my trusted associates are currently out of town on an assignment, and their assistance will be needed. By the time they get back, I should know what it is that you can do for me in return for the favor."

Louie got up from the couch and left Madelyn alone in her suite. He went back to his own office, picked up his now diluted second Walker's Club, and then began thinking of a way to get the information needed that would tell him who those men were that had viciously assaulted Madelyn and her fellow escort.

After pounding back half of the watered down rye, he called Aldo Trivoli; a friend of his whom he had met that very first day he went to the La Famiglia Restaurant Giardino. Not only had the man spent seven years as the athletic director for the University of Chicago, but also he had quietly helped Louie to arrange a few small business transactions during his first year of visits.

With Aldo having a direct connection to the institution, he hoped that his friend could look into all of the fraternities for him, as well as their known and not-so-well known initiation rituals. Louie knew that what he was asking of his old friend had a very good chance at being shot down — he owed him after all, more than a huge favor already because it had partially been his fault that the man's tenure at the university had ended, due to an investigation that 'allegedly' connected him to a Ponzi scheme. Thankfully, Aldo agreed to help. His reason for that was simple — if finding what Louie was looking for would end up doing some damage to the university's reputation, he would be more than happy to have had a hand in allowing that to happen, as he still harbored ill will toward them for what he felt was an unjust reason given for his termination.

8

Even though they had been living in Puerto Rico for a month, Jason Hernandez still feared for the safety of his family. He wasn't even sure if he could ever live a normal life again; he constantly felt as if he had to look over his shoulder, wondering if and when his hasty decision would come back to haunt him.

Leaving Detroit was easy — and though Jason's wife didn't mind living there, she had always longed to one day move back to her homeland of Puerto Rico. So when her husband had suddenly quit his job and told her that they were moving there, she became overwhelmed; with not only happiness, but also concern — this move after all, was rather abrupt. Still, the excitement she had, seemed to offset the apprehension that should be there as it had prevented her from insisting that her husband divulge what the real truth was behind the sudden and unexpected decision that he had made.

On the plane ride to Puerto Rico, she finally became conscious of the fact that her husband was hiding something important from her. As much as she tried, she just could not fathom what it could be or how to go about getting her husband to spill the beans. She could try the direct approach, but she was smart enough to foresee the potential of a full scale argument erupting — that was something she would rather not have taken place inside an enclosed, packed airplane. Therefore, she decided to hold off on her inquiry until a more appropriate moment presented itself.

Once they had arrived at their temporary residence; a place set aside for them by the Puerto Rican Government until they could find a permanent home, she cornered her husband and was surprisingly able to get him to confess to her what it was that had prompted his sudden decision to move. Needless to say, she was beyond upset that he would do something as brainless as selling out his boss; a man with more illegal ties than what Don Cherry owns. But Jason Hernandez was her husband, she loved him with all her heart, and she was going to stick by his side and weather whatever hellish storms may await them because of what he had done.

Since they had come back to their homeland, she had unsuccessfully tried on numerous occasions to reassure her husband that they were now safe and that no one was ever going to find them. She knew that if her husband continued to live in fear, then it would only be a matter of time before he destroyed not only himself, but the rest of the family as well — that was something she wasn't going to let happen.

During all of his years in the casino business, Jason had earned a rather comfortable salary and had been very smart with the money he made — and with the one million dollar bribe added to his rather substantial financial portfolio, he and his wife were easily able to purchase a home in a gated community; one that would be patrolled twenty-four seven by private security. He should have been satisfied that his family's safety would soon be no longer in question, but in Jason's mind, one rather large problem still existed. To anyone else, it would normally be considered just an inconvenience, but for him, not being able to take possession of their new home for two whole months, just intensified the anxiety he already possessed. Unfortunately, it is what it is. There was nothing that he could do to speed up the closing date. Until then, he felt that every possible precaution needed to be taken — and that included having to regulate what his family did. Yes, they were going to hate him, but Jason was not going to allow anyone to leave their temporary place of residence unless it was deemed necessary: work, school, buying food, etc. And even then, no one, not even Jason, could go anywhere unless they were escorted by the security service he had hired. His reasoning for this was simple; the less time that they were out in the public and exposed, the less likelihood there was that something was going to happen.

"This is getting ridiculous, Jason. I understand the need to be cautious, but in my opinion, these restrictions that you are insisting we adhere to are a bit much."

"I don't think so."

"Nothing's going to happen. You are worrying for no reason. Remember, it is no longer that easy for a citizen of the Union to step foot in this country without first having the proper paperwork in place.

It's not like it used to be when you only needed a government issued form of photo identification.

"I know that, dear. I just don't think that I'll ever feel completely safe, no matter what excessive measures we take. Knowing Antonio Marcone and his men as I do, I find it very difficult to believe that they will simply ignore the fact that an employee of theirs chose to hang them out to dry in exchange for a seven figure greased palm. Trust me when I say that they will not take too kindly to what I did."

Camilla didn't know what else to do. She had tried everything she could think of to reassure her husband that they were now safe and nothing was going to happen to them. Yes, she admittedly had thought about taking their young daughter and disappearing into the night, leaving Jason behind to fend for himself, but she was a woman of her word — for better or for worse, she was going to stick by her husband's side. "You don't know for sure that what you handed over in exchange for the money was going to be used in some fashion against them. For all you know, the information wasn't as incriminating as that woman who traded for it, had expected."

"Oh, it is. Names, dates, firsthand accounts; I even documented everything I heard through the proverbial grapevine. What I had collected should be enough to not only bury Antonio Marcone, but liquidate the entire D.U.O."

"Listen, Jason. We can either live out our lives in fear and move from country to country in order to hide our whereabouts, or we can just stay here and hope for the best. I think we need to make a decision."

He wasn't ready to do that. Fear was controlling his common sense; all the pros and cons for some reason, were not clearly being thought through. It was his years of working for a man whom he wanted nothing to do with anymore that had caused him to make that irrational decision in the first place — he had picked his poison, now he had to swallow it. "I don't want us to live our lives on the run. For now, we should just stay here."

Camilla exhaled a sigh of relief, as the last thing she wanted right now, was to keep disrupting the life of their soon-to-be teenage daughter.

"However.., I would feel much more at ease if Florentina did not go to public school. I want our daughter to stay at home and be educated by a private tutor."

"She won't like it.., but under the circumstances, I agree with you."

A smile surprisingly appeared on Jason's face; it was brought on by the knowledge that he now had one less thing to worry about.

"Before we shelter her from the outside world though, I want to make our daughter's upcoming birthday very special. The whole day will be hers and she will get to go wherever she wants to go and do whatever she wants to do."

His smile promptly disappeared, as Jason was very uncomfortable with that idea — but he loved his daughter and he wanted nothing more than to make Florentina's twelfth birthday extra special. It was the least he could do after all, seeing that he was about to force her into exile until basically the day she got married. "Ok, dear."

When the countries of Canada and the United States of America first decided to amalgamate and form the Ameri-Can Union, all native Puerto Rican's were given an open invitation to return to their homeland. Those who did were assured by its government that they would be given a five-year property and income tax exempt, as well as a supplement to their income for that same period. That incentive was all it took for a mass influx of people to quickly push the country's population to almost four point eight million; almost one million more than at the beginning of the century.

It could not have been foreseen, at least not so quickly, but ever since breaking free of the dependence of the United States, Puerto Rico has flourished — not just in population, but business, industry, tourism, and pride. The effects of such rapid growth, had welcomingly created not only a much healthier country, it thrust them right into the top fifty economic countries of the world.

With their ties to the former United States now cut, could citizens of the Union freely visit Puerto Rico? Sure, but it was no longer just a formality; quite a bit of documentation first needed to be filled out. In fact, customs agents tended to display a little biasness of their own and thoroughly, they would scrutinize Union citizens even more so than those of other countries. Being harassed like that, often came close to a violation of one's human rights being committed — but to those who worked the entry points of their country, most felt that they had an obligation to give the people of the former United States a small taste of what it was like to be America's bastard child.

For Zhin and Nicoli, it was easy for them to enter Puerto Rico, as neither one of them were actually Union citizens. Their assignment though, was not going to be so cut and dry. Just because they knew their target had boarded a last minute flight here, didn't mean that the man had already taken up residency. Coming here could simply have been a diversion. Then again, when Connie Yale was giving her opinion on Jason Hernandez' whereabouts, she had also made it known that he had always been a relatively complacent individual. Therefore, Zhin felt confident that their search for the man wasn't going to take too long, even though they honestly had no idea where to begin.

Downtown San Juan was always busy. Most days, the city streets were full of businessmen and women, locals, and of course tourists — that made their presence there that much easier to sell, even though they both really didn't look like the typical tourist type. So instead of wasting their time aimlessly walking the streets and knocking on every door they came to that was owned or lived at by someone named Hernandez, Zhin made the decision to just stay at their hotel that first day and do some research — that decision had surprisingly paid off. After hacking into the country's immigration database, he was able to verify that their target had indeed accepted the government's relocation incentive package.

With their suspicions now verified, all that they had to do was figure out where their target was. Part of the deal of relocating back to Puerto Rico was that, because they were being given tax exemptions, their addresses were considered 'unknown' until the five year transitional period was over. This was a privacy provision in the agreement enacted to protect those who relocated back home, just in case there were locals who took exception toward those returning being given in essence, a signing bonus and a five-year 'free ride'.

That 'clause' now made things much more difficult for Zhin and Nicoli, as it all but forced them to have to conduct their search for the man the old fashion way. Find people who knew Jason Hernandez, or find relatives of his, and then work their way, step by step, until he was found. Unfortunately, the only close relative they had found had been deceased for two years, which made going that route a waste of time. So they instead, concentrated on finding other connections to him.

With the knowledge that Jason Hernandez had an extensive background in the hospitality industry, it seemed only logical that both Zhin and Nicoli should explore that avenue first. Yes, the task was certainly going to be long and tedious, but no other viable option appeared to be on the table.

Starting with the city's capital of San Juan, they split up their search; each visiting every four star and above hotels that they came across — neither felt that their target would take a job at one below that ranking. Once that was complete, if they did not find him, then they would have to move along to the next city.

Thankfully, they didn't have to comb the entire country in their search, as it had only taken them three hours that first day before Nicoli had found their target — or at least, his place of employment. Unfortunately for them, the young desk clerk of the San Juan Hilton had refused to give Nicoli the man's address — the privacy provision agreement by the government being the reason. But that didn't matter, as they had found his place of employment. It also meant that the completion of their first assignment together was going to be a lot easier than what they both had initially assumed it would be.

"Mr. Mazotti,' Zhin said, speaking into his vid-cell from his hotel's balcony. "I have some good news for you. Although we have yet to make visual contact, we have confirmed that the target is in the country and we believe that we have also found his place of employment."

"I didn't expect for you to have such good news so fast. This is exactly why I made you my right hand man. Good job, Zhin."

"Thank you, sir. But I can't take the credit, as Nicoli was the one who found him."

That bit of information immediately became the reaffirmation that Louie sought; he had made the right decision when it came to Nicoli. Though it wasn't yet enough for the man to have now earned his handed position, it did give him some brownie points. "Take your time and don't rush this. I want this mission completed without leaving anything behind that can be traced back to us."

"Rest assured that no remnants of what we will be doing will remain." With his report completed, Zhin disconnected his call and looked over at Nicoli. "You said that Jason isn't working until tomorrow. No use in staking out his hotel until then, so let's go and get ourselves a rental car, explore this city some more, and get to know each other better. I have a feeling that you and I are going to be going on many other adventures like this in the future."

"That sounds good." As they were leaving their hotel room, Nicoli said to Zhin, "Actually, I think that we should just check out of this low-budget hole and get us a room at our target's place of employment. Jason Hernandez has absolutely no idea who we are, so by staying there, it will be much easier for us to keep an eye on him."

That made sense to Zhin; Jason Hernandez only knew whom Antonio, Sal, and Louie were. The man was probably aware of whom he was, but Zhin was confident that the organization's ex-employee had no idea what he looked like.

Since the young desk clerk had already previously seen Nicoli, Zhin went into the Caribe Hilton to book themselves a room. Ten minutes later, he returned to where he had left Nicoli and gave him a copy of their room's keycard. He then suggested that his 'partner' go to the beachside entrance of the hotel, just to be safe, as he didn't want the young desk clerk to become suspicious and do something stupid.

Five minutes later, via the back way, Nicoli had cautiously made his way into the hotel; he then headed up to their tenth floor room where Zhin was already waiting. Again, they thought about renting a car so that they could explore the city, but they both realized that a long day was awaiting them tomorrow and each wanted to make sure that no mental or stupid mistakes were made. So after ordering themselves some room service, consisting of two rib-eye steak dinners and a bottle of chardonnay, they decided to call it a day.

Once Puerto Rico had officially separated itself from any association to the former United States of America, those residences that were serving in the United States military at the time were given two options. If they wished to stay a part of its fraternity, they had to agree to a new posting in their homeland where they would then became part of the Union's secret outpost and munitions' depot. Those who did not wish to accept that offer were simply given an honorable discharge.

<hr />

    Emotional stress was one thing, but now Jerrelle was being forced to suffer through a bad case of sea sickness as well. Never had she liked the idea of travelling by boat; she would have preferred to travel by plane. She had even begged Sabastian to let her go on up ahead and do a little advanced scouting, but her friend could see right through her blatant attempt to avoid the cruise ship. Flying above the water was one thing, but actually being on it was something that she had dreaded her whole life. *"I can deal with my life ending in a plane crash... at least it'll be quick, but having to abandon a sinking ship and voluntarily becoming food for whatever creatures live in the ocean is the least honorable way of dying!"* she'd told Sabastian right before he forced her onto the ship.

    Once the ship had docked in Puerto Rico, Jerrelle literally fell to her knees and thanked whatever ancient mythological god of water there may be that she had somehow survived the trip. But, there was still one more hurdle that had to be cleared before she would be allowed to leave port — she, with her extensive criminal record, had to pass through customs.

    Sabastian and Richard; their military credentials surprisingly were what had prevented them from having to spend more than five minutes at port before they were cleared to enter the country. As was expected though, Jerrelle's checkered past, and a discrepancy on her documentation, was all the reason the Puerto Rican customs authorities needed to pull her aside and spend nearly two hours asking her an excessive amount of questions — most of which, had nothing to do with why Jerrelle had come to their country. Luckily for her, they just could not find a reason to legally deny her entry — which was good because she knew that there was no way that she would be able to survive a boat trip back to the Union so soon.

    After they got into their rental car, they headed out to where the Union's secret military depot was in Trujillo Alto. Honestly,

Jerrelle believed that it was probably going to take most of the trip, nearly thirty minutes to where they were to pick up their weapons, before she would feel somewhat back to normal. And to ensure that happened, she sipped on a small bottle of rum during the car ride — the alcohol, though really not needed, she drank to help calm her nerves after everything she had just went through.

"Don't you think that you've had enough of that rum?"

"No!"

"Well, I think that you've had enough. I need you to be alert and sharp. Who knows when we will come across a member of the A.R.M.? Besides, I'd rather not have you fire off a gun while you're over the limit."

"Don't worry about me, Sab. I'm feeling better now anyway." Deciding to appease her friend's wishes, she put the screw cap back on her rum and put it inside her backpack. "Um… are we there yet?"

Richard Atwater had never met Jerrelle while she was in the army. She had been dishonorably discharged just after both he and Sabastian had become members of the elite S.N.A.F.U. platoon. He had only heard stories about her from his friend over the years and his first impression of her was completely different than what he had expected. From what he had been told about her, he expected this hardnosed, attitude laden, fearless warrior — but instead he saw a self-centered, whining wreck of a human being. "I really don't want to sound like an asshole, Sabastian, but… I really don't think that your friend should be tagging along with us."

Intentionally stepping on the tail of a Rottweiler is not the smartest thing to do. Essentially, that is what Richard had just done, as those feral emotions of Jerrelle's began to awaken. Within a matter of only a few seconds, his unfounded opinion of her had changed. She didn't move, speak, or breathe; she just stayed still, giving off the impression that she was a cobra, waiting patiently to strike when the prey least expected it.

Words are not always needed to get a point across — and in that moment, Richard no longer had a basis to dispute all those stories, as it was now easy for him to see how much of an asset Jerrelle truly was to their team. Nothing had ever caused him to walk on eggshells — until now. He suddenly felt intimidated. And even though he knew

169

that Sabastian would have his back, he decided that for the time being, it was best to keep at least one eye on his friend at all times.

After a few 'by design' tense moments had passed, Jerrelle said, "I'm here because Sabastian asked me to come. He knows that his back is protected whenever I'm with him.., no matter how dangerous the situation may become. You, on the other hand, I may let get killed, as I'm not sure if I should trust you either."

Inside, Sabastian was laughing. The conversation between his two friends after all, had a touch of irony to it, as it was almost identical to the day that he had first met Jerrelle. Right from the very beginning, she didn't like him, and he didn't trust her.

At first sight, they both pegged each other as being the enemy — but it was during the third week of basic training that the animosity toward each other had ended. From day one, their drill sergeant clearly had it out for Jerrelle. At first, Sabastian had thought that she had deserved every bit of it because of her rebellious nature and piss-poor attitude, but as the days went on and the vocal assault given to her by their drill sergeant continued, he began to realize that she had been the one that their sergeant had chosen to be his personal punching bag. That was when he changed his tune concerning Jerrelle; she didn't deserve to be treated the way she was. He knew that this abuse of power was wrong and had to be stopped, so he took it upon himself to find out whether or not his drill sergeant's dislike for Jerrelle was just personal or if there was some other kind of motivation behind it. He wasn't sure, but Sabastian suspected that it was her mixed heritage that was the reason. Two days later, he had the answer he sought.

At three a.m., during a torrential down pour, their drill sergeant came into their bunks and literally dragged Jerrelle out of her bed. Without giving her a chance to even put on some normal clothes, he forced her outside and made her do one hundred push-ups in the mud; then after that was done, he had intended to have her run five miles.

There was no doubt in Sabastian's mind that the man had crossed the line — Jerrelle had done nothing to warrant such a punishment, so he himself got out of bed, and went outside to join her — and like her, he too was in his underwear.

Immediately, the sergeant ordered Sabastian to return to the barracks, but he refused. He just ignored his commanding officer and continued to match Jerrelle, push-up for push-up — his defiance infuriated their drill sergeant. So much so, that the man bent down, grabbed him by the back of his neck, and pulled him up off of the ground. The sergeant then stood nose to nose with Sabastian and tore into him for his defiance; that was what he was hoping for — a reason to get his father, Captain Burelli involved.

With a stoic look on his face, he just stood there and ignored the garbage that was spilling out of the mouth of his drill sergeant. Once the man had finished with his rant, instead of returning to the barracks, Sabastian returned to the ground and finished the one hundred push-ups right along with Jerrelle. Upon their completion, he was sent to see their commanding officer for disciplinary action. He was being accused of insubordination, which was what it actually looked like with him standing there covered from head to toe in mud and wearing only his underwear. But once his father had arrived and Sabastian was able to tell him his side of the story, the mood in the room had quickly changed from disappointment to outrage. Needless to say, the only disciplinary action that was taken that day was against Sabastian's drill sergeant.

When he had returned to the barracks, Jerrelle met him at the doorway. She stopped him dead in his tracks, looked at him nose to nose, and after a few tense seconds, extended her hand. From that moment on, Sabastian knew that he had earned Jerrelle's respect; respect that quickly turned into a life-long bond of friendship.

"What's that smirk on your face for, Sab?"

"Nothing, I was just thinking."

Ten minutes later, they arrived at their destination. The building they stopped at was of a typical construction for the area; one level, stone and plaster construction, with a terracotta designed, almost flat style roof — the building itself did not look that secure.

Unsure if this was the right place or not, Sabastian cautiously approached it as a man exited the building to greet them. "Senõr

Banks... My name is Sergeant Santino Alejandro Lopez. My friends though, call me Sal."

Both Jerrelle and Sabastian looked at each other with a bit of twisted irony on their faces — there was no way that they were going to refer to Santino as Sal. "Well... Since we have just met and are nowhere near close to yet becoming friends, I'll just address you by your given name," Sabastian respectfully declared.

"I don't mean to question how you do things here," Jerrelle said, "but in my opinion, this place looks to be very vulnerable to an unsolicited attack. Not only that, but any lowlife might be tempted to break into it. Where is your security?"

Richard's thoughts went right where they shouldn't have. He had let his mind associate Jerrelle's heritage and attitude with the typical media blamed stereotype. Immediately, he wanted to apologize for what he had just thought — but if he were to, Jerrelle might draw an unfounded conclusion of her own. She already, as it was, did not have a high opinion of him.

After chastising himself for even going there, Richard said, "I'm sure that our military has chosen this place for a reason, so I think that we should just end our current conversation, go on inside, and get what we came for."

The moment they entered the place, their first impressions had changed from uncertainty to confusion. There were only a few pieces of old weathered wooden or faded furniture in each of the rooms they had walked into — and neither one of them had seen anything that would clue them in to where the weapons that they came for were stored.

After passing through two small rooms, they were lead down a hallway to a somewhat smaller room at the back. Once they were inside, they stood there looking at an old beat up leather sofa in what was otherwise an empty space. More unsure thoughts ran through all three of them, as it appeared to each if they had just voluntarily walked themselves into a trap.

Then the room began to change; the floor started to move at the far side and the sofa started to rise up. What they saw next was something that might be written in a Hollywood script, as a huge service type of elevator that had been cleverly concealed into the floor right underneath the couch, now waited to take them down into a secret lair.

"Nice! Hide it in plain sight."

"And you were worried we had the wrong place, Sab."

"No I wasn't, Jerrelle."

"You may not have said it, but we all know you were thinking it," Richard said, as he cracked a sarcastic smirk on his face. "I assume that you would like for us to get on that?"

"That would be a correct assumption, my friend." Santino took them all below the building into what looked like a presidential bunker. They then passed through a solid steel door, followed by another, a long passageway, another steel door, and then another long passageway until they came to a set of metal stairs. They took those down a flight and then took a short passageway that led to a room at the end of it — the room was secured with not only another steel door, but had a retina scan security device, finger print scanner, an I.D. card swiper, and was flanked by two heavily armed guards on either side of the door.

"I take it this is where the big boy toys are kept?"

"That would be correct, Senõrita."

They passed through the secured door and then came to two other normal looking steel doors. The door off to their left, as explained to them by Santino, was their command center where thirty Puerto Rican Union Soldiers worked out of; the door that was straight ahead of them, was where the supply of weapons were kept.

Once inside the artillery room, Jerrelle's jaw dropped. In her eyes, she was looking at a piece of heaven — and she'd have no problem getting locked inside, so long as she had a lifetime supply of beer and meat lover's pizza. Everything that she had ever wanted to fire at least once, was in this room: long range sniper rifles that could easily pick off a squirrel on a wire at five hundred yards away, close range handguns that could blow a hole the size of a softball in someone's chest, small throwing knifes, switch and butterfly knives, and long and short blade close quarter fighting knives of which their edges would make a Ginsu seem dull.

This place even had a supply of various types of explosives such as: dynamite, C4, hand grenades, claymore mines, as well as wet

173

and dry chemicals that, when mixed together correctly, would leave behind a hole in the ground almost as big as what a small asteroid would. But what had snagged Jerrelle's interest more than anything, were the dozens of boxes of Ex-Co (**Ex**tremely **Co**rrosive) patches. This was a relatively new item that the Military or Police S.W.A.T. units used when it came to gaining access into a building. No longer was C4 or primacord needed. You just had to place an Ex-Co patch on any metal door hinge or lock and an instant chemical reaction with the metal would begin. It would only take a few seconds and anything you placed the patch on would be eaten away. "Can I take a few of these Ex-Co patches?"

"They are already in the 'bag of goodies' that we have assembled for you, Señorita."

Curious as to what was in their pre-packed sack, the three of them walked over to where they were lying and each examined the contents. Everything was there that they could foresee needing, so Sabastian and Richard closed their respective packs and thanked their Spanish hermano. Jerrelle though, wasn't quite happy with what was in her bag; there was something in the room she had seen earlier that she now wanted added to the 'bag of goodies', so she walked over to where the munitions locker was and looked over its contents. It only took her a moment to find what she was looking for — a box of corncob darts.

These 'bullets' looked almost like corncob holders — hence the name. They are projectiles that are comprised of three elements: the firing end of the bullet, the middle glass vile section, and the front needle portion. The primer and the rim (back end of the bullet) are constructed out of titanium, and contained within its shell is a small pocket of pure compressed oxygen. The middle section of the dart is constructed out of Pyrex and is designed to hold whatever tranquilizer or drug of choice is required. The front portion of it has three micro-thin, half inch in length needles that are equally distributed around the outer edge, is screwed onto the front end of the middle section, and can penetrate any outer layer: skin, fabric, leather, and even animal hide — the only thing it can't go through is Kevlar. The moment the projectile sticks in its target, inertia forces the compressed oxygen at the back end of the dart up against the substance in the middle section of the bullet, forcing that to flow right through the needles.

Because of the delicate nature of the corncob dart, it is only supposed to be fired from the proper compressed air rifle or air handgun — if one isn't readily available, a paintball gun will also work. Though not at all recommended, the dart can also be fired using a conventional type of weapon — but in order for that to work, a tiny paper wad containing black powder first needs to be placed behind the dart.

"I'll take a box of these; an air rifle and an air handgun, if you don't mind. I have a feeling that we may come across a situation where a non-lethal option will be preferred."

"Good idea," Richard said. He was impressed that Jerrelle had thought about that alternative. *'Maybe Sabastian was right after all... She actually does appear to know what she is doing.'*

After being given a box of one hundred corncob darts, the necessary weapons for them, and enough soporific to fill each, they stuffed them in their bags and left the 'bunker'.

Before they left the building, Santino checked the small monitor in the wall that sat right next to the front door to make sure that the coast was clear. Once he was certain that it was, the three of them exited, got back into their rental car, and drove to San Juan. While on their way there, they had decided that the remainder of their day would be spent in seclusion. First, they needed to make sure that they had a solid game plan in place that they could safely execute the next morning. Secondly, all three of them not only were admittedly starving, they were exhausted — it had been a while since any of them had indirectly travelled as many miles as they had. And lastly, every single corncob dart needed to be filled with the tranquilizer ahead of time, because doing this as needed while in the field could cost them valuable seconds, if not their lives.

She knew that when she had made the decision to become an escort that this was the type of lifestyle that could consume her youth and change her life in a manner that would be difficult to ever recover from. Madelyn had just turned eighteen when she had chosen a career that ended up not even being close to what she had dreamed about

175

when she was a young girl. From the moment she became a teenager, she had wanted to become a runway and fashion model, but her home life had always been so chaotic and out of control — sometimes even bordering on the edge of becoming volatile. It was that exposure which had ultimately caused her own dreams to become less important; survival was all that mattered during that time. So when Madelyn legally became an adult, she took that first step to escape the substance-induced hell that had surrounded her entire youth.

Madelyn was a stunning, beautiful young woman who was obviously aware that she could use her looks to make money. But without a real education, the only thing that she felt she could do to survive was to either become a stripper, or a prostitute — she just didn't know what other way there was where she could use what she had been born with to her advantage.

She was determined to make it on her own, but she never liked the idea of working in an environment where drugs, booze, smoke and drunken people were in her face all night long — that was the kind of situation she had just run away from, so stripping was out of the question. Walking the streets at night and looking for the next 'John' was also something that she was not keen on. But when she came across an ad in the yellow pages for a high-class escort service, she decided that this would probably be her best and safest course of action to take. Seven years later, and what she had feared could one day happen to her, finally did — she had been brutally gang raped.

Two days after going to Detroit to find the nicest, kindest, most thoughtful man that she had ever met since the day she had made her career choice; she made another one — she was done. She picked up the vid-phone in her hotel suite and made the call. This decision was not something that she had made the moment she had experienced the worst night of her life, but after spending a few days recovering in luxury, it became clear to her that there was more to life than using her looks to satisfy the needs of a strange man or woman for money — she was still young and she now wanted more out of life.

Once her decision became official, she called Louie's office and asked him if he could meet her in the hotel lobby and take her out for breakfast. Going back to Chicago was something she had decided she was never going to do again — she wanted to stay away from the city where a large portion of her life had been wasted. And even though Detroit also had a long-standing reputation of not being one of the safest cities in the world to live or be in, she for some reason felt a lot less vulnerable here.

This morning, breakfast wasn't the only thing that she wanted — she wanted Louie's help again. She wanted a new life, and only someone with half a brain would not be able to see that he was a man who not only had power, he had connections. It didn't matter to her what Louie was a part of; all that she needed from him was an opportunity to start over — and she was more than willing to do whatever he needed her to do so that she could move on and start the next chapter of her life.

Once the two of them met up in the lobby, Louie led her down the street to his favorite place. Surprisingly, there was no hesitation from him as they approached the restaurant — even though in the back of his mind sat the possibility that his enemy's essence would again make an unwanted appearance.

Although the Old World Café & Restaurant was mostly known for having an exquisite lunch and dinner menu, Louie could get anything he desired to eat from there — that was of course, because the D.U.O. owned it. So right after Madelyn had asked him to take her out for breakfast; he had called the restaurant and gave them his instructions. He honestly doubted that the thirty minute warning he had given them would be enough time to go and get the requested items they didn't normally stock, let alone have it prepared for them when they arrived. Nevertheless, they promised to make it happen.

He never expected this, but with the company he had at his side, a feeling like none Louie had in years, was present. Immense joy and pride was there — even the reaction he was seeing from those he knew within the restaurant, seemed to be positive. Maybe, just maybe, he might have to reconsider his earlier decision to not become involved in a personal relationship again.

After escorting Madelyn over to his personal table, Louie instructed his favorite waitress to bring them each a cup of their locally famous caramel-chino (a cappuccino that uses real Italian coffee beans blended with caramel malts). Ten minutes after enjoying nearly half of the drink, Madelyn gave Louie a heartfelt 'thank you for letting me discover this amazing drink' smile; a smile that was about to be followed up with a 'Can I get a menu' question, when their waitress returned with literally a seven course breakfast buffet already prepared for them.

Madelyn's eyes nearly popped out of her head when she saw just how much food had been brought to them: pancakes, bacon, ham & sausage, scrambled eggs, cheese omelets, white, whole wheat, and multi-grain toast, four kinds of jam, peanut butter, Nutella, orange, apple, and grapefruit juice, and ten different kinds of fresh fruit for dessert — there were enough calories there to cause her figure to expand just by the smell of it alone. She could not believe that Louie had arranged to have all this food prepared for her. Madelyn didn't even know what to say except, thank you — but even that didn't seem like a good enough response.

Once they had finished indulging themselves on the delicious food, Madelyn looked at Louie and again thanked him for being so kind and generous to her. "I can't even begin to tell you just how grateful I am. I never expected to come here and be treated like a queen."

"I'm not treating you as such; I'm only being me. This is how I treat my friends… and I hope you realize that I now consider you to be one of them."

"Your kindness to me is overwhelming. Thank you again, Louie."

The waitress approached the table and cleared away the remainder of the uneaten food, returning a few minutes later with another cup of caramel-chino for each of them. Madelyn took a sip of her fresh cup, then smiled again as she savored her new favorite drink. "Louie, I um… I have another small favor to ask of you."

"Sure. What is it that you need?"

"I want a normal life. What happened to me the other day, has forced me to finally open up my eyes and see just how risky my line of work really is. I know that it's nowhere near as dangerous as yours, but I now realize just how lucky I am to have survived that night; to have survived every one of those nights in which I had walked through some stranger's front door. I don't wish to put myself in that kind of situation ever again. So I have decided to 'tear up my calling card'. I quit my job this morning. I'm still young and I have my whole life ahead of me. I only became what I was because at the time, I didn't know how else to make the necessary money I needed to survive. I had youth and the looks; two key ingredients required to be an in-demand escort. So in spite of my family, I did it. Now, I want to be a normal woman, have a normal life, have a family one day, grow old, and enjoy playing with my grandchildren. If I didn't take this step today and leave the life that I was living, I'm certain that I would never find the courage needed to get out... and I'd never have a chance at those things that I now know I want to have."

Louie sat back and listened to a young woman who was finally ready to reclaim her life; a life that had been on an unstable path that was highly likely to one day spiral completely out of control and into a dark pit of hopelessness. A bit of pride developed inside of him. If he hadn't called the escort service and chosen her, and if he hadn't treated her in the manner that he had, then she would have just done what she had been paid to do, gone about her business, and probably would have just continued on with her profession — even after she had been gang raped. Louie was happy that he had left such an impression on her that she felt comfortable enough to reach out to him, a complete stranger, for the help that her soul cried out for.

"So, I was just wondering... I remember you asking your manager the other day if there had been any new job openings in the casino. Maybe you could see if there are any possible openings that I could fill? I don't care what the pay is. I just want to start all over."

"That's already been taken care of, Madelyn. I kind of had a feeling that you just might ask me that, so I took the liberty of arranging a position for you. How would you like to be a bartender in the Cadillac Club Room?"

Madelyn exhaled, happy that her desire to start a new life was actually going to happen. "That would be awesome. I can't begin to thank you enough."

"You won't have to start until after our agreement is fulfilled. That will give you some time to finish healing from all of those visible injuries you have and time to learn your drinks. I've made sure that the desktop computer in your room has a digital version of the New Boston Bar Guide installed on it and my executive manager has arranged to have one of our casino's bartenders come up to your suite and give you a few lessons and tips. Take your time and relax and learn. Anything you need in the meantime, just call the front desk and they will take care of you.

They each finished off their second caramel-chino and then left the restaurant; a limo was unexpectedly waiting outside with its door already open. Madelyn stopped in her tracks and stood aghast at what she saw; she immediately wondered what Louie had planned for her next. If she didn't know any better, it felt to her as if he was being more than just an extremely nice and caring man — it was almost as if he was taking the slow steps that any man would take when they were trying to win someone's heart.

Louie walked Madelyn over to the awaiting car, held the door open for her, and then instructed the driver to take her to the closest shopping center so that she could get a few 'normal' things to wear. He knew that Madelyn had left Chicago in a hasty fashion, so he was more than happy to buy her a few items of necessity.

She pulled him into a warm embrace and gave him a gentle kiss on the cheek, thanking him one more time for his kindness and generosity — she then got into the limo and left.

Feeling happier than he had since he could last remember, Louie headed back to the office. He liked Madelyn a lot, and the thought of her did nothing but warm his usually stone cold heart. Mirella had been the only woman that he had ever had any sort of deep feelings for, but now after all these years, another woman had come along and awoken his long dormant emotions; emotions he was unsure of, but welcomed nonetheless. Admittedly, he wasn't ready for something like this, but if the stars one day were to miraculously align, he might have to reassess his earlier decision. Mirella had long ago captured his heart; Madelyn could easily sooth his blacken soul for however much longer his time on earth was to be.

Today was going to be without question, the most stressful of his adult life. Twenty-four hours, it was all that had to pass and then things were going to be how Jason wanted them to be — at least, for the immediate future. Until then, he would have to do his best not to ruin what he and his wife had agreed to do — take their now twelve-year-old daughter out on the town and let her enjoy her birthday.

After spending the morning shopping with the both of them, Jason took his family to lunch at a street side restaurant called 'El Mondo Restaurante'. Outside wasn't where he wanted to be, but the place was somewhat small and unfortunately, busy — they were left with no other choice but to take what available seating there was. At least, a few yards away and flanked on both sides of them, was the private security he was paying for. Still, he felt very uneasy about being in the open. Nearly the entire time, he ignored Florentina on her special day. It had been unintentional and he felt like an asshole, but not relying solely on his security to protect his family was what he felt he had to do in order to ensure their safety.

Once their lunch was over, Jason took his family over to his place of work. It was there that he had kept his daughter's birthday gift. She was way too smart for her age; there wasn't a place in their tiny, temporary home that she wouldn't find a supposedly well-hidden gift, so he had to keep it in a place where she would not think to look.

While Jason's family waited in the lobby area for him to go to his office to get his daughter's present, Louie's associates came down from their room. The day before, Nicoli had been able to quietly break into Jason's office and luckily for him, noticed that the man's vid-cell was lying unattended on top of his desk. So he took out his palm-top, hooked it up to the x-slot on the man's vid-cell, and then loaded into it a small tracking program; a program that allowed Nicoli to keep tabs on Jason Hernandez' whereabouts.

They could have just killed him yesterday while he had been at work, but Zhin and Nicoli did not want to expose themselves. They needed to wait until the right moment to make it look like their target's death was something other than a planned hit. And now, with the tracking program alerting them to Jason's presence in the hotel, Zhin and Nicoli put their plan into motion.

Calmly acting just like any other tourists would, they approached the front desk with their bags in hand, and checked themselves out of the hotel. On their way toward the front door, Zhin greeted Jason's wife and daughter with a courteous 'good afternoon' and smiled as he continued on toward the front door — Nicoli ignored them both, passing by without even a glance. He did notice however, the private security that was present; one inside the lobby and one waiting just outside the front door — those two men, to him, did nothing to change their plans. If either of them got in the way, they would also be eliminated.

After both of them got into their awaiting rental car, Zhin, with an almost compassionate gaze, looked over at his associate and said, "It's a shame that pretty young lady is going to have to live the rest of her life without her father."

"It's not her fault that the man chose to fuck over his employer. She and her mother are just going to have to learn to deal with the fact that the man they both surely love, was forced to pay a high price for making the wrong decision."

Zhin started up their rental car and they headed down the street to a partially secluded area just a short distance away from the Hilton. Once they were parked, their view of what was to soon take place could not have been any better. Yes, they could easily be seen, but no one had any inkling as to what they were doing or who they even were. Besides, they weren't going to be parked for too long, as a few minutes was all that was going to go by before the events they had planned, took place — all thanks to Nicoli and the technology that he had possession of.

Inside their hotel room at the Caribe Hilton, Jerrelle took her early afternoon sim-caf and walked out onto their third floor, street side balcony. It was a near perfect day, and for the first time in a while, she felt like her old self; her worries pertaining to her sister had all but disappeared after the lengthy conversation she had with Bai Lin the previous evening.

This was the first time that she had ever been to Puerto Rico, and other than the issue she had with customs, Jerrelle was beginning to like it here — not because of the climate, but because this was a place where she didn't have to 'hide' the fact that she had a weapon on her. A lot of people who lived here had a weapon of some kind in their possession; it was an acceptance and a way of life in this country. She almost felt at home. In fact, she could even envision Puerto Rico as being a place, when she finally decided that it was time for her to slow her life down, where she could retire to.

When she was halfway done her sim-caf, Richard had joined her out on the balcony. They were planning to leave in just over an hour's time to begin their search for the A.R.M. cell, but he was hoping to learn a bit more about whom Jerrelle really was as a person beforehand. Since they had arrived in San Juan, his perception of her had begun to change. Sabastian had been right — she was a unique individual and it would take him some time to fully understand her. But in the twenty-four hours that they had been in this country, he could now begin to see why his old friend trusted her wholeheartedly.

Richard was just about to initiate a conversation with her when a series of loud screams, followed by a loud crash, filled the air. Inadvertently, Jerrelle jumped back as she was witnessing the events unfold right in front of her; events that caused the remainder of her sim-caf to spill from her cup — some of it ended up on the balcony floor, and some of it went over the edge. Luckily, none of it ended up on her.

In a matter of seconds, chaos had enveloped in the street just below them. Without saying a word, Jerrelle darted back into the hotel room and bolted out the door.

Sabastian had never before seen his friend move that fast as she had come within only a few inches of knocking him right back into the bathroom; he stood there dumbfounded at the threshold of it in his bath towel, having just stepped out of the shower. "What the hell's going on?"

"We were both out on the balcony and we just saw a man and his family get hit by a car." Richard then left the hotel room, knowing that Jerrelle was heading out to the scene of the accident.

Sabastian quickly got himself dressed and hurried out to the street where he found a crowd of people surrounding the victims. He made his way through the sea of humanity and immediately saw Jerrelle kneeling over a man whose body was twisted and covered in blood. Richard was off to the side tending to two other victims: a woman and a young girl. Another person, a man in a suit, was a few meters away and tending to a man dressed nearly identical to him. All three of them thankfully, appeared only to have a few non-life threatening injuries.

As he walked over to Jerrelle, Sabastian could see a despondent look in her eyes. "Is he dead?"

"Yes… and I saw the whole thing from our balcony. This man had bravely pushed his wife and child out of the way from that oncoming car." Jerrelle then motioned over in the direction of the smashed vehicle.

"There was nothing you could have done, Jerrelle?"

"I know, but I still feel responsible."

His friend's statement left Sabastian flabbergasted. "How could you be responsible for this?"

"Sab.., this man is Jason Hernandez. He was the manager at the New Book Cadillac Casino and he is the one I bribed for the copy of that black book."

Sabastian was stunned. This man, a stranger to him, had hastily made a decision to sell out his boss for reasons that at the time, probably made sense to him. Had karma come to collect on its debt? It's possible, but that was something he did not believe in. What he thought instead was that this was just an unavoidable accident. However, he had learned not too long ago to never dismiss the D.U.O. from being guilty of something. They very well could have orchestrated this. It's unfortunate, but there was absolutely nothing that he or Jerrelle could have done to prevent this from happening.

Sabastian gently urged Jerrelle up from her kneeling position; he intended to get her to go with him over to where Richard was tending to the man's wife and daughter — but that was not where she wanted to go. She instead, headed over to where the vehicle responsible for this tragedy now sat. Strangely, she noticed that no one else had gone over to attend to the driver — and when she arrived at the driver's side door, she felt a bit of déjà vu. Just like in Japan, no one was sitting inside the car, nor was there any visual evidence that someone had been and had gotten injured. At that moment, her ever-conjecturing mind took over — she now wanted to find out for sure if what she suspected was the case. There was one obvious problem though. She didn't know what she was looking for; what the S.M.A.R.T. technology she suspected had been retrofitted inside the vehicle, looked like. Time was also not on her side, as she could hear and see the emergency vehicles now approaching the scene. Therefore, she had no other choice but forgo her desire to verify her gut feeling.

Not wanting to get caught tampering with the accident scene, she promptly returned to where Richard and Sabastian were and waited for the police and emergency workers to arrive; she never let it be known to any of the officers that she had witnessed this accident or that she knew who the victim was — she only told them that she had tried to help.

Fifteen minutes later, the three of them were back in their hotel room. Almost immediately, Sabastian could see a change in his old friend. Her mood had resorted back to the way she was when she had first arrived in San Antonio. Something again was bothering her — and whatever it was, it could possible interfere in their assigned mission. That was something that Sabastian could not risk happening. "What is bothering you now, Jerrelle?"

"That car accident out there... I don't think it was an accident."

"What makes you say that?" Richard asked."

"Just like when my sister and I got injured, there was no driver in the car."

Confused, Richard asked the obvious question "What do mean, there was no driver?"

Before she could answer, Sabastian knew exactly what his friend suspected. He told Richard what had happened to Jerrelle and her sister, and then he proceeded to inform him about his knowledge of the experimental technology known as S.M.A.R.T.

"I thought someone was after my sister, but now it appears that they may have been after me. It all makes sense now."

"I agree. It looks like Louie is trying to clean up the mess left behind after Antonio's demise."

"Louie? Antonio?"

"It's a long story, Richard. I'll tell you about it on our way to where we are going this afternoon."

An apparent unsuccessful attempt had been made on Jerrelle's life; a successful one had just claimed the life of Jason Hernandez.

Because of these facts, it didn't take long for an assumption to appear in Sabastian's mind — he was probably going to be the next target. And if that was indeed the case, it now made his current assignment even more stressful than it really needed to be.

He didn't want to, he just had no other choice but to assume that the D.U.O. were indeed back in business and that Louie Mazotti was beginning to tie up any lose ends still out there that were connected to previous regime. Little did the bastard know that Sabastian was no longer the same credulous young man trying only to settle a debt — he was now a confident, self assured soldier who was finally ready to play and win any kind of game that Louie Mazotti might choose to play.

Although no certainty had yet to be established that she had been targeted back in Japan, the fire inside Jerrelle was ready to ignite. However, her sister's safety now appeared no longer to be in question — for that, she was thankful. Was it the D.U.O. who wanted her dead, or was it someone else from her past? Admittedly, she had accumulated quite the extensive list of enemies over the years — but only one of them, she thought, might actually want her dead. Then again, she didn't think that Gino Caravella had the balls to do it.

No thought whatsoever was there that both incidences were not linked to one another, nor had she a clue that the individual responsible for both had actually been staying in the same hotel as they were. Had she seen Nicoli Nemchieve before the accident, she more than likely would have just assumed that it was merely a coincidence that he too was in Puerto Rico and at the same hotel as she. As unfounded as it seemed, she was beginning to lean toward the possibility that Nicoli now blamed her for his brother's death. And if that were indeed the case, then somehow he had gotten his hands on the S.M.A.R.T. technology, with the sole purpose of trying to kill her. What did not make any sort of sense to her though, was that he was a respected, chartered member of the E.C.L. and an association of any kind with the Detroit Underworld Organization would normally be unheard of. There was always a first, but Jerrelle didn't honestly think that to be the case — the E.C.L. had after all, just recently drained one of the D.U.O.'s secret bank accounts.

Another enemy was not what she wanted, but it appeared that she now had one — a very dangerous one. Only one conclusion could be had as far as she was concerned — Helfred's death had made Nicoli's apparent hatred toward her become the sole reason why he chose to throw away what he had long been a part of and go rogue. Of course, she had no viable proof of any of this, but almost never was Jerrelle's intuition wrong.

He walked over to her suite with the most honest of intentions — his caring heart is what made him go there to see her. She had been through a lot over the last few days and Louie just wanted to make sure that everything was all right.

That changed the moment the door to her hotel suite opened up. Madelyn stood just beyond the threshold in a nearly see-through, sheer white laced, tanned accented, full-length teddy. At that moment, all the gentlemanly thoughts that Louie usually had, had instantly disappeared from his head. His heart began to race and his nerves became unsettled.

For a very long time, he had successfully kept suppressed those unabated urges that he once had as a young man, but they suddenly came roaring back to life and rekindled a fire inside of him. Madelyn was a beautiful woman, and it would take all the restraint that Louie had to honor the promise he had made to himself all those years ago, never to 'cheat' on Mirella. But it had been twenty-something years since he had last experienced the wonders of another woman, and his animal instincts were rapidly overwhelming his commitment. He could not control the rising desire he had for the unexpected gift of wholesome beauty that now stood only a few inches in front of him. It wasn't fair, but once Louie's sense of smell locked onto the fragrance of Madelyn's vanilla perfume, his hunger only intensified — it also caused his pallet to insurmountably salivate.

There wasn't any hiding it, as she could easily sense the desire that Louie had for her. So without saying a word, she reached out with her left hand and pulled him completely inside her suite — she then shut the door and promptly pinned his back up against it.

Before he even contemplated objecting to what was happening, Madelyn placed a gentle, hypnotic kiss on his untouched lips. At that moment, she could feel his heart beating outside his chest. She had his full attention and she had him right where she wanted him. His thoughts were now focused solely on her and her alone. Louie was now hers to do with as she pleased.

She had recognized that there was something different; something special about Louie the first day that they had met. And the moment that they finally touched each other's lips, it only confirmed it.

Once she knew that she essentially owned him, she led Louie across the living area of the suite toward the bedroom. As they entered it, she encouraged him to remove his clothes and to lie down. While he was willingly doing this, she turned down the lighting in the room to a more romantic level, lit two opium scented candles, and watched. For a man old enough to be her father, Louie still had the physique of a thirty-five year old. His physical attributes and age though, was irrelevant to her — there was something much deeper that she was attracted to.

As Louie laid vulnerable on the king-sized bed, thoughts of uncertainty began to overtake his mind: uncertain if what he was about to do was right, uncertain if he should break his own promise of long ago, and uncertain if he even deserved this woman who for some unknown reason, seemed to desire him as much as he did her. She was the epitome of perfection. If he were ever going to break his promise, there wouldn't be a better woman on the planet than Madelyn to do it with.

Resistance was quickly becoming futile as she seductively maneuvered herself onto the edge of the bed and then crawled slowly over top of Louie. She hadn't even touched him yet, and he was already standing at attention. With her, any chance of his not being able to perform just wasn't possible. He knew the moment he became ready for action that he would not need one of those blue pills to maintain. She alone was all that it was going to take for Louie to do his part without any help from any artificial means.

Madelyn drank in his eagerness, his desires, his vulnerability. She could sense that he was going to let her dictate what was about to happen — and that was just fine by her. So she lowered herself on top of him and then slid her still covered body across his — just by glancing into Louie's eyes, she could see that he was feeling unfamiliar sensations flowing throughout his body from the contact of her lace teddy up against his bare chest.

Louie's eyes were filled with want and his manhood was ready to be used as a key to unlock and open up the treasure that awaited him. Without even having to jump on an airplane and fly to a sunny, tropical destination, he had found paradise.

Slowly, Madelyn rose up and unlaced her teddy; gently, she let it fall down her backside and onto Louie's bare legs. She then leaned forward, took both of her hands, and lightly combed her fingernails through Louie's mostly-grey chest hair.

That small bit of teasing was all that it took for Louie to lose his mind — and almost something else. He could not take it anymore; this so wasn't fair. If he didn't take over control, then this evening was going to end prematurely, so he grabbed her wrists and attempted to pull her onto him — but she resisted. Instead, she took both of Louie's arms and pinned them back up over his head and flat against the headboard. Madelyn was in control tonight and she was bound and determined not to give it up.

For just a moment, she held him pinned in place, as she only wanted to reiterate that he was to be the submissive one tonight — she then, after believing that Louie finally understood his role, slowly lowering herself until she was close enough to softly nestle her cheek up against his.

The warmth of her skin only intensified his desire to take her — he didn't want to wait any longer. But he had to, as she had made it clear that tonight, she was in control and that she wasn't going to relinquish it over to him. So he closed his eyes and did everything that he could to prevent himself from blowing the moment — but his ability to do that was becoming near impossible; his ruining this once in a lifetime experience was becoming more and more likely. Then, it finally came to the moment when he just could not resist the fire inside any longer. He had been tolerant long enough; he didn't care — he wanted full control.

Sensing Louie's impatience, Madelyn held his hands in place with more force than what a woman should be able to use. A bit of panic suddenly began to surface as he could tell that she was about to do something that he wasn't himself, willing to do. He called out her

189

name, but not in a passionate way — he said it with an uncertainty in his voice. Madelyn didn't respond to his ambiguity, so Louie called out her name again — this time, his tone had a touch of anger in it. What happened next was something so unbelievable, even Louie was left speechless.

Madelyn let go of his wrists, straightened herself up, and then looked deep into his eyes. An almost evil looking smile appeared on her face as she slowly began to change — not her personality, but her actual physical appearance.

Shear horror immediately filled Louie's face as his worst nightmare was manifesting itself right in front of him. He still couldn't move his hands, nor could he even move his body — he was somehow paralyzed by something other than fear. All that he could do was lay there and look at the person, his onetime enemy, who now was hovering right over top of him; right where Madelyn had been.

"Under normal circumstances, people would most definitely get the wrong idea."

"Let me go, you son-of-a-bitch!"

"Um... no!" If it had been at all possible for him to take advantage of his enemy's immobility, Maxwell would have given the bastard a few well-deserved punches to the jaw. But since it was impossible to make any sort of physical contact with him, he simply shifted his hovering position over so that he could then stand on the ground like any normal human being. There, he stood right beside the bed and shook his head in disgust at the man who was partially responsible for his death. "Do you honestly think that Madelyn is the one person in this world who can absolve you of your numerous sins? It doesn't matter if you treat her with kindness and respect; shower her with gifts, and profess to her how much you care. It will not make up for the fact that you are, and always will be, a heartless bastard who deserves to rot in the depths of hell."

Louie still couldn't move; unknown forces kept him pinned to the bed. All he was able to do was talk and listen. He didn't like not being in control of a situation — and he did not like being where he was. "You only ever saw one side of it, Max... the side of the law, not the actual business side of our organization. You tried to prevent the D.U.O. from its evolution; one that has ultimately helped to rebuild the city. We only did what we had to do to you because you would have severely interfered with our progress. And as far as Madelyn goes, I treat her the same way that I treat those who I do care about and love."

"You're full of shit and you know it. You may intend to treat that woman with all the respect she honestly deserves, but she will one day see what kind of man you really are. You can try to hide those facts from her, but she will soon enough discover the truth. For once in your life, Louie, do the right thing and set her free before you ruin her life like so many others before."

"You didn't honestly come here to lecture me about my personal choices, did you?"

"No. I have come here once again to remind you that you will be meeting your maker very soon."

"Again, you are full of shit. I will disprove your baseless prophecy."

"You can't change what the Fates have long ago decided when it comes to you, Louie. Nor is there another religious figure or ancient mythological deity out there who would be willing to show you any kind of mercy."

"I think you've been reading too many Sherrilyn Kenyon novels, Max. The Fates, the Greek and Roman Gods and Goddesses, Buddha, Allah or whoever... they are all just as fictitious as the Almighty Lord is."

"Well aren't you just a cynical bastard?"

"Screw you, Banks!"

Maxwell stood there laughing, knowing full well where his enemy's soul was destined to end up. "Oh... and there's one other thing. If you truly want to do something good before you die, don't ever tell your son who you really are. Save him the same eventual fate as yours."

The next thing Louie knew, he was standing at home plate at Comerica Park. There were two people positioned at the front edge of the pitcher's mound and there was a third one who he could tell was lying on the ground. Curiosity consumed him. He stood where he was, trying to figure out if he knew any of them, but with their backs to him, he just could not get a clear view of what their faces looked like.

191

The only thing that he knew for sure was that of the two who were standing, one was a man, and the other one, a woman. The one lying on the ground, to him it appeared to be a male — but he just could not tell for certain.

Like a moment ago when he was in Madelyn's bed, Louie could not seem to move — but he didn't need to in order to get a better look. The two that had been standing, as if on cue, moved off to the side. One went left, and the other went right — that was what had allowed Louie to clearly see now that it was indeed a young man who was lying on the ground. In fact, it only took him another second to realize that he knew who it was. It was his son, Marco, dead from a gunshot to the side of the head.

Louie screamed out his son's name. The next thing he knew, he was back in Madelyn's bed — still immobile.

"There's only one way that you can change what you just saw from ever taking place. Take my advice, Louie, and do not allow your son to follow in your footsteps.

"Fuck you, Max! Marco is not going to...

Maxwell disappeared, right along with Louie's invisible restraints.

"Come back here you asshole! I'm not finished..."

Louie woke up in his office; his head had been lying against his crossed arms on top of his desk. This had been a first for him. Louie had never before fallen asleep at his desk, and he was uncertain as to why it had just happened — after all, he hadn't been that tired.

He was about to get up and go get himself a drink from his private bar when his vid-phone rang; the display informed him that it was Zhin calling — Louie sincerely hoped that he had some good news to share.

After a few minutes of listening to his associate's report on the events that had taken place, he smiled for the first time in a very long time. Nicoli had done his part and Zhin had nothing but praise for him — which in turn, allowed Louie to feel content. Now, with the success of this first assignment in the books, a confidence was there that he had two men whom he could wholeheartedly trust to do a job and complete it without making any crucial mistakes that could cause more headaches than what someone in his position would normally be expected to deal with.

Once Louie had disconnected his call, he made his way over to the bar, grabbed an ice-cold beer, and brought it back to his desk. After cracking it open and taking a few healthy sips, he smiled. He was happy in that moment, but at the same time, his dream had left a disturbing memory behind. There had to be a logical reason as to why Maxwell Banks was suddenly appearing when he dozed off. Louie was not one who believed in ghosts, premonitions, or déjà vu, but he couldn't dismiss the possibility that what his old adversary had said to him, had showed to him, was going to be the inevitable future for his son.

Louie now had a choice to make. He could either heed the warning that had just been issued, or ignore it all together and accept his two dreams as being just his own stress manifesting what the worst possible scenario might be. And if that was the case, then it was up to him to take the necessary precautions to ensure that such a potential outcome did not happen. So long as he stayed alive, he was confident that his son's future would be bright and not end up in an unthinkable way. He just needed to figure out how to do that.

9

The last few days have been a bit of a challenge for Louie — his: trying to re-organize and restructure the entire D.U.O., trying to correct the mistakes that Antonio had made, trying to help a woman who maneuvered into his life and had unintentionally kept the good that was still within him alive, and his trying to quit smoking those clove-flavored cigarettes, forever. But now, those two unsettling dreams, along with the responsibility of being in charge of an organization as powerful as his, was easily causing the level of stress he normally could keep in check to increase much more than it healthily should. He always understood the enormous amount of responsibility that Antonio carried upon his shoulders, but Louie firmly believed that a lot of the pressure that his former boss had been constantly under was caused by his own obsession with Maxwell Banks. That was something he refused to ever allow happen to him — he needed to find a way of relieving those unwanted stresses before they became his own undoing.

No longer could he delay; it was time that Louie got the organization back up and running again — it was why he had essentially locked himself in his new office. What he wasn't expecting this day though, was continual rejection. After contacting nearly every one of their old clients, and offering every concession and promise that he felt he could as an incentive, without giving away the farm, the answer from everyone was still an emphatic, no.

He sat there scratching his head. In no way shape or form did Louie think that they had burned that many bridges. What reason could there be that no one was willing to give the D.U.O. another opportunity to do business with them? He hadn't the faintest idea. This unexpected failure not only was depressing, but Louie felt insulted. The Detroit Underworld Organization had always done business in good faith, yet the recent difficulties that the organization had, must have somehow become common knowledge and thus, an unfounded opinion had to have been drawn that they were no longer trustworthy.

He felt like giving up — but that was not what a leader did. Besides, there were still two other potential clients left on his list that he had yet to contact. Unfortunately though, one of them he would rather not have to deal with if he could help it. That client of course, was the Communist Revolutionary Assembly Party — it wasn't that they didn't pay top dollar for the merchandise that they had purchased in the past, but he wasn't quite ready to volunteer the information that they were starting back up their trading business. Louie, after all, just wasn't too sure if the C.R.A.P. were angry with the D.U.O. over the death of Vladi Chemzot. If they were, he at least hoped that they were oblivious to the fact that it had been he, because of Antonio's orders, who had executed their leader.

Thankfully, the other organization still left on his list, the U.A.L. (the United Arab League), was one that he knew the D.U.O. had a very good rapport with. However, when Louie made contact with them, it had surprisingly taken quite an effort on his part to convince them to stay on as a client. But he was in a bind and he had no other alternative but to do a little butt kissing, as his organization needed at least one more client in order to get back into the game.

The U.A.L. as a group had always been a relatively small-time local organization. And although the D.U.O. had dealt with them on a handful of occasions in the past, they were a group that Antonio had never really pursued as a steady client. Now, the United Arab League was finally starting to grow by not only expanding their territories, but their ambition as well. It was why the Union Bureau of Investigation had recently started to keep a closer eye on them.

Being watched closely by a government agency wasn't enough to deter Louie. To him, that meant the League were finally getting the respect they deserved — and it was what encouraged Louie to want to do business with them. If he could play a small part in the U.A.L. sticking it to the government, then he was more than willing to be an accessory. Yes, it was a dangerous game to play, but Louie had a point to prove — not only to him that he had the ability to lead an underground organization, but also to those others who just slammed the door in his face and turned down his genuine offer of doing business.

Although the U.A.L. had made it known that they already had an abundance of weapons at their disposal, it was Louie's one final selling point that had sealed the deal; he was able to convince them that he could obtain and supply them with the latest military grade hi-tech weaponry and computer tracking systems so that they not only could stay one step ahead of the U.B.I., but could easily deal with them if confronted.

In seven days time, a meeting would take place. The only thing about it that Louie was uncomfortable with, was that the U.A.L. had requested that he be there when both organizations had their initial face to face meeting — an expectation that he felt he no longer was obliged to make happen. It wasn't like he was not used to having a face to face meeting with a potential buyer, it's just that he was now the boss, and it was supposed to be his associates who conducted such negotiations. However, if meeting the U.A.L. face to face was what it took this time to officially strike a trade agreement, then Louie would comply and do what was being asked of him.

It had been a long day and he was about to go home when his vid-phone rang. He sunk back in his synth-leather chair and answered it. To his surprise, it was the same man who had tracked him down in Chicago a week ago wanting the D.U.O. to send them a shipment of military arms. Curiosity immediately grabbed his attention, as Louie tried to think of a reason as to why the A.R.M., a relatively new organization, would want even more weapons than they already had — then he got his answer. His first shipment had made it to Tijuana as intended, but their cell was raided shortly afterward. A highly trained military assault team had not only shut down the cell, but had confiscated the shipment as well. Now, this man who was on the phone with him was all but begging Louie to ship him some more weapons; weapons that he was more than willing to pay double for.

More money was good, but now he had questions. To him, the A.R.M. had to have some serious holes in it somewhere in order for one of their cells to have been shut down as quickly as it had right after a completed shipment. Having such vulnerability within its infrastructure also meant that a risk was now there to his organization.

With those stolen weapons now back in the hands of the Union's Military, he had to assume that there was a very good chance they could be traced back to the D.U.O.

When Louie inquired about his concerns, the caller hesitated to explain. Instead, the man made a declaration that he hoped would be understood, "It won't happen again. We have an agenda that we intend to complete. Without your help, both of our organizations will eventually fall. What we both stand for and aspire to achieve, will not have a chance of coming to fruition if the Union is allowed to solidify its agreement."

Louie took a moment and contemplated the man's words and what he wanted to do. Yes, re-supplying the A.R.M. with more weapons could produce a serious backlash if what had happened in Tijuana, happened again — but providing what was being asked, after weighing all the possibilities, was still a low enough risk for Louie to take. And although the organization was currently a shell of what it once was, he fully understood the situation. The A.R.M., the U.A.L., and the D.U.O., all had one thing in common — the detestation of those who made up the government, and their self-serving agendas.

After agreeing to help the man, Louie laid down his terms. Doubling the price wasn't good enough — he wanted three times the money. His reasoning for this outrageous increase in price was simple — it would take that kind of money to not only insure that it arrived safely at its destination, but this requested shipment of weapons had to be smuggled into a country that no longer had an open border with the Union — that being Puerto Rico.

After a short bit of hesitation, the man caved in and accepted Louie's terms; the man didn't really have a choice. So with the agreement now in place, he disconnected his call, went over to his wet bar, poured himself a glass of Walker's Club, and then returned to his desk. After taking a moment to relish in his small bit of success, Louie proceeded to do the last thing he needed to do in order to fulfill his end of the agreement — call Casper. "Can you come up with an ingenious way of shipping the same amount of goods to Puerto Rico as you did Tijuana without them being discovered?"

"No problem, as I am a master of illusion."

"Is that one of the reasons why they call you Casper?"

197

"It is."

With a smile on his face, content with the knowledge that what he wanted completed would be, Louie said, "Thanks, Casper. This organization would have never prospered had it not been for you and your skills."

"I certainly appreciate the endorsement, sir. Have a good night."

With that now out of the way, Louie decided that he no longer wanted to go home. He quickly pounded back the remainder of his drink and then left his office; from there he went directly over to Madelyn's suite. He wanted to see if she would like to accompany him to a late dinner, maybe a late night stroll through the New Woodward area, and then maybe join him after that for a nightcap — and if that resulted in his breaking his long ago promise, Louie finally felt that he would have absolutely no regrets afterward.

Unlike Tijuana, there weren't thirty of them to comb the streets in search of the terrorist cell. And just like that Mexican city, no irrefutable evidence was available to them to even suggest that their target was somewhere in San Juan. However, with a population of just over four hundred thousand, it seemed probable to Sabastian that the A.R.M. would have an established outpost located somewhere within the city limits.

Twenty-four hours of searching had come and gone, and as expected, they were no closer to finding any sort of clue that could lead them to where the base camp was for the American Recovery Mission. Thankfully, they hadn't been given a deadline to meet — but that didn't mean that they had all the time in the world at their disposal. Proof of the terrorist's existence in Puerto Rico needed to be found before the group chose to retaliate against the Union for what its military had done to one of their cells.

There was no reason to allow the lack of success on their first day to bother any of them. Sabastian however, was a little perturbed — mostly because he had never before been given an assignment and finished off the day right where he had started. Ending the day with no success at all meant one thing; the same method that they used in Tijuana wasn't going to work in San Juan. Walking the streets in search of any suspicious buildings and blindly knocking on doors was clearly a waste of their time. In order to accomplish their goal, they had to think outside the box — or like, a private investigator. They needed to find sources, who knew sources, which had sources — they needed information no matter how second hand it was. All that they wanted was one small lead to follow, and then they would at least have something to possibly guide them in the right direction.

After racking his brain throughout the evening, Sabastian determined that there was only one realistic option for him to take, so he sent out an inquiring text to the one person that he knew who had plenty of resources at their disposal — his cousin, Sharice Cortland. He hoped that she would be able to come through for him, otherwise the three of them would be stuck canvassing the streets for the foreseeable future.

By midmorning, she had returned his text with a phone call, letting him know of the only lead that she could find. Through a not so trustworthy operative her mother had once known that just so happened to live in Puerto Rico, she was able to find out that a former State Senator named Kenneth J. Harrisburg had moved down there about three years ago. He had done so shortly after his admission of being associated with the Desoto syndicate; a crime family that became famous a decade earlier when they systematically eliminated three of the five long-established New York mob organizations.

Right after his removal from the senate, and just before his conviction, Kenneth J. Harrisburg had disappeared. And although there have been a bunch of unfounded rumors circulating for several years about the former senator, the one that was strongly believed is that he was the one who had started up the American Recovery Mission, for the sole purpose of using it as a platform to one day seek personal vengeance against his ex-country. To this day though, the A.R.M. vehemently denies the former state senator's involvement with them, as they claim that their only objective is to educate and influence an independent way of thinking to all the citizens of what had once been the United States of America.

With what he had just learned, Sabastian felt pretty confident that the U.B.I. was the ones who had requested that the S.N.A.F.U. go on that mission to Tijuana. Was he pissed that a government agency had essentially gone behind everyone's back and asked his unit to acquire the evidence they needed to support their beliefs? No, as he trusted those who made decisions that were in the best interest of his country. Whether or not he always agreed with it, he at least supported it. Personally though, he would have wished that the U.B.I. had taken responsibility for their actions instead of choosing to be surreptitious.

Strangely, he could feel the impatience within him coming to the surface — this assignment called for assuredness. Therefore, Sabastian walked out to his hotel room's balcony and took in the morning breeze. After nearly fifteen minutes of in-depth thought, he felt that a bit more help was needed. So he made a call to his agency, as Baylor and Savanna's talents should be able to get what he sought. And although each were good at what they did; his friend on his computer and his secretary with her researching abilities, Sabastian knew that it would be some time before he heard back from either one of them.

Instead of wasting their time today doing the same thing as yesterday, Sabastian decided to take the entire morning off — he left his supply bag on the end of his bed, didn't change into his searching gear, nor did he strap himself with his piece. He just walked right past Jerrelle, without looking or saying a word to her, and headed for the door.

She instantly became confused. Her first thought was that Sabastian seemed to be acting a bit weird this morning, as if he hadn't a care in the world, and as if this assignment all of a sudden, didn't take precedence. She had never before seen him ignore his obligations like this. In her eyes, something had to be wrong. "Um, where are you going, Sab?"

"Out!"

"Why?"

"Because!"

A stalemate — Sabastian wasn't being co-operative at all. "Should we not be getting ourselves ready to go out and continue our search?"

"Nope!"

"Will you fuckin' give me more than a one word answer?"

"Nope!"

"What's going on?" Richard asked.

"Nothing!"

"Something is going on, but Sabastian won't let me in on what it is."

Like Jerrelle, Richard wasn't one for petty games. He walked up beside his friend and asked him the same questions that she had. "Where are you going?"

"Out!"

"Why?"

"Because!"

He looked at Jerrelle with a perturbed, blank stare on his face; she responded by extending both of her hands out to her sides.

Sabastian just stood there, laughing inside at the little effort it had taken for him to get under the skin of both of his friends. He thought about continuing, but decided not to; his fun was now over and it was time for him to get serious. "I'm sorry... I just could not resist intentionally frustrating you both."

"You know very well what I am capable of doing to you if you happen to piss me off. Do you not remember the last time you decided to speak before allowing your brain a chance to stop you from being a jackass?"

He did. And that day, Sabastian never expected that Jerrelle would hip toss him to the ground and apply a kimura lock. She didn't reef on it to the point where his arm would break, but she kept the pressure on it long enough for Sabastian to regret saying that she was more like a 'man' than a woman. He hadn't intended his words to come across the way they did; he only meant that she was just as tough as any man and didn't really act like a normal woman.

Unwittingly, Sabastian touched his left arm, as for a brief second, a phantom pain had reappeared — but as quickly as that had happened, his mind clued in to the fact that his memories of the jujitsu hold being placed upon him was what had triggered what he thought he was feeling. Hoping that no one had seen him briefly relive an embarrassing moment from his past, he returned his focus to the present. He then looked at Jerrelle and said; "I didn't know you then like I know you now. I've long since learned my lesson."

"Sure you have?" Jerrelle promptly cracked a sinister smile, letting Sabastian think that a day would surely come when she would have to do it again because of another momentary lapse in his better judgement.

Richard was now curious to hear what that piece of history was between the two. He was about to put his friend on the spot and pester him about it, but then he realized that if something embarrassing were to happen to him, he would prefer to never have the incident brought up or made fun of. Therefore, he decided to keep his mouth shut and instead, said, "So... are you going to tell us where you were headed, or are we going to continue this friendly standoff?"

"I wasn't actually headed anywhere. In fact, we are not going out this morning in search of information. At least, not until either Baylor or Savanna calls me back."

"You could have just said that in the first place."

"I know, but I wanted to see if you were really back to being your normal self, Jerrelle. I purposely acted the way I did to test you. And I'm happy to say that I see your hardened personality has officially returned to its normal state of existence."

"You know, Sab... you can be a jackass sometimes."

"We all have unique qualities that separate us from everyone else."

Richard just stood there and listened to the bantering that was going on. It may have seemed unnecessary to some, but he understood exactly what it was; two close friends who could say or do anything and never have to worry about ever really hurting the other. Just from that short exchange of words, he could tell that there was a bond there that wouldn't, and could never be broken — that was something he had to admire. "So if we are not going out today to search, I'm going to head down to the beach and grab some rays."

"Just keep your vid-cell handy. As soon as they call me back, we will get together and formulate a new search plan."

"I'm not going to the beach. I'm going to go have a beer."

"At nine o'clock in the morning?"

"Don't worry... I'll have my bowl of oatmeal with it."

After both Jerrelle and Richard left, Sabastian called for room service and had breakfast sent up; he was hungry and suspected that

202

this might end up being his one and only real meal of the day. And even though they were not going out this morning to physically search for the A.R.M. cell, he had a strong feeling that something was going to be learned by the end of the day that could help them locate what was supposedly here — by either his team back home in San Antonio or by happenstance.

———————————— ◯◯ ————————————

Louie woke up in the morning, happy that Maxwell Banks had not invaded his dreams again. Yesterday's disturbing experience still bothered him somewhat, almost to the point of becoming slightly paranoid. Fearing that another visit was imminent, he immediately went to his personal computer and spent time on the Internet looking for information about the possibility of ghosts haunting someone's dreams. With what he had found, Louie had to concede that the possibility was there that his old adversary was invading his mind during its most vulnerable period — then again, he also came across some information that suggested it simply could be his immense guilt that was behind these unwanted, haunting images. Either way, Louie wanted to find a way to prevent these disturbing occurrences from ever happening to him again.

He had thought about contacting and making an appointment to see a professional hypnotherapist, but he honestly believed those who practiced that kind of therapy were on the same level as those who sold snake oil. So instead, Louie arranged for a team of personal masseuses from the hotel to come up to his office and pamper him. Relaxation and the removal of stress was what he had hoped would be the solution to his psychological problem, not someone who by a few simple commands, took control over your mind and manipulated you like a puppet.

Forty-five minutes into his session, Louie felt himself dosing off, but he quickly snapped back to reality when he heard his office door open. The thought of Maxwell Banks walking in uninvitingly had promptly crossed his now relaxed mind, but he quickly dismissed that thought, remembering that his enemy was no longer alive. When he turned his head in order to see who it was, a smile of relief appeared on his face; his associates, Zhin and Nicoli, had returned.

Louie promptly ended his pampering session and instructed the masseuses to swiftly pack up their equipment and leave. While they were doing that, he got dressed. Not wanting to have to wait ten minutes or so for their privacy, Nicoli helped the massage team to pack up. While he was busy doing that, Zhin distributed the fresh sim-caf that he had brought with him for everyone.

After accepting his, Louie sunk back into his office chair and enjoyed his first sip. A minute or so later, the masseuses were gone and the office was theirs — he then intently listened as both Zhin and Nicoli give him their detailed report on everything that had happened in Puerto Rico. Not only was he happy with the results, but Louie was also impressed that his recent hire had been willing to use the S.M.A.R.T. technology that he possessed and had assimilated it into a car; an unmanned vehicle that did the dirty work for them.

Jason Hernandez was now dead, which left only one more loose end for him to tie up — Sabastian Banks. But then again, that was something that needn't be done right away. Louie had a basic plan already in place when it came to Maxwell's son, and the young man's immediate disposal was no longer priority one — retribution on Madelyn's behalf was what he wanted done next.

Zhin listened intently to what his boss was saying. And although it was not his place, or his nature to disagree with any given orders, he wasn't quite sure what the reasoning was behind the new assignment. "I have no problem doing whatever it is that you ask of me. I'm just unsure as to what this has to do with the organization."

"Once you and Nicoli complete this assignment, then the person that I am doing this favor for has agreed to do one for me in the near future."

"I have a question, if you don't mind?"

"What is it you want to know, Nicoli?"

"Do you want us to just send a message, or do you want us to leave a lasting impression?"

"I want you to send a message that is clear as day. That way, those who did what they did, will think twice about every doing it again. I know it may sound hypocritical of me, but the line they crossed is the one that I would never."

"Understood!" Zhin and Nicoli said near simultaneously.

Forty minutes later, and right after consuming a healthy brunch, Zhin and Nicoli were ready to leave for Chicago, but before they headed out on the road, Louie passed along the information that he had received the previous evening from his friend. Not only was Aldo Trivoli able to use the few connections that he still had at the university, he was able to supply much more information than what had been expected.

According to Louie's old business friend, there had been several reports of forced sexual occurrences over the past few years that all pointed in the direction of one fraternity at the University of Chicago — Sigma Del Phi. Yet, for some reason, all filed complaints were oddly withdrawn a few days later. It wasn't proof, but it was a coincidental pattern. Also, Louie had given Zhin a copy of the descriptions of those who had viciously assaulted Madelyn; the somewhat vague ones that she had given to him the day she first had asked for his help.

Although what they knew was not so apparent, Louie figured that he had assembled enough information for his two men to easily find those responsible for the heinous act they had committed against Madelyn Kinsworth and her fellow escort. Only following the completion of their assignment, could the first phase of his plan pertaining to the last of the loose ends, then commence.

Richard Atwater could hardly remember the lone vacation he and his father had taken when he was eight years old. Several opportunities had been there afterward, he recalled, but another vacation never happened. Once he turned eighteen, his life's direction had been chosen. The military was what was most important to him. Taking time off, he felt had no purpose. It just seemed like an unnecessary waste of valuable time and did not do anything to help him achieve his goals.

Like Sabastian's 'adopted' father Terrence Burelli had been, Richard was driven and determined to rise through the ranks of the military as fast as he possibly could — which was why he had been thrilled when Sabastian had asked him to be a part of this undercover mission, as an assignment such as this greatly increased his chances of another promotion — much sooner than it normally would come.

Technically, his morning alone on the beach in San Juan was not a real vacation, per se, but this would probably be the closest thing that he'd get to experiencing, as an adult, what one was actually like — after seven years of service, he was finally willing to take a little break. So he just lay there, soaked up the morning sun, and watched the incredible buffet of delicious eye candy as they walked along the shoreline in their 'should be illegal' swimwear.

He himself was in near perfect shape; this had caused a few of the ladies passing by to either pose a smile or take a hungry, indiscreet glance at him. Yes, it was shallow of him to allow himself to be ogled and drooled over like that, but this situation had never really happened to him before and Richard was going to enjoy every bit of being thought of as a sex object or an afternoon snack.

As noon was approaching, a hope came to him that the remainder of this day would also be his to enjoy. Strangely, he really wasn't in any hurry to return to his responsibilities and look for the A.R.M. — he was having too much fun watching the ladies walk by and doing absolutely nothing. He also realized one important thing. He had let his adult life become consumed by his drive for military prestige. And in doing so, he had ended up becoming oblivious to what else was out there in the world. He liked this little taste of freedom that he was now experiencing, and he wanted to sample more of it. He wasn't quite ready to put his military career on hold like Sabastian had, but he hastily had made a game-changing decision. From this moment forward, his plans were going to be altered. No, he wasn't going to forget about his long-term goals — he instead, was going to find a way to include in his life what else was out there for him to discover instead of just walking the path he had originally chosen to take.

As he sat there on his beach towel and stared out across the ocean, he reflected upon his life up until this point — he had no regrets whatsoever. He knew that his career choice came with some sacrifices, and he had missed many other great opportunities because of it — but no more was he willing to do so. It wasn't going to be easy, but he wanted to try and make up for some lost time. Therefore, when this current assignment of his was over, Richard was going to put in a request for an extended leave of absence and then take a tour of as many exotic places as his time off would allow. Then, when that was over, his batteries were either going to be fully recharged and he would be ready to resume his military career, or he would come to the realization that civilian life was what he wanted.

His never before tanned skin was now beginning to show signs of redness; sun block was something foreign to Richard, so he had just lain out there in the sun unprotected. After finally realizing his mistake, he stupidly thought that a quick dip in the ocean would help his now tender skin, so he got up and headed out into the water. The coolness of the water felt great; relief was instant. Unbeknownst to him though, the salt water that now coated his body only helped the sun to cook his skin even more.

Out of the corner of his eye, he saw the same pair of perfect redheaded sisters that he had seen earlier walk past him twice. Both ladies, who in Richard's opinion were hotter than the afternoon sun, had made their way together into the ocean roughly seventy feet away from where he currently was. *'I think that it's time I made my move on these two beauties. I'm gonna purposely swim over toward them and pretend that I didn't notice them like an oblivious fool.'* But just before he did that, he heard his vid-cell ringing on the beach. *'Damn! That better not be Sabastian.'*

By the time Richard had made his way back to where his beach towel was lying, his call had been missed. He looked at the screen and sure enough, it had been his old friend. For a moment, he thought about ignoring the call and going back out into the water, but reality quickly reminded him of why he was in Puerto Rico, so he called him back. "Sorry for missing your call. I was… distracted. What's up?" Richard didn't even need to hear his friend's reply to his question. He knew right away that his brief vacation was already over. So he disconnected his call, gathered up his belongings, and headed back to their hotel room. *'I knew that I should have intentionally left my vid-cell in the room — or buried it in the sand.'*

They spent about an hour putting together a game plan. With the information that Baylor and Savanna were able to gather for them, Sabastian, Jerrelle, and Richard, all felt confident that they were going to achieve their goal of locating the base cell of the American

Recovery Mission. However, once they did find what they were looking for, it was going to be somewhat tricky to completely shut down the group's operations. They had no backup, as it was just the three of them.

In order to increase their chances of success, it made sense to be patient and systematically take them apart. That strategy though, came with a big risk. They had no idea just how many cell locations there were, so they needed to figure out which one was the smallest, shut it down, move onto the next smallest, and then so on. It was going to be a time-consuming operation; one that would open the door to their presence in San Juan being discovered — but it was the only way each of them felt that they could safely complete their mission.

Once it was clear that everyone was on the same page, Sabastian contacted Sergeant Lopez. With him being one of the few Union soldiers who were in Puerto Rico, it made sense to ask him for some help — not to back them up with this, as it was a deadwood mission, but to set up a temporary holding cell for those whom they would capture until the prisoners' return to the Union could be arranged.

Once it had been explained to Santino what their mission was and what was needed from him, he immediately offered his services to his fellow brethren. Luckily, the man's family owned a small shipping company whose warehouse complex was not too far away from where one of the suspected A.R.M. cell locations were. He did however, inform Sabastian that he would need at least the remainder of the day to prep one of the warehouses for such a purpose as detention — and he also told him not to worry about the security of the warehouse, because he would bring as many men with him from the secret underground Union Military facility that he felt would be needed on that day to help secure the place.

Now feeling satisfied that everything was set, Sabastian opened up the hotel bar fridge and grabbed himself a beer. He walked outside onto the balcony and sat in the lone chair that was out there. Richard followed him outside a moment later, beer also in hand — one look at his friend and he could see that Sabastian was in deep thought.

"What's wrong there, bud?"

"Nothing really, I'm just anxious to get this assignment over with."

"So am I. Meanwhile, I have no qualms about taking advantage of every free moment that I have to enjoy the sites."

"You've only gone down to the beach."

"Oh trust me when I say, there was a lot of sites to take in." Richard then displayed a cheeky grin.

"Well then, I suggest that you quickly finish off your beer and go have some more fun. It won't be until tomorrow morning before we can begin to do what we came here to do."

"How come?"

"Santino needs the remainder of the day to prep a warehouse for us to use as a temporary holding facility."

"Oh, ok. Do you want to join me?"

"Where the hell are you going?" Jerrelle asked, as she stepped out onto the balcony.

"Sabastian just told me that we won't be going after the A.R.M. until tomorrow morning."

"Then where the hell are you going?"

"I'm not sure? I just thought about walking the main streets of the city for a while and checking out what Puerto Rico has to offer."

"That sounds good. Do you mind if I tag along?"

"You kids go and have some fun. Just remember not to get too drunk, as I want to start looking for the A.R.M. just after the morning sunrise."

"We'll be back by ten, Sab."

"You're welcome to come with us," Richard stated.

"I appreciate the invite, but I'm just gonna stay here. I want to call my grandmother and let her know that I'm all right. I also want to review our plan of attack and make sure that we haven't missed anything that could unintentionally fuck everything up for us."

Disappointed, but also understanding his reasons, Richard pounded back his beer and then both he and Jerrelle left the hotel. After his beer was finished, Sabastian spent just over an hour on his vid-cell. His first call was to Captain Swilling, as he wanted to bring his commanding officer up to date on their progress and subsequent plan; the man seemed very happy with the progress that had been

209

made, including their learning of a few possible A.R.M. cell locations. The captain then assured Sabastian that those who will end up being taken as prisoners would not be his responsibility once they were dropped off, as the necessary arrangements would instead be made by those who had authorized this covert mission to have them all discreetly transported back to the Union afterward.

Once his conversation with Captain Swilling was over, Sabastian placed a call to his uncle and then to his grandmother. He wanted to let each of them know that he was all right and that he would be home more than likely by the end of the week. Once those calls were completed, Sabastian changed into his swimming trunks and headed down to the beach.

He hadn't been there for more than two minutes before he realized that his head was spinning around like the character of Regan MacNeil in the exorcist; it was swiveling back and forth in directions that it wasn't meant to go. *'Well... Richard was certainly right. This beach is full of incredible 'sites'.'*

He almost felt guilty; not with the kinds of thoughts that were forming in his mind, but by his not doing anything constructive when it came to the assignment he was expected to complete. But there was nothing that he could do until everything was in place, so he liberally put on his sunscreen and just laid there watching the parade of scantily clad woman walk the shoreline — and he admittedly enjoyed every chauvinist moment of it.

When they walked out of their hotel room the next morning, a windowless, extra long grey van was parked out front — just like Santino had promised. And although the man was on their side, Jerrelle's suspicious nature insisted that they still be cautious, so she took out her vid-cell, turned on the bug sweeping app it had, and thoroughly checked the vehicle for any type of tracking or explosive device that may have been attached. Once she was satisfied that the van was clean, she opened up the side door and invited Sabastian and Richard to get in. Before they could object, she quickly made her way around to the driver's side door.

"What makes you think that you should be the one who drives?"

"(A) — You were just too damn slow at claiming the driver's seat. And (B) — I'd like to see you try to stop me, Sab."

Not wanting to waste time this morning over something so petty, he claimed the passenger seat — Richard entered the side door and sat in the back. It wasn't until they started down the road that it dawned on Sabastian that this arrangement actually made more sense, as it would be a lot harder for him to drive the van and look for the suspected A.R.M. cells at the same time.

Baylor had given him four potential locations in San Juan to investigate: two were privately owned buildings by Kenneth J. Harrisburg and the other two were owned by a long-time friend and former business associate of his, Paul Killingsworth. Mr. Killingsworth was a man who was at one time, the vice president of the second largest computer corporation in the former United States. Like Kenneth Harrisburg, Paul Killingsworth had been accused of and found guilty of a crime. The man had successfully embezzled a third of the company's profits over a fifteen-year period, only to be unexpectedly caught by an overzealous intern who brought her suspicions to the company's chief operating officer.

It didn't take the three of them long to find the first place that they had been looking for. By the appearance of the outside of the building, it looked as if it had once been an art studio, as the entire facade was covered in different kinds of cultural murals. You can't always see the forest for the trees; that was an idiom that Sabastian and Richard always tended to use. Being a part of the S.N.A.F.U. meant that they could never take anything for granted. Just because the outside of this building looked like it was one thing, didn't mean that it was that. So they parked their van just past the building, got out, and the three of them took a brief tour around the perimeter. With no windows except for the ones in the front of the building, and no outside mounted cameras, they knew that this place was going to be easy for them to secure. That didn't mean though, that what they were about to do was going to be a walk in the park — they needed to be cautious until everything was firmly in their control.

With their immediate surroundings now familiar, Richard returned to the van and pulled it around to the back alley to cover the exit; Sabastian and Jerrelle waited a few moments and then walked through the front door, posing as tourists.

Upon entering the front of the building, the only thing that they saw was an empty room; empty except for the half a dozen or so rolled up sleeping bags and pillows that were on the floor and tucked into a corner. Sabastian's initial suspicions told him that this place may just be a makeshift hostel or mission — but Jerrelle had her own suspicions, and they were nowhere near what her friend's were.

Within a few moments, their attention was quickly drawn to a young lady, not of Puerto Rican decent, as she walked into the room; she had appeared from a center hallway that looked as if it lead right to the back of the building. "You must be the two newbie's that we are expecting?"

A slight smile broke across Jerrelle's face, as her suspicions seemed to be spot on. This, she believed, was a recruitment center for the A.R.M.; a place where people who wanted to be a part of the American Recovery Mission's cause came to be assessed, scrutinized, and then educated on the objective of the group.

The situation they had just walked into couldn't be more straightforward. The information they came looking for; learning exactly where the other cells in the city were, as well as exactly where the A.R.M. headquarters was at, should be easy for them to extract from this unsuspecting subordinate. "Um... yes we are. But before we commit to your cause, we have a couple of questions we'd like answered first."

The recruiter looked at them a bit confused. No one had come to join the A.R.M. and had asked questions before committing, as they generally knew already why they had come there in the first place. "I... I suppose. I'll do my best to answer your questions. What would you like to know?"

"How many people are here in this building right now?" Sabastian asked.

The recruiter looked puzzled by Sabastian's strange question, but answered it anyway. "Normally there are six of us here processing the new recruits. Four are currently not here though, as they have gone out to gather us some supplies."

"So then… what would you do if someone came in here with a gun?" Jerrelle and Sabastian both looked at each other, and without another word having to be said, drew their weapons. "As you can see, that is what we have. So I ask you again, what would you do if someone came in here with a gun?"

It became obvious to the two of them that the recruiter had never expected something like this to ever happen. She clearly hadn't been trained nor had she any idea as to how to handle a situation such as this — which was what they both knew they could exploit.

Confidently, Jerrelle took two steps forward, keeping her gun at a level so that the recruiter could easily see it. She then ordered her to sit down on the ground over against the east wall. Once the woman was where she had wanted her, Sabastian walked down the same hallway that the recruiter had exited from, searching for the other person who was supposed to be in the building; it didn't take him long to find a young black man sitting at a desk in a makeshift office at the back of the building.

After ordering the man to get up, Sabastian walked him out to the front lobby area, brought him over to where the recruiter was sitting, and told him to join her on the floor. He then opened up his supply pack, removed a few heavy-duty zip ties, and handed them over to Jerrelle so that she could bind the hands of the two A.R.M. members together behind their backs.

While she was securing their first two prisoners, Sabastian removed his vid-cell from his front pocket and called Richard. He informed him of their situation and then asked him to keep an eye out for the eventual return of the remaining four members of the A.R.M.

Twenty minutes later, Richard called Sabastian back to let him know that the other four were now returning. After disconnecting his call, he made his way toward the front of the building, careful as he did this not to let the four A.R.M. members know of his presence in the area. Yes, they technically were outnumbered, but Richard wasn't worried. His team would have the inside covered and he had the front guarded. Anyone possibly making a break for it out the back of the recruitment center would find that decision of theirs to be a mistake, as he had nudged their van right up against the back exit door of the building, just before he abandoned it to keep watch.

This had been by far the easiest sting operation that any of them had ever been on. Mind you, their prisoners had turned out to be a pencil pusher, a computer geek, and recruiters — not soldiers, mercenaries, or terrorists. Nevertheless, they were a part of the A.R.M. and surely they had to know something.

After they were all loaded into the cargo van, Jerrelle drove it to their makeshift holding cell. There, Richard and Sabastian escorted the prisoners into the warehouse; Jerrelle decided to stay behind in the vehicle. It's not like she wasn't able to help, but she was no longer a military officer so the extracting of what could end up being sensitive information, technically could not be done by her — or so that was her argument.

Thirty minutes later, they had acquired all of the information they felt they needed, including exactly how many members of the A.R.M. that were currently in Puerto Rico, confirmation on the other locations they had suspected, and where the base camp was located.

With this now in hand, Sabastian and Richard exited their makeshift holding facility, leaving the prisoners in the capable hands of Santino and his fellow Union soldiers, and joined Jerrelle back in their van. They then promptly took off to roundup the thirty members of the A.R.M. that were equally dispersed between two other Puerto Rican satellite cell locations. By early evening, their capture had been completed.

Now came the difficult part of their mission — invading the base camp. There was a very good chance that the A.R.M. was now aware of what had been taking place this day, so a surprise assault was probably not going to happen. The base facility also probably had some serious security measures protecting it. That was something that they would have to figure out and then determine a way around. They also did not know how many members of the A.R.M. were stationed there, or if the head of the A.R.M. was even present. All that they knew was that this was why they had come to Puerto Rico, and they had to do what was necessary to ensure that any potential or future planned terrorist attacks against the Union, did not happen. If this mission cost them their lives, then they died protecting their country. Even Jerrelle would accept death in this situation, as it would be her own way of making amends for having disgraced the uniform and being dishonorably discharged because of it.

This last raid was going to be much more difficult than what they had first anticipated. Unlike the other three cell locations, the A.R.M. base camp was located just outside the city limits. The landscape that surrounded the two-story stone structure was very distinctive, insofar that each side of it had its own unique characteristics. East and west of the property, the somewhat rocky terrain gradually graded upward to a height of about fifty feet, and then it tapered off flat. The front, north side of the property was also tapered upward, but it was only about half as high. At the top of the front, there sat a manmade burm. Right in the middle of that berm, was a ten-foot gate that gave access to the property — and at the back south side of the building, sat a dense grouping of not overly tall trees that was equal in distance away from the house as what the front burm was.

To the three of them, it was plainly obvious that this location for the cell's base camp headquarters was strategically chosen because of the unique terrain surrounding it — not for the beauty of it, but for the natural shaping of the area. It easily allowed the terrorist group to feel safe in their surroundings due to the rugged landscape of the natural U-shaped hillsides and the wide open area between it and the house — a sneak attack would be near impossible for an enemy to conduct. Likewise, with the thick woodland area behind it, navigating through from the backside would be an exhausting task, as it was roughly two kilometers long. Undoubtedly, the A.R.M. would have set numerous, unsuspecting traps throughout, assuming that an approaching adversary would be more focused on their trek through it instead of what could be awaiting them within the area.

Unlike their three previous engagements, their plan this time around was to conduct this last part of their mission the same as they would any surgical military assault: distract, confuse, and surprise. However, due to the unfriendly landscape in front of their target, their only option appeared to be a long distance strike. For that to work, they first had to wait for the sun to completely set. Total darkness would also allow Jerrelle to move into position and furtively set up their initial diversion. And so long as the perimeter wasn't protected with motion sensors, or some other kind of unsuspecting trap, everything they had planned should go off without a hitch.

Jerrelle had a basic knowledge of explosives; that skill of hers hadn't been learned during her time in the military, as it was something that she had educated herself on during her mischievous teenage years. Neither Sabastian nor Richard was really comfortable when it came to anything volatile, so she gladly volunteered for this part of their operation. After all, it had been a good year before she had joined the military that she had last blown something up intentionally, and she was looking forward to doing it again, but for the right reasons this time.

After carefully navigating the down slope of the eastside hill, she cautiously headed about twenty feet into the woods. Once she had found the ideal spot, she removed a block of C4 from her bag of goodies, attached a remote detonator to it, and then carefully, she set it down at the base of a somewhat rotting tree — there was really no need for her to do this, but the tree was almost dead anyway. She then headed toward the western side of the woods to bury another block, but before she got even halfway to where she wanted to go, she stopped. Their mission almost ended at that moment. Cleverly hidden amongst leaves and the twigs on the ground was a snare. Had she stepped one foot further, Jerrelle would be hanging upside down from a ceiba tree.

After cursing under her breath, she did what she knew she should not — she just hoped that with her being as far back from the front tree line as she was, what she was about to do, would not be seen. To ensure that there was no more unsuspecting traps on the ground or in the trees themselves, Jerrelle used the light function on her vid-cell to illuminate the way. Once she got to where she wanted to go, she attached a remote detonator and then she set it down on top of an ant hill — her mischievous teenage ways had apparently never completely left her. After that, she headed about fifty feet deeper into the woods and stopped only when she had found a tree large enough in diameter for her to take shelter behind. Now, she just had to wait until it was the right time to use the app she had on her vid-cell to trigger the explosives and light up the night.

Sabastian and Richard stealthily maneuvered to the front burms and each found a concealed position, about one hundred feet apart from each other. Near simultaneously, they opened up their bag of goodies, removed a Beretta CNML 86-B; an air compressed mini scud launcher, and then loaded them with tear gas grenades. Once they were both ready, they strategically aimed their weapons at the two lower front windows of the stone structure. Now that everything was set, patience was needed — soon enough, the right moment would come.

At nine p.m., Sabastian sent Jerrelle a brief text, letting her know that it was time. The sky lit up a few seconds later, the ground shook, and the distraction that they had wanted, had worked. The lights inside the A.R.M. headquarters immediately turned on, illuminating the entire property.

With his long range night visual enhancers pulled over his eyes, Sabastian could clearly see through the front windows of the building — those who were inside the house were now haphazardly moving toward the back; everyone was curious to find out what the hell had just happened.

The plan was to wait ten seconds after the detonation of the C4 before they began phase two. They didn't even have to look at each other to make sure that they were on the same page, as both Sabastian and Richard fired their Berettas in sequence, sending both scuds of military grade tear gas through each of the front lower windows. They then quickly reloaded and each sent another scud into the upper level front windows.

Panic ensued, as those inside the building scrambled for the front and back exits. Like what would happen when disturbing a beehive, they all exited. Unlike how bees would be though, they were not angry — they instead, all had their hands across their mouths and were coughing. So far, their plan was working to perfection.

Now it was time for them to have some fun. Sabastian, Richard, and Jerrelle all left their positions; each with a portable breathing apparatus dangling against their chest, and made their way toward their targets. With their compressed air handguns aimed at the confused members of the A.R.M., one at a time, they began to pick them off with the corncob tranquilizer darts. The closer they made it to the stone building, the more sleeping bodies on the ground they stepped over. Less than two minutes later, there were twenty tranquilized bodies that lay strewn across the property and out for the night.

Those, they knew, weren't all of them, so they put on their gas masks, entered the structure, and searched it. Three minutes after that, the last ten members of the radical group had been neutralized.

With what now seemed to be their biggest obstacle out of the way, each armed with everything that they may need, Sabastian, Richard, and Jerrelle conducted a thorough search of both levels. Upon completion, they found the place to be rather sparse of any materialistic items as well as disappointingly, nothing that could be used as incriminating evidence.

The inability to find the smoking gun wasn't all that discouraging; they had after all, captured thirty more suspected terrorists. Nevertheless, it would have been nice had they been able to at least solidify the reasoning for this mission.

The only thing left for them to do now, was to clean up their mess. Sabastian was just about to call Santino and inform him of their pending arrival and delivery of thirty more prisoners when Jerrelle accidently discovered a trap door that was in the floor of the back closet next to the kitchen. Unlike the one she had luckily discovered in England, this one had a complex locking mechanism on it.

Before Sabastian or Richard could even suggest a way that they might get past the lock, Jerrelle had set her compressed air handgun down on the shelf in the closet, dug into her backpack of goodies, and removed two Ex-Co patches from it. After ripping one of them in half, she placed both pieces over each hinge, and then placed the other one completely over the lock. Within ten seconds, the complex locking mechanism and the hinges were no more.

Carefully, she removed the access door and stepped aside, allowing Richard to go first. He stood at the foot of the old wooden, rather steep stairs; a gun in each of his hands (one had bullets and one had the corncob darts), and then he slowly made his way down the stairs. Sabastian went next, followed by Jerrelle.

Unlike the other two, she didn't enter the basement with a gun in each hand; she instead, left it clipped to her hip and removed her honor blade. The badass that she was known to be, relished an opportunity whenever present, to fight hand-to-hand instead of simply shooting someone with a gun. To her, there was no honor in that type of victory.

The basement smelled rather musty and was dimly lit with overhead lights that looked to be from the early twentieth century — you could easily tell that it was dug out as an afterthought once the place had been built. After all three of them had made it to the bottom of the stairs and were able to determine that the air was breathable, they removed their portable breathing apparatuses and set them down onto the floor — they then cautiously moved forward. Off to the right, they noticed a rather narrow hallway where a small wooden door at the end of it, caused curiosity to appear in each. Once they got to it, Richard brought his leg up and was just about to attempt to kick it down when Jerrelle stopped him. She then removed her vid-cell and brought up her latest security-detecting app — it was a good thing that she did as she instantly saw that it had identified the door as being booby-trapped.

Richard exhaled some relief; his eagerness could have cost them their lives. Inexplicably, he had forgotten his training and almost blindly barreled right through the door — maybe this near mistake was the first clear sign that it was time for him to step away from his military life for a while and take some time to actually smell the roses instead of just looking at them.

In all reality, this mission had been a success. If only Kenneth Harrisburg or Paul Killingsworth had been one of the thirty individuals that were now currently asleep and waiting to be transported to their holding facility, then Sabastian probably wouldn't feel as let down as he did. He had hoped that by the end of this day, his services were no longer going to be called upon, but unless what was behind the door in front of them gave them the hard evidence they sought, another day would come in which he was going to be needed. "What are the chances that Harrisburg and Killingsworth are hiding behind that..?"

'Click! Click!'

No one needed to say a word because they all recognized that sound. Slowly, they all turned around to look down the hallway from which they came and saw two men walking toward them with guns drawn.

"Don't be stupid! Toss your weapons out in front of you and drop down to your knees. I don't know who you are, but you have made a very big mistake."

All three of them complied and set down their weapons, never taking their eyes off of the two men who had their guns pointed at them. "It doesn't really matter who we are, Senator."

"Ah… So you know who I am."

"I would bet that these three are the reason why we can't get a hold of anyone at our other three cells," Paul Killingsworth said. "I think that we should just kill them now and get this over with." The man intently aimed his gun at Jerrelle; the one that he incorrectly assumed would be the most vulnerable of the three.

"Be patient, Paul. Don't forget what's behind that door. If you fire and miss, you could end up accidently blowing us all to smithereens."

"Why do you want to liberate the Union?" Sabastian asked.

"It's not so much that I want to liberate the Union. I just tell the world that is what the A.R.M. is all about. I only really want to pay back all those fucking government officials who stuck their noses where they didn't belong."

"You were one of them at one time… and I'm sure you did the same thing," Richard said, accusingly.

Kenneth knew he was a hypocrite, but he didn't care, as his own interests were all that mattered. And now that there was a very good chance the Union government was aware of his plans, it no longer made sense to him to go through with them. "You were responsible for what happened in Tijuana, weren't you?"

Sabastian could not help but produce a smile.

"Well then… all thanks to you, I am now forced to scrap my initial plans and go with my back-up… which by the way, is a bit more drastic than what I had planned for the G8 conference."

"Attacking that conference sounds pretty drastic to me," Richard stated.

"It is. But since Paul and I now seem to be the only ones left from our organization that can complete our objective, it only makes sense to do something that will all but force those governmental bastards to comply with our demands."

"What exactly are your intentions?" Sabastian asked.

"I intend to blow up Wall Street."

"What?" Sabastian and Richard said simultaneously.

"You truly are crazy!" Jerrelle declared.

"Actually, I'm not. It was Paul's idea… and a brilliant one at that, I must say. There's nothing like another 9-11 to grab the world's attention. And since you all know what we are now planning on doing, we obviously can't let you leave here. So why don't all of you just close your eyes now, count to ten, and pray… because ten seconds is all the time that you have left on this earth to make peace with whatever religious entity you submit to."

They were cornered with no way out. If they were out in the open, then it might be possible to win this fight. They could rush the two men and hope that their numbers would at least prevent one of them from taking a fatal bullet, or they could simply end it all right there and force open the wired door behind them. Sabastian didn't mind sacrificing his life for his country, but he had a problem doing it in order to stop two crazy and insane men.

The three of them looked at each other and knew that it was over. They had gotten themselves into another no-win situation. This time, neither Sabastian nor Jerrelle thought that they had a chance in hell of surviving. If ever a miracle were to happen, now would be a perfect time for one.

"One… Two… Three…" As Kenneth and Paul were counting, they made their way behind their three captives. It's not that they wanted to kill them this way, a bullet to the back of the head, but they didn't want to take a chance of an accidental wayward bullet hitting the door behind them. "Six… Seven… Eight… Nine… Ten…"

Nothing happened — except for the sound of two bodies hitting the floor. Unsure what it was that had just taken place, Sabastian hesitantly opened up his eyes; he fully expected to see that both of his friends were dead — they weren't. What he saw behind him instead was Kenneth Harrisburg and Paul Killingsworth — they were lying on the floor and sound asleep.

Befuddled was beyond what Sabastian was; he couldn't figure out what the hell had just happened. "Open your eyes, Jerrelle... Richard! I don't know what just..." Sabastian was shocked. Out of the shadows stepped an individual he never in a million years expected to see — a pleasing smile was on her face and a just fired weapon now rested down by her side. "So... which one of you knew that I was coming and left me their air gun on that shelf at the top of the stairs?"

"We ah... I ah... never left it there for you on purpose."

"You know, Jerrelle. I kinda like these three pronged dart thingies."

"What are you doing here, Sharice? And... how did you know where I was?"

"Like I told you before, cuz.., I will be there whenever you need me."

The first time Jerrelle had seen Sharice she had held open a cab door for her and had no idea that she was Sabastian's first cousin. She only knew that she had an immediate physical attraction — now she had a completely different feeling toward her. Again, she had been in the right place at the right time to save their asses — for that reason, Jerrelle had just gained a whole new respect for this mysterious beauty. "I'm glad that you came... but now I owe you my life two times over."

"I'm sure you'll repay me one day, Jerrelle."

Richard was thankful as well, though his curiosity was now focused on the door behind them. He studied it for a moment to see if there was some way to disarm the security that was attached to the door. "I have a question. Does anyone have an idea as to how we might be able to disarm this wired door? I am sure that I am not the only one here who is curious to see what is on the other side."

"I can take a look." Sharice walked over to the door and studied it, and then she studied the readings that Jerrelle had taken with the app on her vid-cell. "I believe that I can defuse it, but this is a very complex piece of work. It could take me anywhere from thirty minutes to several hours to do so."

"Take your time, Sharice. We'll start zip tying and loading up all those tranquilized bodies into our van so that we can take them to our holding area."

Just over an hour later, Sabastian's cousin had successfully bypassed the wired door. He, Richard, and Jerrelle had kept themselves busy during that time, thankfully under the cover of darkness, making several trips with their unconscious prisoners to their makeshift holding complex. By the time they were ready to take their last trip, Sabastian stayed behind in order to help Sharice investigate the contents of the room — and like they had hoped, it contained explosives and every kind of military weaponry imaginable; all of it more than likely had been stolen from multiple Union depots. "So… why did you come here looking for me?"

"I had just wrapped up a deal of sorts in Miami when I had thought about going to visit you in San Antonio. However, since you had texted me inquiring about some information, I knew that you were up to something that could be dangerous and thought that you might need my help. So I called your uncle Sydney and he told me that you had been recalled by the Union Military and had been sent here to Puerto Rico… but that was all he knew."

"Still.., how did you find me?"

"Sergeant Lopez. His father and my mother were 'friends'. Whenever my mother would get some time off, either she would come here to Puerto Rico and spend time with Santino's father, or he would come to England. Nothing serious ever came from it; they both just enjoyed each other's company. That is how I first met Santino. I've known him ever since I was about ten years old. And because I knew that he had chosen to remain a part of the Union Military and what his posting was with them, I gave him a call. He had confirmed that you were indeed here in Puerto Rico and that you were on an undercover assignment."

"Santino doesn't know exactly where I am."

"He gave me the frequency of the tracking signal on the van he had lent to you."

"What tracking signal?" Jerrelle asked as she and Richard returned to find Sharice and Sabastian snooping through the contents of the room. "I swept the entire van when we first got it and I found it clean."

"The tracker on the van has the latest frequency sweep detection system shielding on it; plus the tracker stays dormant until it is needed. Using one of the Union's military satellites, Santino sent out a signal and turned on the tracker. He then gave me the frequency to track your van."

"I'm gonna have to have my tech friend update my app to look for frequency sweep detection system shielding now. I don't like being followed."

"But if Sharice hadn't tracked us down then we'd all be dead now."

"I don't know about you, Jerrelle, but I'm glad that she showed up," Richard said as he too began to curiously look at the rather large assortment of weapons that were in the room. "I guess we'll be here all night loading up these stolen weapons and bringing them back home where they belong."

"And how do you expect to get them all past customs?" Jerrelle asked.

"I don't know.., but we just can't leave them here."

"We will load them into the van and then bring them over to Santino at the secret depot," Sabastian stated. "I'm fairly certain that these weapons came from one of our military's storage facilities, so the depot is the only logical place for us to bring them."

Five minutes into the process of loading all of the weapons into the van, Richard saw a single small piece of paper lying on top of a small makeshift desk up against the wall. "Hey, bud! I found something rather odd. Do you have any idea what these two sets of numbers could be?"

Sabastian took a closer look at the paper and was unsure of what the numbers could be for — except he did notice that both sets coincidently began with 313. When Jerrelle re-entered the room a few minutes later to grab another box of weapons, Sabastian showed the paper to her. She looked at it and immediately knew that both numbers were not random, but actual phone numbers for the City of Detroit.

"Where's Sharice?"

"Like before, she couldn't stay. But she did tell me something interesting while we were outside."

"I don't understand why she likes to disappear before I can say goodbye?"

"I don't either, but she did say before she left that she had hoped to find me here with you so she could tell me personally that she had found out Nicoli, Helfred's brother, had gone rogue and left the E.C.L. — which I actually started to think might have been possible shortly after Jason Hernandez' death."

"The E.C.L.? What is that, another terrorist group?" Richard asked.

"No, um… They are sort of an activist-type of group. I'm sure that Jerrelle will tell you more about them later. But right now, I'd like to get this room emptied before sunrise."

It took them about two hours to finish loading the remaining weapons into the van. Now the hard part was to move those weapons all the way to the secret depot without drawing anyone's suspicions — which was going to be hard for them to accomplish, seeing that the van's shocks were compressed down almost all the way to the top of the tires.

After they had successfully returned the van full of the confiscated weapons to the secret depot, Santino gave them a ride back to their hotel. By midday, the three of them were on another cruise ship and headed back home. This time, Jerrelle was prepared for the trip with a forty of Jack Daniels, a two-liter bottle of coke, and a large bottle of Gaviscon.

10

As with the typical summer climate in Berlin, Germany, rain continued sporadically throughout the day. Those who lived there were more than used to it; Nicoli for some reason though, loathed it. Many times throughout his early adult life he had thought about leaving this continuously depressing weather that bombarded his homeland. Sun, sand, and paradise was the kind of lifestyle that he dreamed about living — but he was a proud German and he loved his family very much. So for those two reasons alone, he chose to deal with the unpleasant environment as best as he could.

Helfred had just been granted a two-week leave from the service and today he was scheduled to come home. It had been more than a year since Nicoli had seen him and he just could not wait to share the news he had with his baby brother. And if all went according to plan, Helfred no longer would be missing from his everyday life.

Nicoli met him at the train station and immediately embraced him — the way only close brothers would. Almost immediately, he could sense that there was something different about his younger brother. This past year had somehow changed Helfred — and Nicoli was both curious and eager to find out what it was. However, his brother wasn't forthcoming. He instead, just brushed it off and denied that anything had happened to him while he was away. But Nicoli wasn't that stupid — he knew that something was different and he was bound and determined to find out what it was.

Yes, Helfred was being unusually difficult, but not even this atypical crappy weather could put a damper on their reunion. Therefore, Nicoli decided to take him to their favorite watering hole, 'The Weimar Club' and see if a few pints would cause his brother to slip up and divulge what it was that he was hiding. The place wasn't much to look at, but it had been the establishment in which both brothers had experienced alcohol for the first time, each at the ripe *young age of sixteen. Of course, that had only happened because the owner of the pub was their mother's first cousin.*

Two pints into their reunion and Nicoli decided to press his brother once again for the information he sought. But just like before, Helfred had stood his ground. It wasn't his plan to get his brother drunk right after he had returned home, but Nicoli was bound and determined to find out what it was that had changed in him — so he ordered another round, and then another. A few sips short of finishing off pint number four, Helfred had finally let it slip, admitting to his brother that things had indeed changed. His life had taken an unexpected turn two months earlier, as he had met his soul mate.

This revelation wasn't what Nicoli had expected. A promotion was more like it, but a girl — this was bad. That was the kind of obstacle that would undoubtedly ruin what he had planned. Helfred had less than a year to go before his initial commitment to the German military would be complete, and when that day came, Nicoli had wanted his brother to step away and officially close that chapter of his life. The plan was to then bring him into the fold and have him become a member of the E.C.L.— and now, that want of his was seriously in jeopardy of ever happening.

Even though Nicoli had never once hinted what he one day intended to do, Helfred had suspected that an invite would soon be coming. Joining the E.C.L. was surely an alluring proposition, but he enjoyed being in the military and was seriously thinking about signing on for another five years once his current commitment had ended. What made things even more difficult for him though, was that there was a known roadblock in his way. With whatever decision he made, that would first have to be addressed. There was a pending issue that he knew he would soon have to face/fight pertaining to his military career. If he decided to follow in his brother's footsteps and join the E.C.L., the situation would be similar and in all likelihood, Jerrelle was going to have to be let go from his life.

That unwanted inevitability nevertheless, was something that his brother need not become aware of. In Helfred's mind, a chance at his own happiness was more important than his older brother's. He hated it, but if Nicoli asked him the question he expected, he was going

227

to have to do what he honestly did not want to — break his brother's heart.

"Listen, Helfred. I certainly hope that you don't allow a relationship with a woman to nudge you off of the path that you should be taking. I mean.., you've never committed more than three days to someone before. What makes this one any different than those other brief flings you've had?"

"I was hoping that you would at least try and be happy for me, Nic. I honestly never thought that I'd find someone that I would want to spend the rest of my life with... but I really think that she could be the one."

"Well.., I'm not happy. I just assumed that you'd finish your military obligations and then join the E.C.L. with me. And you know that can't be done if you are attached to a typical housewife."

There it was. Although Nicoli had not officially asked him, his intent was now known. "Trust me... she won't be a typical housewife."

"Then what will she be?"

"She'll be everything I've always wanted, and more."

"Listen, Helfred. There isn't a woman in Germany, military or not, who'd be able to fully understand and accept what the E.C.L. is all about if you were to ever join."

"I never said that she was from Germany."

"Then where is she from?"

"The Ameri-Can Union"

Nicoli nearly spit out his beer. He wasn't about to let some hybrid American dumb blond, big-breasted bimbo, poison his brother's mind with false hopes and dreams. So for the next ten minutes, he didn't let his brother get a word in edgewise as he read Helfred the riot act. There was no way that he was going to let his brother ruin his life and he was going to do everything in his power to make sure that he understood that.

He loved his brother, but it finally got to a point where Helfred had enough. He was either going to punch out his brother right there inside the Weimar Club, or he was going to just walk away. And since he didn't want to cause a scene in their family bar, so he got up off his bar stool, put on his jacket, and headed for the exit. Nicoli followed *right behind him, only to be quickly halted by Helfred's cold and piercing stare at the threshold. One look into his brother's eyes and again Nicoli could see a change. This time he saw pure anger — it was something that he had never seen before from his younger sibling.*

Helfred didn't say a word... all that he did was get into a cab and head back to the train station. Nicoli was furious: at himself and at this woman who had poisoned his brother with thoughts of unattainable happiness. He was never going to forget about what she had done to his brother and promised himself that the day would come when he would send her a message; a message that would ruin her life the same way it was ruining Helfred's. And of course, that message now would only be intensified because Nicoli blamed Jerrelle for his brother's unwarranted death — and he wasn't going to wait much longer to make her pay.

Nicoli woke up just as they had arrived at the Chicago City limits. His dream had brought to the surface his contempt for Jerrelle Dakota Robinson. If she hadn't walked into his brother's life, then Helfred, he firmly believed, would still be alive, right by his side, and part of the E.C.L. with him. Now Nicoli wasn't part of the Liberation anymore either. He was going to kill Jerrelle and leaving behind what he loved being a part of was a sacrifice that he had to make in order to accomplish what he emphatically believed, had to be done. What made this necessary task difficult though, was that his enemy's half-sister, Bai Lin, was also a long-time associate and friend of his. He had no desire to hurt her, but if she just happened to get in the way of his personal mission, then so be it. He was glad that she had not been seriously hurt during his first attempt at killing Jerrelle. The next time however, if Bai Lin happened to be close like before, her unnecessary death likely would be the result of his actions.

When they finally arrived in the residential community for the students of the University of Chicago, it was just past eight in the evening. Zhin Wi had pulled their car up in front of the frat house in question and he immediately could see that there was quite a bit of activity going on. He didn't mind being the muscle for Louie once in a while, as it kept his skills sharp, but Zhin wanted to be one hundred percent sure that his intended targets were the correct ones. He didn't like making mistakes, and mistakes could easily be made when there were multiple, innocent individuals in the way. He knew that he had to be sure of who each of the accused were before he sent them the message that Louie had wanted delivered, because what he hated more than anything was cleaning up a rather large mess that should not have been made in the first place.

Both carrying concealed weapons of their choice, Zhin and Nicoli left their car and approached the frat house. Neither wanted to raise any suspicions the moment they entered the residence, so they each brought with them a few bottles of booze, trying to blend in with the sea of arriving party goers.

Once they were both inside, Zhin approached a young woman; more than likely a fellow student at the college, and asked her if she knew where the head of the frat house might be. Luckily for him, she knew who and where he was. He respectfully thanked the young lady for the information and then went up the stairs to the back bedroom; Nicoli followed only a few steps behind. When he opened up the door, the first thing he saw were two naked people doing what naked people usually do. Of course, the fully exposed man wasn't happy that his fun had just become a public spectacle, so he sprung up off of the bed, junk freely hanging loose, squared up his shoulders, and looked Zhin in the eyes as he heaved a stern visual warning his way for him to immediately leave the room. Yes, the young man was rather tall and large; more than likely a football player or wrestler, but his size was irrelevant to Zhin.

Without enough time passing for a word to be exchanged between the two of them, the man suddenly decided to back off his stance and deflate his ego — only because a man, much larger and meaner looking than he was, joined the stranger in his room.

Once he was sure that his weapon had been clearly seen, Nicoli closed the door behind him and asked in a rather stern, demanding tone, "Are you the head of this frat house?"

"Um… yes I am," replied the now nervous naked man.

"Good! Get dressed. We have an issue that needs to be sorted out."

Zhin could see the panic that was beginning to surface from the young, naive woman who had been sharing the bed with the head of the frat house. She wasn't his concern, yet he could see that she could end up being a problem if he didn't calm her down. "You have nothing to be afraid of, miss. Our issue is not with you. As soon as you get dressed, you can leave this house, so long as you keep quiet as to what is going on here."

She nodded her head in compliance. She might not have been smart enough to realize who she was willing to open up her legs for, but she was smart enough to know when to keep her mouth shut. So after hastily getting dressed, she exited the room, and promptly headed down the stairs.

Once the girl was gone, Zhin reviewed the images in his mind that Louie had passed along to him — and sure enough; the head of this frat house looked a lot like one of the supposed 'guilty' parties. "What I need from you little man is for you to follow us out of this room and have everyone in this place, who is not a member of this fraternity, leave immediately. And don't be stupid, because my associate is not the only one with a weapon at his disposal."

The head of the frat house finished getting dressed and complied with Zhin's order. He walked down the stairs; followed closely behind by Zhin and Nicoli. Two steps before he got to the bottom of the stairs, he stopped and promptly grabbed everyone's attention with a high-pitched whistle; a series of unexpected words then came out of his mouth, "The party is over! Everyone who doesn't live here, get the fuck out!" The room was filled with stunned people at first, but they soon all realized that the head of the frat house was serious — everyone who had come to have a good time, quickly complied and emptied the place.

Once the last person left, Nicoli closed the door behind them, and then he locked it. This now left twelve frat brothers standing inside the living room area of the residence; all of which were a bit unsure as to why the head of their fraternity had put a sudden stop to their biweekly party, and who the two unknown men were that were still present.

Zhin and Nicoli stood in front of the group and looked them over; some of them looked like the type to actually do what they were being accused of, and some looked like little lost dogs that had to be led around by a leash. Eight of them had partaken in the 'incident' that

Louie had wanted resolved; four of them were innocent — this was an unforeseen issue that Zhin wasn't too sure he could figure out.

Although he didn't know his new partner all that well, Zhin got the feeling that Nicoli would have probably just punished all twelve of the frat brothers for the committed crimes — but he was not like that. He could be cold and callus whenever he wanted to, but he also had a conscience and would rather not hurt someone who didn't deserve it. Should the other four be considered guilty by association? That was a question that Zhin had to quickly deliberate over, as the last thing he wanted was to waste more time than was necessary trying to figure out whom exactly should be punished and who should not be. "One quick thing before we get down to business. There was an initiation about a week ago that involved two escorts. Those of you that did not partake in that initiation, please give me a show of hands." As expected, not one of the frat brothers did what he asked. Solidarity was part of being a member of a fraternity, and Zhin could at least respect that. "I expected everyone to stick together. Sometimes though, you will come across a situation where you need to worry about yourself and your own wellbeing instead of your friends... and this is one of those times."

While Zhin was trying to determine who should stay and who could go, Nicoli had taken a quick tour of the main floor of the frat house, making sure that all the doors and windows were closed, locked, and all the blinds were shut. Once that was done, Nicoli returned to the living room area and stood behind the group of frat brothers, just in case any of them might think about attempting an escape — that would be a stupid mistake on their part.

"I'm sure you're all wondering why we are here and what we want. Well, we were sent here because eight of you decided that it would be cool to viciously rape two escorts... one of whom is a good friend of our boss. And for those of you who are curious, our boss is the head of the Detroit Underworld Organization." Zhin paused for a moment to let this revelation sink in — and sure enough, he could hear some nervous rumblings amongst the frat brothers. "And so that all of you do understand what I had just said to you, I'll repeat myself using plain English — you idiots went and pissed off a mob boss!"

232

That got their attention, as the four innocent frat brothers immediately spoke up, hoping that it wasn't too late to save their skin from what they only assumed was soon to be a not too pleasant experience.

Zhin had always thought himself to be relatively good at reading people, and he was pretty sure that those who now were claiming their innocence were all telling the truth. But just to be sure, he called those four men forward and looked each of them in their eyes to confirm his initial assessment. He was satisfied that they were the four who were not a part of the gang rape and allowed them to leave, but not before first warning them that they would be hunted down and dealt with in the most unpleasant way if they ever spoke a word of this to anyone.

Now that the numbers were where they should be, Zhin split the eight frat boys up into two groups. Nicoli took four of them upstairs; the four who came across as being the kind of arrogant assholes who would be capable of influencing their brethren to do what they had done, and marched them straight to the back bedroom. Once there, he told three of them to sit on the front edges of the two beds in the room that were positioned side by side. Nicoli then turned and faced the head of the frat house — which he had kept standing just off to his side. He then said, "Although you aren't the only one who participated in this, you are the one responsible for what we are about to do in retaliation." He then turned his attention back to the three on the bed, aimed his gun with a silencer, and precisely shot the three of them in their lower right legs.

The frat boys fell off the beds, dropped to the floor, held their wounded legs, and screamed in pain. Nicoli then did it again, this time shooting each of them in their left thighs. "I'm sure that none of you will be doing it doggie style anytime soon." After using his vid-cell to take a few photos to document the deed, he holstered his gun, grabbed a hold of the frat house leader by the back of his collar, turned him around, and then marched him back down the stairs.

Purposely, Zhin had waited for Nicoli to complete his task before he began his. He wanted to let the other four frat boys hear the screams of their fellow brothers; he wanted to make them stop and think as to what they had done and what was about to happen to them.

"You four boys are in college for a reason. And you should have used the brain that got you here in the first place instead of allowing that jackass," Zhin pointed with his eyes in the direction of the frat leader as he was nearing the bottom of the stairs, "to convince you to do something as stupid as raping two defenseless women." He then did exactly what Nicoli had done — shot a bullet into each of their legs and thighs. "At least now, you four won't be able to be led around on a leash. And once your wounds are healed, maybe you'll have finally learned how to walk all by yourself."

Seven punished, one left to go; the one who had orchestrated the gang rapes. Zhin could have just done the same thing to him, but the leader of the frat house needed to be made an example of instead of just hurt for organizing the initiation. In fact, by the time that he was finished with what it was that he was about to do, Zhin was certain that this conceited asshole will have learned a lesson more valuable than any being taught here at the university.

After placing his gun back into its holster, he walked up to the frat leader and essentially wedged his nose right underneath his. "Once I'm done with you, I hope that you will remember that a woman is to be treasured, not treated like a used car that you can ride, beat up, and abuse until it breaks down. And just because you know that you can go out and get yourself another one anytime you want to, doesn't mean that it no longer has any value." With surgical precision, Zhin used his martial arts skills and broke both of the frat boy's legs, just below the kneecaps. As he collapsed from a lack of vertical support, Zhin grabbed him by the right forearm and snapped it as easily as you would a toothpick. After he let the young man's useless body drop unceremoniously to the floor, he gave him one more parting shot for good measure; the frat leader's nose met the downward thrust of Zhin's right palm, breaking it in three places.

"If any of you think that calling the police is a good idea, remember that we could have easily executed you instead. Don't make us come back here and do just that."

Before they left the frat house, Nicoli again used his vid-cell; this time to document what Zhin had just done. They then retrieved the booze that they had brought with them, along with a few abandoned full cases of beer and six unopened bottles of Tequila, Jack Daniels, and Southern Comfort, and headed out to their car.

Now that their assignment was done, Zhin had hoped that anymore 'favors' that Louie would want done would at least be business related and not personal. Nicoli on the other hand was happy that they had done this. This was exactly the kind of assignment that he needed to be a part of to show Louie that he could be trusted. He needed to prove that he could be a big asset to the D.U.O.; an asset that Louie had to acknowledge he simply could not pass up. He also needed to quickly gain the man's trust, because it would be that trust that would eventually allow him the best opportunity he saw possible to accomplish his real objective — kill the bitch responsible for his brother's death.

With the success of the mission, a sense of pride filled all three of them. Sabastian and his best friend in the military, Richard Atwater, had again performed their duty, served their country, and in the process, eliminated a potential serious threat. For Jerrelle, some personal redemption had been attained. One thing still bothered Sabastian though — the A.R.M. had again somehow acquired stolen Union military weapons and had been able to get them smuggled into Puerto Rico. The seemingly easy availability of them was something that not only Sabastian felt had to be stopped, but Jerrelle did as well. This kind of theft wasn't something new, it had been happening for years — and he firmly believed that he knew where its trail began.

As soon as the cruise ship that had taken them back to Texas had docked, Richard Atwater went directly back to the military base in Houston to rejoin the platoon, while Sabastian and Jerrelle returned to San Antonio. He was eager to get on with his life, but he had to admit that in order for him to do so, he no longer could procrastinate when it came to dealing with the one obstacle that was still standing at the end of his destined path — the one that he had initially chosen to temporarily go around.

Jerrelle wasn't sure what she was going to do. She had wondered what it would be like to move down to San Antonio and help her friend with his detective agency; that type of career actually appealed to her. That thought had first started to float around in her mind during her flight from Japan to Texas, but she really wasn't sure that she was ready to leave the city that she had called home for her entire life. For as much trouble as she got herself into, as much trouble that followed her nearly everywhere she went, she felt more comfortable being in Detroit than any other place she had ever spent time in. But she also was smart enough to realize that she'd be a stupid fool to just throw away a chance at a normal life; a chance to start all over, fresh, where nobody knew her or her reputation.

An opportunity was there that she honestly thought would never be — and although he did not actually come out and say it, Sabastian had all but hinted to Jerrelle on the cruise ship for her to let him know whenever she was ready to try something new. However, there was one thing that was preventing her from taking that big step — she was admittedly, afraid. She didn't have the same kind of trepidation that would appear when facing an opponent whose skills were equal to hers — that kind of situation she was comfortable dealing with. What she honestly was afraid of, was stepping out of her comfort zone, taking that huge leap of faith, and making a real change in her life — one that she knew deep down inside had to be done.

Less than an hour after they had returned to the Union, they arrived at the agency. The first thing that Sabastian did when he entered was walk straight over to Baylor, lean up against his new desk, and ask him to trace the two phone numbers that they had found in Puerto Rico — a simple task that didn't take Baylor more than a minute to complete. Jerrelle had been correct in her initial assessment, as those numbers were both phone numbers for an individual who lived in Detroit. And once Sabastian heard exactly to whom those numbers had belonged, he smiled — his enemy's hand had all but been caught in the cookie jar. Both of those numbers were associated with Louie Mazotti; one was for the man's personal vid-cell and the other one was for the Detroit Underworld Organization's headquarters.

After everything that had happened the previous month, Sabastian had just been content to wait until the stars aligned before he finished what had long ago been started. Now, he was being pulled right back onto the path he had been fated to walk. Much sooner than he would have hoped, the enemy was going to see his unwanted face.

There had been no doubt in Sabastian's mind that Louie Mazotti was going to take over control of the Detroit Underworld Organization, but he clearly misjudged exactly how long it would be before that took place. He honestly figured that it would be months, maybe even a year from now before that occurred — oh, how wrong he had been. Whether or not he was even ready to re-enter the game was irrelevant; he had no other choice now but to. Sabastian had sworn an oath the moment he joined the military to protect his country; a pledge that he refused to disregard. But on the day he learned who he had been born as, an obligation had been bestowed upon him — and it came with a debt that he knew he had to collect on. What his father had started all those years ago, Sabastian was going to complete — no matter how long it took.

Knowing full well what he was soon going to face, he walked purposefully into his office; Jerrelle followed closely behind him. After closing the door for some privacy, Sabastian picked up the vid-phone off his desk and called Captain E.J. Swilling. He started off his conversation by first explaining to him everything that he knew about the stolen weapons that they had recovered. From there, he went into detail about the suspicions that he now had about the D.U.O.'s involvement, as well as everything he knew that could connect them to all of the missing stolen weapons over the years.

Quietly, Jerrelle just sat back and listened to her friend's conversation. The moment they had first found those weapons, her mind had begun to formulate a possible scenario with the limited amount of information they had at that time. But with what they now knew, it had become obvious to her that they very soon, were going to restart what they had put on hold — and she was more than ready to do just that. At least now, knowing that her sister was no longer in danger, her focus could be right where it needed to be.

It didn't take much of an effort on Sabastian's part before he was able to convince Captain Swilling that it would be in the best interest of the military to temporarily hold off on conducting their own investigation into the stolen weapons. His winning argument was that if it ever became public knowledge that the Union's military had major security breaches within their own ranks, and that weapons had continuously been stolen from underneath their noses for decades by a well known mob organization, who in turn would sell them to the highest bidding terrorist group, then that not only could be a huge political embarrassment, but could cause other terrorist or religious fanatical organizations to falsely believe that the Union's combined military forces may actually have some major cracks within its structure that they in turn, could exploit. He hated to make the fraternity he belonged to appear like a bunch of brainless fools, but there was no denying the facts. In his mind, there was only one way to save the reputation of the military from becoming tarnished, and that was for Sabastian to take down the one responsible for it all.

Before he finished off his conversation with his captain, he made him a promise. Once he had accomplished his goal of shutting down the D.U.O., he would use his friendship with the Governor of Michigan to encourage him to share whatever information was available pertaining to all of the past stolen weaponry. This would then allow the military to begin its own internal investigation into just how exactly the weapons ended up disappearing in the first place. Only then could it be 'swept under the rug' and sealed with all of the rest of the classified documents.

After Sabastian had disconnected his call, he sat back in his chair, looked at Jerrelle, and exhaled; he didn't even have to speak, as she knew exactly what he was thinking.

"It has to be done, Sab!"

"I know, Jerrelle. But I was hoping for a bit of a reprieve. I was hoping that Louie would have crawled into a deep hole and hibernated for at least the winter."

"Well, he hasn't. The one thing that I believe though, is that he probably doesn't even know that those two shipments that were confiscated have been traced back to him, or that you were responsible for their seizure."

"I agree. His not knowing, gives us an advantage. We need to use the element of surprise and show up on his doorstep unannounced."

"Ok… but I am not wearing a blonde wig again."

Sabastian could not help but chuckle at his friend's light-hearted comment. He got up from behind his desk chair and exited his office; Jerrelle followed closely behind. He then invited Baylor,

Savanna, and Sydney to join them in an impromptu round table discussion in the lobby area. He wanted to inform everyone else of what had happened during his conversation with Captain Swilling and what he and Jerrelle had subsequently decided to do. As expected, both Sydney and Savanna wanted to protest, but they both knew in their hearts that Maxwell's death had yet to be fully vindicated and that Sabastian needed to finish off what his father had long ago started.

The temptation was certainly there for them to leave for Detroit right away, but Sabastian wanted to be sure that he was ready; emotionally and physically. His brief time spent back in the military had taken him out of his new routine and he needed to make sure that when the time finally came for him to face Louie one on one, he was fully rested and prepared. So Sabastian said his evening goodbyes, got up from his chair, as did Jerrelle, and they both left the agency to go and get some much needed rest — but not before they went to the gym to get in a good workout.

In the world of underground crime networks, like life itself, failure will occur at one time or another — though it is generally not accepted. To learn and grow from failure is what drives those who have, to move past those utter disappointments and strive for ultimate success in the future. But there are times when failure means that it all has to end. When that happens, you can either move on into a different direction or you can seek retribution against those who caused you to fail. If retribution is what you really desire, then once you commit to go that route, there would be absolutely no way to reclaim the life that you once had — you will have officially reached the point of no return, and you will have no other choice but to accept the consequences that will surely follow from your decision.

Louie leaned back in his office chair and contemplated the unexpected news that he had just received from Casper. According to his 'shipping clerk', the A.R.M. was suppose to receive the remaining third, already paid for shipment of weapons tomorrow, but he had been unable to make contact with the A.R.M. to confirm exactly where the shipment was supposed to go — he only knew that it was supposed to go to a different location than the previous two had. So Casper took it upon himself to contact an old friend of his in Puerto Rico, who told him that the A.R.M. no longer had any operating cells in that county. And although his friend refused to give him any specifics, due to the fact that they were an active member of the Union's military, he was able to confirm that three individuals, that were a part of an elite specialized unit, were responsible for shutting down those cells.

This news was not good for Louie. The A.R.M. had been the only remaining client that was left over from Antonio's regime, and now that welcomed source of income had unwittingly been removed. If Louie hadn't been ordered to put a bullet into the head of Vladi Chemzot, the leader of the C.R.A.P., then the D.U.O. would still have at least one major client left to do business with. Now, the success of their upcoming meeting with the U.A.L. was of the utmost of importance. Still, there was no guarantee that a business agreement with them could be reached.

Louie's sudden confidence had just been dealt a rather large blow. He knew that he could not let this situation influence his future decisions, as unforeseen things do tend to occur in the business he is in. It was something that he was always mentally prepared for; however, the last thing he needed right now was the same elite unit banging on his front door. He truly hoped that a connection between the D.U.O. and the A.R.M. had not yet been made.

After a short period of trepidation, Louie suddenly produced an unexpected smile. He had already received the final payment from the A.R.M. for their last shipment, so he in essence, had gotten a bonus check. Their misfortune meant that the profit margin on those unshipped weapons would eventually double — a buyer for them though, would first need to be found.

Because of what he now knew, Louie made a decision — it was the only one that he could make. He no longer could follow the playbook that the D.U.O. had used for years when it came to expanding the empire. He had to start all over from scratch, make his own rules, and blast right on through whatever may be in his way — the old way no longer seemed to be working. So as soon as his associates returned from Chicago, he was going to spend quite a bit of time with them and try and determine what possible new clients there were out there that they could make contact with in order to possibly start up a business relationship with. Louie had always hated it when Antonio had asked for him to solicit new business partners, but he knew that there were times when it was a necessary thing to do — at least now, he didn't have to be the one to make first contact as he had Zhin and Nicoli to do that for him.

Louie got up from behind his desk and walked over to his wet bar to grab himself a glass of Walker's Club — for some strange reason, he was beginning to prefer the rye over his usual beer. Once there though, he changed his mind and grabbed a Red Bull 2.0, as he was feeling just a bit sluggish. As he was returning to his desk, his vid-phone rang; he was pleasantly surprised to see that it was Madelyn calling him — she wanted to see if he was busy because she wanted to come to his office for a brief visit.

There was something about her that Louie had a hard time resisting — he had even done what he should not have; given her a scan card for the new security panel inside the main elevator, thus freely allowing her access to the top floor. He couldn't ask her to give it back; he would come across as being the asshole that everyone else knew him to be. She saw him in a completely different light and Louie did not want to drive a wedge in between the friendship that the two of them were quickly building.

After agreeing to her request, Louie returned to his wet bar. There, he poured a glass of merlot for Madelyn, then took it back to his desk where he waited for her arrival. Only a few moments had passed before a knock resonated on his office door. In that moment, whatever stresses Louie had, seemed to disappear. His mind stayed focused on only one thing — his new friend.

In front of Louie's extra long synth-leather couch, sat an oak coffee table; there, he set their drinks down. As he did this, he said, "The door is open."

Louie could not help but smile the moment Madelyn entered; he promptly invited her to join him. After making her way over to his side, she graciously accepted her awaiting drink and then sat on the couch. As she was about to thank him for his hospitality, the office door opened back up — Louie's associates had returned from their assignment.

Unsure as to what he had just walked into, Zhin knew enough to keep his mouth shut and his opinions to himself. So he just walked over to the front of Louie's desk and sat in one of the available chairs. Unlike his 'partner', Nicoli's curiosity wanted him to inquire about this obvious uncomfortable situation he had just walked into. But after a moment of thought, he remembered that he had yet to earn his position within the D.U.O. — his desire to know what was going on might not sit well with his prospective boss. Therefore, Nicoli decided that it was best he just take up a seat next to Zhin and keep quiet.

"I honestly didn't expect you two back so soon. I can only assume that there were no unforeseen problems with what I had asked of you?"

"Everything went according to plan. The message that you asked us to deliver was received loud and clear."

Madelyn set her glass of merlot down on the coffee table and attempted to leave the office, because she was unsure if the conversation that was taking place was something that she should become privy to. Louie's business wasn't her business as she was just a guest at the hotel, but he immediately reached over and gently placed his hand on her left arm. "There is no reason for you to leave, Madelyn. It is okay that you hear what my men and I are discussing, as it actually pertains to you."

It took her a moment to comprehend what Louie had meant — but then she finally clued in. *'Message… delivered'?* She had asked him to help her to pay back the men responsible for viciously raping her and her cohort, and now she realized that her request had just been fulfilled — but what exactly had his men done for her to constitute payback, was a question that Madelyn was uncertain that she wanted the answer to.

This was the first time that they had met their boss's 'friend' in person — and at first glance, Zhin could understand the infatuation that Louie obviously had for her. She was without a doubt a very stunning young woman who obviously did not deserve what had happened to her. Yet, he himself was not sure as to why his boss had made the rash decision to send them to Chicago to pay back those responsible for the attack. To Zhin, the big picture was certainly not clear — just because his status within the organization had changed, didn't mean that

242

everything now had to be shared with him. From what he understood, Louie had only spent roughly an hour with this woman. In that time, a bond of friendship could not have been established. The foundation for one though, could.

A speculating thought suddenly appeared in Zhin's mind. Quite possibly, after learning about the brief encounter between Louie and Madelyn, someone could have used that knowledge as a means to get what they wanted. The heart was known to make people do things without first thinking them through, so maybe the raping of the two escorts could have been planned so that revenge would be gained for someone else via a proxy. Similar instances had been reported in the past when it came to that same fraternity, and having the deed done by an underground organization instead of hiring someone else, meant that it was highly unlikely any suspicions would come their way. What else was possible was that those eight frat boys and the escorts were simply used as pawns in order to distract the D.U.O. long enough so that they would not see an attack of some kind coming.

Although all those scenarios seemed rather farfetched, Zhin felt assured about one thing — somewhere down the road, Madelyn Kinsworth was going to become a thorn in their side. For now though, his opinion about her would be kept to himself.

The next several minutes were spent filling in everyone on everything that had taken place. The report and the photo evidence that Nicoli had supplied produced a genuine smile across Louie's face. His men had done exactly what he had asked them to do and he now felt more confident that he had two reliable individuals who would complete any assignment that he would ever ask of them without any questions, misunderstandings, or mistakes.

Madelyn sunk as far back into the couch as she could; almost farther than what the couch would normally allow a body to. She had asked Louie to help her gain some retribution for what had happened to her, but what his men had done was something that she never imagined. She thought that maybe he would send his men to Chicago and just have them threaten those eight frat boys until they either pissed their pants or felt obligated to turn themselves in and confess to their crimes. She never imagined that these two associates of his would be as brutal and callous as they had been: broken limbs, a broken nose, and multiple bullet wounds — thankfully, no one had been killed.

'What have I gotten myself mixed up with?' she thought. Regret immediately consumed her. She could have changed her mind about wanting revenge right after Louie had come clean and informed her about who he really was, but she didn't. She had come to Detroit specifically to seek out his help; and that help is what she got. Now, it was up to her to live up to her end of the bargain — she had picked her poison, now she had to swallow it.

Louie looked over at Madelyn and could see the uncertainty in her eyes. In that moment, she became nervous; she honestly expected that he was going to put her on the spot and inform her of what would now be required of her in return for that favor. She really wasn't sure that she wanted to uphold her end of the agreement, but her word was something that she had never once in her life, gone back on. Besides, she did not want to end up in worse shape than those eight frat boys if she were to refuse.

Without looking at Zhin and Nicoli, he asked them to leave his office. Once they had, he took her left hand in his and gently caressed the back of it. "Don't take this the wrong way Madelyn, but I do care about you — the same way that a friend cares about those who are close to them." Louie stayed silent for a few moments, just long enough to finish off the remainder of his Red Bull. He then let go of Madelyn's hand and asked her the obvious question. "I can see that something is bothering you. What is it?"

"I don't know? It's just... I honestly never expected that your men would do what they did. I mean, I asked you to do me that favor, but I never imagined what the outcome would be. I guess... even though I wanted those responsible to pay, I never wanted them to be hurt as badly as they were."

"Those eight young men are just like me... I however, expect that there will one day be consequences for my actions. They did not, as they viewed you and the other girl as individuals who were well beneath them and did not deserve any sort of respect. They treated both of you like you were their possessions because they paid for your services."

Madelyn just sat there and listened. As much as she wanted to deny the fact that, as a prostitute, she was considered rental property, she had no other choice but to agree with his assessment. For seven years of her life, she had accepted that the exchange of money for sex was all right. Unfortunately, it took an evening of having her dignity being stripped completely away from her before she had finally recognized the truth — she was worth far more than any amount that any John could ever pay her.

"Intolerant people like that need to be sent a clear cut message — a beating might do that, but then it might not. However, I can guarantee you that those young men will never forget what they did for the rest of their lives."

"I know. And I know that I owe you for doing what I asked of you. I do not wish to have an unpaid debt, so... whatever it is you want me to do, I will do it with no questions asked."

That was the commitment from Madelyn that Louie was hoping to hear, as he didn't want to force her into doing what he wanted. "Good... because I would like for you to seduce someone for me."

That surprised Madelyn — she never thought that being the 'poisoned rose' was what he would want her to do. "So... you want me to be an escort again?"

"No. I want you to go to San Antonio, Texas, and seduce a man for me. Make him fall in love with you. He has caused us a lot of trouble and I want him out of my way for awhile so that I can finish restructuring and restarting the organization."

"You want me to become this man's girlfriend and then keep him away from you?"

"That is correct."

"Then I am going to need to know all that you know about this man before I do this. It is the only way that I will succeed."

"I will make sure that you know everything there is to know."

"So what exactly did this guy do?"

"Let's just say that he is responsible for the death of my former boss and my former trusted partner and friend (that was a hard pill for Louie to swallow lying about Sal like that). His unfulfilled obsessions will only interfere with my ability to properly run and rebuild this organization. I need him out of my hair for a little while. And then, when the time is right, I will ask for you to hand him over to me."

"Do I want to know what you will do to him when I hand him over?"

"It's best that I not tell you my intentions… but I know that you are a smart enough woman to figure that all out on your own."

What Louie was asking of her was something that she could do. She was though, a bit uncomfortable with having to eventually lead someone to his or her own impending death. But what could she do about that? She owed him a huge favor and had no choice but to comply with Louie's wishes — she would just have to learn to deal with her conscience afterward. "When do you want me to start?"

"I've booked you a flight for Texas tomorrow morning — until then, if you would care to join me for dinner, I will fill you in on everything that you will need to know about Sabastian Banks."

They left the office together; Louie then escorted Madelyn to his favorite Greek restaurant. Two hours later, he returned to his office alone and had asked Zhin and Nicoli to be there waiting for him; he needed to begin to find some perspective clients for the D.U.O. to conduct some future business with.

By midnight, they had a list of twenty organizations and individuals whom they all felt would make good clients — now, the hard part was to get at least some of them to agree on a business relationship.

The next day, Sabastian felt like a million bucks. The two hour intense workout that he had put himself through yesterday at the gym was all that it took for his overworked body and stressed out mind to fall into a well needed, deep, and peaceful evening of sleep.

The first thing that he did when he walked into the agency the next morning was give Savanna a hug and kiss on the cheek. He knew that she had spent a lot of time during the past month worrying about him, just like she used to do every time his father went away because of one of his cases — Sabastian just wanted to re-assure her that he was okay and that this was really his home.

She and his uncle Sydney had only been a part of his life for a short time, yet almost immediately, he felt a deep connection to them both; one connection being blood, the other a kinship that united two people through a common bond. He now understood why his father had connected with Savanna like he did, and he himself was beginning to feel similarly toward her. This was his family, and he would do everything in his power to be there and protect them.

Sabastian went into his office, sat in his chair, and as what has become an unconscious habit, picked up the photo that sat on the desk; now finally displayed in a new-brushed steel frame. There was something special about this picture. Maybe the essence of his parents now resided within it, or maybe it was the fact that this was the only photo that had ever been taken of the three of them. Whatever the reason for it, it now held a special place in his heart.

At the same moment that Savanna had entered his office with a fresh cup of English sim-tea with a touch of lemon rum, Sabastian place the photo back in its usual place. "Thank you.., but you don't have to bring me a tea every morning. I can get it myself, you know."

"I know.., but I used to do this for your father every morning, even though he would say the same thing to me. It's just my way of letting you know that I am happy you're safe and back at home."

"As am I... and thank you again for the tea."

As Savanna was about to leave Sabastian's office, Jerrelle entered. "Morning, Sab. How'd you sleep last night?"

"Like a baby. Best sleep I've had in weeks."

"Then can I assume that you finally feel like you are home?"

"Yup! I am home. So what about you? Have you decided to accept my offer?" Sabastian had taken the opportunity he had at the gym yesterday and all but insisted that he wanted Jerrelle to move down to San Antonio and work with him.

"I'm still not sure. There are things in my life that I have to sort out before I make that kind of decision."

"I trust you'll let me know when that is done."

"Of course." Jerrelle excused herself, and then left Sabastian's office to go and get herself a fresh cup of sim-caf. As soon as she had cleared the threshold, Savanna re-appeared with an odd look on her face. "Um, Sabastian... There is a call for you from someone who refused to show me his face or identify himself... but he insists on speaking with you. Should I tell him that you're not here, or do you want me to transfer the call?"

"I'll take the call. It's probably someone who is a little leery of speaking with a private detective. They probably just want to get a little information or assurance before they fully disclose who they are."

Acknowledging that possibility, Savanna went back over to her desk and transferred the call, just as Jerrelle returned to Sabastian's office with her morning sim-caf. She took a seat upon the synth-suede chair just off to the far side of the desk and took her first sip as her friend answered his call.

"Hello, Mr. Banks. It's good to speak with you again."

"I'm sorry... Do I know you?"

"Yes. We do go back a long way."

Sabastian took a sip of his tea and curiously thought for a moment. Though the caller hadn't been willing to show him his face, Sabastian somehow thought that he should know that voice — it did sound somewhat familiar, but he just could not figure out who it may be."

"Are you perhaps looking to speak with my father, Maxwell Banks?"

"No, Sabastian. I called to speak with you."

More confusion now enveloped him, as this man apparently knew who he was. He thought that to be rather odd, considering that he only found out who he was just a short time ago — still, his curiosity made him interested in knowing more. Maybe this mystery man had known who he was his whole life and had chosen to keep Sabastian's true identity a secret. Everyone has their own motives for doing what they do, so for that reason, he knew that he could not assume anything until he found out the purpose of this unexpected call. "So... what is it that you wish to speak to me about, sir?"

"First off, I want to thank you for what you did."

"Thank me?" That was a declaration that immediately threw Sabastian an even bigger curve ball. If the man would only show him his face, then maybe he would understand and be able to answer some of the questions that were formulating in his mind. "I'm sorry, but you've lost me."

"I'm thanking you because you are the one who took care of my problems. And because you did, I now have complete control of what I've always wanted."

Jerrelle was listening intently to what was taking place, and like Sabastian, was confused as to what this mystery man was talking about. She admittedly was someone who did not have a lot of patience with those who intentionally beat around the bush, so she got up from her chair, walked behind Sabastian, and then spoke her mind. "I think this is pretty rude of you, whomever you are, that you would call my friend and thank him for something for which he has no idea what he did for you. The least you can do is to have the decency to show us your goddamn face!"

Sabastian was stunned by the abrasive tone that his friend had just used. In fact, for a brief moment, he was certain that this mystery man was going to disconnect the call. He didn't. Instead, the man did what Jerrelle demanded of him.

In that moment, Sabastian would have wished that this individual had kept his identity a secret. Who he was now looking at was someone that he never wanted to see again unless he was lying dead in a coffin.

Jerrelle went from agitated, to furious in less than a second; Sabastian could immediately sense this and turned to his old friend. With only a glance, he was able to get her to settle down, knowing that she was close to reaching her boiling point.

"Come on now, Sabastian. You can't be that stunned that I tracked you down and gave you a call."

"What the fuck do you want, Louie?"

"I just called to thank you for eliminating Antonio and Sal for me. Thanks to you, I am now in complete control of the Detroit Underworld Organization."

His belief had now been confirmed; Louie Mazotti was in control of Detroit's mob. No longer could Sabastian procrastinate and put this on the back burner until a later date, he had to finish this feud before the bastard and his organization became an unstoppable entity. "I didn't do that for your benefit. I was actually content to forget about hunting you down in the hopes that you'd disappear for more than just a few short weeks, but now that I know you are back in Detroit, and can assume that you are more than likely planning something that has to be stopped, you have left me no choice but to…"

"Listen to me you over confident little punk! You got lucky and took out two of us. But I will not be anywhere near as easy to eliminate. You are nothing but a puss filled pimple on my ass that I can easily pop… and it will also be just as easy for me to dispose of that pile of trash that is rotting right behind you."

If it wasn't for the fact that it would be impossible to accomplish, Jerrelle would have tried to jump through the vid-phone so that she could rip Louie to shreds. And even though he did not use one of those key words that she hated, he did after all heave a non-flattering, derogatory insult her way. Therefore, the only thing that she could do at that moment was fire an insult back of her own. "You know Louie, I'd tell you to go and fuck yourself, but I'd just be wasting my breath knowing that 'it' is nowhere near long enough for you to ever come close to accomplishing that feat."

The temptation was certainly there for Sabastian to follow up Jerrelle's insult with one of his own, but he chose in that moment not to. Now was not the time to childishly be slinging mud at each other. Now was the time to just listen, observe, and learn. So without trying to be too obvious, Sabastian was able to get his old friend to understand his desire for her to back down; it was a task that he knew wasn't always easy for her to accomplish — especially when that 'bitch' switch of hers was close to being turned on.

He suspected that there was more to this call from Louie than just insults and threats. The man had gone out of his way to find him and make contact with him for a reason — what that was, Sabastian just could not even begin to fathom. He could have just hung up on the man, but that would be a response that Louie would have expected from him. If he had learned anything from his recent military expeditions, it was that there was always something unexpected to be learned about your opponent that you just might be able to use against them — you just had to be patient and wait for the information to be unwittingly given.

Hoping that Louie would do just that, Sabastian decided to humor the man for a while longer. "I know that you didn't call me just to exchange insults, Louie."

"You're right. I called you because I have a proposal."

That was something Sabastian would have never expected; he was now curious — but that didn't mean that he would seriously consider whatever bullshit offer Louie Mazotti had for him. "What logical reason would there be for me to even consider agreeing to any sort of proposition that you present?"

"Because, Sabastian.., you're smart enough not to readily dismiss something that is obviously in your best interest."

Whatever it was that Louie was about to offer him, Sabastian was certain that it would not be what the man was claiming. Nevertheless, he let him continue. "Ok, I'm listening."

"Since I do owe you for removing those who stood in my way of controlling the D.U.O., I am willing to do what you said earlier. I am willing to leave you alone forever, if you agree to leave me alone — forgive and forget."

"I did say that, but now... I am not so sure that I can?"

"Let's just say that if you don't, then I will be forced to eliminate those few remaining people on this planet who mean the most to you. And seeing that Ohio is closer to me than Texas is, I will start in that state."

Now it was Jerrelle's turn to restrain Sabastian from jumping through the vid-phone. "Listen to me you bastard! If you go anywhere near my grandmother, I will find you and..."

"I never said that I would. But if you don't leave me alone so that I can resume the daily operations of the D.U.O. without having to constantly look over my shoulder, I will have no other choice but to kill Edith Burelli."

Of all the things that Sabastian had thought that Louie would say to him, that threat against his grandmother was not one of them. But before he could speak his mind and send the man back a threat of his own, the line went blank. Louie had disconnected the call, leaving both he and Jerrelle at a loss for words.

Every terrible thought instantly went through Sabastian's head. He was tempted to leave San Antonio that very minute and go back to Ohio to protect his grandmother, but his instincts told him that she would be all right; that it was only an empty threat by Louie to get him unraveled and upset. If the man was true to his word, which Sabastian

believed that he intended to be, then his grandmother would be safe —
so as long as he left him alone. Besides, if he really wanted Sabastian
to show up at his doorstep, killing his grandmother would not be
necessary — an invitation is all that it would take.

Was it worth the risk to finish off what his father had started,
or would it be best that he just forget about everything and live a quiet
life, far away from any involvement with the D.U.O.? That was
something he would have to mull over. Then again, he had a promise
to keep and a responsibility to his country to get the evidence needed
that connected the D.U.O. to the recovered stolen weapons. He knew
that a decision pertaining to those things could not be ignored; nor
could his heart. He had to somehow find a solution that would
accomplish what he knew had to be done, and at the same time, not put
those whom he loved in danger.

The conversation with Sabastian went exactly as Louie had
expected it to go. Unlike Antonio, he didn't feel the need to kill
someone just because they were in the way, or to merely send someone
a message. He had no intention of killing Sabastian's grandmother —
although the thought did briefly cross his mind to do it anyway, simply
because it had been Terrance Burelli who had pulled the trigger and
ended Antonio's life. The man's recruitment all those years ago had
also been one of his biggest regrets. Two very good reasons were there
for him to even the score. However, Louie only wanted to make
Sabastian aware of the fact that he was willing, and capable of hurting
anyone that he cared about if he foolishly decided to continue on with
that senseless vendetta his father had begun all those years ago.

Now, all that Louie had to do was to wait and see if Sabastian
decided to accept his ultimatum. He hoped that he did, because he had
a plan that he'd much rather see be executed. No, he had no intention
of following in his predecessor's footsteps and commencing an
extensive game. He was more interested in using his 'bait' to lure
Sabastian to him when he was good and ready to deal with the young
man instead of resorting to having to get his attention by striking at his
heart. Dealing with the young man on his own terms instead of having
to deal with what would surely be an angry individual, was a much

more appealing way to get rid of the last thorn in the organization's side.

He walked over to his bar, opened up the fridge, and grabbed himself a cold beer. After carrying it over to his desk, instead of sitting down in his office chair, Louie stopped in front of the only window and took a moment to enjoy the view. Site seeing wasn't something that Louie enjoyed doing, but today, the city skyline looked more picturesque than he had ever remembered — maybe, he just never noticed the beauty of it before because he had been so preoccupied and consumed with things that only pertained to the D.U.O. or his son.

Just by taking those few moments, he now could see that there was a lot more out there, a lot more to life, to living, and to existing, than just his work. It was a gesture that was uncharacteristic of him, but Louie nevertheless, raised his beer and toasted his city below. *'I must not let this life of mine consume me like it did my predecessor. From this moment forward, I promise myself that I will allow some personal time to experience more of the things that life has to offer and not be so regulated when it comes to the ever changing world that is around me.'*

Once he had finished taking in the entire view, he turned around with the intention to sit down at his desk — instead, he stood there frozen. His past was sitting at the far side of the room on his extra long synth-leather sofa. This was not possible. Louie knew for a fact that this time, he was not dreaming. He had always believed that ghosts were just a figment of one's own wild imagination, but — how in the hell could Maxwell Banks be in his office?

"What's with the surprised look on your ugly face, Louie?"

"This is not possible! You are dead and I know that I'm not dreaming."

"Anything is possible. The mind is a powerful thing that even the greatest of scientists have yet to fully understand. I am here because you are allowing me to be here."

"Bullshit!"

The ethereal image of Maxwell Banks stood up from the sofa, and walked over toward Louie; he stopped at the other side of the desk and looked his enemy directly into his eyes. "It's not bullshit. Your guilty mind has allowed me to be here for a reason that only you can

253

figure out. And I would bet that there is a small corner in that diluted brain of yours that is trying to stop you from doing what you plan on doing to my son."

Unsure of what was really happening to him, Louie took a quick look at his beer. This was the first one that he had today, and he had only taken one sip out of it — so it wasn't the booze. He was far from tired, so that wasn't it either. Maybe Maxwell, or this unexplained likeness of the man was right. Maybe it was his mind that was creating this unwanted confrontation? "Are you a real ghost, or are you just a figment of my imagination?"

"I am whatever you think I am, therefore I am real. But if I were to guess, I'd say that there is something inside of you, possibly what little good there may still be, that is forcing you to second guess whatever it is that you are planning on doing."

"You are wrong! I have no reservations whatsoever about what I plan on doing. My intentions toward your son will not change. In order for me and this organization to prosper, he must be eliminated."

"I doubt that will happen."

"It will! So you need to quit worrying about what I am going to do and start worrying about your son."

"I'm not worried about Sabastian. I know that he will survive."

"If you were alive, Maxwell, then I'd lay money on that not happening as I have a guarantee in my back pocket to ensure that I will win."

Maxwell just stood there, arms crossed, and shaking his head. "Nothing's guaranteed. More so than you, it annoys me that you would stoop as low as you have and decided to use someone like Madelyn Kinsworth to do your own dirty work."

That statement was something that Louie did not expect to hear. It was as if this ethereal entity had tapped into his thoughts. "How do you know about her?"

"How I know is irrelevant. You claim to care about her, but you and I know that is nothing but a lie. If you truly did care about her, then you would not be using her as a pawn in your game."

"You have no idea what you are talking about. I am not using her; she is only returning a favor."

"She may believe that she is returning the favor, but you know very well that is not true. You planned on using her from the very moment that you met her in Chicago. Your malevolent mind immediately began to formulate a way to use her benevolent heart by making her believe that you were the nicest, most honest man in the world. No wonder she sought you out for help when she needed it the most. And just like your mind foresaw, she became the perfect person for you to try to use against my son. For once in your life, be that nice, kind and caring man that you tell Madelyn you are and distance your life from her before it is too late."

Louie was getting pissed off — not only at the ethereal image of Maxwell chastising him, but also at himself for more than likely, conjuring it up. He couldn't believe the insinuation that his own mind had convinced himself from the very beginning that he only wanted to use Madelyn for his own personal gain and not to just get a favor in return for his apparent good deed. Louie did not want to acknowledge the possibility that everything Maxwell was telling him might in essence, be true. In fact, he was getting tired of the man's unwanted presence all together. "I think that it's time for you to leave here... for good! I demand that you exit my thoughts.., if that is where you are really coming from. Either way, you can fuck right off!

Maxwell didn't leave. He stood still for a moment and looked stone faced into the enemy's eyes. Louie wasn't the kind of man who openly showed any sort of uneasiness, yet the moment that his adversary began to walk toward him, right on through the desk, he involuntarily started to back up — but a few feet was all he could go before he was backed right up against the window that he had been looking out of.

Unsure of what Maxwell's true intention was, Louie decided not to wait to find out, so he threw a wild punch at Maxwell; the punch knifed right through the air and unsurprisingly, hit nothing. Stunned, Louie turned back around and saw Maxwell standing in front of the window with a conceited look on his face.

Desperate to get rid of him, Louie did the only thing that he could think of at that moment. "Get the hell out of my head!" He screamed, as he threw his nearly full bottle of beer at Maxwell. That worked, as his enemy immediately disappeared. However, the beer bottle had shattered up against Louie's office window, causing a spider-web crack in the windowpane, twelve inches in diameter.

After a few moments of uneasiness, Louie was able to regain his thoughts. *'I think that I need some rest... well, maybe not just yet — Maxwell might return to torment me some more.'* Louie took a moment and gathered his thoughts, *'My long-term plans now have to change. The complete reassembly of the organization is going to have to wait. The only thing that matters now is dealing with Maxwell's pain-in-the-ass son. Once that is complete, I am going to go back to my homeland of Sicily and take a very long, much needed vacation.'*

Louie went back over to his wet bar; he needed a much stronger drink than a beer, so he poured himself a double shot of Walker's Club on the rocks, walked over to his desk, pulled out a small stainless steel container from within the top drawer, opened it up, and removed the last cigarette that had been inside it — so much for quitting, but after what he had just been through, he needed this vice to help him relax. A clove-flavored cigarette had been the only thing that ever had helped Louie to keep his nerves calm — especially during all those years of having to put up with all the headaches that Sal used to cause him. Now, things seemed to be almost as bad.

Strangely in that moment, he had come to a realization — something, other than smoking those cigarettes was going to be his undoing. That he could not let happen. He needed to figure this all out, and soon so that he didn't end up fulfilling the enemy's prophecy.

With his last cigarette and most of his rye gone, Louie finally felt relaxed — too bad what was ahead of him wasn't going to be nearly as easy to get rid of as his brief bout of anxiety had been. If only he could kill his pending large amount of stress with a simple stimulant, his obligatory task would be much easier for him to complete and his life could then return to the version of normal that he envisioned it to be.

Epilogue

Another decisive victory should have been claimed, as he had finally figured out how to make an appearance on earth in an ethereal form. However, what Maxwell had accomplished seemed rather hollow. Yes, he had succeeded in bringing fear into the man and yes, he was certain that he had succeeded in bringing forward some doubt in Louie's mind. Unfortunately, this visit of his just didn't seem to have quite enough persuasion behind it to have prevented his longtime advisory from giving up on his plans to kill Sabastian. But the Apollo's Stone had not been given to Maxwell so that he could use it in order to stop the enemy from trying to kill his son — it had been given to him so that he could ensure that Louie's destiny became fulfilled. And if allowing the man to continue on with his intention to kill Sabastian was what it took for that to happen, then Maxwell had to permit it to take place. That left him with only one other option to ensure that his son did not prematurely die. He had to visit him.

Using the Apollo's Stone for that purpose was something that he had decided he was not going to do until after Louie's demise had occurred — or at least, until he and Nefieti had built up more of a trust between them. But now, Maxwell knew that it had become absolutely necessary — he just hoped that there were not going to be any repercussions to follow. However, before he even contemplated doing this, he first needed to figure out a way to appear and not have too much emotion overwhelm Sabastian.

Like all fathers are supposed to be, he had not been there for his son. This pending visit that he was planning wasn't how he envisioned fulfilling his responsibilities — but he just didn't have a choice. This way, in the form of an apparition, was the only method now available for Maxwell to be able to let Sabastian know that he would be there to help and guide him along the way — it was also the only way for him to finally be able to let his son know just how much he loved him. As long as he was careful how he went about doing this,

his son would stay the course and eventually create a legacy that one day far exceeded his.

To be continued...

About the author

Steven F. Deslippe was born in Canada on September 24th, 1966. He grew up in a rural community, right next door to his Grandparents' farm, just outside of the town of Amherstburg, Ontario.

Farming wasn't of interest to him; however music was. Beginning in late 1987, and lasting for fifteen years, Steven worked as a disc jockey, playing music and emceeing weddings, parties, dance clubs, rock clubs and gentleman's clubs. It was during this time period where he discovered a passion for reading and writing — both of which he admittedly did not like, nor was very good at when he was younger.

As the years went by, both of these skills greatly improved — the result of his dedication and hard work, now forever captured in each book that he writes.

Facebook
https://www.facebook.com/Author.Steven.F.Deslippe.Official/

Goodreads
https://www.goodreads.com/author/show/16559506.Steven_F_Deslippe

Youtube
https://www.youtube.com/channel/UChXnJAOrOEv0vnWNdQWJbqQ

Amazon
https://www.amazon.ca/s/rcf=nb_sb_noss_2/134-6867989-8132316?url=search-alias%3Daps&field-keywords=steven+f+deslippe

https://www.amazon.com/s/ref=nb_sb_noss?url=search-alias%3Daps&field-keywords=steven+f+deslippe

E-mail contact
sdeslippe@sympatico.ca

*** Other releases ***